HARNESSING FIRE

LEGENDS OF BERLA
BOOK ONE

AMELIA J. RIVERS

UP CURRENT PRESS

NORTH OCEAN

Gillons

Red Ice

Mist Forest

Cliffs

Teffar Mudpits

Mosa River

Peras River

NEPTA OCEAN

Scarlet Mountains

Drylands

Ice Caves

BERLA

Blue Plains

Monoc

Ask Fields

Grasslands

Trotten Forest Treble lake

Whismor Forest

Castle Traitors

Mosa Plains

Sea Swamp

Silver Forest

WIND OCEAN

Winter Forest

Lunar Plains

Castle King Malik

Winter Plains

Hirk

KENNARD

Wyllen Forest

Phantom Islands

Spirit Strait

Einhorn Forest

Southern Port

WIND OCEAN

To the characters within. You were my escape through the roughest years.

NOTE

Chapter 1

VAYSA

The smell of sweat and incense clogged Vaysa's throat. Her white eyes watered as she stifled a choke, and yet a thrill of excitement skittered down her spine. Gripping her dagger, she silently crept barefoot over the tree branch, watching a noble and his attendant beneath her.

Each of Shad's lessons echoed in her mind. Now muscle memory, the thoughts helped keep her grounded and focused on the task at hand instead of the bounty waiting for her.

Their yellow-painted cart was perched lopsided on the incline of the traveling path. They'd fallen for her trick: a rock lobbed at the wheel. The racket had stopped them, and while the noble rebuked the attendant for the delay, he took the opportunity for a meal break in the shaded path.

She hadn't expected a noble in such simple accommodations. A niggle of worry slithered in her nerves and dulled the excitement that accompanied most robberies. Again, she searched for the sign that more footmen or escorts were coming. A plume of smoke. A haze on the air. A nicker on the wind. Or the smell of soap or perfume.

The path remained silent.

Through the skewed drapery, the single trunk in the cart meant they weren't planning a long stay. Anything of value would be on the noble. She glanced at him again. He'd be an easy target. No weaponry on him. Attention diverted. The attendant distracted. A gold crescent moon hung low on the cart's front, sparkling in the few rays of light. He was from the Lunar Plains region, a place known for fertile fields and which supplied much of the wheat for the country.

It'd be a fast and easy score. Based on the bulge of the velvet purse at his side, Vaysa would have plenty of gold to trade in the village for the winter.

Despite the smile dancing on her lips, her gaze darted down the trail in both directions once again. Any robbery was a risk. No smoke plumes blurred the blue sky, and the paths were silent save for the scuttle of forest creatures.

The curl of excitement fluttered again in her stomach, matched by the dormant fire that snaked through her veins. The feeling was both familiar and unsettling. For the past few weeks, it had pulsed more urgently, spiking with her emotions, but like all the other times since she first arrived in Kennard, it never manifested. Just a shadow lurking.

The attendant saw to their horses, distracted with the work while the aristocrat sat perched on a small stool, holding a drumstick in one hand and a silver goblet in the other. Vaysa's stomach rumbled at the spiced meat. She'd only sampled such fancy cuisine a few times, her food normally coming from nightly hunts.

The juices ran down his fingers and pooled around his rings on each finger. Spilling over, they dripped down his hand and onto his wrist where he wore three gold bracelets. On his other wrist was a gold cuff.

Each ring or sleek bauble would buy her a few weeks of food. The jewel-encrusted cuff would provide a few months' worth of supplies. If she were human, all the items would buy her at least a year's worth or more of food and a house in a village. But non-humans weren't allowed in Kennard to trade items or to live.

Fumbling her bottom lip between her teeth, she eyed his black velvet pouch of gold coins and the beaded gold chain around his neck. The ornate jewelry would be recognized in any city she traded in. Only a few merchants would traffic them when their shops were closed, and at steep costs. They weren't worth her trouble.

Gold coins and beads, however, were universal and untraceable, and everyone welcomed them. Even when she went in cloaked and at odd hours.

With an exhale, Vaysa launched herself from the gnarled tree branch, landing in the thick shadows behind the noble. The attendant screamed and darted to the cart.

She bit her smile down, centering herself. This was her favorite part, but she needed to stay focused. Her gaze flickered to the attendant. He cowered behind the horses, tightly scrunching his cap down over his eyes as he hid behind the horses' rumps. He'd only be a threat if he startled the horses.

The noble gasped at Vaysa and dropped his drumstick. His blue eyes widened, and his manicured hand flew to his powdered face.

She licked her lips and smirked. Pointing at his purse, she bent her finger and gestured for him to give it to her.

His eyes flared when his gaze met her white eyes.

The noble launched up, sending the stool to the ground. He held the goblet in front of him, fashioning it as a weapon, and swung it at Vaysa. He bared his teeth, making a sound between a squeal and a growl.

Vaysa tightened her stomach to keep from laughing. Nobles had more ego than brains.

"This could go fast," she said, stepping closer, hoping he'd have a moment of smarts. "Give me your purse and you go free."

He chucked the goblet at her head, missing her by a few feet. His eyes bulged as it landed in the foliage.

She sighed, the excitement curdling in her stomach. They always chose the hard way. Flames flickered in her veins, sending heat through her body. She sucked in a breath, but the moment passed. The pulse extinguished as quickly as it came.

His mouth trembled.

Before he could voice his insults, Vaysa lunged at him, kicking his legs out, and then jumped on top of him, pressing her dagger to his throat. Her muscles vibrated with the hunt. Even if the pursuit exhilarated her, she preferred when targets let their fear control them and just fled. When they fought, she always ran the risk of hurting them. Despite their uselessness, their blood wasn't worth the gold.

He sputtered nonsense, his eyes darting around for nonexistent help, and flailed his legs trying to free himself.

"Make this easy on yourself," Vaysa growled, pushing her oversized jacket sleeves up her arm as she worked his beaded necklace over his head. Her dirty hands left smudges on his blue silk collar.

The noble nodded but tried to kick out again while slamming his head toward Vaysa.

Vaysa dodged to the left, dropping her dagger. Flaring her nostrils, she punched his face. After hearing the satisfying "humph" as he fell backwards, unconscious, she finished removing his necklace and gold pouch.

As an afterthought, she removed the ring from his left pinky. It had a square green stone with silver flecks that sat on a smooth, thick silver band. She slid it on her pointer finger and fanned her fingers out. She shrugged and dropped the ring back on his lap.

It would only trace her back to this encounter.

Securing the pouch, Vaysa left her victim in the shrubs. She rescued the silver goblet and her dagger from the mud and frowned at seeing a chip in her blade. She'd have to waste some of their new gold to replace it. Weighing the purse in her palm, she blew a breath out. They'd still have plenty left over.

With a flick of Vaysa's hand, Shad, a shape-shifting Cuma, emerged from the forest in her human form and joined her. Her gold eyes shined as she scanned the path and trees, and her jutting fangs glistened in the receding light. Only a few whisps of gray fur around her eyes showed additional decades. Her nose twitched as she took in the scents from the travelers and forest. Her eased demeanor meant there weren't others around. To Vaysa's dismay, Shad smiled and leaned over the nobleman.

Vaysa shook her head as Shad eyed up the victim. Even though Shad was in her human form, her strength was far superior to a human's and her hefty size dwarfed the others.

Shad snorted but left the attendant alone.

"This will feed us," Vaysa said, forcing a smile and patting the pouch. Shad rolled her eyes.

"You're evil!" the attendant wailed while cowering in a ball.

The common sentiment settled on her skin like embers. She'd heard it since the first night she arrived in Kennard. The first night in foreign lands. The first night in a human village. The first night without her mother. The only time her powers manifested before becoming nothing but phantom pulses in her veins. The normal twist of annoyance unsettled her stomach, but she swallowed down her desire to punch him. He wasn't a real threat.

Vaysa turned to him. Before thinking better of it, she pushed her black hair out of her pupil-less white eyes and laughed. "Evil?"

Shad smiled and licked her lips. "I'm good with being called evil."

"Have anything better to call us?" Vaysa asked.

"You monsters, you heathens," the servant whimpered. "You attacked an innocent man."

Vaysa looked back at the noble sprawled on the ground. The mud darkened his rich velvet robes and caked his smooth hands.

"Innocent as hell," Vaysa said.

She sighed at the streaks of red and purple that crossed the sky and colored the clouds in shades of pink. The sun kissed the forest canopy and would soon drop behind the eastern mountains. Playing with the human would only lead to issues, as she learned the hard way the last time they moved. They needed to get off the trails, but she couldn't leave someone unconscious on the side.

Before she could tell the attendant to go for help, a faint nicker sounded on the air. More humans were coming.

The familiar curl of heat twisted beneath her skin, singeing her excitement.

She swallowed.

Shad didn't turn toward the sound, her gold eyes fixed on the two humans before them. She gave a nod to Vaysa though, indicating she'd heard what was approaching and knew about the flare up in Vaysa's veins. Their time was limited.

Shad's choice would be to kill them. Vaysa knew it without asking, but Shad wouldn't do it and risk a fight with Vaysa unless Vaysa was in danger. They'd had the argument countless times, and it had reached pointlessness. Neither would budge.

A few humans had tried to kill Vaysa as a child her first night in Kennard, and she learned distance provided safety. But these humans weren't worth an argument with Shad or the cost of killing.

Her stomach growled and the growing pangs of hunger clawed at her. Any other discussion would have to wait. At least now she had some gold for the village and some for winter. The incoming humans could help the attendant.

Vaysa launched into the trees, knowing Shad would follow. The trees swallowed them, full canopies providing protection from the humans. The forest creatures paid the figures no heed as they ran along the branches. Following the well-known path for several miles, her mind wandered, focusing on needed preparation for the coming winter and the limited food.

This was their time to stockpile items for trade. The number of travelers increased with the start of the cold winds, either for the weather or holidays or something else humans did. None of it mattered to Vaysa as long as she got supplies before they stopped traveling when the days were only a few hours, and the nights were long and cold. They wouldn't return until the winds were warm again. The surplus of travelers now meant she would have items to trade in the villages when the travelers stopped.

She landed lightly on top of their home. Abandoned years ago, it was a simple unpainted wooden structure weathered with age and nestled high in the trees. They'd covered their window frames, unlike most of the similar tree structures used by hunters throughout the forests of Kennard. Vaysa didn't remember well the time before she landed in Kennard, and with no hope or desire to travel the strait back to Berla, she'd made a secret home here in the forest.

Shad silently joined her and leaned against the doorframe. Her golden eyes glowed slightly in the dim light.

Finally, she spoke, "You let them go. They'll look for us."

"Maybe," Vaysa mumbled. She didn't want to have this fight. Again.

"I was serious earlier. We should consider moving to a different location. There've been more soldiers lately. There shouldn't be. Not at this time of year. I don't like it."

Vaysa waved Shad off. She had been cautious with the noble. Even if she had a little fun. She didn't want to move again. They'd just settled here after the Royal Guard became more prevalent in the area surrounding their previous home, taking too much interest in the accounts of the forest's monsters. The soldiers didn't normally look too hard for them, were easy to pilfer from when they were drunk, and they had great supplies. But when the Royal Guard settled in a place or took the travelers too seriously, Vaysa and Shad had to keep moving.

With winter coming, they needed a place to hunker down.

"How long do you think it'll take before they send a group to search for us?"

Vaysa sighed. Shad wasn't wrong. But one noble shouldn't ruin their plans.

"We're way off path," Vaysa said, adding the coins to their collection. "We'll go to a different section of the path for the next few days. Or just take cover. We have a few weeks to build a reserve to trade. Let the soldiers think they're just drunk."

"He called us monsters," Shad said through gritted teeth.

"So?" They always called them monsters. It was the best the humans could ever come up with. It's not like they knew the individual species of Berla. Well, neither did she other than Shad.

Shad snorted in response. She opened her mouth but licked her lips instead of voicing the comment. Still, uncertainty twisted in Vaysa's stomach knowing the comment was likely related to her increased flare-ups in her veins.

"You're in human form. You mostly had your fangs hidden. The only odd things about us are my eyes. We're fine," Vaysa muttered as her stomach tightened. The unease agreed with Shad. They'd probably have to move again. No place would ever be home.

Shad rolled her eyes and flicked her fingers. The long, dagger-like claws made a clicking noise as they rubbed together, and she ran her tongue over a fang. "Yeah, I look real human."

Vaysa sighed again. Shad's point was too accurate. Shad's human form was really more humanoid. She was taller than most, her eyes glowed in dim light or when she was mad, which was often, and, even in human form, she had cat-like claws, and her fangs often jutted out of her mouth. She could keep them hidden but preferred not to.

Vaysa finally met Shad's eyes and said, "Well, I look human."

"Then why do you wear a cloak into the towns and only go when it's dark?"

Vaysa growled and threw her hands in the air.

"Vaysa, I'm sorry," Shad started, her yellow eyes dimming and her lips turning down.

"It's fine, you're right," Vaysa mumbled.

Vaysa ran a hand absentmindedly over her arms. Her white eyes weren't as big of an issue as her opaque white skin. Through the years her body had become laced with angry, raised red scars as most injuries left a permanent mark. They drew alarm whenever a human saw them. So no matter the temperature, she wore long sleeves to avoid questions. However, the cover of dusk and dawn with a hood and cloak were the best to not draw immediate attention to appearance.

Her biggest issue, though, was her powers. Or her lack of ability to use them. They were always bubbling like magma under the surface. And recently, more often, taunting her. Their promise felt closer and farther all at once.

Vaysa knew what they were supposed to be. She'd known since her first night in Kennard when she'd burned a human village and learned the difference between human and non-human.

She'd only displayed them that one time, the irrevocable proof she wasn't human, and as the unwelcome curl of heat twisted in her veins, she clenched her teeth until it dissipated. Though she experienced rushes of heat, nothing ever materialized. Even now, as they swam bolder and angrier through her veins. She was a mute siren. A powerless Berlan in the human land of Kennard.

The pulse passed quickly, like normal, but Shad still noticed. She stilled as she surveyed Vaysa, her lips curled into a grimace.

Vaysa cursed and folded her arms over her torso. Shad's concern about the soldiers had increased as her surges became more frequent. It's why they moved twice in the summer instead of once like normal.

"I need to go into town tomorrow," Vaysa said quickly, ignoring Shad's expression, and tossed the damaged dagger on the weathered crate that served as a table.

Shad narrowed her eyes and raised an eyebrow. "No. The villagers will be nervous after what just happened."

"I know the smith. It'll be fast. I'll go in before sunup. Then we can find another place to move to, but I need a blade." The reality of it settled like needles on her skin. Another home gone.

Vaysa watched as Shad stalked out of the structure to find the night's dinner. Shad was only concerned about her. She'd been like a mother to Vaysa since she lost her own, but Vaysa wasn't Shad. Vaysa couldn't use her powers.

Chapter 2

VAYSA

*V*aysa cast her eyes to the ground and sunk deeper into the folds of her hood. It didn't matter if others couldn't see her eyes or skin in the dark hour, or that no one was out on the streets yet. Her heart rate quickened regardless, and she licked her lips.

Like all villages in Kennard, only humans inhabited Hark, a small village on the outskirts of the forest south of the Winter Plains. The buildings were made of the traditional Kennardian blue stone base with clapboard siding in shades of white, gray, and tan. A few completely stone buildings, made of the northern violet-hued stone, sat on larger lots announcing the owner's wealth.

The town served as a stopping point before entering the lush forest to the south, or the several days' hike to the castle if heading north. There were several pocket towns that dotted the forest's edge, but Vaysa liked the smith here best.

The first haze of golden light warmed the horizon as she wove through the familiar streets until she found the forge. A greater warmth emanating from the building meant that the smith was already at work. She involuntarily lifted her hands to the welcoming heat but quickly retracted them back into her wraps.

She considered knocking, but the sweet smell of pastries lingered in the air and her stomach rumbled. She scanned the buildings, focusing on the shadows. Shad was there, but Vaysa couldn't see her. A few minutes wouldn't hurt.

She backtracked slightly and found the whitewashed building with red shutters. Saliva pooled in her mouth as the sweet aroma of sticky buns wafted out of the slightly opened window. It was a fabulous gimmick. Vaysa always promised she wouldn't waste money on one but had yet to honor the oath. She rapped lightly on the door and shuffled her feet as she waited. Her eyes darted around as the seconds ticked by.

The door finally swung open, allowing a wave of heavenly smells to escape. Vaysa closed her eyes slightly and smiled. Catching herself, she nodded at the plump elderly lady with steel gray hair. The woman's frown faltered. Shaking her head, she left the door open as she meandered back into the kitchen. She returned with a small, warm bundle. Vaysa slipped her a gold coin worth dozens of buns.

Her stomach growled as she unwrapped the bundle for a roll. Grabbing two instead, she ate them before returning to the forge. The sweet goodness was a welcome comfort after the previous night. She knocked loudly and watched the shadows as she waited. A few others were now out on the streets as the sun rose higher, but they were more concerned with their own business. Even so, she needed to hurry before the sun rose too high. She sighed loudly and pounded again on the door. It finally swung open and, with a flash, a blade was pointed at her. She rolled her eyes and raised a bun in surrender.

"You," the man hissed but grabbed the bun and stepped aside, allowing her to enter. He greedily ate the bun in two bites, letting the crumbs remain in his red beard, which matched the shock of unruly red locks on his head.

Vaysa held her cracked dagger out with her gloved hand and, with the cloak covering most of her eyes, looked expectantly at the smith.

"How do you break so many?" His gruff voice was laced with admiration.

Putting the dagger on his table, Vaysa shrugged and walked toward his finished pieces. Despite the heat, she kept her cloak on and her head bent. Sweat beaded down her neck and dampened her shirt.

"It's hot as hell in here," the man said, but went back to his piece he was working on.

"Your supplies are low," Vaysa said.

"The Royal Guard is helping with that."

Vaysa's head shot up and she looked back toward the door.

The man chuckled, His sweaty chin bobbled and his hands clasped his stomach. He wiped his dark eyes and said, "That look was priceless. I should almost give you a dagger for free for that."

Vaysa shot him a curious look, and he replied, "Almost."

"More training?" Vaysa asked, keeping her voice steady despite the lump in her throat. The buns she'd eaten turned in her stomach.

"Nah, something about a new mission."

"Oh?"

What could they be up to now? It wouldn't matter. She and Shad would relocate and stay off the trails for a week or so until the Royal Guard and the noble's tales passed.

"Eh, when aren't they moving?" he said, waving his hand dismissively. But his eyes narrowed on his piece, his jaw working. "Word is some monsters attacked a nobleman yesterday."

Vaysa stilled, her fingers curling into fists beneath her cloak. She didn't have a weapon of her own, but plenty lay around her if needed. They'd never talked about the monster rumors before.

"Rumors are flying about some Berlans being here."

Her muscles tightened but only her eyes tracked to the smith. Was he warning her or setting her up?

"Nothing's been official yet." He lifted his dark eyes to her. The fire of his forge glinted in them. "But the biggest rumor is one of the princes is missing. With rumors of Berlans on the land..." His voice trailed off.

Berla meant nothing to Vaysa. She'd left as a toddler, but that didn't mean she was welcomed in Kennard. There was a reason she chose specific hours to visit and only specific shops. If half of what he said was true, she and Shad would need to move immediately. Find a space deeper in the woods. They'd have to stay off the trails even if it meant losing out on gold for the winter. What good would the gold be if they were dead?

Moving to quench his sword, he continued, "It be best for anyone with a reason to hide from the Royal Guard to stay real low for the next few days, probably weeks. It's not like Berlans are just going to walk into a human town. The Royal Guard must be desperate to set up stations here in Hark. Especially near the river."

Vaysa nodded, but her heart slammed in her chest. She needed to leave. She didn't want to be trapped in a town with them. For some reason, even knowing she had reason to avoid the Royal Guard, he was warning her. Even if he suspected her to not be human. Without time to process it, she quickly selected a new dagger and paid three times its worth. She preferred to overpay at select shops. That way the merchants were always welcoming of her money at any hour and never asked many questions.

He pocketed it with a wink. "Quick feet home," he offered.

Slipping out of the forge and keeping to the shadows, she trekked back toward the edge of town. She smiled as the bakery came into view. Maybe another bun would help with the trip back to her home. Especially since it would be weeks before she could have another.

Hearing a crash at the inn, she flinched and stepped deeper into the shadows. The inn door burst open and two Royal Guards stomped out.

"Where the hell did he go?" a half-dressed soldier growled. He ran a hand through his messy hair as he searched the darkened streets.

"I don't know, Teo, but Gren better not have run off," the other said as his pale hand fell momentarily on his sword. He was fully dressed and stood a few inches taller than Teo. His light hair was slicked back. "Stupid assignment. We don't need him."

"Tell General Closs that or shut up, Ben," Teo said.

Vaysa retreated deeper into the shadows at hearing the general's name. Was he really back? A pulse of fire coursed through her. At the same instance, her skin prickled, and she whirled around to face the person standing behind her. She hadn't heard him, and she couldn't blame the sleeping city for distracting her.

"Sh," the figure said. The figure shifted to watch the soldiers and revealed dark red eyes in the dim morning light.

Vaysa stepped back, blinking repeatedly. She opened her mouth to ask about his eyes and abruptly stopped herself.

"They're going to wake the entire town up," he sighed. Although he spoke the common language of the area, his voice held a unique clip. "I just wanted air."

Vaysa followed his gaze to the soldiers who were unceremoniously moving trash cans, looking under porches and in shrubbery. She turned back to him and arched an eyebrow. Her mind finally caught up with the events. He was Gren. He wasn't a human and the soldiers were looking for him. Her eyes darted to the tree line. Shad would be furious, but she couldn't just leave him, a nonhuman, to the guards. They'd imprison him, torture him, or worse. The guards probably had worse weapons than the town she'd been in. "Do you need help?"

His jaw twitched, and he averted his gaze. "No."

"You sure?"

"I doubt you'll make it out of the village alive and, sadly, I am with them." He moved out of the shadows into the faint glow of dawn. The hunter green Royal Guard uniform clashed with his blue skin. His light green hair was neatly combed and slicked back, but tufts were already cowlicking.

"What the hell!" Vaysa realized her volume too late. She shoved him back and drew her dagger. What new trickery had the Royal Guard devised?

"Run, non-human," he breathed, a slight smile tugging on his lips.

Heat bloomed on her cheeks and radiated up her neck and into her ears. The blood pounded, and she had to fight to clear her head. She was in the shadows and cloaked. He shouldn't know she wasn't a human.

"Gren, what the hell!" Ben yelled, running toward them. He pulled up short and stared between Vaysa and Gren. He placed his hand back on his sword and took a step toward Vaysa. "What're you doing with Gren?"

Vaysa ducked her head and stepped back into the receding shadows. She licked her lips, surveying the paths back to the forest. An unwelcome warmth pulsed in her veins. Her fingers curled, and for the first time in over a decade, her fingertips burned with heat. Startled, she tried to relax her fingers, breathe in fresh air, but the air only fueled the building heat. Her eyes unfocused momentarily as thoughts of the village flashed forward. Voices echoed in her brain. No. Not now. She needed to get out of here. She needed to think. To assess what just happened. She needed Shad.

"I asked you a question."

"Nothing," Vaysa seethed and turned to leave. Forcing her breath even, her eyes to blink, and falling to the calming techniques Shad had taught her, her body relaxed. The raging fire soothed to a river. Her fingertips cooled.

Ben took a step forward. "I am the Royal Guard. You will not leave until I dismiss you."

Vaysa looked back at him over her shoulder and chortled. It'd be a cold day in hell before she listened to the Royal Guard. No matter what coursed in her veins. She bolted for the forest line.

His feet pounded on the cobblestones behind her and she gripped her new dagger. She hadn't planned on christening it so soon.

"Ben, no!" Teo yelled, backing out of an alley.

Vaysa didn't wait to see if Ben had listened. She ran and jumped, grabbing hold of the wooden post holding a shop's sign up. Using her momentum, she propelled herself onto the roof. She landed softly and tore off toward the next roof. She slipped slightly and decided she didn't want to run on the steep-sloped roofs.

She leapt onto the next roof, swooped back, and used the post on the building to guide her back to the cobbled street. She faced Ben. His pale face burned in surprise and his step faltered slightly.

Fire spiked through her. This time, fueling her. The uncontrolled heat promised to help. She'd make him regret following her.

Vaysa lunged, knocking him to the ground. She punched his wrist and elbowed his face, disorienting him enough to loosen his grip on his sword. She yanked it from his grasp and punched him again. A satisfied smile curled her lips.

"Please, stop!" Teo yelled. He and Gren had caught up to them. "He's just an idiot."

"I'll cure him of it," Vaysa said and punched him again. Fire twisted in her veins, urging her to let loose. To let go.

Ben's eyes enlarged when her hood slipped back slightly.

"Berlan," he mouthed.

Red hot heat spiked in her veins. He saw her. Her eyes. He knew. She slammed her fist into his face. Ash from her knuckles smeared on his cheek. Her hands throbbed to punch him again. Her body pulsed with satisfaction as he went limp in her hands.

"More soldiers are coming. Go back home," Teo pleaded.

She blinked. The lure of the power receded enough below the current of fear for her to assess the situation.

Vaysa tugged her cloak closer and glanced up at him. He ran a hand through his black hair. His amber eyes darted back toward the inn. He didn't know. He thought she was human. Of course he did. That's all that was supposed to be in Kennard. He was trying to save her from the Royal Guard. If he only knew she wasn't human, he'd probably lead her to the gallows. She sucked in a ragged breath. Three soldiers at once weren't favorable, nor however many joined them. And in a village filled with them.

Still holding Ben's sword, Vaysa scooted away from him and rushed back to the city's edge.

Vaysa darted into the woods, not stopping to reconvene with Shad. Shad would follow. Images flashed in her mind. The red eyes, the smirk, Ben saying, "Berlan," and the fire that coursed in her veins and burned her fingers.

The path whirled by her, her vision swimming. Too many thoughts clouded her mind, blocking her senses. Vaysa launched herself into their home and threw her cloak against the wall.

"What happened?" Shad asked, following her inside. Her golden eyes narrowed as she glanced back toward the trail.

"Who has red eyes?" Vaysa yelled, whirling around to face Shad, focusing on the one thing she could admit to.

Shad pulled back in confusion. "Huh?"

"What species has red eyes?"

"Vaysa, back up and tell me what happened."

Vaysa let out a breath between her clenched teeth. "I got some buns, got a dagger, and on my way out two soldiers left the inn looking for another soldier. That soldier was hiding in the shadows with me. I didn't hear him. And he clearly had red eyes... and blue skin and green hair. What is he?"

"Are you kidding?" Shad asked, but it wasn't a question.

"What is he?" Her anger edged toward curiosity. Shad had to know what it was. And it was in Kennard.

"A horrible species from Berla. What is it doing here?" Shad stared out the window, and when Vaysa cleared her throat, she turned her gaze back to her. "It's called a Silver. Never trust one. They are nasty creatures from the Silver Forest. The same forest I'm from in Berla. They can see in any light, including pitch black. They're known for their stealth, but waste it on having way too many celebrations."

Vaysa blinked. Too many questions swam in her mind. A Berlan was in Kennard? Shad hated Silvers but never mentioned them before. What did this mean for them? Breathing through her nose, she focused on the most pressing matters.

"Is he a threat?" Vaysa asked.

His ability to see in the dark would explain how he knew she was a non-human and would be an advantage against them, especially for the Royal Guard. But he was a non-human. It didn't make sense why he was with them.

Shad snorted. "A Silver, a threat? Only if you listen to it. They're more annoying than dangerous. The bigger question is why is he in Kennard and what are the Royal Guards doing with him?"

"He was in uniform."

Shad's eyes widened and her mouth fell open. "As I said, never trust one. We need to avoid him, and whatever his and their agenda is. We should move."

"Do you think there are more?" Other than Shad, she hadn't seen a non-human in Kennard.

"I don't know, but we don't need to get involved. It's not our problem. We all come here fleeing something."

Vaysa scrunched her face in disbelief but said nothing. Ignoring it didn't feel right. A non-human in Royal Guard gear wasn't right. But they had other things to discuss, too.

"Shad," Vaysa started but stopped. How could she tell Shad about her powers? That she'd felt them in her hands? That Ben had recognized her?

Shad's chest heaved, her eyes narrowing. When her gaze drifted to Vaysa's hands, her jaw flexed. "Did they see it?"

Vaysa's alarmed eyes met Shad's gaze.

"One called me a Berlan," she admitted.

It was always monsters, or evil, never just Berlan. Somehow Berlan seemed the bigger threat than the other names.

"I don't know why..." Shad shook her head. Her gaze fixed off in the distance on something only she could see. "Your powers shouldn't materialize here. They shouldn't."

Heavy silence sat between them.

She'd heard it all before. She'd been too young when she arrived in Kennard. Kennard didn't have the resources needed for them to develop. No one was there to train her.

But this was something else.

Vaysa waited, holding her breath for the words she knew Shad didn't want to admit to.

"We aren't safe here anymore," Shad finally said.

"We'll move," Vaysa agreed.

Shad shot her a sad look. Her glossy eyes scanned her before continuing. "I don't think that'll be enough."

"Then what?" Vaysa forced out, unsure what more they could do.

"Your powers are becoming unpredictable. More fierce."

Vaysa stared at her hands, the dirty, opaque white flesh not belying what happened earlier. Maybe she had imagined it. Just a rush of adrenaline.

"There's something that can help."

"What?" Vaysa breathed. So many thoughts and hopes slammed in her brain. She could control her powers? "But you said…"

Shad shook her head. "I know what I said, and it is the truth. Your powers shouldn't manifest here. I don't know why they are now. I think we need to go to Berla."

"What? Why?" Vaysa roared. Shad wasn't thinking. The Spirit Strait, Phantom Islands, and so much stood in the way.

Shad sighed, staring at the ground. "It's…"

Vaysa waited, letting the silence sit between them.

"You wouldn't believe me if I told you."

Vaysa furrowed her brow and crossed her arms. Shad slowly raised her gaze to Vaysa and groaned.

"There's a way for you to control your powers."

"There is?" Vaysa asked. Hope started to bloom in her chest but wilted. "But you haven't mentioned it before. Why not?" The words hardened her stomach.

"It hasn't mattered. Until recently they've been dormant. There hasn't been a need until now, and now the dam is ready to burst."

"But maybe it could have helped me develop them."

Shad's eyes narrowed. "Fire would have only drawn more attention. Your powers shouldn't materialize in Kennard. Ever."

"But they are, somewhat." Vaysa swallowed back at the lump of embarrassment in her throat. Her meager moments of power had been nothing and now Shad was right. She was ready to burst. "I could have learned… Had some control."

"The risks far outweighed it. They shouldn't have materialized," Shad repeated, her nostrils flared.

The few blips of her power in her veins hadn't felt that threatening, nothing more than an angry blush, but she'd never felt anything on her skin before other than the first night in Kennard. And now a soldier had seen them. "What's the way?"

"You need a dragon scale."

"What?" Vaysa chuckled, the tension breaking. She sobered at Shad's miserable expression.

Shad held her gaze.

"Seriously, a dragon scale?" Vaysa asked, her eyes shooting up in amusement. Shad wanted to go to Berla, and face everything, for a dragon scale? There had to be easier ways in Kennard that didn't require so much risk. Or they could keep moving until the powers went away like they had after that night.

Shad passed her a dark look. "Yes."

"Wait, you're saying dragons are real?"

"I'm saying they used to cover Berla."

"And they just left scales behind before going extinct?" She forced herself to not laugh again.

"I didn't say they were extinct. They used to nest everywhere, but there's a location that was known for large quantities of nests."

"You're being serious?"

Vaysa's stomach dropped. Shad had lost reason, and for what? A bit of heat in her veins? They knew she was a Berlan, and whether her powers should materialize or not, they didn't leave because of Shad's powers. They'd figure out a way to deal with this that didn't involve going to Berla, crossing the strait, or looking for something as ridiculous as a dragon's scale.

Shad stared at Vaysa in disgust.

"Okay, okay," Vaysa said, holding up her palms and shaking her head. The least she could do was hear Shad out before saying no. "Why would a dragon scale help?"

"Their scales are filled with magical properties. They are used to center..." Shad hesitated, and slowly said, "...elemental wielders."

"What does that mean? Elemental wielders?"

"Fire, water, ground, plants, etc. It will help anchor your powers."

"How?"

"I don't know how it works. It just does." Shad ran a hand through her dark hair.

"So you're saying it's a legend that dragon scales can do this? So you want to do this based on a myth? You want me to believe a myth?" A disbelieving chuckle rippled up her throat, but the acidic burn of betrayal pushed it back down. Shad wanted her to believe a myth.

With everything that was going on around them, she wanted to chase a legend instead of prep for the actual coming winter.

"No, I want you to believe the truth. It is not a myth. You believe in the power of your fists and strength, not an inanimate object. I believe in you, and I know a scale will help."

When Vaysa fell silent, Shad blew out a breath. Her frame deflated. Without looking at her, Shad exited the treehouse for their dinner, leaving Vaysa with her thoughts.

A dragon scale was ridiculous, and going to Berla was suicide. But Shad was right, they needed to move, again... because of her.

Chapter 3

TEO

Teo stared at the cold porridge solidifying in his bowl. A shiver of unease wormed through his spine. He should have eaten, but his stomach tightened. The murmur of voices surrounded him. The small tavern next to the inn even tighter with so many soldiers packed inside with the hopes of a hot meal instead of trail rations.

With a shove, he stood. Now was as good a time as any to triple check his roll was packed.

Someone had attacked them. In the middle of town. No, attacked Ben. No, not even that. They hadn't even drawn their sword until Ben had. Even if Ben had made wild accusations about the person, they hadn't done anything other than retreat until Ben tried to exert his control. Teo shook his head. It didn't matter. If anything, the other soldiers were more alert, more ready after Ben's rants.

Pfft. Who could be ready to face Berla? Face the monsters there?

With a flick of his eyes, Teo confirmed Gren had stood with him. A non-human. The first he'd ever seen outside of his grandmother's book. One his troop was to protect. He certainly wasn't a monster type. The pamphlet about Silvers confirmed it. Still though, he was from Berla. General Closs had assigned Gren to his and Ben's care, which meant sharing quarters. So far, Gren had been tidier than any of Teo's siblings and mostly kept to himself. Of all the bunkmates Teo had been assigned, he was the easiest to live with outside of his mumbled quips and random slips outside. But Teo couldn't really blame Gren. He always had to have someone with him in case a townsman got too emboldened. And he was always stared at. Always whispered about. Or yelled about.

Teo could imagine the look of disapproval in his parents' eyes. He was protecting a Berlan. The war with Berla and the non-humans before his birth had taken a toll on his family. His uncle never returned. Unrealistic crop expectations from the castle to feed the troops had worn the land, depleting nutrients and his family's meager gold.

His fingers fell to the satchel at his waist. Inside were the typical tools for a medic and the last bit of cookie his sister had sent. Even if his family hadn't wanted him to join the Royal Guard, his twin Mariah had supported him and sent him gifts. This time a birthday treat she'd made for one of their younger siblings. The treat made possible from the money he sent home. His parents had to know it was from him, even if they refused to write. Even if they called him a disappointment when he left.

He'd hurt his family's pride, but he'd make it right. Like his father had taught him.

"Watch out," Gren growled.

Teo stiffened his spine as he turned to Gren, his finger instinctively inching toward his blade. Instead of paying Teo heed, Gren brushed off crumbs and goo the tavern owner had spilled on his uniform from a stack of dirty plates.

From the sneer and hardness in the owner's eyes, it had been intentional. "Careful, Berlan," the owner snarled. "Wouldn't want any more accidents."

"Jards," Teo breathed.

If only they could explain Gren was helping them, then the people would leave him alone. Hark was the second town they'd stopped at for supplies, the first one shuttering up when they saw Gren's blue skin. The town of Hark hadn't cared since they brought gold. Even if not everyone was welcoming. Once they got to the forests, at least there'd be space to spread out. Breathe. Adjust to the changes, figure out what having a Berlan in the group really meant. Maybe share the watching detail.

With a step to the right, he blocked the path of the tavern owner from Gren, taking the brunt of the broom handle in his side swung at Gren as the owner swept. Biting back a curse, Teo curled his fists but urged Gren to walk ahead of him.

"I can handle their hate," Gren murmured. His red eyes flicked to Teo and then the owner.

"Sure," Teo agreed. "But their hate comes with sharp blades if we're not around."

Gren cocked an eyebrow and flicked his head in dismissal of the comment.

Ben's clear voice rang out. "Attention."

As if pulled by a string, Teo and the others straightened their spines and fell into a line with arms at their sides.

The air shifted. Harsher, thicker, heavier. General Closs strolled from his chambers. His weathered white skin was tanned and reddened from the harsh eastern elements. His normal scowl darkened his face, growing more pronounced the longer he stared at the recruits. Then his gaze found Gren, and his lips curled almost into a smile.

"Gear and in formation in five minutes," Closs bellowed. "The Silver with Ben."

Gren's face darkened at the comment, but otherwise didn't respond.

"Remember," Closs threatened. "Gren is our key. Protect him."

There was no need for "or else". Death would be merciful compared to what Closs would do to them.

Even if he was a non-human, Gren was more important than any of them.

One of the Kennardian princes had been kidnapped. Everyone

knew the Traitors of Berla had to have done it. And Closs had a Berlan willing to help traverse the land.

With a breath of relief, Teo moved toward the last room he'd see before they returned to Kennard from Berla.

His parents hadn't wanted him to join, to go to the eastern mountains like the others had. Over the years, a few returned wounded, or word of their death came. The others had stayed on for the wages. Something Teo hoped to provide for his family. The famine had taken his older brother and one of his younger brothers. With Teo's absence, they'd have one less mouth to feed but without mourning. Hopefully. The thought churned his stomach.

Although he couldn't tell his parents, his assignment wasn't in the east. No, he'd drawn a lucky straw. After basic training, Teo had been assigned to Closs's platoon. Now, Teo was with a secret group to rescue the prince.

He'd be able to send his stipend home, provide his family with seed and resources, and stop a growing war and the likely requirement in a few years for his siblings to join. Even if it had cost him his engagement to Adrienne. Had drawn his father's silent scorn, and his mother's tears. All he had to do was follow Closs's orders, rescue the prince from Berla, survive Berla's monsters, and make it back to Kennard.

Chapter 4

VAYSA

A few weak rays of light left the foliage a dark labyrinth. The first wave of night insects began to sing, and a wisp of fall wind rippled through the leaves. The cloak of night would bring the necessary cover and protection as they gathered berries and lumber before the rain set in. Tomorrow they'd head deeper into the forest to find a winter home. For the evening, they'd camp.

Shad's words buzzed in Vaysa's head. They hadn't talked about Berla since the morning. Nor had Shad argued when Vaysa mentioned moving north in the forest.

Vaysa stilled, a sound flittered in the air. With furrowed brows, she shot a glance at where Shad was in the trees. They were far from Hark and far from where Vaysa had attacked the noble, on a path rarely traveled on the best of days, much less so close to winter.

Tying her cloth into a sack, Vaysa stepped around the bushes dwindling with berries. They would dry out the batch she had and save it for winter.

Strapped to each of their backs were the essentials from their home, which was left abandoned once more in the trees. With their bedrolls, gold, some utensils, and a few extra garments, they'd be able to settle anywhere. Until the Royal Guard found them again.

The uniform clicking of heels carried over the wind, echoing in the trees. Her stomach twisted. Had the troops come looking for her after what happened in town? There was no way they'd know where they lived. Hark was more than a two-day hike for soldiers with gear, and they were west of Hark. Soldiers only went to the eastern mountains. The smith's warning turned in her mind. The rumors of the prince. Of the Berlans. Of her. Her throat tightened.

Shad silently joined her, the feeling of calmness alerting Vaysa to her presence.

"Soldiers," Shad growled.

"Do you think they're after me?" Vaysa asked. "The ones from the village?"

"Doubtful," Shad muttered as she ran a hand over her neck, but she didn't meet Vaysa's eyes.

Doubtful but possible. It was even more unlikely the soldiers would know where to find them. Shad and she hadn't left a trail. But uncertainty tugged at Vaysa's mind, unsettling her nerves. She hadn't been the most cautious when they fled. Even if they had left their home, they couldn't be too careful.

Another curl of heat twisted in her, but as it had for so many years, it flicked out as quickly as it came. A whispered promise on the wind.

She needed to assess the risk. To be certain. Were they being followed or was it simply coincidence? Was it even too dangerous for her and Shad to be out at all, or did they just need to stay off the paths?

Vaysa left her sack of berries with Shad's lumber. With a quick leap, she was in the trees and heading toward the troops. Curiosity and fear twisted in her veins, fueling her muscles.

Shad growled but followed.

Halting a distance from the troops in the direction they approached, Vaysa shifted in the tree, clenching her fists. Her stomach tightened and she tensed to control her fidgeting.

The wet leaves muffled the sound of the approaching soldiers' march. They were heading southwest toward the ports, instead of the eastern mountains like the troops usually did.

Shad cut her eyes to Vaysa.

Vaysa braced for the expected rebuke. The reminder of the village.

Shad's voice was barely a whisper. "We shouldn't be here. We need to get off the path, even the trees above it. Soldiers are too dangerous after the noble and the village."

"Soldiers shouldn't be here. Not on this path. They should be going east, not west. They shouldn't have a Berlan with them. Same troop or not, we need to know what is going on. What are they doing about the prince? They are in Hark. Where else are they? Do we need to move to the South instead of North? The mountains? They'll talk about plans. They always do."

Shad snorted and rolled her eyes. "It's dangerous."

"You know I'm right."

Shad growled but didn't argue.

Vaysa searched the marching guards below her. She recognized a few faces in front from previous encounters, but most were new, young, scared faces that made up the rest of the line.

Her eyes darted amongst the sea of faces until she caught sight of blue skin. Her breath hitched. Toward the end of the line was the unmistakable face of the Silver, the only non-human in the group. Her stomach twisted and a lump bobbed in her throat. It was the same group. How had they made it this far?

She scanned the group and noted their light packing, unlike all the soldiers going to the eastern mountains who wore gear and carried packs. No wonder they had made it so fast. The group below only carried trail essentials for a few days, not the weeks required for the mountains. But they had a Berlan, were headed in the wrong direction, and didn't bother with the normal rations. So the rumor was true. Had something happened to one of the princes? If so, she and Shad would be in more danger. They wouldn't be able to get more supplies. The troops would follow up on all the tales of monsters in the forest.

She licked her lips as her gaze darted back through the line. Unease rattled her muscles, but she didn't move from her position.

"Vaysa," Shad warned. Her warning to not pursue the guards, ample supplies or not.

Vaysa gave a single nod in response. She wouldn't engage.

The smith had noted the Royal Guard's increased presence and now these particular guards were acting unusual and had a non-human. Why would they go west? The only thing west was the Spirit Strait. The Wind Ocean sat to the south. A breath caught in her throat. West of the Spirit Strait was Berla. But the strait was impassible without a cruiser... which the Royal Guard had in the southern ports.

The prince wasn't in Kennard anymore. They were sending troops after the prince and the Berlans. A cold spike speared her heart. More and more troops would come their way. They'd have troops to the east and west of them. They'd be surrounded without a direction to retreat to. The troops would be in Berla. One more reason they couldn't go there for a dragon scale.

An unexpected curl of fire rolled through her veins. She flinched but didn't bother to look at Shad to see if she'd noticed. Shad most likely had, and Vaysa didn't want the worried look or inane comment about going for a dragon scale.

Where could she and Shad go now? Would north be any better? It was closer to the castle. The horrific Sentinels. And probably more Royal Guards to protect the other princes.

With the troops' gaze focused ahead, not scanning for signs of life or habitats, whatever their mission was, they didn't care about the trees or what lived in them. Relief didn't settle on her as she expected with the assumption they weren't pursuing her, instead fire flickered in her veins and her neck hair raised. A hum danced on the breeze.

The smell of rain intensified, even though the sky was clear, pulling her from her thoughts.

"Vaysa, let's go," Shad hissed.

She nodded but allowed herself a few moments to drink in Gren's oddness. His movements were like the other soldiers', but his red eyes reflected the few hints of light. He didn't seem stressed in the group: his gait was normal, he wasn't rigid, and instead of watching the other soldiers, his focus was on the trees. He appeared oblivious to the others' leers and distance.

Most of the others seemed to give him extra space. Then she noticed Ben scowling next to him. Vaysa snarled. Fire pulsed in her hands and a raw curl of fire flickered in her stomach. Her vision tunneled and whispers licked at her ears as she watched his moves, his disdain-filled glances at Gren.

An insatiable pull tugged at her. A moth to the flame.

Instead of slipping back into the forest as Shad wanted, she crept along after them, her focus bouncing between Ben and Gren. A curl of fire skidded through her.

She watched the Silver as he trekked along. Each time Gren's gait brought him closer to Ben, Ben would recoil and grimace.

Vaysa caught Gren smirking when Ben jerked to the side. He sauntered on, unperturbed by the others. The Royal Guard was notorious for their hatred of non-humans, but he said he didn't need saving, and he seemed safe. And he was wearing a Royal Guard's uniform. For whatever reason, he was one of them and would be gone soon.

They finally came to a clearing that forked into several paths. The troops pulled up and began the process of setting up camp. The platoon posted two guards at each path while the remaining soldiers set up tents and cooked dinner.

The wind had grown colder and gustier and bit at exposed skin. The insect noise lessened with the cold, and distant calls of larger animals sliced the night air. To compensate, the soldiers built a large fire. Although the fire illuminated the area nearest to it, it made the surrounding area darker.

The troops broke off into small groups and lounged with their meals. The quiet of the forest thrummed in the air, and several soldiers leaned back with their eyes closed. Vaysa snorted. They made it easy to rob them. Too bad she wouldn't be able to tonight.

Her eyes flickered to the non-human soldier and then the rest of the troops. The others continued to give him and Ben a wide berth. In the flicker of the firelight, their youthful faces stood in contrast to their uniforms.

Gren and Ben sat on the edge of the path against a large deciduous tree away from the camp. Ben's annoyance darkened his face, and he mumbled under his breath while he stared into the distance. Gren's red eyes searched the trees, ignoring his companion.

Vaysa grinned. They were separated and distracted. It would be so easy. She sucked in a silent breath and slowly let it out. No, she was already taking a risk following them. She couldn't engage, couldn't garner more attention. Wouldn't risk what happened in Hark. She and Shad were already moving again when they should be hankering down for winter.

A familiar voice cut through the forest's murmurs and idle chatting. Her neck hair rose, and she searched the area.

"Closs," Shad hissed.

Her stomach clenched and Vaysa stole a glance to make sure Shad wouldn't launch out of the tree onto him.

Shad gave a slight nod, acknowledging Vaysa's concern.

Vaysa swallowed and leaned back on her heels. Closs was Shad's favorite to target. He just hadn't been in the area since he was sent east a few years ago.

General Closs was at once a familiar and annoying sight. He'd marched troops across Kennard for as long as she could remember. He was short and heavy, with disheveled peppery gray hair, weathered pale skin, cold, light blue eyes, and bulging shoulders tapered into thickly muscled thighs. His constant snarl matched his one eye that permanently squinted.

The soldiers near him picked at their meals and avoided eye contact, and those who could snuck out of view.

General Closs surveyed the group and narrowed in on the soldier Teo, who'd stopped her from pummeling Ben in the town, and spat, "Your turn to watch the Silver. If anything happens to him, you're responsible."

Shad sucked in a breath and her eyes flashed gold at the word "Silver."

Teo nodded sharply at Closs's order and sat down by a few of the younger soldiers. His gaze drifted to the Silver and he sighed. His sullen face matched the other soldiers' faces.

Ben sneered at Gren as he moved away, finally relieved of duty.

Everyone's attention was focused on Gren.

Vaysa gestured to Shad to retreat. With Closs there, she didn't want to risk Shad's reaction or her own toward Ben.

To her surprise, Shad ignored her sign to move back toward the canopy, her gaze locked on Gren. A wicked smile danced on Shad's lips, her eyes golden and bright.

General Closs grumbled and finally went into his tent. Teo sighed and pulled out a deck of cards, raising it questioningly to the soldiers near him. His threat level was nil.

The Silver peeled off his boots and leaned against the tree. His eyes slowly shut, and he let out a long breath.

Vaysa released the breath she had been holding. She gestured to Shad again. One encounter was enough.

"A Silver," Shad breathed.

Vaysa licked her lips, hesitation stalling her step. "Shad," Vaysa mouthed. Shad had shown hatred earlier toward the Silver, but Vaysa hadn't expected her to focus on him.

A dark look passed over Shad's face.

Vaysa frowned as Shad's breathing escalated into raspy waves and her chest heaved up and down. Drool dripped from her revealed fangs as they grew. The full coming of night brought with it the stubbles of her gray fur. Her hair merged with her mane, her shoulders bulged, her claws extended out several inches, and her human form became feline-like. The silent transformation took only a few seconds. A smile tugged on her lips as she gauged Gren.

Vaysa put a hand up to warn Shad. Shad could be impulsive in Cuma form. Now she had both Closs and a Silver in her sights.

Vaysa blinked away her reservations. While drawing her dagger, she slid up to the tree trunk. The bark rubbed against her calloused palm. There was nothing more to learn. The guards would be every-where. She gestured again at Shad to go into the canopy.

With a roll of her eyes, Shad moved back.

Before Vaysa could pull herself up after Shad, a bark of laughter rang out, followed by a chorus of hoots. A group of guards were playing cards, including Gren's babysitter Teo. Several stood around, watching. Teo slammed his hand down, bringing on a wave of laughter from the card players. The roars were greeted by grunts and groans of the sleeping men. Vaysa retreated into the shadows when Teo trudged over to Gren while gesturing to the soldiers still snicker-ing. Teo slumped down next to Gren. Although she was silent, she didn't want to tip their attention to her.

Vaysa bit her lips between her teeth, stilling all other motion, including her breath. She'd need to wait for their attention to be diverted again. A curse twirled on her tongue. She'd led Shad here and now got them stuck.

Shad snorted. Her gaze remained fixated on Gren as she waited for Vaysa. Her lips danced in a snarl and her fingers flexed, extending her claws. Unease chilled Vaysa's veins.

"You'll get your money back tomorrow," Gren said without looking at Teo.

"Yeah? Maybe if you play," Teo said and punched the dirt. He sighed and then ran a brown hand through his black hair. He was so close his amber eyes were distinguishable.

Gren rolled his eyes in response, but finally asked, "Do you think we'll find the prince?"

Confirmation. The smith was right. They were looking for the prince.

"What?" Teo barked.

Vaysa's stomach tightened when several soldiers turned from the card game to stare, but they quickly turned back to gambling when Teo made another gesture at them.

Teo returned his gaze to Gren and said, "We are the Royal Guard, of course we will!"

A muscle twitched in Gren's face and his eyes narrowed. Recoiling to the side, he muttered, "Cockiness has sent many people to their death. What if something has happened to him? What will we do then?"

"Then we'll kill the Traitors. I don't give a jards if they have magical powers. I have steel." Teo stopped when he saw Gren staring at him. His eyes widened and he licked his lips.

"Killing Traitors didn't work the first time," Gren said and rubbed his forehead. "King Russom was still alive then and in control of Berla before the Traitors took over. The Traitors survived his troops and King Malik's Royal Guard. Forced them both out."

Teo frowned. "King Malik and the Royal Guards know more this time. We'll sneak in and out before they know."

Gren raised an eyebrow and tilted his head to look at Teo. He shrugged and nodded noncommittally. "Perhaps."

Teo's face darkened as he perused Gren, and he asked, "You don't think we'll succeed?"

"Oh, I'm certain you will succeed with the goal," Gren said and met his eyes. "Otherwise, I wouldn't have joined."

Her stomach turned. Hopefully they'd find the Kennardian prince fast, be done, and go back to their focus in the east. Then their lives could return to normal. But this felt more than a simple retrieval. They were mobilizing troops.

Teo stared at him, his jaw working to stop the retort, his face red and his eyes narrowed.

Gren stood, wiping his pants off, and said, "I need to take a walk."

Teo sighed and slipped his hands beneath him and pushed himself up. "Where to?"

"I can go alone."

Teo's eyes darted to Closs's tent and back to Gren, then tracked to the other guards. "I need to protect you."

Gren snorted, his red eyes flashing. "I'm better equipped for the dark than you. Besides, what'll happen with all the soldiers here?" he asked, gesturing to the guards in various stages of relaxation.

Vaysa smirked. It was that same sentiment that made the troops easy targets.

Teo's lips pinched. Finally he nodded as his gaze took in the number of soldiers. "Okay," he relented, and then joked, "Watch out for thieves."

"Least of my concerns," Gren said while his gaze flickered to the Royal Guards.

Vaysa mirrored Gren's step as he backed away from Teo and then strolled down the path, unencumbered by the humans near him and not fearful of what lurked in the dark forest.

His eyes darted toward the trees. Vaysa stilled as his gaze lingered. He seemed indifferent to everything, blasé about the dangers. But then he'd somehow made it across the Spirit Strait and to Kennard. It had almost killed her when she came to Kennard.

Teo looked up as Gren slid into the forest instead of walking on the trail. The darkness enveloped Gren. Teo's eyes bulged and his mouth hung agape. Swearing, he clambered to his feet. Teo whistled and pointed with trembling hands.

Several guards scrambled to their feet and crept into the forest. Teo whimpered and cursed and then dashed back to the campsite toward General Closs's tent.

Pausing, Vaysa glanced toward where Shad would be. Even without seeing her, she could feel Shad watching her. A calm settled on her skin, and she let out a silent breath.

"Let's go," Vaysa signaled to Shad. They could use the guards' clumsiness to cover their retreat.

Grabbing onto the branches, Vaysa pushed her feet against the welcoming bark and launched up effortlessly into the foliage. The slight rustle of leaves meant Shad was following her in the trees. She'd head north until they were far enough away so that they could regroup for the night.

The soldiers drew closer, fumbling below in the darkness in search of Gren. Agitated curses floated up. The soldiers were blind and disoriented in the dense forest. They weren't focused on her or Shad.

Tuning out the forest's noises and the cold, Vaysa followed Shad.

The branches got thicker as she ventured farther into the dense flora. Wind skimmed against her neck and tingles shimmied down her back. She moved forward, her feet gliding on the familiar branches, but her eyes scanned all around her. Discomfort slithered down her back. The thin strips of moonlight that penetrated the branches were more than enough light for her to see. She felt his presence before his hand could land on her back.

Chapter 5

VAYSA

*H*is bony fingers dug into her shoulder, reaching for muscle. Vaysa crouched, grabbing the assaulting hand, and then yanked. Her muscles screamed as she tore his grip from her. Gren flew over her head and crashed into the tree trunk. The rush of the attack flooded her body with warmth. She smiled and licked her lips in expectancy.

Gren stirred and slowly stood up. He smirked. "Hello, non-human."

Vaysa growled, gripping her dagger, then lunged toward Gren. She smashed him into the tree trunk, her dagger pressed against his throat, stopping any additional attack.

"I saw you watching the camp. I came to warn you." Gren gulped and sweat beaded on his brow.

"Already saw the Royal Guard, thanks." Vaysa's jaw twitched, but she otherwise contained her surprise. Shad said they could see in the dark.

He tried to pull back, but she held him in place. He finally eased under her grip and sighed.

"They're looking for you."

Her body froze except for an intake of breath.

"They sent me earlier to find your home."

A wave of red warmed through Vaysa. Her mind played back her carelessness when she'd fled the village.

"But I saw you packing. I delayed them as long as possible."

Instead of responding, she let her muscles ease and took slow, deliberate breaths.

"What do you want?" she asked, calm despite the fire singeing her nerves. Berlan or not, he was in a Royal Guard's uniform. He was with them freely.

"I owe you," he shrugged. "You offered to help me. So..." Gren chuckled, the sound hollow and dark. "All I have to say is run while you can. You attacked an officer. A prince is kidnapped. You obviously didn't do it, but they don't care."

Vaysa shoved him back. His jacket wrinkled where her hands had been.

Instead of straightening it, he smirked. "Tick tock, they're coming," Gren taunted.

"Fine, if you're trying to help us, then where should we head?" Vaysa asked. Without a doubt, he'd lie. His word was as good as his uniform.

He shook his head. "Nowhere is safe. If they see you, they'll strike first. They're headed right now to your tree house."

Vaysa growled, baring her teeth. He wasn't any better than the Royal Guard. He was one of them. "A big help you are, leading them to my house."

"I said I delayed them. I already knew you left."

"Why are you helping them?" The words were out before she could stop them.

"They offered me passage home."

Before Vaysa could retort, Shad landed behind them.

"Cuma?" Gren whispered, his eyes large.

Shad ignored him and hissed, "They're coming."

Below them, alarmed, muffled voices filled the air. The guards were closer than she thought. Her muscles tightened. Twice in one day he'd distracted her. Twice the Royal Guard had taken her by surprise. A new twist of fire tangled in her veins. With a gasp, she sucked in air to focus her mind, but the inferno welled beneath her skin.

Regaining his composure, Gren smirked. "Told you. Your time is almost up."

Vaysa swore.

"Go," she growled to Gren. Her eyes darted around the canopy for the best escape route. "Before they hurt you, too."

"There's someone with him," a voice bellowed below.

Shad shot Vaysa an "I told you so" look with an arch of her eyebrow but said nothing.

Vaysa sighed, embarrassment reddening her neck. They had no new information, but now the Royal Guard was closing in on them. Again.

"There's an archer," Gren hissed, pointing to a figure moving up the trees. Their dark green uniform blended into the surrounding foliage.

"Aim for the big one," a familiar voice demanded. Ben. "Take it out first."

"Duck," Gren growled and tugged on Vaysa's sleeve.

Vaysa was able to dodge before a folly of arrows ripped through the air. Only one snagged Vaysa's jacket, tearing flesh. The others, Shad batted away. Fresh blood blossomed from Vaysa's wound. She cursed as pain radiated up her arm. The tang of blood twisted in the air.

Shad bellowed, the roar filling the trees and momentarily silencing everything.

When she fell silent, her body heaved, her breaths short and angry. Her eyes flashed gold.

"You," Shad snarled at Gren. "You led them here."

She bared her teeth and breathed in his face.

His eyes watered.

Drool dripped from the side of Shad's mouth and she snarled.

Gren licked his lips and looked toward Vaysa.

"I... I had to..." He sucked in a breath. "They were testing my loyalty. I made sure you had left. They'd only find your abandoned home."

"He warned us about the archer," Vaysa gritted out.

"Silver," Shad roared, ignoring her. "You're never to be trusted. I should end you now."

"No!" Vaysa screamed. Shadows swarmed in her vision. The hiss of whispers licked at her ears.

"What the jards," Gren breathed, staring at Vaysa.

A whine filled the air. Her veins pulsed in an angry inferno.

"Take out the other one, now!" Ben's voice ricocheted through her thoughts.

Before Vaysa could think, respond, act, Shad howled and dove for the scattering soldiers.

Vaysa swore in confusion and leaned over the branch and watched as Shad landed on all fours and spun around, daring the soldiers to attack.

One of the guards, stupid enough to comply, raced toward her with his sword. Shad batted him away, but another drew closer, and then a third.

They'd destroy Shad. No, Vaysa couldn't let that happen. Couldn't let them take her only family.

No!

Vaysa dove from the branch using another limb to control her descent. She landed squat on the ground, and her eyes flashed as she growled at the men surrounding them. She'd destroy them if they hurt Shad. A bolt of thunder sliced the sky, pulling the soldiers' attention up.

A hiss sounded on the air. Tingles raced down Vaysa's spine.

Shad made a surprised noise in her throat and backed up from the men. Her gaze swung to Vaysa and back to the sky. The soldiers took it as a sign of fear and edged closer.

Vaysa pulled her sword from its scabbard. The one she'd taken from Ben. She could take at least three out.

"Leave her alone," Vaysa seethed. Black edged her vision and faint, familiar whispers skittered in the air. Fire raced in her veins and she panted.

"What the?" Ben flinched, but then his face hardened, and he stepped forward brandishing his sword.

"No," Shad growled, her fangs glistening with saliva.

"You're the creature from the village," Ben sneered, pointing his sword toward Vaysa. "You owe me a sword. I've come to collect."

"Come and get it."

"No," Teo's voice moved toward Ben. "Don't make it worse, again."

Vaysa sneered. Always Ben's shield.

"What's going on?" Closs's voice boomed through the forest, pulling Vaysa's attention from Ben.

"No," Shad yelled and leapt toward Ben as he swung his sword.

Darkness clouded Vaysa's vision, and the whispers grew. Their voices a shrill scream. Power welled within her core, burning her veins and straining against her muscles. Dormant power she'd been unable to tap, but yearned to be released, and she couldn't hold it back.

The dam broke and the surge of power flooded her body, leaching into her veins and clawing at her resolve.

Fire coursed through her muscles, constricted and then released as a wave of power shot from her toward Ben. The ball of fire slammed into a tree when Ben fell to the ground to dodge it, setting the dried leaves on fire.

Vaysa blinked. The world swam back into focus. She stared at her hands, unscathed but pulsing with remnants of heat, then to the horror-filled faces of the soldiers around her.

How had she done it?

It was like the night in the village when she first arrived. With a blink, she saw the fire that had shot from her hands toward the villagers' weapons. Echoes of the screams filled her mind that had faded as she fled into the forest. But now she had soldiers as witnesses.

"Is it a dragon?" a voice called out.

"You idiot, there aren't dragons, it was her," another replied.

"She's one of them," another voice whispered, and others joined in the murmur of fear.

"It's the Berlans. Here to kill us."

"It's the forest monsters."

She stepped back. Shad was by her side, her form blocking Vaysa from the prying eyes.

"You'll pay," Ben spat and scrambled to his feet. "Both of you monsters."

The hot pulse of anger rocketed through her veins again, the motion causing her to tremble, but she tightened her muscles to control it as another burst of thunder tore across the star-speckled sky.

"You." Closs's voice was near, and the soldiers parted as he crept closer. His gaze locked on Vaysa. "I know what you are."

How? She didn't even know what she was.

Vaysa heaved, her vision tunneled toward Closs, everything else filtered out. How did he know anything about her? Her fingers curled into fist as fire welled again in her veins. Promising to end everything.

A wicked smile spread over his face. His gaze darted over her form, an appreciative look in his eyes. He stepped closer, his hand reaching toward her. "You're even better than I imagined you could be."

Before Vaysa could respond, Shad had them in the branches above the soldiers.

The crackle of fire consuming the trees deafened the soldiers' voices, pulling Vaysa into the situation as Shad positioned herself to run in the canopies.

"Wait," Vaysa said, her eyes catching sight of Gren.

"Let's go," Shad barked.

Vaysa flinched, staring at Gren and then the approaching inferno. The soldiers were screaming about monsters and fire. No one was trying to help Gren or stop the fire. No one cared. He was in danger of the soldiers' zealousness and the blaze. He'd burn because of her. He had helped them. "He warned us twice."

"Dammit," Shad spat at Vaysa's hesitation and lunged toward Gren.

Gren jumped back and tried to cower in a ball. Shad grabbed him anyway, and without a word, Vaysa crawled on her back.

Vaysa stared at her hands, unmarred except for the normal red scars, as the trio flew through the treetops. She looked at the sky, the normal stars on display without a trace of a storm. She looked backwards, but the sky remained clear except for a hazy plume of smoke blotting out the view, growing smaller and smaller as they covered the vast terrain.

What had she done?

They landed atop their old roof. Shad sniffed vigilantly and then tossed Gren into the shack. She followed with Vaysa still on her back.

The barren walls offered no reprieve from the coming calamity. The place that had once promised shelter and protection during the winter was a waiting beacon for the enemy.

She moved her gaze from her hands to Shad. Shad was assessing her, her face pinched in concern.

"I don't know," Vaysa started and stopped. What didn't she know? How? Why?

Shad shook her head. "It's been building. It was going to happen. We need to move, now."

Shad's eyes bore into her. She didn't just mean somewhere new in Kennard. She meant Berla.

"They know about this place, they're coming here," Gren said. "I'm sorry. They were testing me. I couldn't lie... Not if..."

Shad rolled her eyes. Her gaze darted to the sky and then back to Vaysa.

Vaysa huffed a shaky breath. Now the soldiers had seen her fire, and Closs. She sucked in a shakier breath, her gaze losing focus. Closs seemed so intent on her. Claimed to know what she was.

"We could—" Gren started.

"Shut up, Silver," Shad warned, and looking at Vaysa said. "Ready?"

No. Not to go where Shad wanted to go.

Vaysa searched the room in wide sweeping glances, seeing nothing as her brain processed the night. Where could they go? No town would protect them. The Royal Guard was following them. If they went east toward the mountains, they'd run into the troops there.

"Are you a Traitor?" Gren asked.

He tilted his head, his eyes pinched, seeming to already know the answer.

"A what?" Vaysa hesitated.

It was a word Gren and Teo had discussed earlier. Something about them being in Berla. But Berla didn't matter.

"Watch it," Shad hissed as she moved closer to Gren to block Vaysa.

Vaysa raised her eyebrows at Shad in question but remained quiet.

Shad shook her head at Vaysa, but finally relented, "They watch over Berla since they dismantled the monarchy of King Russom."

Vaysa had no idea what that meant and didn't care. It was more about Berla, and they were in Kennard. She snorted. "No, I'm no Traitor."

"I can help you get out of Kennard, then," Gren said, resting back with a large smile spread across his face. "It won't be a breach of my stupid oath I made to leave Kennard. I can't help Traitors... but you're not."

Vaysa frowned in response. She needed a place to hide. She didn't want to leave Kennard, and if she did, she wouldn't need his help.

Shad slid a glare to Gren before locking eyes with Vaysa. She mouthed, "You need a dragon scale."

When Vaysa opened her mouth to protest, Shad shook her head. Her eyes cut to Gren then back to Vaysa. "Between us only," she mouthed.

Vaysa blew out a breath. Phantom heat snaked over her hands, reminding her of her exhibition. How could a dragon scale help? Why was Shad mentioning it now, after all these years? It was ridiculous. She and Shad had to move north, away from the ports. Somehow bypass the Royal Guard descending on them.

"I can help," Gren whined.

Shad shook her head at Vaysa and put her hand up to stop her from commenting. She said to Gren, "You expect us to just believe you're going to help us? You're in Royal Guard gear. A jarding Berlan in Royal Guard gear."

He shrugged. "Probably not."

"We should have left you in the trees with your troops."

"Shad," Vaysa warned. They both knew it meant death.

"But I have information you don't."

"What does it matter?" Shad roared. "We can see the Royal Guard is everywhere."

"But I can help."

"This is why you don't get involved with Silvers," Shad said to Vaysa, pointing at Gren. "They just play games and change sides as it benefits them."

Vaysa's breath caught in her throat as Shad's eyes flashed gold. Despite his annoying personality, he didn't deserve death.

Shad took a few steps toward Gren, her head tilted to the side. "All right Silver, you want to help? You have info we don't? Why are you here, in Kennard?"

"I'm on a mission." He paused and, turning toward Vaysa, smiled darkly and said, "You could help me with your... skills... and reap the reward."

"No thanks," Vaysa said.

Shad snorted and furled her fist. "True to Silver form." She snapped her fingers at Gren and spat, "Look at me. Why are you with the Kennardian Royal Guard?"

Gren swung his dark gaze back to Shad. "It was the only way to survive here, and now there is a reward to get."

Vaysa sighed loudly, cutting off Shad's retort. She'd finally met someone more irritating to Shad than humans. "Enough. You warned me about the archer, and we got you out of the fire. We're even."

Gren chuckled. "Sure."

Shad's lips pressed into a thin line. Her golden eyes darkened. With a shake of her head, she growled. "Let's just leave him. We need to move now. They're coming. We know they are. Knowing what we do about the prince and..." Shad flinched, her eyes falling to Vaysa's hands. "We have to go."

Vaysa cursed. A dragon scale wouldn't help. They needed to hide. Get ahead of the Royal Guard. Not focus on nonsense. Or secrets.

"Wait, wait, wait," Gren said hurriedly with his hand in the air and his palm facing Vaysa. "Take me with you."

"What?" Both Vaysa and Shad said in unison.

"I can't stay here. They'll blame me for your escape. I can't just join another group. Not with everything going on. You want answers. You want to know why we're headed west. We're after a reward. We're after the prince."

"The jards." Vaysa rolled her eyes. "I don't care about your reward."

"No matter where you go, the Royal Guard will be there. You need to stay ahead of them. Whoever saves the prince will be rewarded. I can help. You can earn their favor."

Vaysa scoffed. "I don't want the Royal Guard's favor."

"Okay, then I know the main routes the Royal Guards are taking. I can help you avoid them."

Vaysa's eyes widened. A sliver of hope wormed in her veins.

Shad rolled her eyes and crossed her arms over her chest, muttering, "Don't trust a Silver."

"Hey, I'm not a liar. The goal is to get the prince and get out." Gren unrolled a piece of parchment from his vest and tossed it at Vaysa's feet while glaring at Shad. Vaysa scanned the reward poster; it was typical propaganda. She knew they would never give her and Shad the reward. Only a noose.

"It doesn't matter," Shad said, taking the poster and tearing it up.

"We could tie him up and leave him for the Royal Guard," Vaysa said. "He told them where we lived. They'll be here by morning. They can find him here. They can add it to our list of charges."

Gren's eyes widened.

Tilting her head, Shad sniffed and scampered outside. She came back in ashen. "I smell fire."

"What? Why would they burn the forest?"

How had the Royal Guard tracked them so fast? Another pulse of heat flared in Vaysa's veins. Her fingers curled on their own, beckoning it forward. She sucked in a ragged breath. Instead of recessing, it coiled into her stomach. A faint whisper sounded.

A crack of lightning sliced the sky, drenching the forest in brilliant silver light.

The heat dissipated, rolling through her limbs in receding waves. She stared at her hands that showed no hint of the power coiling in her.

"Who knows? Let's go," Shad said, frozen and staring at the sky.

Shad had been right; as long as her powers were awry, they were no longer safe in Kennard. And neither was Gren. The Royal Guard would kill him in an attempt to get her and Shad. They had to move.

Vaysa roughly grabbed Gren before he could protest and tied his arms behind his back. He didn't need to die in the fire, but Vaysa didn't trust him, either.

She tethered Gren to Shad's back and slid on behind him.

Shad glided out of the shack and into the treetops. Vaysa turned for one final look at their past home. The bile taste of fear crept up her throat and she suppressed a scream. After turning back, she focused her gaze west.

Chapter 6

TEO

Teo stared ahead. His mouth trembled, but he stood silently in front of General Closs.

Closs was ranting about losing Gren. Word of the prince's kidnapping had spurred troops into action. Berla had to have done it. Even if they hadn't claimed it yet. Closs had marched back from the Eastern side of the mountains with a non-human in tow. After a private audience with King Malik, Closs had been granted permission to join the other Royal Guards heading to Berla. Teo had been selected for the private group.

And Teo had messed up.

All the troops were starting to be rerouted to rescue the prince, but General Closs had the key to a quick recovery. The ability to end this before it was war. He had a Berlan willing to help traverse the land to expedite the process.

Closs had made it clear: the troop was to protect and watch Gren. He was invaluable to their mission.

And Teo had messed up.

He'd let Gren walk away.

Even with other guards around, it was still his mistake. He was supposed to protect Gren. Even if Gren made it hard to. Teo had treated him like a normal soldier.

Jards.

Gren wasn't close to normal, though. He was a Silver. There was a pamphlet on his species. His species didn't fall into the monster spectrum, but he was still non-human. Not only did he have blue skin, green hair, and red eyes, the guy could pretty much see in the dark. He wasn't a normal soldier.

The pamphlet didn't compare to Teo's grandma's book, a book of fairytales from her youth. Gren looked more like the night-watchers in her book, trickster people who became one with the night. They'd protect others from mythical monsters prowling in the woods.

Teo blinked and focused back on Closs, who continued to bellow, eyes bulging and spittle flying out of his mouth. The words had passed intelligible and moved to ranting.

Closs had been yelling about the Cuma and how it stole from him. Stole their best tool to find the prince. But he'd roared the most about the woman getting away.

Teo's cheeks flushed as the others stared at him. It was all his fault. Gren, the key to rescuing the prince, was gone, and it was Teo's fault. He let a monster get him. He wasn't sure why, but it was also his fault the men couldn't catch the woman with fire powers. He sucked back a whimper and stared forward.

He had let his troop down and he'd be damned to fail them again. He'd joined the Royal Guard to provide for his family after the famine. They depended on his stipend. He wouldn't disappoint them. Again.

"Sir," Teo said, surprised to hear his own voice.

He flinched when the men around him gasped at his stupidity.

Closs stopped mid-word. His face contorted with rage. "You dare to interrupt me?"

Teo winced, unsure what to do or say.

"Answer me, boy!" Closs yelled.

When Teo hesitated, Closs stormed the distance between them. Teo swallowed as his lips trembled.

Closs shoved his face so close to Teo's that the warmth and moisture of Closs's breath dampened Teo's cheek.

"Sir, I will bring him back."

He didn't know how, but his family didn't raise cowards. And, as his dad always said, "You fix what you did wrong." Teo had made the mess, and he'd fix it. He wouldn't be an embarrassment to his family. He'd find Gren and do whatever it took to protect him until he could reconvene with General Closs.

Closs chuckled and Teo froze. "You already failed. You're a worthless sack of jards."

"Yes, Sir."

Closs sneered. "I bet Gren is following that girl."

Teo's brow furrowed but he didn't interrupt. Why would Gren follow anyone? The Royal Guard would keep him protected.

Closs snorted. His voice dropped low and calm. "You bring him to me, or you'll be an example to the world of why you don't cross me."

Teo gulped and blinked. Sweat dripped down his neck and his fists involuntarily clenched and unclenched.

"Yes, Sir."

Chapter 7

VAYSA

Shad had soared through the trees, but she didn't slow down throughout the night. Vaysa watched as the blackness of the forest canopy lightened, revealing hints of green, red, and orange leaves. Few peeks of the sky were visible through the foliage. Each glimpse showed the brightening of the morning, and the star-speckled sky became streaked with blues and oranges. The familiar stars faded in the encroaching light as they fled deeper into foreign trees.

The morning would warm up quickly. They'd have a few more weeks to stockpile.

She stopped herself. Their stockpile was gone. Her home was gone.

She shivered despite the mild temperatures. They'd make it work. As long as she had Shad, everything would be okay.

The smell of the salty ocean assaulted Vaysa long before she saw it. The briny odor clung to the trees and left a coating on her tongue. Goosebumps prickled her skin, sweat trickled down her face and neck, and dread crept up her throat. She looked frantically around for the invader.

She flexed, ready for the imaginary assailant, and then cursed.

It was the damn strait again.

She didn't want to face it, or the memories of her first trek across it. The memories of her mom.

But to get to Berla, she'd have to.

Shad slowed and found them an overgrown patch of weeds to rest in. Plush bushes had spade-shaped, flame-red leaves. Trees provided cover from above and anyone venturing in the area. The distant crash of waves thrummed in the air and the pungent smell of salty water masked the earthy smell of the foliage.

Vaysa helped unload Gren on to a pile of brush.

Dawn broke and Shad morphed back into human form.

Shad stretched and then tossed Vaysa their pack of matches, which was already dwindling low.

Vaysa stared at Gren. He'd fallen asleep on the ride. If he had any matches, they would have been in his travel pack still back at camp. Sighing, she used one of their matches to start a small fire. A blaze quickly grew, and she absentmindedly added twigs, dry grasses, and leaves to fuel it.

"I'll get us food," Shad said. Her eyes cut to Gren and then back to Vaysa. She growled.

"Shad, how are we going to hide?" Vaysa asked, standing up. They were too close to the human villages on the coast.

"I don't know if we can," Shad sighed, her dull cream eyes gaze skimming over Vaysa.

Shad was doing all this for a legendary token. A chance. Something she'd kept from Vaysa. If they went for it, what other secrets would be uncovered?

"Are you sure about the dragon scale?" Vaysa asked. Her eyes flickered in the direction of the strait. To the unknown.

"Yes," Shad confirmed.

Vaysa's stomach settled hard. "Aside from the Royal Guard, will Berla be safe?"

"Probably not."

A spike of fire tickled her veins. She tightened her muscles to suppress it, but based on Shad's expression, she hadn't succeeded completely. "Why?" Vaysa whispered. "It's a land of non-humans."

"There's so much I haven't told you about Berla, that hasn't mattered in Kennard," Shad said and shook her head. "None of it mattered until now. They saw you. They'll hunt you to death to control you. Your powers."

"You know what I am?" Vaysa asked, the sting of betrayal piercing her heart. Shad had always told her she didn't since they met the night Vaysa set the village on fire. "You know what my powers are?"

Shad shook her head. "No, I don't know what your powers will be. We know you created fire, but I don't know how or what else you can do. But I do know what I saw, and I know what the Royal Guard saw."

"But—" Vaysa started. The familiar words felt hollow. Shad knew something, and she'd withheld it. Even if it had been for Vaysa's safety, the sting of it twisted in her veins.

"I can't help with this. Your powers should be dormant here, but you started a forest fire. I don't know what else to do. I can only morph at night here, otherwise it's too taxing. You saw that when we were attacked all those years ago. You were so young when you came here; your powers hadn't developed in Berla and shouldn't have developed here. The water and land here are nutrient poor. I don't know what other powers you should have, but fire is dangerous. You don't know how to control it. I don't know either. You need a dragon scale before something else happens."

Acid pooled in Vaysa's stomach. Of all the times her powers manifested, they had to manifest when the Royal Guard were on a crusade to bring a prince back. There wasn't time to think or plan. Nothing was as it should be. She remembered this normal lecture about Shad's morphing. Vaysa's powers weren't supposed to develop here. She'd accepted it years ago. But they'd displayed again. Something wasn't right.

"The Royal Guard are headed there, too," Vaysa said. "Berla's unknown. How will it be safe?"

Shad closed her eyes and rolled her lips between her teeth. Sighing, she looked back at Vaysa. "The Royal Guard is everywhere. The only way for you to have a chance to survive is to get out of Kennard and across the water. There's so much to tell you, and I will, but for now, just trust me. I'm going to get you the help you need."

Vaysa turned in the direction they had come from. To see her home. To see something familiar to calm her. But it was pointless. It was gone, as was her life in Kennard.

She nodded and looked down at the fire flickering in the morning light. Her hand landed on her gold pouch. Filling it two days ago had led her here. Would it even be useful in Berla?

She blew out a sigh. It didn't matter. They'd figure out a way to survive no matter where they landed.

Shad silently left, slipping into the forest to get breakfast.

Vaysa leaned against a tree. She'd put them in this position. Shad had warned her, and she didn't listen. The urge to lash out, kick something or scream, filled her, and then an inferno burned in her core and swam through her veins. She clenched her hands to stop the fire, but it burst out, popping in a shower of sparks.

She stared dumbfounded at the display. Never had the fire pushed out through her muscles. Now it had, multiple times in a day. She slumped back.

Her stupid powers, which she couldn't control, and never showed until now, were why they had to run. If she'd listened, not gone to watch the guard, they'd still be at home preparing for winter and living the life she knew. Not heading to Berla. And Shad wouldn't be talking about a ridiculous dragon scale.

But playing what-if wouldn't help and neither would self-pity.

She could block the fear and emotion if she just focused on the basics. Guilt would only make her vulnerable and distracted. They would be fine. They would find a new home in Berla. She just needed to believe it. Once in Berla, she'd be able to figure out her powers without the threat of the Royal Guard. Perhaps once they reached Berla, Shad would forget about the dragon scale, and Vaysa could forget about the secrets, and they could work on finding a home for the winter.

Gren shifted in his sleep when the fire's heat reached him. He groaned and then lurched against his restraints. His eyes flew open in surprise that morphed into horror, and he started jerking against his constraints.

Vaysa chuckled and then went to release him from the bindings.

"Aren't you afraid I'll run?" Gren asked.

"You aren't our prisoner. I didn't want you to burn in a fire. You're free to go. I'll warn you, though, uniform or not, the people on the edge are violent, paranoid folk. You don't have any weapons left on you, and you stand out."

Gren nodded. He felt around his hiding places and cursed.

"I'm alive."

"Yep."

"She's a Cuma."

"Correct again."

"They're...." Gren's voice faded, and his eyes bulged as he stared at Vaysa.

Vaysa laughed. Very few understood the awesomeness of Shad.

"Why didn't you kill me?" Gren asked. "She wanted to. You could have let the Royal Guard do it."

"You're not my enemy."

He narrowed his eyes. "Really? She thinks I am."

Vaysa shrugged and gestured behind her. "There's the way out."

"You think I'd make it back?"

"Your choice," Vaysa said and looked away. If he left, he wouldn't survive. He didn't have the means for survival in the forest and the closest villages wouldn't ask questions before killing him. She'd protect him in Kennard, even if Shad wouldn't like it. They had taken him there after all, but she would not force him to stay with them. "But you're safe with us."

Gren gave her a bewildered look.

"I didn't know non-humans could join the Royal Guard," she said after a long silence. His story hadn't added up last night and now, in the daylight, it was even more suspicious.

Gren shifted and mumbled, "I want to help Berla. Get the prince out. Get the Royal Guard out."

"Why did they let you join?"

Gren sighed, and his jaw twitched. He was trying to decide if he was going to tell her the truth. She'd seen it many times watching the soldiers.

Gren said, "Since I'm from Berla, they let me join to help travel over the terrain. I'm simply a tool to them."

"You're in a uniform. You aren't in chains. They've accepted you as one of them."

He scuffed. "Accepted? You think most soldiers have to have escorts in every town? That I can't breathe without someone being suspicious and it means I am one of them? They'd much rather kill me than anything, but I'm useful for now."

Vaysa nodded. He was just a pawn. "They'll use anyone."

Gren shrugged. "Yes, but it was mutual. I get a ride home and Kennardians out of Berla."

Vaysa shook her head. Neither of them believed that was his reasoning, but they also didn't trust each other.

"Aren't you from Berla?"

Vaysa shrugged. They both knew she was.

Gren rolled his eyes. "What species are you? I don't know of any with pure white eyes, especially those who can control fire."

Vaysa glared at him and set her jaw. He knew about other species with firepowers. Shad had said it didn't matter since her powers wouldn't manifest in Kennard. But now they had, and she knew nothing about her kin. But if she asked about them, she'd be indebted to him. "I don't know. What's with your red eyes? That's not very common either."

"Actually, it is. The adaptation helps Silvers to see in the Silver Forest. Most people go blind spending time in the forest because of light reflected from the silver bark," Gren said.

A low growl filled the air, interrupting them, and Gren's smile faded.

Shad returned with bread, cheese, berries, and a flask of liquid. As she passed by Gren, she brushed against him. Gren pulled his head back and shuddered. Vaysa waited for him to question where the provision came from but was pleased when he just shook his head and looked away.

AFTER THEY ATE their meal in silence, Vaysa stood and brushed the sandy dirt from her clothes and stamped out the fire.

Gren scrunched his face and muttered, "It'll get cold."

"Only if we stay."

"Is he coming with us?" Shad mouthed to Vaysa.

Vaysa met Shad's gaze. Her eyes flickered to Gren. There wasn't really a choice. She hadn't thought about taking him to Berla—only protecting him in Kennard—but they'd have to take him there.

She couldn't explain her willingness to help him further than surviving the fire, and it was unsettling. She didn't have the resources to care about anyone but herself and Shad, especially with the Royal Guard looking for them. She sighed inwardly and looked away. It didn't matter. He needed help because of her, because of her outburst, so she'd offer it to him.

Shad rolled her eyes and muttered, "Fine, but I warned you about Silvers."

Vaysa mimicked Shad but didn't engage in the argument. Her choice didn't make sense to her, either.

Shad and Vaysa packed up the remaining food, gathered their belongings, and started walking off.

Vaysa looked back at Gren and couldn't stop herself from jerking her head gesturing toward the path and saying, "We're going to Berla if you want to tag along."

He stared back in confusion.

She shrugged and followed Shad.

Gren sighed and jogged through the brush to catch up.

Vaysa swallowed at the dark look Shad cut to her. Once they were in Berla, Gren could be on his way. Then Vaysa would face Berla with Shad at her side, like always.

Chapter 8

VAYSA

After a short while, they reached a village with buildings of various sizes and states of decay. Vaysa stared in disbelief at the place, distant memories flooding her mind. The smell of fire clogged her nose and watered her eyes.

A few buildings she recognized remained, and new ones had been erected in place of the ones she burned down fifteen years ago.

Despite age, the few dozen weathered structures had chipped paint and stains of mildew wiped away. There were no stone structures like in the Hark village. Beyond the town lay a small beach, then a massive waterfront. The strait's water lapped at the sand, leaving trails of white foam.

One of the Phantom Islands was in clear view. A volcano covered in dark trees with no specks of birds flying about dominated the imposing large mass. It loomed like an old relic void of life. A scar of blackened earth snaked down the mountain and a stream of gray smoke marred the blue sky. The smell of sulfur wafted from the island and clung to the town.

Few people were in the town, as most of them were fishing in the shallow parts of the water where the current was manageable.

The people in the town leered at the trio, but did not ask questions nor bother to approach them. They wore simple garments that age had frayed. The droughts of past years left marks on the town, but the fish kept them fed.

Vaysa shuddered in revulsion. She had only lived in the town one night, but visions of it burning still haunted her. She'd never bothered to learn its name, nor return to it in the past fifteen years.

Her hands flexed and she licked her lips. Despite the time away, vivid memories were reminiscent of the previous evening with the soldiers. A phantom curl of fire rolled through her. She'd lost control then, too. The town looked more run down, but little else had changed. At least she and Shad weren't staying.

Noticing a sign painted with a fish, boat and tackle on it, their group started that way.

Gren tagged along a few paces back. Vaysa rolled her eyes at his failed attempt to distance himself.

She put her arm up to block Gren from entering the store.

Shad smiled at Vaysa and walked into the store, leaving the two alone.

Vaysa stared at the ground.

Their presence wouldn't go unnoticed, and even though the town was unwelcoming, the Royal Guard could follow them here and hold the town liable for their escape.

She'd partially burned it once. After last night, the Royal Guard could finish it. And despite how much she hated the town, there were innocent people here who knew nothing about that night.

If they weren't being pursued, and had time to spare, she'd have gone in at dusk or dawn like she did in the other towns. Now their odd appearances were exposed, and the villagers were openly staring at Gren's blue skin. Maybe in Berla their appearance wouldn't matter. That would be odd and refreshing.

Gren flinched when a crash broke the calm air; it was followed by some yells and then sudden quiet. Vaysa closed her eyes and snorted. His fear of Shad was understandable even if she didn't share it.

Shad emerged with a small rowboat, paddles, and a sack bulging with goods. Gren and Vaysa peeked into the store. A short, rotund man with a few wisps of dark hair lay sprawled on the counter, breathing heavily and staring at the ceiling.

Gren turned to Vaysa with wide eyes. She shrugged in response and pulled a coin out. Stepping inside the store, she put her finger to her mouth and hissed, "Shh."

The man weakly nodded without looking at her.

He was familiar. He had been the first to say she needed to leave the town. He had gained many pounds and had lost most of his hair since she last saw him. He didn't seem so frightening now, but Vaysa involuntarily snarled and stepped back.

Fire licked at her resolve and pulsed through her body, yearning to escape. She blinked and it passed. Shad was right. She needed help. Even if they disagreed on what could help and Vaysa thought it ridiculous. Shad was certain a dragon scale would help. Maybe she was right.

"That coin's worth more than what she's carrying," Gren said when she left the store. "Maybe that's why you have to rob so much."

"That coin is worth silence," she said, ignoring Gren's latter comment. It only showed he didn't understand humans. She slapped him on his shoulder and directed him toward the water's front.

She took a long breath to quench the flood of memories and choked slightly on the air.

Shaking his head, Gren walked with her to the shallow beach.

Shad slid the boat into the water.

The three quickly climbed into the vessel and Shad took the paddles with her powerful strength. She heaved them off, and the boat rocked violently in the harsh current.

As they pulled away, Gren's gaze turned to the village. The townspeople gathered around the shop.

"It's not over," he said, still staring at the village.

"Probably not."

The town was likely fearful enough to involve the Royal Guard in the non-humans. Before yesterday, it'd have been a delay to the Royal Guard, but now it was possible the town would be punished for letting them pass. It was a shame what fear could bring. And she was responsible for what happened. She went in during the daytime. She stirred their fear. It was another mistake to think about later.

At least she hadn't shown her powers in the town again.

Shad grunted and Vaysa looked up. Shad smiled softly and said, "It'll be okay. Focus on what's next."

Vaysa nodded and looked away. Shad was right. She couldn't dwell on what she couldn't change. She had to face the now.

THE VESSEL ROCKED in the rough current, and Vaysa rubbed her forehead with her fingertips.

"Vaysa, it'll be all right," a familiar but out-of-place voice called to her.

She looked up, but instead of the sunny warm weather, night surrounded her, and her throat tightened. She whipped around in the too-familiar vessel. A cloaked figure sat beside her, a song starting on their lips, calming the air and sea.

"Mom?" Vaysa croaked and reached her hand tentatively out to the figure.

The waves slapped against the ship, and lightning slashed across the sky, leaving glowing veins before darkness again masked them.

She gasped as frigid water encased her feet and crept up her legs. She jumped up to escape the water's grip, but the boat rocked violently, and more water lapped in.

"Sit down," the figure coaxed, and patted the seat. "There is nothing to fear."

Another bolt of lightning rocketed across the sky, lightening the watery world and illuminating the figure. The familiar warm smile on olive skin and metallic copper eyes with black slit pupils shone brightly at her, and Vaysa held her breath to maintain the moment.

Lightning flashed again, but as it lit up the sky, the dark clouds dispersed in the intensity and brilliant sunlight ripped through the image.

Vaysa blinked and found herself again on the vessel with Shad and Gren.

"You okay?" Gren's voice cut through the slosh of the water.

Vaysa jolted when he laid a hand on her shoulder.

"Vaysa." Shad's welcoming voice pulled her attention through the fog in her mind. "We're here." Shad nodded toward the shore.

Vaysa nodded and rubbed her cheeks. Part one of the strait was completed. Her mother's memory would hopefully fade again, back into the strait where she'd returned when she left Vaysa in Kennard.

The three hauled the boat up to where the tree line started and the beach ended. Black sand clung to their wet pants. The wind shifted and the smell of the salty strait masked the slight sulfuric smell of the island.

She glanced back at the strait, looking for a glimpse of the unwanted memory, but the watery surface rushed by with dark debris and the mountain peaks shimmered in the sun.

Shad patted her shoulder as she walked up the beach, pulling Vaysa's focus back to the island.

Vaysa swatted a bug that landed on her face and surveyed the land. These trees differed from the ones in Kennard. The long thin tubes clawed at the sky with short, jagged limbs dotted with indigo fan-shaped leaves. Alone, the trees were meager, but the forest was imposing as the trees grew close together, choking out other vegetation and creating an impenetrable-looking wall.

Vaysa cringed at the screeches and calls of the monsters lurking in the mass of trees. She couldn't see the eyes watching her, but her skin crawled.

Her shirt quickly stained with perspiration in the stifling heat. She pulled it away from her skin and shook it a few times to get airflow.

"I didn't know anything lived on the islands," Vaysa said, focusing on the other two.

"Nothing worth meeting," Gren replied.

Vaysa shrugged. At least no humans lived here. With Shad, they'd be safe for the night on the beach. She pulled her damp hair from her face. She pulled her shirt away again and used the droop in fabric to collect pieces of timber that washed up on the beach while Shad sniffed the forest.

Gren sat and picked at his dirtied uniform dampened with sweat. His green hair cowlicked in the humidity. He jumped when Shad let out a roar.

The forest became instantly quiet. After a few seconds, growls floated out of the forest again. Shad responded with roars. Then all noise stopped. She snorted and entered the forest.

Sighing, Gren got up and started collecting firewood, too.

Vaysa started a small fire. She maneuvered the boat to hide the flames from view.

"She okay in there?" Gren asked and gestured behind him as he dropped a load of wood.

"Shad? Yeah, she can handle herself. If you're worried, though, you can go help." Vaysa smirked at him.

She blinked away her reservations. Shad was tenacious, but this was a new land with new creatures. Vaysa took a breath and breathed out. She and Shad would get through the Phantom Islands and then whatever Berla offered.

"What happened with the fire last night?"

"What?" Vaysa asked as a spike of fire raced through her veins. She rubbed her fingers, willing it to stay inside.

"You looked terrified when it shot out." His eyes searched her face. "Like you do now."

She glared at him.

"Haven't you done that before?"

She snorted at him and went back to tending to the fire. He was a Berlan; he had powers, which meant he'd grown up in Berla. He couldn't understand her limitations growing up in Kennard.

She may have been born in Berla, but she'd spent fifteen out of her eighteen years in Kennard undoing anything from her birth. She'd learned how to survive, but learning about Berla and its creatures or her possible powers wasn't a part of it.

Even if she'd been born there, she remembered nothing of it. Not her father. Not the lands. Even her mom was a ghost of a memory.

She knew Shad, she knew the trees they were leaving, and she knew how to survive.

Vaysa looked up and caught Gren staring at her. She met his gaze and gave him a cold glare. When Gren didn't look away, she barked, "What?"

Gren blinked repeatedly and, clearing his throat, asked, "How long you and the Cuma been together?"

Vaysa cut her eyes to Gren. "Awhile."

"How'd you meet?"

"Why all the questions?"

"Well, all I know about you is you like gold, you lived in a treehouse, you're from Berla, and you're one of only two non-humans I met since arriving in Kennard. You are with a Cuma, one of the most dangerous creatures from Berla, but seem to care about others. Don't get me wrong, you're a thief, but despite the reckless, don't-care attitude, you tried to save me in Hark. You saved me from a fire you created and one you didn't, and then you offered me protection from the coastal village. My gold can't be that important. I'm guessing you're a decent person."

Damn it. She couldn't explain that weakness.

Gren stared at her for a bit, and then said, "Okay, I see I've flustered you. I'll talk. I'm Gren. I'm momentarily a member of the Royal Guard. I joined several months ago so I could get home. I'm from the Silver Forest of Berla. My family was killed when I was younger. I left Berla so they wouldn't haunt me in the forest. They still haunt me, and I miss the Silver Forest. I'm ready to go home."

Vaysa narrowed her eyes at him. It seemed rehearsed. Whatever his reason for joining the Royal Guard, there was more to it than going home. She asked dryly, "Why Kennard? It's the most dangerous place for non-humans."

Gren nodded and sighed. Emotions battled on his face.

He finally said, "I wanted revenge. I wanted to find the captain in charge of the troops who killed my parents."

"How'd that go for you?"

"He's already dead," Gren said flatly. "Died on the Eastern front."

"And now?"

"It's time to go home, and what better way than a warship?" Gren said, throwing his hands in the air.

"You traveled all the way to Kennard to find and kill the captain who killed your parents. You found out he's dead, and now you've joined the people who murdered your parents to find their prince, and are turning around with your tail between your legs? I call jards. Try again."

Gren looked away and said, "I want the reward."

"You think they'll give it to a Berlan? Jards. Try again."

"Fine. I don't know how else to get home," Gren's voice grew lower and angrier. "There aren't trade ships. No one's for hire that'll travel the Spirit Strait. Kennard is horrible. You have a better idea?"

"There's most of the truth. I guess you could get quasi-kidnapped and flee a burning forest with a Cuma and me," Vaysa said with a crooked grin.

Gren snorted and then smiled himself. He asked, "What about your past?"

"My time began when I met Shad. Everything before that is no longer important." Even if it were, she would not share it with him.

"That bad?"

"Don't know. Don't remember. Don't care." She'd lie any day to not have to relive coming to Kennard and her mother leaving.

Gren raised his eyebrows slightly. He opened his mouth and then closed it again.

"You ever try to go to Berla before?" he asked.

"Why would I?"

"As you said, Kennard is the least safe place for non-humans, and I'd imagine keeping fire powers hidden is a challenge."

Vaysa snorted. It hadn't been a challenge until a few days before;

before then, they'd displayed once. They hadn't been a constant surge in her veins. "I know how to survive the Royal Guard."

"You think we'll be safe here?" Gren asked, turning toward the forest.

Vaysa sighed inwardly. The Phantom Islands were only transitory; Berla being safe was the most important question. "We don't have any place better."

Shad emerged from the forest. Her face looked washed, but a few smears of blood remained. She dropped an armful of various fruits, nuts, and tubers. It was meager, but would keep them fed.

She nodded to Vaysa and slumped down by the fire. Vaysa smiled, glad for the quiet her friend brought.

Gren quickly scrambled up to collect the food. He carried it to the water to wash it.

Vaysa and Shad watched him.

He came back and grabbed a few large, dark purple leaves. He washed them and then mashed a few red and orange berries around the leaf skins. He jabbed a stick into the tubers, creating holes. After wrapping the tubers and nuts inside the leaves, he buried them in a shallow pit and placed hot rocks from the fire on top of them.

"Did you just destroy my food?" Vaysa asked, her eyebrow raised.

Shad's lip quivered into a smile when Gren's face flushed. "You thought I was the only one you had to be afraid of. I wouldn't get in the way of Vaysa and food."

Vaysa stuck her tongue out at Shad. She returned her gaze to Gren waiting for an answer.

He sputtered, "No, just cooking it."

"We'll see."

After a bit, aromas wafted up, causing Vaysa's stomach to rumble.

Gren dug them back up and offered a pouch to Vaysa. He took his and gingerly opened it. He took some leftover fruit and spread it out before him. Looking about, he asked, "Do you have a fork, or should we eat with our fingers?"

Vaysa handed him one from the sack. After watching him greedily dig in, Vaysa stabbed her food with a fork and took a small bite. The tangy mix surprised her, and she devoured her remaining portion.

Maybe the Phantom Islands weren't so bad. There weren't humans. They had food. And maybe Gren wasn't so bad, either. He could cook. Neither she nor Shad could.

Shad took first shift that night since she needed little sleep. Vaysa relaxed, knowing Shad would protect her. She didn't want to think about what new things the Phantom Islands would offer them in the morning.

Chapter 9

TEO

Teo gasped as he reached the sandy shore. His boat's pieces lay scattered on the water's surface and slipped silently into the ocean. Some creature of the strait had wrapped its tentacles around the vessel, crushing it and almost him. He clung to the sand so the water wouldn't rip him back to the terrors of the sea. He swore and then coughed a laugh when he realized he'd survived a part of the Spirit Strait.

"Now I got you to deal with," Teo muttered to the island. Blackness surrounded him and he swallowed back at the fear creeping up his throat. He needed to keep moving forward. Gren could be lost in the strait, or on an island, or already in Berla. But he had to find him. He wouldn't go back without him alive or proof of his death.

The dizziness from the sea fight and the smell of sulfur spun his vision and stomach. He suppressed the urge to vomit and slowly pulled himself up to a sitting position. He rubbed his neck and surveyed his situation.

His uniform hung in tatters around him, and he had lost almost everything he had carried. Taking stock of what he still had, he found one knife hidden in one of his boots, a small pouch of medicine, and a canister of matches that had not washed out of his shredded jacket.

It was too dark to explore the island, but he had to find some kind of shelter. He had to stay uneaten by the monsters on the island. He had to fix his mistake.

TEO AWOKE to his body aching and his legs like jelly. He ran his tongue over his dry mouth and coughed. Despite it being early morning, his clothes were already damp with sweat. More pressing, his stomach rumbled for food.

The heavy smoke dimmed the rising sun. He needed to move. In a few hours, the heat would be insufferable. He stretched the best he could, but his body fought every movement he made. He shouldn't venture into the forest. It was a waiting death trap. However, the perimeter canopy would offer some cover from the brutal sun.

He stared at the water. His grandma's words subconsciously tumbled forth. "Evil may come, but always by sea, For within the land, the protectors stand. Evil may come, but always by sea, For within the air, the protectors snare. Evil may come, but always will flee."

His eyes darted from the sea to the sky and then the forest. There was nothing there to protect him. He shook his head at the old tale. He couldn't take to the air, but the sea and forest were death traps. He had one option.

Skirting the woods, he drew his knife and held it at the ready. After an hour of looking, his stomach pounded with hunger, and he was lightheaded. The sun had warmed the air and sweat drenched him despite the shade.

Anger and fear welled in his eyes. He blinked the emotions back. His mouth trembled when he thought about returning to the kingdom without Gren. A death here would be less painful and less humiliating. He'd face Closs and deal with the consequences, but at the thought of seeing his dad's disapproval, he forced his feet forward.

Voices whispered through the wind, taunting him. He shook his head to ward off the hallucinations, but the hushed tones grew in ferocity.

If only the protectors were real.

He needed food and noticed berries dangling in his path, just a few inches above his head. He blinked but they remained. The dark red berries looked like the common snapper fruit. He sniffed the air, and the citrusy aroma tickled his nose. They smelled like snapper fruit, too.

"Poison or starvation?" he muttered to himself. Both would be painful. At least poison would be quicker.

His hand hovered suspended in the air around the berries when something landed on him, flattening him to the ground, his face pushed into the sand. The sharp sand cut his eyes. Filled his nostrils. Choked his throat. His body was too fatigued to fight back.

One of the forest's creatures was going to eat him. Would it kill him first or just start gnawing?

A low hiss tickled his ears and sent tingles down his spine. His body tightened in response.

"Why are you here?"

He couldn't lift his head to clear his mouth of sand, and he couldn't find the air to talk.

With a quick, hard yank from the attacker, he was on his back facing it. He panted, choking on the sand lodged in his throat, and blinked as the towering figure's piercing gold eyes bore through him.

"What are you doing here?"

He sputtered, the sand scraping at his throat and words, "I'm... looking for... a... soldier."

"Why?"

"He was... taken."

A low laugh emerged from the creature pinning him down. Teo's eyes blurred from the sand, but when the figure backed up, it appeared to be human. He had never seen a human so large. Or one with fangs.

It was a non-human.

His mind raced. There weren't supposed to be any humans or non-humans on the islands.

"Shad," a sharp voice carried from a distance.

The non-human growled.

"Aren't you lucky?" it seethed.

Lucky? There were more non-humans, and he was lucky?

Before Teo could respond, the non-human grabbed him, threw him over its shoulder, and carried him off.

A scream bubbled up his throat but lodged in his mouth. His eyes darted around. There were more of them. If he screamed, who would hear him? Or care? He'd just attract something else. Likely a bigger, meaner monster that ate both of them. Teo paused. Neither would escape then.

Before he could call to any monsters, the creature threw him roughly to the ground. His eyes stung, but he could see. Through the sulfur and fear he could smell... was that food? The salty tang of crackling fish caused his mouth to water and his stomach to rumble in anticipation.

Jards. He was about to die and all he could think about was food.

Rolling over to get away from the gaze of the creature, his head smacked into two sets of soldier boots. Someone snickered. Looking up, a woman with evil white eyes stared down at him.

Another non-human.

He screamed and pushed his hands against the sands to back up, but he only fell forward.

"Careful," she chuckled and held out a hand to help him up.

He stilled and shook his head. He blinked and looked beyond her eyes. She was young and muscular. About his age. She didn't look like a monster. She almost looked human. Almost. Her mouth formed words, but he didn't hear them as he watched her lips move. He took a ragged breath.

"Do you?" She demanded. The words snapped his attention.

"Pardon?"

"Need help up?" Her lip hooked in challenge. She flicked her fingers at him.

Without taking her offer of help, he pushed to his feet. He rubbed at the heat building in his cheeks. His thoughts were wandering because he was distracted from hunger and dehydration. Nothing else.

All his thoughts shattered when he saw the most miraculous thing possible: Gren was sitting there trying to hide a laugh.

He was alive.

Teo had found Gren.

He'd succeeded...

His gaze darted back to the woman. His eyes lingered too long on hers before reason caught up. She wasn't the woman that had created fire. The fire woman had copper eyes that glowed, not completely white eyes. Nor did she have fur like a Cuma. She looked familiar but he couldn't place her. Her eyes narrowed at him the longer he stared.

Shad snorted, drawing his attention. She was large with fangs but looked almost human. Nor did she glow.

His mind raced through what he remembered from the pamphlets about Cumas: monster class, fur, fangs, looked like a panther, couldn't be reasoned with, and were killing machines.

He blew out a breath. The Cuma and fire woman weren't here. Just two weird non-humans that almost looked human.

Now he just needed to rescue Gren from the non-humans and face the strait. He wasn't sure how he would do that, but at least he'd found Gren.

Gren asked, "Teo, what are you doing here?"

"I'm here to rescue you," Teo stammered.

"Good job," the woman chortled. "Now all you have to do is get back to Kennard."

Teo swallowed. Without looking back, he knew the land would barely be a speck on the horizon. Besides, he was supposed to get Gren to Closs in Berla, which wasn't even visible yet on the other horizon.

"And how do you plan on taking me back? Where's your boat?" Gren said, ignoring the woman. His red eyes were dark and belied his half-grin.

Teo cursed inwardly. "Well... that is a problem, my boat's toast. It was destroyed."

His eyes scanned the shore landing on an intact vessel. This group had a boat, but he wouldn't be able to get it from them. They may not look like monster type non-humans, but not only could they beat him in a physical battle, he didn't have a weapon to attack from afar.

"So, you're stuck with us then?" Gren grinned.

Teo gulped. Was he? They hadn't moved to bind him. Maybe if they planned to stay on the Phantom Islands, he could escape with Gren when they fell asleep.

He stared at the two for a moment. They were non-humans, but were they Traitors? Had the Traitors found out about Closs's plan to rescue the prince? Teo's brow pinched. That just didn't make sense. No other troops knew about their secret weapon, so no one could divulge it.

But both of them wore odd pieces of Royal Guard uniforms, including pants and the military's traveling jacket but not a uniform rank jacket. Their weapons were smith-forged but looked better than the typical Royal Guard-issued fare. They'd been to Kennard. Had another Royal Guard unit come up with the same idea to use non-humans to traverse the foreign Berlan lands?

No, it was Closs's plan. Besides, how many Berlans were unknowingly just living in Kennard? They had to be Traitors.

Teo pointed to the two and mouthed, "Traitors?" to Gren.

Gren smirked but shook his head.

A smile flittered across Teo's face but fell. Something was still off. His hand involuntarily fell to his sword. His heart sank as he realized the scabbard spot was empty. He had nothing to defend himself.

"No, you can't eat him. Even if he is Royal Guard."

"What?" Teo squeaked and looked to Gren for help.

Gren smiled and winked. "I wonder if your steel can protect you now?"

Teo's face paled. He had said that to Gren back at the camp. He couldn't back up the comment now without his sword or the rest of the troops.

How was he going to get him back when faced with non-humans with unknown powers and all he had was a medicine pouch and a knife?

Teo looked at the woman. She was shaking her head at Shad, chewing on her thumbnail and looking bored. She then turned to Teo. His stomach turned, and he stepped back.

"I'd be nice to Vaysa," Gren mouthed to Teo and pointed to the woman. "The other one listens to her."

Vaysa rolled her eyes. Emotion warred on her face before she said, "We don't have time for this. You got three options. One, Shad eats you. Two, you stay here to survive on your own. Or three, you help us get to Berla."

She didn't have time? He was supposed to have had Gren back before he even walked away in the first place. His life and his stipend were on the line.

"I like option one," Shad said, tilting her head and smiling.

Teo gagged. He was trapped with a cannibal. Wait, she was apparently a monster-type Traitor, so it wasn't cannibalism. Just horrifying. He stared at Shad. She didn't look like a monster, but he wasn't sure what species she was either.

Shad noticed his staring and snarled, revealing her shortened fang, and fanned her claws out in the air.

He gulped. Yep, she was definitely a monster type.

"As long as you don't annoy me, she won't eat you." Vaysa smirked. "Maybe. Most likely."

Teo's breath caught. His life was a game to them.

Vaysa's expression sobered. "I'm joking."

Shad mumbled, "Mostly."

"Seriously, though," Vaysa said. "We need to get moving. The choice is yours."

Gren lifted in his brows toward Teo. "What'll it be?"

He needed to get Gren back. He didn't have a boat or real weapon. They were planning to go to Berla. So was Closs. It was a simple decision.

"Okay, I'll join you."

Chapter 10

VAYSA

The four finished their breakfast and packed what little gear they had in the vessel. The fourth body would make things even tighter, but Vaysa couldn't leave Teo there alone to die, even if he was Royal Guard. That was another argument she hoped to avoid with Shad, but based on Shad's growls and mumbling, it would likely happen soon.

She'd immediately recognized him as the soldier from the inn, the one who begged her to let Ben go and had been saddled with watching Gren the previous night. He was there because of her. Like they all were. She owed him help.

The island wasn't vast, but it took a full day to walk the perimeter. Going directly through on foot or around in the boat would have been quicker, but significantly more dangerous with the choppy water and other monsters at sea and whatever else lay in the thick foliage. Shad even warned against going through. At least if something attacked them on the island, she had ground beneath her feet.

Regret gnawed at her decision to go the slow path as the insect swarms grew in numbers near the waters pooled between all three islands. She licked her dry lips and pushed her sweaty bangs from her face. She smacked at another bug and blew out a sigh of relief when Shad reached out and ate it. Vaysa grimaced and then gagged when Shad smiled at her with bits of the bug still in her teeth.

The smell of rot and decay clung to the air as they neared the waters. It coated Vaysa's throat and blurred her vision. She kept stealing glances at Shad. If she was that affected by the surroundings, it meant Shad had entered hell.

Having enough, Vaysa finally called for a rest. Teo and Gren flopped on the ground. Shad eyed them and then gave Vaysa a dark look before entering the forest. At least she could have a break from the smell, even if Vaysa calling a break annoyed her.

Vaysa closed her eyes and pinched her nose. Flashes of her home passed through her mind, and then the fire, the looks on the soldiers' faces when flames shot from her. The memories of the strait. She growled and opened her eyes. She didn't have time to wallow in the past. Or about why her powers were displaying now. Going back wasn't an option. She didn't belong in Kennard, anyway. Maybe Berla would be able to help, as Shad said. She snorted and balled the thoughts down to a small kernel in her stomach. She'd dwell on them later.

Vaysa finally knelt to the ground and lay back. The forest sounds mixed with the gurgles of the waves. The subtle rhythm eased through her muscles. She pinched her nose and breathed through her mouth to block some of the smell.

"Why were you in Kennard?' Teo's question pierced the tense quiet.

Silence. But the feeling of being watched skittered on her skin.

With a flick of her gaze, she found both Teo and Gren watching her.

She grunted in response.

"Where you there for reconnaissance?"

"Of what?" Vaysa laughed.

Teo's brow pinched. "You are wearing pieces of Royal Guard gear. You obviously were there. To track the royal family. To monitor the Royal Guard."

"Don't flattered yourself," Vaysa said. "I don't care anything about humans other than what goods they have."

He blinked and his eyes clouded in darkness. "So you're just a thief?"

"Believe what you want."

"You were in town," Gren said. "You used money."

She tossed him a dark look before leaning back to stare at the canopy of dark leaves.

Teo mumbled something to which Gren laughed in response.

"Were you following Gren?" Teo asked.

Vaysa blew out a sigh.

"No, she wasn't," Gren said. "Our paths just crossed."

Vaysa growled.

Both cast a glance at her.

"I don't need you speaking for me." She pinned Gren with a pointed look. Then she shifted her gaze to Teo. "And I don't owe you any answers."

"So, Ben was right." Teo snorted. "Jards."

The name sent a spike of anger down her spine.

"He's a jarding waste of breath."

"Is he?" Teo challenged. "From what I saw, sure he was a jerk, but he was trying to protect Gren and is risking his life to rescue the prince."

"Then why'd you leave his halo of greatness?"

Teo flinched, his gaze falling to his lap.

Then the camp and Closs came to Vaysa's mind. The forest. The flames.

"Was it his idea to burn the forest to find Gren?"

"What?" Teo lifted his hard gaze to her.

"Who decided to burn the forest?"

Teo blinked. Then again. Realization dawned on his face. His expression morphing to one of horror.

"Jards." He breathed.

She knew it.

"Yeah, he's a real hero."

"It was Closs's, not Ben's," Teo whispered.

"What?" Vaysa said.

Teo shook his head as if trying to make an image leave his mind. "Closs burned it. Said he'd burn anyplace that offered you reprieve."

"And that's who you're following directions from?" Vaysa chortled in disgust.

Teo worked his lips. "Not all of us can survive on robbing others. Some of us have families to take care of."

His words likely meant to hurt, did little but numb at the anger building in her heart. She had Shad. It was better than what most had. She didn't need numbers of people. Especially not humans. They only brought more issues and pain.

"Don't worry," Vaysa snarled. "Once were in Berla go your own way."

"You're welcome to just go on without us," Teo shot back.

"Hey, leave me out of this," Gren warned.

Teo's glare matched Vaysa's.

Gren was the source of them both being here. Vaysa scoffed. Too bad she couldn't go back and direct herself to the forest instead of trying for another bun. Or stop her curiosity of the guards.

"No offense, but I prefer my chances in a boat with those two than swimming back with you," Gren said.

Teo's expression fell as he looked at the one lone boat they had.

He was stuck. He'd come to rescue Gren but was marooned. Jards. Once they got to Berla, they could separate. Until then, she could just avoid talking to him.

Hard silence fell on them. The weight of her choice pulled on her shoulders.

"Oh great," Shad muttered when she returned from the forest and then tossed Vaysa a canteen from their home.

"That one's ours," Shad said, and then, not masking her distaste, tossed another one at Teo and Gren. "That's yours."

"We have to share?" Teo asked. His eyes bulged in surprise at his own words, and then said, "Um, thanks."

Shad snorted and rolled her eyes, but didn't retort.

Vaysa chose silence instead of responding.

Gren looked longing at the canteen but refrained from it and asked, "Is it safe?"

Vaysa uncapped hers and sniffed it. There was an odd, unrecognizable odor to it. She looked questioningly at Shad, who shrugged in response and half-heartedly nodded.

"You're welcome to get water from the strait if you'd prefer," Shad said to Gren and directed a thumb toward the bank.

The three's heads involuntarily turned toward the water.

"This is great," Teo said and took a sip, only gagging slightly. "Really."

Shad rolled her eyes and sat on the ground away from Teo and Gren but continued to watch them.

Vaysa watched the strait. Odd chunks floated in the current. One object bounced up and down and seemed out of place compared to the dark masses of foliage. Vaysa walked closer, squinting to see it better. Gren and Teo called after her to stop and come back, but she waved them off.

Shad narrowed her eyes and called out, "You probably don't want to."

Vaysa stared back at her. She should have turned back, but her curiosity won out and she inched closer anyway. The water lapped the black sand about thirty feet from where she stood, leaving trails of debris and white foam. She saw the eyes first. They were whitish blue and attached to a swollen blob of hanging flesh, showing bone and muscle. Her stomach turned and she swallowed hard to keep her food down, stumbling back a few steps.

It was a human head, and it looked strangely familiar. Another presence joined her, and she turned to find Gren standing beside her. His skin turned a tinted green color. He clasped his hand to his mouth and turned, but that didn't help. He fell to his knees, heaving his meal up. After he vomited, he sat dry heaving.

"You recognize him?" Vaysa asked, grimacing as Gren finished. She absentmindedly cupped a hand over her mouth.

"Yeah, he was the shopkeeper from the boat store," Gren said, his voice raspy.

The familiar features swam into focus, warring with the ones from her youth, blurring with the injuries into a mosaic of disgust.

Blackness edged her vision and faint whispers skittered in the air. A clap of thunder sounded, vibrating through her core.

"Hey," Gren yelled and touched her hand.

Vaysa jerked from the contact and, shaking her head, looked away. The Royal Guard had followed them to the village. They must have punished the shopkeeper for selling to them.

She blinked several times and let out a slow breath. She couldn't help the village now. If she could make the Royal Guard pay later, she would.

"How..." She gestured toward the head. "...did it get here so fast? We were there yesterday."

Gren stared back toward Kennard. "It probably got caught in the tides."

Vaysa looked at him and back toward the waters.

"Or," Gren said, and gagged, "it was dragged upstream by one of the creatures."

Vaysa shuddered.

Sighing, she extended her hand. After helping Gren up, she headed back to the duo still waiting.

Shad's eyes scanned Vaysa and raised an eyebrow in question.

"They found our trail." Vaysa turned to Teo and narrowed her eyes. Something unexpected twisted in her stomach when his amber eyes met hers. It should be annoyance and hatred. Not whatever quivered in her stomach. Swallowing back against the flush burning at her neck, she said, "Who killed the shopkeeper?"

"Whoa! What? I have no idea what you're talking about," Teo said. His confusion appeared real. He searched her gaze.

Vaysa pressed on, ignoring the flutter in her stomach. The water must have been a bit rancid. It couldn't be anything else. "Ok, then who followed you, knows what you're doing, or sent you?"

"Ah, no one," Teo said, throwing his palms toward the sky.

Gren turned to him. His red eyes darkened, and his voice was low and soft. "One is already dead. You want to be next? How did you know to come to the Phantom Islands?"

Vaysa raised her brows in surprise at Gren but turned her gaze back to Teo.

Teo backed up from the group. His eyes darted between Vaysa and Gren. Sweat beaded on his brow. Trembling, he sputtered, "After the fire, we found the ruins of a shack in the trees that had Ben's sword in it. We went to the nearest town, and it had a lot of money. They started yelling about a blue non-human and the strait. I left from there."

"You came by yourself to look for me?"

Teo nodded. "I traded a gold piece for a boat. No one wanted to come."

Even with Shad, Vaysa hadn't wanted to cross the strait. She never would have tried by herself. But she didn't have to answer to Closs. Or the Royal Guard.

Vaysa's stomach pinched. He wasn't more than a pawn. One held accountable for her actions.

"Weren't you afraid of the creatures that grabbed me?" Gren asked, a smile growing across his face. His red eyes narrowed.

Teo nodded, and his gaze tracked to Vaysa and Shad. He hesitated before saying, "But neither one is a Cuma. A Cuma took you."

His gaze slid to Vaysa's. Hope and realization warred in his eyes.

Gren bit his lip and closed his eyes. He shook slightly with laughter. He finally opened his eyes and nodded his head toward Shad.

Teo backed up, his hand brushed against his empty scabbard, and he looked toward the strait. His gaze returned to them. "But neither of you are a Cuma, you don't have fur or look like a panther, nor are you glowing."

Vaysa stared at him with a raised brow. Shad didn't glow and neither did she.

Shad straightened. Setting her jaw, she stepped in front of Vaysa, facing Teo. "You keep believing that. It'll keep you safer."

Teo's eyes darted between the three. He opened his mouth to ask another question and then stopped. He nodded and gulped. Keeping Shad's gaze, he said, "Understood."

Vaysa stepped around Shad, pulling Teo's gaze to her. He stared at the oddity of her white eyes. He didn't trust them, and Vaysa didn't blame him, but like the others, he was here because of her. She owed him protection. Even if he was a Royal Guard. It was nothing more. And it be over soon. The odd twisting in her stomach uncoiled. She sucked in a steadying breath and flexed her toes to settle her reactions.

"Will more of them look for you on the islands?" Vaysa asked Gren.

"Most likely not. Even if they thought we made it here, they wouldn't think we'd make it off alive," Gren said.

"How fast can the Royal Guard cross the strait?" Vaysa asked.

Gren rubbed his temples and said, "They won't cross without the ocean cruisers. It's too dangerous otherwise. They already planned to meet up with the cruisers in Southern Port. With travel, they'll probably reach southern Berla in about a week. We may have an extra day from the detour they took following our trail. If we go north, it may buy us a few extra days. They're aiming for the southern part of Berla, not the coast."

"Dude," Teo muttered. His face darkened, and his fists furled as he glared at Gren.

"They're not Traitors," Gren said, rolling his eyes.

"But they're..." Teo's voice tapered off.

"Berlans? Non-humans? Monsters?" Gren offered.

Teo stared at him, his amber eyes dark and cold. He took a step forward.

"If you don't like the company, leave." Shad's voice caused Teo to jump. "There's the way out," Shad said and pointed to the water.

Gren and Teo went silent.

"Vaysa offered you help. If you stay with us, you're agreeing to help everyone get to Berla," Shad said. "Once safely in Berla, go your own way. Until then, shut up. Understood?"

Gren and Teo nodded without looking at each other.

Vaysa looked around at the small island. It provided shelter, food, and a water source. If the Royal Guard wouldn't look for them here, it seemed safe. They didn't need to go to Berla. They didn't have to look for a dragon scale. They could make this their permanent home. She could learn to control her powers on her own, in her own time; she didn't need Berla's help. Gren and Teo could take the boat and leave. Turning to Shad, she said, "Why don't we just live here? We've avoided the Royal Guard, and it meets our needs."

Shad shook her head. "Vaysa, we're not safe here. He'll come here."

"What do you mean?" Vaysa asked.

"We need to get to Berla," Shad echoed. Her eyes bore into Vaysa. She still wanted to get the dragon scale.

Vaysa opened her mouth to protest.

Shad's eyes darted to Teo and Gren and she shook her head at Vaysa.

Vaysa turned away but didn't push her further in front of them.

Chapter 11

VAYSA

Both Gren and Teo remained quiet the rest of the trip around the island. They set up camp on the other side of the island next to the tree line. As night approached, Gren and Teo huddled under the upturned boat. Shad lay by Vaysa's side outside of the vessel, away from Gren and Teo.

Vaysa claimed the first watch since the horrid smell and days of little sleep wore Shad down.

Night fell, bringing some relief from the intense sun. Smoke drifted from the islands, hazing the moon and masking the stars. She stared at the sky for a glimpse of a familiar navigational sight.

Everything was changing. Their home. Her powers. She swallowed hard as fear crept up her throat. She needed to focus on the current night. The fire. Keeping watch.

For all the treachery the island held, it was still the safest place to keep humans from finding them. If only Shad could see this was a good home. They could make a home in the trees, away from the strait's smell. It'd be theirs. She could figure everything out.

They had so much to face just to reach Berla, and it was her fault.

She'd forced Shad into this situation. She'd chosen to attack the Royal Guard Ben in the village and knew better, even if he deserved it, and she'd chosen to trail the Royal Guard, and she couldn't control her powers.

Now Shad was doing everything to get them to safety. And Vaysa had invited Gren along and then Teo. She cursed. She wasn't helping Shad or their predicament.

Still, she couldn't send them away now. Gren could take care of himself once in Berla. And Teo... He'd probably try to meet up with the Royal Guard. She could make him stay on the island. But he'd be trapped, and she couldn't live with herself for leaving him to die or suffer. Shad could, but not her. That'd be another battle to fight once she got to Berla.

She laughed to herself. She was assuming they'd even make it there. She needed to focus on the strait, not Berla. They still had to make it to another island and across the rest of the strait.

The other island could be an option for a home if she could convince Shad to stay there.

But Shad was insistent on going to Berla, going for a dragon scale, and wouldn't budge or discuss it even when Teo and Gren weren't close by. Even with the unknowns, and the Royal Guard invading the land, Vaysa would follow Shad there.

But there lingered in her mind. Where was Shad headed in Berla? In what place had dragons once nested in droves? A tingle shimmied down her spine, curling her toes. She let out a long sigh to relax her muscles. Now wasn't the time. She could see the physical challenges ahead just to make it to the next island. There was no point in worrying about farther than that.

VAYSA REFUSED to acknowledge Gren's probing eyes as they maneuvered the boat in the water. She steeled her face and entered the vessel.

They headed to the north island. It was closer in distance, farther from Royal Guard's eyes, which Shad insisted were there, and it had fewer of the smaller islands surrounding it that would tear apart their boat if they got close.

The western side of the strait was darker and more humid with rolling fog. The gossamer clouds billowed on the waves. A few larger ones brought pungent smells of decay. Vaysa coughed and covered her mouth and nose.

Amidst the ethereal presence, random creatures slithered in the current beneath their vessel. Vaysa killed a few of the things that whacked their ship and nudged their oars.

Teo muttered under his breath, continuously saying, "Evil may come, but always by sea..."

The almost chant tugged at Vaysa's resolve. Were they the evil? Did it wait for them? The words wrapped around her, and she rocked in motion to them.

"What are you saying?" Gren finally asked.

"Huh?" Teo's eyes darted to him.

"That phrase," Gren said.

"Just something my grandma said," Teo muttered and looked away.

"Was it to keep you from going to Berla?" Gren asked.

"If he went to Berla, he'd be coming by the sea and be the evil," Vaysa said.

Gren chuckled.

Teo's dark eyes cut to Vaysa. "We were the ones on the land. Traitors stole the prince."

Vaysa snorted. "Why would anyone want that jarding—"

"Enough," Shad said, bringing silence, but then she dry-heaved a few times.

Teo turned to Vaysa with an eyebrow raised and nodded toward Shad.

"She okay?" he mouthed.

His concerned seemed genuine, adding weight to the lump in her throat. But it couldn't be real. He was only concerned about making it to Berla and reuniting with his troop.

Vaysa started to tell him to shut up and that everything was fine, but the lie stayed on her tongue. She turned her gaze toward the shore and the trees. Teo grunted and finally looked away. Vaysa went back to staring at Shad. Her friend wasn't okay. The strain after yesterday's trek was taking its toll, and the heat and smells were wearing her down.

As Vaysa plunged her sword into an eel-like creature, she saw a metallic reflection from the tree line. Her heart jumped and her stomach clenched. Fire swirled through her veins, and she fisted her hands. She looked at Shad, who nodded and looked back toward the island. Metal meant people.

Someone was on the island. Vaysa bit her lip as she scanned the horizon. They were likely visible from the island despite the hazy smoke and debris. There were no large structures or other signs of humanoid habitation.

She looked to the southern island, now even farther away because of their progress. Smaller islands jutted out of the water with foamy rapids rushing over them. Their boat couldn't survive it.

She looked at Gren and Teo, both staring at the strait and the creatures lurking below.

Shad caught her gaze, shook her head at them, and mouthed, "We don't have another choice."

Vaysa's muscles tightened, and fire coursed through her veins. The intense burst of heat singed her nerves. Flashes of Kennard skittered in her mind. With nothing but the putrid waters surrounding them, she curled her fingers to clasp at the power. But as quickly as it rippled through her, it extinguished, leaving her muscles raw and aching.

She set her jaw and focused on finishing the trek instead of staring into the forest. They were only staying a night. Hopefully, whoever was living there would leave them alone.

She helped her team drag the battered boat ashore. The beach had similar black sand and indigo-leafed trees to the last island.

They were drenched with sweat and seawater and breathing heavily, but no one said anything. She ignored Teo and Gren, who lay against the boat to dry out as she collected firewood. Shad stuck to the tree line, collecting various fruits and roots.

Gren's eyes followed Shad as she skimmed the foliage but didn't enter the forest. He turned to Vaysa questioningly. She raised an eyebrow at him, and he wordlessly turned back to the campsite and washed what Shad brought over.

Shad passed Gren a dark look and then went to gather more. Gren kept his head bowed but made a face as she turned away. Vaysa rolled her eyes but didn't intervene.

Teo hovered by Gren after Shad returned to the tree line and whispered, "What do I do?"

Gren stared back at Teo and blinked. Saying nothing, he turned back to washing the food.

Teo turned to Vaysa and flinched but asked, "What can I do?"

"Something useful," Vaysa said, frowning.

He stared back at her with his mouth agape and raised his palms slightly.

"What did you do with your platoon?"

"What they told me," he mumbled.

She rolled her eyes. "Seriously? You didn't learn to assess a situation and see what needs to be done?"

He rolled his tongue against his teeth. "I grew up on a farm. I didn't scavenge off a hellish island," he bit out. With a sigh, he rubbed a hand over his face. "You're right. I should be able to tell. Shad's getting food. Gren's washing it. You're getting firewood. We don't have tents. Are we sleeping on the sand tonight? I can gather brush to sleep on. Or make some overhead coverage in case it rains."

Those were good options, but it wasn't just the weather they had to worry about. They needed to prepare for possibly meeting the humanoids. "Build a lean-to, or something similar but sturdy. We might need more protection than branches."

Gren and Teo looked at each other and gulped.

"You think the animals will attack us?" Teo's gaze flicked to the dark forest.

"Maybe a warship would have been safer," Gren mumbled and wrapped his arms around his torso.

"What?" Vaysa asked and narrowed her eyes.

He chose to follow them to Berla. She was trying to protect him. He saw what the Royal Guard did, and he thought he'd be safer with them.

Gren's eyes bolted up to her, fear mirrored back. He blinked, and it was gone. His gaze shifted to Shad.

Her vision tunneled and she clenched her fists. If he thought Shad was a bigger threat than the Royal Guard, then they'd all be safer with Gren on a warship.

Shad's snort carried from the forest.

Gren pulled back slightly, his eyes darting between Vaysa and Shad.

Shad walked back with another armful. Looking between Vaysa and Gren, she said, "Enough."

Gren opened his mouth to say something but shut it again when Shad glared at him.

Shad patted Vaysa's shoulder and then flopped down by the boat.

Vaysa sighed and let the tension ease. He had a right to be scared. The last two nights were unfortunate and even she doubted everything. Besides, they'd separate once in Berla.

THE FOUR SAT SILENTLY around the fire, each lost in their own thoughts. Vaysa ached to turn toward Kennard. To see a glimpse of something familiar. But it'd only lead to resentment and guilt. There was nothing she could do to undo what had happened. The idea of Berla and all that waited bobbed like a lump in her throat. Unable to focus on either direction, she allowed her vision to fixate on the fire and the embers twirling in the air like blinking stars.

When night finally fell, blackness embracing them, Shad morphed.

Teo looked at her and screamed. The other three stared at him with wide eyes.

"What?" Shad growled.

"You're really a..." Teo fumbled backwards and tried to tug Gren with him.

"Cuma," Gren finished, brushing Teo's hand off his shoulder.

Teo nodded weakly and let his arm hang by his side.

"I told you," Gren said.

"Yeah, but I thought you were likely lying. Trying to scare me. Be a jerk. I mean, come on, she didn't have fur. Cumas have fur."

Shad passed Vaysa a dark look Vaysa didn't acknowledge.

"She does now," Vaysa said.

Gren chuckled.

"Shut up," Teo said and sat back down.

"In the morning, she'll shift back to her human form." Vaysa offered. A smile tugged on her lips.

"What?" Teo sputtered. "The pamphlets never said they shapeshifted."

"Pamphlets?" Vaysa asked.

Teo shrugged. "To help us learn about what we'd encounter."

"You were made into a pamphlet," Vaysa said, smirking to Shad. "I bet you're proud."

"Very," Shad deadpanned and glared at Teo. "They knew so much they omitted shapeshifting."

Teo's eyes fixed on Shad.

"What else did they say?" Shad prompted.

He stared at her.

"Oh, this will be good," Vaysa said. "Do they have horns? Maybe wings? Shad would look good with horns."

Teo scowled at Vaysa. "How else were we to learn about what we would encounter?"

"They obviously haven't helped much," Vaysa said. "You were with one for multiple days and didn't know."

"Maybe I didn't want to know."

"What else did it say?" Shad said.

Teo swallowed.

"Oh, just tell her." Gren grinned. When Teo remained quiet, Gren finished, "You're a monster class that eats flesh. You're animalistic and only destroy. You cannot be reasoned with, and you don't follow a moral code. Just destruction."

"You enjoy that?" Shad asked Gren.

His smile faltered and he shifted slightly.

"You're more like a Prowler," Teo said.

"A what?" Shad asked, her gaze shifting back to Teo.

"Never mind," Teo said, his cheeks reddening.

"Is it from your grandma's book?" Gren smirked.

Teo's eyes darted up to Gren and narrowed. His jaw ticked, and he said, "Yes."

"Interesting book," Gren said when Shad passed him a dark look.

"More Royal Guard literature?" Vaysa asked.

Teo shook his head. "It was my grandma's when she was a kid. Just poems and songs about made up creatures."

"Sounds more accurate than the pamphlets."

Teo met her gaze, but questions danced in his amber eyes. The same odd flutter as earlier rippled in her stomach. The circumstances had to be getting to her.

"What are you?" Teo asked.

She shrugged but thankfully her stomach dropped in a familiar disappointment chasing the earlier feeling. She had no idea what species she was. Shad said she wasn't sure. She'd only been called monster, heathen, or something else similar by humans. Ben had been the first to call her simply Berlan. And just like a human, he was focused on her being a non-human.

"None of the species listed glow," he said, leaning closer.

A breeze stirred the embers of the fire. The air seemed to warm.

"I don't glow," Vaysa said and leaned away. For some strange reason, her heart beat faster.

"But..."

"Teo," Gren started.

Before Gren could finish, Shad reared up, clawing at the air, and her roar filled the night sky. Arrows whizzed by her. She collapsed on top of the boat, smashing the fortification Teo had assembled. Her limp body heaved slowly.

Vaysa bellowed and fire curled into the air. She jumped up and grabbed a piece of the smashed fortifications and, using it as a shield, knelt over Shad. Gren and Teo ducked under the small shield as a few more arrows tore through the air.

Vaysa had the men help her turn Shad over and pull her behind the boat, away from the forest, while careful to keep the shield facing the tree line. Teo and Gren grabbed more pieces of wood to use as additional shields.

"I only saw one person moving in the trees," Gren said when the arrows stopped. "They went deeper back. They're gone for now."

Vaysa barely nodded toward him, his words nearly lost in the wind.

With hands trembling, Vaysa searched Shad and found a silver arrow embedded in her heart.

Shad's eyes rolled back, and she gasped for breath. A small trickle of blood escaped her mouth. Blood blossomed around the arrow.

Words fell from Vaysa's lips. Promises. Pleas. Prayers. She grasped the arrow with both hands but couldn't dislodge it. Her vision tunneled and her heart pounded in her ears, deafening all sound. She couldn't lose Shad. She needed Shad.

A crack of thunder sounded, and she jolted.

Teo hurried over yelling something and tried to push Vaysa back. She shrugged him off and growled. She'd kill him if he tried to prevent her from helping Shad.

He pushed her hands away from the wound and again tried to yell at her. She bolted up and punched him squarely on his left cheek. He swayed and then fell over.

She took shaky breaths, fumbling back to her spot by Shad. She needed to get the arrow out and then dress the wound. She flinched. She was better at inflicting the wounds than tending to them.

"That wasn't smart," Gren said, kneeling by Vaysa.

She growled in response and then cursed when her hands slipped again on the bloodied arrow shaft.

Gren continued. "He was training to be a medic."

"Could have said something sooner," Vaysa said, swallowing the fear down her throat. Her best hope at helping Shad lay unconscious by her feet. Because she'd made another mistake. A scream bubbled up her throat, but she swallowed it down. She shouldn't panic. Panic was the enemy.

Chapter 12

TEO

Teo blinked his eyes open. The world swam around in a haze. A sharp, searing pain consumed his face, and he worked his jaw to ease the pain.

He searched around trying to piece together the jumbled images. Raspy breathing broke the silence, followed by someone crying, and someone rifling through his pockets.

A crack of thunder and burst of lightning filled the sky, pulling his attention upwards and sharpening his focus. He looked toward his feet. Gren was rummaging through his stuff. Stealing from him. The person he was supposed to protect.

He was on a Phantom Islands with three non-humans. Including a Cuma monster. He sucked back a sob and shoved Gren away from his jacket.

Gren flew back. Jards. How much more of a mess could he make?

Teo pushed himself up. He swallowed a cry of pain with a grimace and rubbed his temple in an attempt to relieve the headache. He squinted as he surveyed the camp.

Vaysa hovered over Shad. Tears trickled down her face, leaving dirty smudges on her cheeks. Words caught in his throat. Jards. She was a Berlan who had taken Gren, the reason he was on Phantom Islands. And yet, he swallowed back at sympathy bubbling up. Focus.

Shad was barely breathing, and her eyes no longer glowed, having turned a light cream color.

Teo cursed. He didn't have an option. He wanted to survive to reach Berla, and they needed Shad to do it, even if she had taken Gren.

He grabbed his small medicine case stashed in a hidden pocket of his pants by his waist, along with his knife. He shuddered looking at Vaysa. Blood covered her, and her hands could no longer get a solid hold on the arrow's shaft.

He nudged her and waited for her to look at him. He sucked in a breath. Despite her frightening white eyes, her face crumbled in emotion, and more tears spilled down her face as she sucked back a sob. She'd finally stopped glowing, but her white eyes still shimmered. Something more than pity twisted in his stomach. It had to be heightened fear messing with his emotions.

Another bolt of thunder cracked through the sky. He shook his head to focus and pointed to the fire. "Please get me some light."

She did so wordlessly. She held the burning stick in her hand without flinching.

Taking a shaky breath, Teo took his knife and cut a small incision around the protruding part of the arrow. He flinched when Vaysa yelped for Shad, who was too weak. He slowly cut away flesh until he found the arrow tip. It had twisted and lodged in her ribs.

Sighing, he looked at Vaysa. "This will really hurt her, but please trust me."

Vaysa nodded dully.

Teo paused and shook off the hypocrisy of helping Shad. He took part of his uniform and wiped her blood off the arrow. He grasped the arrow handle and twisted the grip to release it.

Shad arched in pain and gasped loudly. Teo ducked when Vaysa tightened her grip on the branch and let out a breath when Vaysa stopped herself from clubbing him with it.

The arrow slid out of Shad. Vaysa and Teo both sighed with relief. Teo's hands were soaked in Shad's blood, and he stared at them for a moment. Vaysa would destroy him, but he could kill Shad. He could do exactly as Closs wanted. And ordered. He stared a moment longer and then his training kicked in.

Teo diligently washed the injury, stitched it up, and placed a pink salve on top. He then grabbed a scrap from his jacket, boiled it, and wrapped it around Shad's wound, shoulder, and torso.

"What now?" Vaysa choked.

The attacker had poisoned the arrow. The rank smell of it was unfamiliar. Without knowing by what, he couldn't treat it effectively. There was little hope outside of whatever Berlan magic she could muster.

The truth turned on his tongue.

"She needs rest. She looks tough, she might make it." Teo lied to console Vaysa. He blinked. What did it matter if she had hope? They were nothing. Just strangers. No enemies... Enemies with a common goal until they reached Berla.

"Thank you," Vaysa said and tossed Teo a small leather pouch.

"You're welcome," he mumbled in surprise, rubbing his swollen face.

The leather pouch was heavy for its size. He carefully dumped the contents out to find small vials of different medicines, creams, and such. He looked questioningly at Vaysa.

She shrugged and said, "You're better equipped to use them."

Teo shook his head. Whom hadn't she robbed?

Gren's groans jerked Teo's attention away from the pouch.

"You okay?" Teo asked. Standing, he shuffled toward Gren to assess his injuries.

"I was till I got suckered punched."

"I thought you were stealing from me." It was lame. He'd been wrong and should apologize, but he just couldn't bear to see or hear Gren's smug response.

"You just saved a thief!"

"Yeah, one who fed me and helped get me across the rank currents." And one he wanted to use to help him get to Berla and the Royal Guard. At least those reasons made sense, even if he couldn't explain why he really did it.

Chapter 13

VAYSA

Vaysa snorted at the two bickering. They didn't matter when Shad was injured, and she turned her attention to the forest line. Someone was living on the Phantom Islands and they attacked. And obviously they had poisoned the tip, otherwise Shad would have started to heal, like she always did.

She scanned the foreign tree line, the reed-thin trunks clustered into a wall. It was too risky to enter when everything behind it was masked. She'd leave the other three exposed and risk getting lost or injured if she ventured in.

Their attackers would likely be back when they thought the Cuma was nullified.

She'd be ready. She'd protect Shad.

Vaysa moved Shad under the boat. She made Teo and Gren stay on the side of the boat away from the forest. The attacker would have to come out in the open to get them.

Gren and Teo watched as she made shields and checked on Shad but said nothing.

Vaysa glared at Teo when he finally opened his mouth. He rolled his tongue over his teeth and looked away. Vaysa snorted in satisfaction.

As she crawled under the boat to check on Shad for the umpteenth time, she let out a wail. Her limp body was covered in sand and blood smeared across her jacket and face. Revulsion clawed at her throat and stole a choking breath from her. Bawling, she pounded her fists and kicked the boat. She emerged and fell to the sandy beach.

Gren and Teo turned to her, and tried to help her up, but she shoved them away.

"What? Is it... Shad?" Teo asked, staring back at the upturned boat.

"She... she... she's dead," Vaysa screamed, the lie painful to utter.

Teo and Gren looked at the ground and slumped beside Vaysa.

"I'm sorry, Vaysa," Teo whispered. He reached for her shoulder but stopped himself and ran it through his hair. He shook his head and said, "Jards, we're never getting off this island."

Gren groaned and smacked Teo half-heartedly.

"Well, we're not."

Not if she didn't do something about it. Not if she didn't help Shad.

Keeping her fingers laced over her face, Vaysa studied the trees from her position. A glint of metal flashed in the moonlight. Staggering to her feet, she grabbed the shield and stumbled toward the tree line.

Teo and Gren chased after her, pulling her back.

"You'll die in there!" Gren scolded.

"Don't be stupid," Teo yelled when Vaysa shrugged his hand off her shoulder and headed for the forest.

Leaves shuffled gently in a nonexistent breeze a few paces to her left. She focused her gaze in that direction and loudly said, "You two are soldiers; you'll be fine. Get back behind the boat."

Gren and Teo stared at each other.

"What?" Teo mouthed to Gren.

Gren shook his head and shrugged. His gaze sharpened on the trees. He staged whispered, "Vaysa, someone's there. They're watching us."

Vaysa turned momentarily to the forest. She'd forgotten he could see in the dark. She could have done this so differently. But it was too late now. She turned to the trees and whispered, "Where? How many?"

Before Gren could respond, an arrow sailed through the air, tearing into Teo's arm across his Royal Guard insignia. He howled and collapsed to the ground. Another whizzed by, grazing Gren's leg as he dove for cover behind the shields.

Vaysa didn't run to their aid. Even if she didn't like it, she had to use them as bait. It'd have been easier if they'd listened and hid behind the boat. Or if she'd remembered Gren's skill. Either way, it was too late. She ducked behind her shield and yelled, "Come out and show yourself, cowards!"

She didn't know what to expect. If it was a whole tribe, she'd have to let them take her to their prison, if they hopefully had a prison. There was no way she could take them all on the beach. Otherwise, they were all dead. If she could get to their settlement, she could get the cure. Somehow.

If it was a solo stranded person, hopefully she could reason with them. Or at least overpower them.

Her stomach knotted as an arrow landed at her feet. Vaysa kept the shield up as she reached for her sword.

A rough, deep voice escaped the forest. "Keep your hands in the air. No weapons."

Vaysa let her hand hang in the air and smiled; she didn't need a weapon.

A single man emerged. She searched the line but didn't see anyone else.

The light was dim, even with the fire. The low light diminished his features, but he was taller than most humans. Shad was still bigger. He had long dark hair and wore leather pants, a tunic, and a duster despite the immense heat. Without light, it was hard to determine if he was human or not, but he was likely non-human.

"What do you want?" the man asked, his weapon drawn and aimed at Vaysa.

"Are you alone?"

The man glanced toward the injured soldiers behind her and nodded.

"I want the cure for the poison."

The man laughed.

Vaysa bristled. She hadn't said anything funny.

He asked, "Why are you here?"

"We're running."

"You have two soldiers with you."

"Deserters."

"Hm." Keeping a sharp eye on Vaysa, the man moved over to Teo and knelt down. "Quite the interesting group. A Cuma, Silver, and two humans."

"Only one human."

The man raised an eyebrow but didn't respond. He looked at Teo and Gren and finally back toward Vaysa.

Red clouded her vision and warmth tingled in her veins. She flexed her fingers at the sensation. Shad didn't have time to wait. She sucked on her cheeks to keep her anger contained.

Finally, the man asked, "Berlans joined the Royal Guard?"

Vaysa let out a bark of sarcastic laughter.

"Cumas and Silvers are now allies?"

Vaysa stared back at him and shrugged. How would she know?

"Is there another war?"

Vaysa cocked her head to the side and gauged the man. He didn't look like he had been stranded very long. He looked well fed and healthy. He was too shrouded in clothing to get a good look at his features, but he certainly wasn't human.

Vaysa finally asked, "How long have you been here?"

"Too long." He sighed, sheathing the arrow in his hand and stowing his bow. He wiped his hands on his jacket and stood up again.

Vaysa eased the shield to a resting position and put her hand down. The two stared at each other. He didn't feel like an enemy. He just looked bored. Or broken.

Gren thrashed around and Vaysa suppressed a growl when he said, "Excuse me."

"What?" she said without looking at him.

"Teo will die from the poison on the tips, and I'll lose my leg or worse. Either kill each other or help us."

Without looking away from Vaysa, the man asked Gren, "Why are you here?"

"We are fleeing the army."

The man smirked at Vaysa and said, "Fine. I will leave you be. Just be gone at morning light. Also, I recommend ditching the uniforms if you're going to Berla. It's why I attacked."

"Wait!" Vaysa yelled as he started to turn around. "You shot three members of my group, poisoned them, and just plan on walking away?"

"What else would I do?" he said, turning back to her with interest.

"Tell me how to cure the poison," Vaysa said in a low, controlled voice. Fire licked at her veins. Powers or not, if he turned away again, he'd never make it to the tree line. She understood why he'd attacked, but he still needed to fix it.

Thunder rumbled above, and the man glanced up and frowned. He looked back to Vaysa and tossed her a small vial filled with a brownish sludge. "I'll work on the human."

Vaysa's eyes fell to Gren. The arrow had only grazed him. He could wait. She scampered under the boat with the vial clutched in her trembling hand.

Shad lay there breathing better than before, but still unconscious. Vaysa lathered the brown gunk all over Shad's wound. Her heart pounded in her ears. She stroked Shad's head and softly prayed for her friend. Shad was breathing, and that was all that mattered.

Reemerging, she came face to face with Gren and the man. Teo stirred in the distance and started to moan. He would be okay.

However, Gren looked furious. The fire caused shadows to dance on his dark face. She set her jaw and braced herself.

Vaysa tossed him the remaining mixture in the vial.

He glowered but caught it.

The man looked to Gren and then Vaysa. He stood straighter and pointed to the boat. "I thought it was dead."

"How do you know she's not?"

"Boats snore?"

"You wouldn't have come closer if she wasn't."

"You risked our lives!" Gren interjected. He took a step forward and pointed a finger at Vaysa. trembling with anger.

"She was obviously poisoned, and I needed to know by what." Heat clawed at her neck.

"Again, you risked our lives!"

"We'd have been dead without her, anyway. Besides, I told you to hide behind the boat and you chose not to listen." Vaysa replied through clenched teeth. They were all okay, and they needed Shad. Shad was more important than they were.

Gren growled and stormed off pouting. The attacker moved to the side and watched Gren with amusement. With his back now to the fire, his gaze fell back on Vaysa, and his eyes bulged in surprise.

"What's your problem?" Vaysa spat.

His mouth hung open, and his eyes squinted shut. He gripped the bridge of his nose with his forefinger and thumb. "Your eyes are white?"

Vaysa's face scrunched up, and she snarled. No matter where she went, they focused on that. "I was born with them."

"The curse hasn't..."

"Yeah, they're a curse. People always need to point them out. What's your point?"

The man looked down and shook his head. "That's not what I meant... I'm... Solon."

"Okay."

"You?"

Vaysa walked away. This man, Solon, was creepy. They didn't need another enemy, but she didn't need another friend, either.

THE MEDICINE HELPED Gren and Teo doze off. Vaysa stayed away from Solon. He had offered to stay to help make sure everyone was okay. Vaysa had declined the help, but Solon had stayed anyway.

Even if she could drive him into the forest, she couldn't do anything about him lurking there. At least on the beach, she could watch his moves.

Adrenaline fled, exhaustion tugging at her eyes, Vaysa sat on the boat to provide one more line of defense for Shad. Vaysa startled awake when Shad started thrashing around. She jumped down, sword drawn. The other three were still sleeping in various spots on the beach.

Vaysa whispered, "Shad, sh."

Shad's eyes flashed and darted to Vaysa. She sighed and slumped back, panting.

Vaysa scooted under the boat and lifted it. Shad pulled herself through the opening and, breathing heavily, slumped against the boat.

"What happened?" Shad asked.

"You were shot and poisoned. So were Teo and Gren." Her vision blurred with the truth. She'd almost lost Shad.

Shad growled and scanned around and asked incredulously, "We have another one?"

"He's the shooter."

Shad tried to pull herself up as she balled her massive hand into a fist and snarled. Her fangs glistened in the light.

"He also helped heal everyone. I was pretty clear we had soldiers with us to draw him out. I can't imagine people coming here willingly... It could be a good place to live," Vaysa said. "A safe place..." Her powers didn't matter here.

Snorting, Shad fell back again. She rolled her eyes at Vaysa's mention of staying on the island. "Are the two guards okay?"

Vaysa swallowed at Shad's choice of term and nodded.

"Great," Shad drawled.

"He obviously lives here. He might be able to help us regroup, heal, and get safely to the mainland if you still want to go there," Vaysa said, studying the islands. Even with Solon, they were safer here than in Kennard. And they wouldn't have to face the Royal Guard in Berla or whatever else awaited them there.

"He's probably stuck."

"Or he's chosen to stay here. It's away from people and has plenty of food."

Shad furrowed her brow and shook her head. "No one stays in this hellhole willingly."

Vaysa swallowed but didn't respond.

She left Shad there to rest while she collected breakfast, but found Solon had awakened and was already preparing a plentitude of foods. She stared at Solon over the fire while he cooked.

She studied his appearance in the gray morning light. He had long jet-black hair. His eyes were the same deep black. From a distance it wasn't odd, but up close it was noticeable that light didn't bounce off of them. The few bits of skin that showed from beneath the long, dark coat were bone white. His skin should have been tanned from living on the hot island. He wasn't human.

He stared back, also not engaging in conversation.

Teo and Gren awoke to delicious smells wafting from the fire and stumbled over, interrupting their silent assessment.

Gren limped slightly but could move around.

Teo was slower moving and tentatively rotating his arm.

"He's still with us? Great." Teo deadpanned, plopping down by the fire. Seeing the food, he smiled and said, "At least he can make breakfast."

Vaysa hid a smile as she stole a glance at Solon. He seemed oblivious to Teo's comment.

"How's..." Teo asked and jerked his head toward the boat.

"She's okay," Gren said and gestured toward Shad, who had stood up from her spot by the boat and started their way.

"She didn't die?" Teo asked, his face lighting up.

"Careful, you almost sound happy," Vaysa said.

Solon turned around. He dropped the food he was holding and stared at her. "Shad?"

"Solon? It's been a long time." Shad barely hid her grin.

Vaysa stared at both of them. How did they know each other?

Chapter 14

VAYSA

"What's going on?" Vaysa demanded.

"We're old friends," Shad whispered. Her smile faltered and her eyes dimmed.

"Did you know he was here?" Vaysa asked in a tight voice while pointing down at the sandy beach. Her heartbeat thumped in her ears.

Shad averted her eyes and shook her head.

"She probably thought I was dead. That's why they sent me here," Solon said, stepping between Shad and Vaysa.

"You were exiled here?" Gren asked. His red eyes gazed across the island with interest.

"No one stops here willingly. Either you're a prisoner or running," Solon said.

Shad flinched and her face contorted in sadness.

How many secrets did Shad have? First a dragon scale… and now this?

Vaysa's nostrils flared and with a deep, shaky sigh, she walked away from the group. Nothing made sense.

Gren tried to follow her but sighed in resignation when she brushed him off with a flick of her hand.

Teo asked, "Why'd you shoot your friend?"

Solon glared at him, and Gren covered his eyes with his hand.

Solon finally shook his head and answered, "Not all Cumas are friends. Like humans, some are good and some are not. A Cuma helping Royal Guard soldiers? That's a nightmare."

"The pamphlets said Cumas were killing machines," Teo said, and then flinched when he saw Shad staring at him.

"Yet, you're still alive," Shad spat.

Solon snorted and said, "They can be, just like humans."

Gren hid his smile and mumbled, "Idiot."

Shad staggered up and limped after Vaysa. Despite her injury, her stride was immense. Vaysa stopped and grunted when Shad placed a hand on her shoulder.

"I know Solon from Berla, from the war." Shad's voice broke, causing Vaysa to wince.

Vaysa blinked. The war. Shad rarely spoke about it.

"Did you know he was here?" Vaysa rubbed her arms, her eyes unable to meet Shad's.

Sighing, Shad sat down. "I figured as much."

"Why'd you leave him here?" Vaysa took a step back from her friend. The Shad she knew wouldn't leave a friend. But the Shad she knew had many secrets, too.

"I didn't. Kennard captured him. I had to help the others out of Berla. Solon made me promise not to come back for him. I knew the routine. They'd torture him. If he was lucky, he'd die quickly. If not, they'd drop him off on an island. That's how they handled prisoners." Shad's head fell to her hands.

A gnarled pang rippled in Vaysa's heart. With a step forward, her fingers rested on Shad's shoulders.

"Didn't you want to help him?" she whispered.

"Yes!" Shad threw her head back. Her glowing eyes squinted.

"Then why?" Vaysa didn't step back despite Shad's outburst.

"I thought he was dead."

"What did he do?" Vaysa asked and glanced back at Solon.

"Made two kings angry in the last war. However, it's his story to tell."

Shad had been a part of the war on Berla. She never said much about it, and Vaysa didn't pry. The war had seemed mythical; more fantasy than reality. But a ghost had resurrected to validate the stories.

Finally, with a twist of her stomach, she sank beside her friend. Whatever was in Shad's past, she'd only ever looked out for Vaysa. Helped her. Even with partial facts and secrets, Vaysa knew Shad would only have left him if necessary. "Were you two close?"

"Yes." Shad's voice trailed off, and her gaze fell on Solon. Shaking her head, Shad turned back to Vaysa. "They tortured him. They broke him. I don't know how he survived."

"He survived here. We could be safe here, too," Vaysa said.

"Vaysa, no. It's not an option. We'll get a dragon scale."

Vaysa growled. Too much was happening. Too many secrets. Too many unknowns. Too many truths.

"Is he coming with us?" Vaysa asked, her gaze flickering to Solon.

Shad's face fell. "That's up to him if he wants to come to Berla. If he does, we can get him to some people who can help. We'll have a long, dangerous journey ahead of us in Berla."

Help. From people. More unknown friends. More parts of Shad's past Vaysa never heard about. And in dangerous parts she had no experience with. On that thought, Vaysa said, "Then let's stay here. It's safe here."

"No it's not!" Shad roared, and after taking a shaky breath, she said softer, "He'll come here."

"Who?"

Shad glared at her and said, "Closs. He saw you."

"So? We left. I'm nothing to him."

Shad licked her lips and averted her eyes. "Vaysa, I can't help with your powers. They're growing rapidly."

"I'll figure them out. There's no one here to hurt. I'm in control of them here." They wouldn't need to go to Berla for a dragon scale or face the Royal Guard.

"Vaysa," Shad chortled. "Fire not shooting from your hands every few seconds isn't control."

"It's something," Vaysa said. "They aren't triggered here."

Shad snorted. "You burned a village and started a forest fire. If you start one here, we're doomed."

Vaysa rolled her eyes. "I lost control twice."

"How many times have you been in control of them?"

Vaysa flinched. She looked at Solon and then Shad. Her stomach twisted and heat thrummed up from her chest through her arms and neck. "I didn't lose control last night."

Shad followed Vaysa's gaze and growled softly. She rubbed her forehead. "They'd have us pinned. If we stay here, it'd be the same as being in prison. They can surround us here. Berla will be safer. We can get you the help you need."

"I'm sorry," Vaysa said. She didn't have control of her powers. She was a danger to them. If she lost control, she could destroy everything. "This is my fault."

"No, it's not." Shad said, shaking her head. "The powers shouldn't be materializing."

"So what about the powers!" Vaysa spat. Fire curled through her veins. "We're here because I didn't listen. I attacked Ben and followed the soldiers. They saw me because I was reckless."

"What you did didn't warrant them burning a forest."

Vaysa snorted. Shad's lie sounded nice, but it was still a lie.

"Vaysa, we'll get the help you need to control them. A dragon scale. We'll find a home, again."

Vaysa looked around. They had nothing left. They were on an island in the Spirit Strait with two non-humans and a human, secrets coming to life, her uncontrolled powers increasing, and the Royal Guard was coming for them according to Shad. Even possibly on the Phantom Islands. How was this really any different than before? A curl of fire raced in her veins, yearning to be released. She stilled, holding her breath, wondering if it would escape. When it passed, she looked at her hands. No signs of fire or the destruction they could cause were visible.

But she wasn't in control.

Looking for a dragon scale would at least keep them moving, focused. Comfort Shad. Even if it was a wild chase, it was something to work toward. She'd even learn more about Shad. And she couldn't deny Shad's conviction. She owed Shad. She'd cost them their home when she didn't listen. And there was a glimmer of hope that Shad was right. Shad believed she could control her powers with a dragon scale. An odd calm eased her tight stomach.

Pride and disbelief were of the same mindset; they ignored reality.

Both had blinded her. Both had cost them their home.

Another reality, lingering in the recesses, came to mind. "You hid the idea of a dragon scale from me and that you thought a friend was on the Phantom Islands."

Shad sighed as she nodded. "I did."

Vaysa flicked her gaze to Shad. Shad's hard face belied nothing. No regret, guilt, pride. "Why?"

"It didn't matter in Kennard. It would have only complicated... everything."

"How much have you kept from me?" The words were barely a whisper but filled the chasm between them.

"Vaysa, I had a life on Berla before we met in Kennard."

"I'm aware."

Shad snorted. "I don't even know how much I haven't shared." She swallowed. Her golden eyes dimmed as she stared into the distance. "But we're going to have to face a lot of it."

We. Shad was including Vaysa in it. Finally sharing her past with her. It didn't fix the ache in Vaysa's heart or satisfy the questions, but it was a start. And no matter what had happened in Vaysa's life since arriving in Kennard, Shad had been there with her and for her. Vaysa could give her more time, but she couldn't be a risk.

"Then we go for a scale."

Shad licked her lips and looked back at Vaysa. "No matter what someone asks you, don't tell them we're after it."

Vaysa snorted in disbelief. "What do I say then?"

"Say nothing."

"Why? If dragon scales are so powerful, don't a lot go for them?" Vaysa challenged.

"Vaysa, I know you don't believe what I'm saying."

"I believe and trust you," Vaysa said. "And you seem to believe it."

"I do. Not many living beings remember the tales of the dragons. It's become a myth to most. But it is not. Those who do know won't venture into the nests."

"And we are?" Vaysa's vision blurred, settling on the reality of what Shad was saying. They were going to Berla, an unknown world to Vaysa, with the Royal Guard swarming, so she could go after an elusive dragon scale in a nest that others were too scared to enter. Whichever way she looked, death or worse faced her.

"We don't have a choice. I promise, once you have a scale, you'll be in control. Otherwise the elements will try to control you."

It was a nice promise. One Vaysa wanted to believe. But her powers were already trying to control her.

Chapter 15

VAYSA

"We've spent four days here already," Gren said. "At most we would've had eight days to avoid the Royal Guard when we landed on the island."

"Gren and Teo filled me in. Another war is starting," Solon added as Vaysa and Shad rejoined the group. "We're working on a plan."

"We" meant he was coming. Jards.

"I think we should stay here until we're healed," Teo said.

"Once again, no!" Gren said, almost shouting. "The Royal Guard will set up posts along Berla's coasts from the Wind Ocean, through the Spirit Strait, and into the Dark Ocean. We need to slip in before them if we don't want to deal with them."

Teo mimicked Gren and mumbled under his breath.

Vaysa frowned, her stomach clenching. Teo wanted to get caught. She looked around the island. Maybe they could leave him here. There was no good in taking him to Berla. Sure, she was responsible for Gren being here and by default Teo, but he joined the Royal Guard and followed orders to bring Gren back.

She looked at Shad, who was staring intently at Teo.

Shad looked up at Vaysa and rolled her eyes. Shad would let her leave him, but Vaysa couldn't leave him here in good conscience. Even knowing he'd rejoin the Royal Guard once they made it to Berla. The reality settled like lead in her stomach.

"Gren is right, since we don't want to get caught, and we likely would if the Royal Guard landed before us," Solon said.

Teo sighed and said, "Okay, great, but the largest section of water to cross still awaits us. My arm is useless, Shad's seriously injured, and our boat is pretty beat up already."

"You could stay," Gren offered.

Teo made a gesture with his finger.

"Enough," Shad said.

The two fell silent.

Ignoring them, Solon gestured for Shad to follow him.

Vaysa ran her tongue over her teeth and looked away when Shad's gaze turned to her. A heated spike coursed through her veins.

Shad growled but followed Solon. They left the group and disappeared into the woods.

"Vaysa," Teo started.

She flicked her gaze to him. "What?"

He sighed.

"Whatever," she blew a breath out. He was wasting time.

"Thanks," he said.

"For?"

Teo chuckled. "Really? You're a Berlan. I'm a Royal Guard. You could have killed me. Instead, you're letting me tag along to Berla."

"I hope I don't regret it," she muttered.

Teo's eyes locked on hers for a long moment before his gaze fell to Gren and then the sand.

Bitterness tanged in her mouth. They both knew their realities. The tenuous truce would evaporate on the shores of Berla. She just had to make sure they separated before he could turn on them.

Shad and Solon reemerged half-dragging, half-carrying an ancient-looking vessel. The weathered, mismatching wood slabs had reinforced sides. There were weapon-like contraptions sticking out of it, and he'd built the sides up with various pieces of wood. It was slightly bigger than their boat. Not by much, but the five of them would fit.

Shad wrapped the sack she and Vaysa had brought from their home carefully around her back, avoiding her wound. Teo still had his two medical kits and knives. Gren had nothing left after they had stripped him clean in Kennard.

Solon pulled from the vessel a satchel each for Gren, Teo, Vaysa, and himself to carry. Solon had loaded them down with an array of items from coins to food and blankets. It was odd he was so well supplied, but she didn't question the origins of the goods. She'd use them, anyway.

Vaysa looked at the group and groaned internally. She was bringing two strangers and Shad was bringing Solon. It was against everything she'd done to survive in Kennard. But this wasn't Kennard.

The odds weren't great that they'd make it to Berla. She looked at the island again and wished she could convince Shad to stay. She glanced at Shad and suppressed a smile when Shad shook her head "no" at her.

She took one last glance around the island and in the direction of Kennard shoreline. The longing she expected wasn't there. Just an emptiness in her stomach and a dull ache in her heart. She couldn't see the land, but she knew what was there. She turned her gaze west to Berla and prepared herself for what they may face.

Berla it was.

Despite her injury, Shad took up an oar with Teo. Solon flanked Gren with an additional set of oars. Vaysa stood to help navigate and defend the boat. His vessel had raised sides to protect them and bladed sticks they could use with their feet if something attacked them in the water.

They gained distance from the island as morning brightened to midday. The air wasn't as heavy, and the odor lessened in intensity. Vaysa leaned back on her heels, watching the haze ease. Despite the serenity, her muscles tightened, and she swallowed down the acid of uncertainty. A gentle breeze skimmed her arms and she strained to see a sign of Berla on the horizon. Instead, flashes of brilliant light shot across the water.

She cursed and rolled her eyes in expectancy of what new terror she'd face in the strait.

She searched the horizon to see if they could avoid the spectacle, but there were only pops of color.

"Incoming," she said and took a defensive pose. She exhaled a breath, pushing out thoughts of Berla, Kennard, and the unknown.

The others grumbled, but they maintained their course.

As they neared, the pops of light turned into fish. She snorted a laugh and grabbed a spare paddle to use instead of her sword. She rolled her shoulders, readying for fun.

A few thuds hit the ship's armor, harmless, but then a swirl of orange and yellow Koi arched over the ship. The dizzying display swirled in a kaleidoscope of colors.

Pulling her arm back, she used the paddle to slam them back into the water. Each one disappeared into the putrid dark waters. She smiled until one fell into the boat.

"Jards," Teo and Gren cursed.

"They tear flesh," Shad yelled. "Stop it!"

Tossing her paddle down, Vaysa dove for the slippery creature. The bite of the wood skinned her arms but she crawled after the fish toward Solon. Before she could reach it, the fish bit Solon's foot. His leather boot provided some protection, but the teeth tore through it to his flesh.

Solon's bellow filled the air, rattling Vaysa and sending a curl of fire through her veins. Blood wept from his boot, slicking the belly of the boat.

"Gross," Teo gagged. With eyes pinched closed, he turned his head.

"It'll take his toe off," Gren said. A wave of green clawed at his face.

Shad reached across the packed vessel and bit the fish's body in two. Blood and scales dripped down her fangs, but the jaws remained attached. Vaysa gagged but dropped down and tugged on them. Her fingers slipped on the blood.

"I can't get a good grip," Vaysa groaned.

Solon bent down and pulled on the topside of the jaws. Vaysa dug her heels into the boat for leverage and pulled. The sickening crack of the jawbone filled the air.

Panting and gray, Solon returned to rowing while Vaysa dug the teeth out. Solon's blood covered her hands as she collected the teeth in a metal tin.

"Infection will set in," Teo said. His amber eyes swept over Solon. "Did it reach bone?"

Face still pinched, Solon nodded.

"It should be washed out, cleaned and wrapped," Teo said. "But we don't have all the supplies. Clean it as much as you can. In the bag you gave me, there's a brown glass bottle. Put a few drops of it on the wound and then wrap it with the cleanest cloth you can find."

Instead of focusing on why he was helping, Vaysa grabbed the damp packs. Her gaze flicked to the others as she dug in the sacks. She licked her lips. They could still turn around, go back to the Phantom Islands. Not deal with the strait or what waited in Berla.

Shad's gold eyes met hers. She lifted her chin toward the bag in Vaysa's hands and then set her eyes in the direction of Berla.

A hollowness settled in her heart, robbing her of breath. This was their path. They weren't going back. Swallowing, Vaysa dug in the sacks and made some strips of cloth from something Solon had packed. When Teo nodded at the third bottle she lifted, she put a small amount on the wound and wrapped Solon's foot.

"Thanks," Solon muttered between clenched teeth.

Vaysa's gaze flicked to Teo. His body rippled as he rowed his paddle. When his attention flicked to her, she wanted to see mockery or disgust. Instead, concern burned bright in them. She swallowed. Jards. "Thanks."

With his lips pressed tightly, he nodded.

Vaysa turned to Solon. "I don't have anything for the pain."

"I've had worse."

Shad growled. Vaysa slid her eyes to Shad. A snarl rippled over Shad's lips. Her eyes flashed in golden hate.

This was just the beginning. She blinked and stopped herself from rubbing her bloodied hands in her hair. Now wasn't the time to get lost in what would happen and what had happened. Before them lay frothing waters teeming with more obstacles.

Vaysa quit playing with the Koi and started pounding them back. When the Koi vanished, her stomach tightened with unease. The waters lapped by, pungent and fierce, but unblemished by objects or fish. Something wasn't right. She leaned over the side and beneath her a large shadow trailed their boat.

She groaned. Another new creature would attack them. Then likely another. The Spirit Strait was proving why no one wanted to cross it.

Speeding up, the plump creature started circling them in choppy circles, dipping deeper and then bobbing up close to the surface but never breaching. As it came broadside, she saw it was twice the vessel's size, yet it stayed a distance from the blades from the ship.

She swallowed the lump in her throat and stared at the water and the creature beneath. They had to face it.

Turning to her crew, she said, "Start your feet thing."

They stared at her for a moment, and then their faces lit up with realization. The four ran the poles with their feet. Teo's clogged up, and a red glob floated to the water's top.

Vaysa's stomach twisted and acid burned at her throat, the desire to wretch overwhelming. Saliva pooled in her mouth, and she braced against the side of the boat for a beat.

The beast lashed at the boat, rocking it back and forth, tossing Vaysa back from the side. She swallowed, fighting her stomach to keep its contents. As sweat beaded on her brow, she caught sight of Gren shaking, his face and neck tinted green.

The creature broke free of the blade and rammed the bow of the boat. Vaysa fell to the belly of the boat, her side taking the impact. She swore and touched her side. Other than a bruise she'd be fine. But looking at Gren and his ashen face, she yanked the oar from him and nudged him over. He didn't argue as she climbed into his seat.

Swaying, he tried to stand. It took three attempts. He grasped the sides of the boat, leaned, and then the air filled with the sound of him sending his breakfast into the sea. He repeated it several times, including a few dry heaves. His breathing slowly returned to him as he clutched the side of the vessel.

He lumbered back into a sitting position. Looking at Vaysa, Gren said, "Wait a few minutes before going back up there."

She nodded, unable to meet his eyes. Dipping her head over her knees, she took long breaths to steady her reaction.

When her breath steadied, she returned to the helm. The smell still hovered, but the current had carried the actual debris away. She watched as the monster swam in odd lurching motions before disappearing into the depths. Her eyes flickered forward, wondering what new hell they would face.

Chapter 16

VAYSA

The sun nestled on the horizon, dipping below the waves when Vaysa spotted land. She swallowed and leaned back, taking in the sight. Looming ahead was a vast expanse of land unlike anything she'd seen. There were large trees, but the roots twisted above the land. The spindly branches did not appear strong enough for shelter, and massive sepia leaves hung in droops, causing the branches to bend toward the earth. The land was a mushy, dark brown mess of murky water.

"We've made it... somewhere."

The four slowed their rowing. Solon stood and winced at the pain. He cursed when his gaze swept across the swamp before him.

"We missed the Blue Plains and landed in the Sea Swamp," Solon said.

Shad and Gren groaned.

"What's the problem?" Teo asked. "We made it to Berla."

"The swamps are close to the southern tip. It's also, well, not very safe. The plains would have been better. The humans there would've probably given us food," Gren said.

"There're humans in Berla?" Teo asked, his eyes and nose scrunched.

"Most are farmers. Russom was a human," Gren said, staring southwards.

"Russom?" Vaysa murmured. Gren had mentioned the same name that night in Kennard.

Solon and Shad flinched. Vaysa cursed. A shared secret.

"The dethroned king of Berla," Gren said, glancing back at her. "The Traitors overthrew him. He died. The Traitors now oversee the lands. They even overtook his castle. Unlike Russom, the Traitors won't trade crops with King Malik and Kennard."

"Traitors?" Solon whispered. His dark eyes found Shad.

Vaysa looked at Shad, who avoided her eyes.

Shad shrugged in defeat.

Solon's face darkened and he clenched his teeth, a muscle ticking in his jaw.

"There are humans in Berla?" Teo asked again. "I thought..."

"Only monsters?" Vaysa finished for him and rolled her eyes. She wouldn't have to face that term much longer.

"Yes, Teo. There're humans in Berla. There aren't nearly as many as when Russom ruled, but there're humans in the Blue Plains," Gren said. "Traitors won't trade with King Malik because he tried to help King Russom."

"I thought the humans were in the Mosa Plains, by the castle," Solon said, turning to Gren.

"The Traitors moved them a few years after they overthrew King Russom," Gren said and fell into a coughing fit.

Shad and Solon shared another subtle exchange. It was another secret. Vaysa didn't try to stop the heat that radiated from her heart through her limbs.

"We should free them," Teo said passionately.

"What're you talking about? They aren't prisoners, you moron. They're protected. The Traitors moved them to fertile fields. The humans have to eat, too," Gren shot.

"Interesting," Vaysa said. "Traitors will feed the humans who live here while Kennard tries to kill any non-human who steps foot on their soil. No wonder the Traitors won't trade with them."

"It's not—" Teo started.

"Kennard isn't like that?" Vaysa challenged.

Teo's face turned crimson, and he looked away, muttering and making faces.

They'd land soon and then he could go on his way. Back to the Royal Guard and humans.

"We could jog to the plains," Solon said, pointing to the northern shore.

"Current's too strong." Shad turned to Gren. "If I remember correctly, the swamp merges into the Silver Forest away from the strait."

Gren's face paled and he averted his eyes. He doubled over coughing and gasped for air.

"Are you okay?" Vaysa asked, trying to lean away from him.

"Yeah, just swamp air." He leaned against the side and slid to a sitting position and let Solon take both of their loads. His blue skin had a faint green tint.

Shad narrowed her eyes at Gren and then shifted her gaze to the shoreline. "If we can get through the Sea Swamp, there are forests on all sides. We can camp there tonight."

Vaysa grimaced. This land looked worse than the Phantom Islands. The ground on the islands was solid versus the loose terrain. A long sigh escaped her lips. She couldn't look backward. Only forward.

Scanning the horizon, Vaysa noticed bubbles popping from the brown goo. Small, round red rocks started bobbing by them. The small rocks, connected to another red rock, grew to about two feet in diameter as they came out of the water. Attached to the top of the first rock were two thin, long red antennae.

She swiped at Shad and pointed. Shad followed her gaze and yelled, "Cypress Ants!"

The ants streamed out of the water. Solon and Shad bolted to the oars, and Solon yanked Vaysa down.

"Don't let them see you!" Solon hissed and pointed at Gren's oar.

Vaysa bit her tongue to stop her retort and took over Gren's position. They'd found their next hell to face already.

Gren rolled to the center of the ship and just lay there. His skin turned even greener.

"We need to back up and get out of here!" Solon shouted.

It was too late. The ship jerked and bounced as the ants lifted it from the murk and carried it out of the water. Vaysa tried to get a view, but Solon and Shad yanked her back down. The bumpy ride ended when the boat banged into a large, dense object. There was a scratching sound, and then more tugging.

"They're trying to figure out how to get us in their nest," Solon said.

"If they do, we aren't getting out," Shad said.

"Great." Teo deadpanned.

"Maybe Gren could vomit. It helped with the sea thingy," Vaysa said, waving backwards.

Gren groaned and slumped backward. His red eyes narrowed into slits and he shot Vaysa a dark look.

They hadn't even officially landed in Berla, and its creatures were attacking them. How could Vaysa defend them from these things? Did she even have to? The agreement was to get everyone to Berla. It was where both Gren and Teo wanted to be. She had gotten them there as agreed. Well, close enough. The ants got them to the land.

Vaysa looked up at the trees. Shad could get the two of them into the branches from the boat. The ants likely wouldn't climb the trees after them if the three men remained.

She looked back at the others. It was doubtful Shad would leave Solon behind. Also, as much as she didn't want to admit it, and despite her better judgment, Vaysa couldn't leave the others either. Even if they had only agreed to make it to Berla together. She couldn't leave them on Phantom Islands, and she couldn't leave them to the ants.

"What do they fear or dislike?" Teo asked.

"Vinegar, spice, and mint," Solon rattled off.

"Great, let's make them a salad," Teo said.

"What about a sword through the head?" Vaysa asked.

"There's only five of us, and a swarm of them," Teo said, gesturing at the ants.

Of all times for her powers to kick in, this would have been a good time, but nothing stirred in her veins. She tightened her core and willed fire to swirl, but nothing happened.

Shad frowned at Vaysa, and her eyes darted to the trees. They didn't have these weird creatures in Kennard. Then it hit Vaysa. She pulled on the interior planks of the boat and pulled off her own seat. Taking the tin of matches, she struck one. The wood, wet from travel, was hard to light.

Catching on, Teo tore off more of his jacket. He sprinkled something from one of his jars on it. Hesitantly, Vaysa handed him the plank when he reached for it. He wrapped the remnants of his jacket around it. Vaysa lit the swatch and fire leapt onto the plank.

Teo dropped it when the fire licked his fingers, causing the fire to extinguish. Vaysa swatted him, stopping herself from punching him.

Teo grabbed the plank again and sprinkled a few more drops onto the charred fabric. This time Vaysa held it as it was lit. The fire spread over the board. The flames licked at her fingers and the warmth of the fire heated her cheeks. Her body hummed in response, but the dormant flow of heat still didn't spark within her.

She flung the board blindly out of the ship and was met with thumps, roars, and more scratching noises.

"I think you made them mad."

Before anyone could grab her, Vaysa peeked over the edge. One ant was on fire, and part of the hoard was trying to put it out. A smile danced on her lips and adrenaline rushed through her. They had a chance.

Vaysa ducked back down, grabbed her satchel, and before anyone could stop her, grabbed the lip of the vessel and pulled herself over the edge. "They're flammable."

The ants scattered when the five leapt from the ship.

They strapped Gren to Shad's back. Solon carried supplies from his stash and Shad's sack. Teo crested the vessel cursing.

Vaysa suppressed a shudder at the giant insects. If this was what Berla had to offer, the Royal Guard in Kennard was preferable.

Vaysa gestured toward Teo, Solon, and Shad. They joined her and smashed Gren in the middle. His body was warming with a fever. Solon led the way, with Teo and Vaysa flanking the sides. Shad defended the rear.

As Vaysa swung her plank, flaming embers sizzled in the mud. The thin tree branches danced above her head. The leaves bobbled and swayed, darkened from the fire. The bitter taste of fear crept up her throat. It would be easy for the fire to trap them.

In front of her was a sea of bobbing ant bodies. She glanced back toward the strait. The current had ripped the ship back into the sea. Her heart squeezed and her limbs numbed. She was stuck in Berla. A whine filled her ears and her vision tunneled.

She stumbled on a root and fell face-first into a branch. Blood flooded her mouth and she spat. She needed to stay focused. They'd made a decision. She could think about it later.

"Watch out!" Shad roared.

Teo's fingers tightened around Vaysa's arm and he tugged her to the right before another branch swayed in her path. Just as quickly, he released her to step around a jagged tree stump jutting into their path.

Fear balled in Vaysa's stomach, and she tried to swivel to see where Solon was leading them. It didn't matter. Swarms of the ants were coming from everywhere.

Darkness ebbed at the corners of her vision. Fire finally swam in her veins, ready to surge forward, and she cursed. Now wasn't the time. She'd kill them all.

Teo yelled, and Vaysa turned to help him. She ducked as he swung his plank too wide. Heat singed her face. Before she could react, his plank landed in a thick bush. The dried top came to life with flames. The ants scurried away from the shrubbery and the fire. Vaysa cursed and pulled Teo backward hard as he stumbled in surprise toward the inferno.

She needed an advantage.

The ants streamed back together, forming into a red river of bodies and antennae. The fire provided a small gap of reprieve, but the ants swung right around it to regroup.

Seeing a chance, Vaysa put her plank in one hand and hopped onto the back of an ant that had skirted the fire. It reared at the unwelcomed rider, but Vaysa hung on. She swung at the ants next to them, smacking several and setting them aflame, but they continued their attack.

The ants nearest balked as their antennae caught fire. She smiled and swung again. In response, the ant she rode bucked, trying to knock Vaysa off.

Vaysa grasped at the slippery skin, but with only a one-handed grip, she slid off. With her other hand, she aimed for the ant's antennae. The plank crashed into the thin appendage, snapping it and setting it ablaze. The ants bumped into her as they raced to the other ant's aid.

A snap sounded in her body and pain seared up her side, extinguishing the fire building within. Moaning, she stumbled back toward the group's formation.

"Aim for the antennae, they light quicker than the body," she gasped between jolts of pain.

Solon turned as Vaysa limped back into line. Her breath was still ragged. She paused momentarily at his expression. It was anger or fear, or both. She shook her head and turned back to the ants charging her. She stopped when Solon's eyes flickered with what appeared to be fire.

He turned to his left and growled at Shad. She ducked, and when she did, Solon yelled into the torch he carried. Fire curled into the air and set the pack of ants nearest Vaysa on fire. Solon gasped for air and swayed. Taking deep breaths, he continued forward.

Vaysa stared, mouth agape, as he sucked in another breath and sent a swirl of fire toward another section of the ants.

Shad shook her head at him. "Risky."

"We need to get to safety," he mouthed back.

Vaysa's stomach tightened, and she looked to see if Teo witnessed it too. He, however, was swinging his branch and swearing at the ants.

Solon could control fire. Shad knew it, too. Granted, his fire seemed powered by his breath and hers from her hands. Shad knew someone else who could make fire, an elemental wielder, and hadn't told her. He could have helped her on the island. They didn't need to be in Berla. They didn't need a dragon scale.

But Shad wanted to be here. Shad wanted Vaysa to have a dragon scale. Had risked everything for it. An odd numbness edged at her heart. There were too many secrets. Too much unknown. And Shad knew too much about it. Had kept it from her. The numbness turned to a pang and Vaysa gasped.

"Get behind me," Solon ordered and stumbled.

"Dammit," Shad growled. She shoved Vaysa and Teo behind Solon.

Solon turned toward the ants. His breath and hands shook and his white skin grayed.

Vaysa curled her fists and stepped forward to help, but Shad threw an arm around her and dragged her back.

The heat curled back, and the wave of fire consumed the trees. The flames clawed toward the sky and blocked the ants. The sizzle of the fire deafened the squeals of their retreat.

"Another forest fire," Vaysa murmured and stared at the flames.

A crackle of lightning ripped across the sky, drawing their attention up.

"What the?" Shad said and stared at the sky.

"A thunderstorm? Now?" Teo said.

"It'll put the fire out," Shad said and glanced nervously at Vaysa, then Solon.

Solon gazed upwards, and confusion darkened his face.

"What's wrong with a thunderstorm?" Vaysa asked as Shad ushered them farther from the flames. The storm should put the fire out, and they wouldn't be responsible for another fire.

Solon stumbled and then crumbled to the ground.

Teo knelt down and wrapped Solon's arm around his neck and lifted Solon up.

Vaysa stared at him. Teo was helping a Berlan. Even though Teo was in Berla and didn't need Solon's help anymore. She glanced back at the wall of fire. Even if she didn't want him there, Solon had saved them. Damn it. She stooped on the other side of Solon and, biting back the pain in her ribs, helped Teo support him. They followed Shad as the first gust of wind and rain bit at her face.

Chapter 17

VAYSA

S had stopped them at a small creek. The ground was solid, and cypress trees were interspersed with silver trees. The metallic bark reflected the few remaining streams of sunlight. Vaysa ran a hand over the bark and flinched at the rough surface.

Solon had walked the last hour on his own and slumped on the ground. His face was no longer gray, but his breathing was still raspy.

She bit back at a stab of pain in her side as she tried to crouch down, and instead leaned against a tree. She gritted a breath between her teeth. They'd made it to Berla to die.

Vaysa shifted to measure the group and suppressed a groan as another shot of pain rocketed up her side. She licked her lips and tasted blood. She looked at her hands and arms and saw fresh red lines over her dirty skin.

With rest, she'd be fine. She wouldn't get rest soon, but the others looked worse. She owed them help. They were in this predicament because of her.

Gren was still unconscious and green, and sweat beaded down his face. The fever that had started in the strait had worsened.

Shad was still protective of her chest and took ragged breaths from the exertion, but she was recovering.

Teo sat holding his injured arm, his head rested on his knees. He had burn marks. There was a large gash on his leg and yellow puss oozed out.

"Teo, your leg," Vaysa said, forcing herself up from the tree. She winced as stars popped in her eyes and her muscles screamed in protest.

"I know. An ant bite." He didn't look at her, and his voice sounded defeated.

"When?" He hadn't complained about it while helping Solon.

"Shortly after we landed. I'd guess I have a day at most." He didn't bother to hide as he wiped at his teary eyes. He sniffed and mumbled, "I just want to see my family again."

She looked around at the group startled. What type of ant bite killed?

She met Solon's eyes. He grimaced and, shaking his head, looked away. Teo likely didn't have a day.

It'd be so easy to make things simple again. Gren had a fever. Teo had less than a day. Solon, although looking better, still looked weak from his fire show and was limping from the fish bite.

All she had to do was slip into the trees with Shad and they would be free to find their own home. Find the dragon scale like Shad wanted. They'd met their goal. They were in Berla. She looked at the trees. Her stomach knotted, and she looked toward Shad.

Shad stared at her, her expression unreadable. Her glance flicked to Solon and back to Vaysa. Her jaw twitched, and she looked away. Shad couldn't do it either. She didn't want to leave Solon.

Vaysa shouldn't care about these people. She didn't have any resources to start life in Berla with Shad, and she was adding three additional people. Yet, she was going to help them.

NIGHT FELL QUICKLY. The humid air was filled with animal calls Vaysa had never heard before. She suppressed a shiver as a distant raspy howl pierced the air. The moon hung low in the sky, bright and round, but dimmed by thousands of scraggly tree branches.

The musty smell of the swamp was more pleasant than the sulfuric smell of the Phantom Islands, but it wasn't as safe as the island. It didn't matter. This was home now. This was where Shad wanted to be.

Vaysa made a fire and then gingerly climbed a tree.

Even if she blinked, she wouldn't be back in Kennard. Her heart pounded, and numbness evaded her. Berla was home now. Even if Berla hadn't welcomed her upon landing, she stood a better chance of belonging here than in Kennard.

She let out a breath when Teo finally fell into a fitful sleep. Gren was still unconscious but breathing. She stilled when Solon knelt by Shad, closing her eyes to slits. It still stung knowing about their past. He spoke in hushed tones.

"We need Zara," he said to Shad.

"You think she'll help you?"

Great, another new friend of Shad's.

"She's a fair woman."

"Her husband died saving you."

"I know." Solon bowed his head. "But I'm going. Gren and Teo don't have more than a day. I'm sure Vaysa has broken ribs, and you're still healing."

"This is crazy."

"Any better ideas?" When Shad didn't respond, he looked toward Vaysa and back at Shad.

Shad growled and shook her head.

Solon disappeared into the trees, and Shad sighed when Solon was out of earshot.

"Give him a chance." Shad said.

Vaysa remained quiet instead of saying "no."

VAYSA GROWLED as she woke and grimaced at the trees swaying above her. She was in Berla. Most of her group was injured, and Shad was still keeping secrets from her. However, her festering anger with Shad wouldn't keep them safe.

Rubbing the sleep from her eyes, she stretched and instantly regretted it as she doubled over when searing pain shot up her ribs. Grimacing, she clutched her side and hobbled over to where Shad lay and knelt by her.

Shad wrapped her arm around Vaysa.

"What is Solon?" Vaysa asked.

Shad sighed. Her gaze turned to the ground, lost in the past. "He's a Monocian."

Vaysa mulled over the word. She'd never heard the term before. "Did he breathe fire?"

"Yep."

Vaysa stared expectantly at Shad. Waited for her to admit another truth.

After several long seconds, Shad swallowed. "He's from Monoc. They can control fire and heat elements like lava."

"You didn't think that was important to tell me?"

"You'd have tried to stay on the islands," Shad said, giving voice to Vaysa's thoughts.

"Of course. It's safe from humans."

"No, it isn't. He's looking for you. I won't let you stay trapped in that prison."

"Closs is not looking for me," Vaysa said through clenched teeth.

"I wish that were true," Shad said, rubbing her forehead.

"Why do you think he is?"

"He recognized your powers."

"Yes, I'm a non-human. I have fire powers, just like Solon does. Gren said others did too. He's not going to come to Berla to kill me. There's plenty here he hasn't cared about."

Shad sighed and, leaning back, closed her eyes. "Fine then, we're in Berla with an invading army who hates non-humans. We could be in Kennard with the same soldiers looking for you and every human there willing to rat you out. We could be on a Phantom Islands which is just a land prison and be destroyed when they set fire to it just in case."

Vaysa stared at her. She hated her truths. But not as much as her lies or secrets. She growled, but dropped the subject and said instead, "He's an element wielder like you said before."

"Yes, he's a fire wielder."

"Does he have a dragon scale?"

Shad sighed and pinched the bridge of her nose. "No, Vaysa. He grew up with his powers and trained with other Monocians. You didn't get that privilege."

"Couldn't he train me instead of getting a dragon scale?"

Shad shook her head and shrugged. Finally, she said, "I don't know. Maybe. Doubtful. Being a fire elemental wielder doesn't mean he can train you. Especially him, especially now. The dragon scale is our best option."

Rubbing a hand over her face, Shad's head lulled to the side to look at Vaysa. The weight of everything pulled on her face.

Vaysa swallowed back the lump of guilt in her throat. She had too many questions, but Shad had kept too many secrets. "He looked exhausted back there. He looked gray."

"He's weak from the foot injury and trip over the Spirit Strait. He's a good fire wielder, but it wasn't his strength. He didn't train for battle."

"Didn't train for battle? What did he train for?"

Shad leaned back to stare at the sky. "All Monocians can control fire. Those who excel train to protect Monoc either from the volcano or invasion. Solon was more involved in the leadership of Monoc."

"Can they train me?" Vaysa asked and grimaced at the thought. She didn't want to go to his home.

"Doubtful," Shad said. "Their methods are from birth."

"Is it close? Is he going to go home?" Vaysa asked. Hopefully his land needed him.

"He's going where we go," Shad said and turned to meet Vaysa's eyes. "Give him a chance. Please."

Vaysa snarled. She didn't want to, but she'd try for Shad. Even if she was keeping secrets. Shad had always been there for her. Always protected her. She was family. Solon wasn't her biggest issue, anyway. She was in an unfamiliar land. The Royal Guard was coming. It would be better to have a fire wielder who could control their fire, trained for battle or not, on their side than not to have one. She'd use any tool she could to survive. Even one she didn't like.

"Who's Zara?" Vaysa asked to change the subject, remembering the name Solon mentioned.

"The Widow Warrior."

Vaysa snorted. "Ah, okay."

"She helped Solon many years ago in the war. Her husband died in the battle. She hasn't been the same since."

Sadness dimmed Shad's eyes. The odd reaction twisted Vaysa's stomach and stopped her next question about Zara.

"I take it we're close to your homeland?" Vaysa asked. Shad hadn't morphed back into her human form yet. It was odd to see her friend in full Cuma form in the sun.

"Cumas are native to the Peras River. It's one of the two big rivers that run the length of Berla. As long as I have Berla's water, I can shift as I want without strain like in Kennard."

"You missed it?" Vaysa whispered, already knowing the answer.

Shad wrapped an arm around Vaysa and drew her to her side. "I'd take you over morphing at-will."

Vaysa smiled and pushed against her. A welcoming warmth swam in her heart.

"Where's Zara from then?" Vaysa asked.

A raspy laugh escaped Shad. "Wherever she wants to be from. She's half Gillonite, and half something else."

"What's a Gillonite?"

"Someone from Gillons, a nasty, inhospitable wasteland. It's in the far northwest. Some call them shamans and some call them witches, but they're considered pacifists and are the best healers in Berla. She's definitely a powerful healer, but pacifist not so much."

Vaysa nodded. Zara was another ghost from Shad's past. She finally asked, "Are we close to where you wanted to go?"

She wanted to know but feared what she'd learn. Shad was home. It just wasn't Vaysa's home.

Shad hesitated and sighed, "No, we're not."

"Where are we going?"

"Gillons."

"What?" Vaysa yelled. "You just said it was an inhospitable wasteland."

"It is," Shad said, and shrugged. "But they used to have many dragons."

"But…" Vaysa trailed off.

"It will likely mean nothing to Teo, but Gren may know the legends. Don't bring it up to them. Zara obviously knows about it being from there, but she hasn't been back since she had a falling out with her family years ago."

"Solon?" Vaysa asked, her voice higher than normal.

Shad gave her a sideways glance but said, "Yea, he knows about the legends."

"Is he going there with us?" Vaysa whispered, already knowing the answer.

"Probably," Shad said, wrapping an arm around Vaysa again. "He's going where we go."

Vaysa gritted her teeth as acid pooled in her stomach. She swallowed down the bitter taste as it clawed at her throat.

"Where are we now?" she finally asked.

"We're on the outskirts of the Sea Swamp. When the cypress trees change to silver trees, we'll be in the Silver Forest."

"Isn't that where Gren's from?" Vaysa almost added, and you?

"Yes. He acts like he doesn't want to go back."

"His family's dead. You can't blame him."

Shad frowned. "He wanted to go back to Berla. It's why he joined the Royal Guard."

"Sometimes getting what you want isn't what you really wanted." Her fingers curled into fists. No heat pulsed through her veins. The chill was a reminder of what she wanted and what it cost.

VAYSA WENT to check on the others. Gren was still unconscious, and his fever was even higher. His blue skin was still green, the same color as his hair. He shivered despite the humid heat around them. Shad joined her with a blanket from Solon's sack.

"I'll see what I can find for the fever and breakfast. All the food Solon packed is waterlogged," Shad said, then disappeared into the overgrowth of vegetation.

Vaysa moved to Teo. His skin was tinted yellow, his leg oozed yellow goo, and he tossed in a fitful sleep. Sweat covered his face, and his breathing was raspy and heavy.

He didn't want to be with them, and yet had helped Shad, helped in the boat, and even helped Solon over the terrain. She sighed. It also helped him get to safety. There was no point in trying to attribute his actions to anything other than duty and necessity. Still though, he had risked his own wellbeing to help.

"Teo?" she whispered, placing a hand on his forehead to check his fever.

His eyes opened and darted around, unable to find the attacker. He lashed out with his hand to defend himself, catching Vaysa in the shoulder.

"Ow, you jerk." She rubbed her arm but restrained herself from slugging him back.

"Vaysa?" he said in a whimper.

"Yeah. Can you see?"

"No," he squeaked.

He was Royal Guard. She shouldn't mind him being sick. Shouldn't care. It'd be one less Royal Guard. But she did. For now, at least, he was part of their group. She cursed at herself but asked, "You hungry?"

"No." He slumped back and closed his eyes.

Vaysa frowned in response. "You should eat though."

"It won't matter," he whispered. His chin quivered as he fought the emotion. "Save the resources."

Her heart thudded in her chest. He'd accepted death. After making it to Berla, reaching his goal, he'd accepted failure.

"Teo..."

"It's..." he sniffed.

"It's not fine," Vaysa growled.

With effort, he swallowed. "Just leave me. Hide and stay safe."

Her spine stiffened. They hadn't done everything to just die after landing on the shore. Even if Berla wanted to kill them. Or the Royal Guard. Or the Spirit Strait creatures.

Even if he wanted to give up, she wouldn't let him.

Vaysa swallowed against the odd fluttering in her stomach as she watched Teo. Each of his labored breaths caused her to hold her own. Waiting. Hoping...For what? Solon to return? Or stay away? For Teo to get better so he could rejoin the Royal Guard? For everything to just go back? Hope was a poison to reality. She needed to focus on shelter, food, and figuring out how to get the dragon scale. Not how to protect people she wasn't supposed to be with. Perhaps the ants had bitten her or hunger was finally catching up and causing weird reactions.

There wasn't much to find in the swamp, and all the plants were foreign. She found a few berries but wasn't certain if they were edible. Unable to take the waiting, Vaysa moved the canteen to his lips for him to take sips. The safest plan was to wait for Shad.

Shad finally returned with little, but she had a gray, odd-looking, fist-sized fruit and a few yellow curly leaves.

"We are in luck. A few silver trees are close by." She tossed Vaysa the fruit. "Don't eat a lot of the fruit, or you'll look like Gren." She grinned.

Vaysa cut the fleshy fruit into thirds. The gray skin hid a vibrant blue interior. She put the pieces by Teo and moved his hand next to them. His fingers curled for a moment around hers. The odd sensation caused her to freeze.

"You need to eat," she choked out.

"What is it?" he managed.

"Something Shad found. She says it's safe."

He nodded but didn't take the food.

"Do I need to force feed you?" Vaysa bit out harder than she meant.

He sighed in defeat. "It's pointless."

She picked a piece up and pressed it against his lips.

"Eat."

Either to eat or protest, he opened his mouth, and she shoved the piece of fruit in.

He coughed but ate it.

"Do you have this?" Vaysa moved his hand back to the fruit. "Or should I help you?"

"I got it," Teo muttered and moved another piece to his lips.

Making sure Teo ate a few pieces, Vaysa turned to Gren. She squeezed the juice into Gren's mouth. The slightest twinge of blue rippled across his face and then disappeared, leaving his skin green again. She ate hers without thinking about the color, odd taste, or aroma.

Teo had eaten a few pieces of what she gave him. He didn't look blue, so Vaysa figured she didn't either.

Shad toasted the curly leaves over the fire, and then she put them in strained boiling water, giving off a minty aroma. Despite being strained, the water still had a brown hue. Shad let it cool slightly and then poured small amounts at a time down Gren's throat. His temperature dropped for a while and then soared back.

"These leaves won't work for long," Shad said as she made another batch. "He needs something more powerful."

Vaysa swallowed. There wasn't anything they had that would help.

She didn't know any of the fauna or flora. If Shad couldn't find something, and Solon didn't return with Zara, she'd watch both Teo and Gren die. The thought shouldn't matter. They were royal guards and not a part of her plan. She wouldn't have to help them get to a safe place. If she wanted, she could just walk away and be done with them and any connection to Closs. And yet, her feet remained planted, her breath rising and falling as she watched theirs.

Chapter 18

VAYSA

Teo, no longer able to sit up, weakly waved his hand for Vaysa to join him.

She knelt by him and touched his arm. A jolt shot through her, and she yanked her fingers back. She'd spent too much time too close to them. The weird reactions would diminish once they separated.

"Please stay by me. I don't want to die alone," he croaked. He sniffed back the tears welling up. His body trembled and he gasped for air.

She wanted to say, "then don't die," but there was nothing she could do to help with the poison.

With pinched lips, Vaysa took his hand in hers, ignoring the odd sensation, and settled down by him. After threading his fingers with hers, he sighed and lay back down.

She stared at their joined hands. Something unfamiliar bubbled in her gut. Shifting her stomach, she grimaced and forced her eyes to look anywhere else.

Vaysa didn't bother rationalizing why she was helping. She shouldn't care. He was Royal Guard. She got him to Berla as promised. She growled and smacked her forehead. And now here she was holding his hand.

Her ribs ached in the kneeling position but, looking down at Teo, she decided she wouldn't leave him alone to die, despite everything. She relaxed, lying down beside him, providing relief to her side, and turned to put her head on his torso. The odd sensation intensified, but fatigue kept her from moving. There was no point in fighting how tired she was. She needed rest, too.

Shad stayed by Gren, continuing to pour the leaf medicine down his throat.

Teo's breaths were shallow and his heartbeat faint when the sound of galloping horses broke the silence.

Vaysa instinctively reached for her weapon and gasped from the shooting pain in her side.

Shad said, "Solon," and Vaysa eased back.

He arrived in his normal foreboding appearance, which made his companion even more stunning. She was much shorter than Solon, but more muscular under her green leather and gold armor. She had long wavy dark brown hair that ended in a single curl. Her amber eyes sparkled against her golden-brown skin.

"Zara?" Vaysa mouthed to Shad.

Shad grinned and nodded.

Zara scanned the dreary scene with unblinking eyes before dismounting. Her friendly smile didn't meet her eyes. Her voice was soft and airy as she slapped Solon's shoulder and said, "They're as bad as you said. Tsk, tsk. You should take better care of your companions."

Zara rummaged around the horses that were both loaded down with rolls, canteens, and an assortment of pouches. Zara grabbed a few canteens and vials and went to Gren. Shad backed up to give her room.

"Not good. This Silver's almost dead. I know, I know, Silvers are very sensitive to environmental changes," she said to the shadows, and then started sorting through her items. She mixed several things together and had Solon prop him up, but Gren folded in his arms.

As they worked on him, Vaysa scooted over to Shad.

Shad said, "She's one of the best healers in Berla and makes the best weapons."

"So don't cross her?"

Shad snorted and nodded in agreement.

Whispering, Vaysa said, "I expected her to be in black."

"You mean as in mourning as the Widow Warrior?"

"Yeah."

"She doesn't realize she should be," Shad said and gave Vaysa an awkward smile.

Vaysa stared at her with questioning eyes. Zara looked sane enough, even though she appeared to be talking to the air.

VAYSA SLAMMED a hand over her mouth and gagged as Zara dug the yellow junk out of Teo's leg.

He howled and thrashed against the pain. After Zara removed the yellow puss, a long crater engulfed most of Teo's leg. It was puffy and pink with blood pooling inside. Zara mixed another concoction and lathered it in, filling the entire wound with medicine, and then wrapped it with gauze.

"We need to get them back to my place," Zara commanded.

"Why?" Vaysa said.

Even if her decisions hadn't been the best lately, she wouldn't blindly follow this woman. Even if Shad knew her.

"You want to watch your friends die?" Zara asked and fixed her gaze on Vaysa.

Vaysa stared at Zara, bewildered. She didn't want to go to Shad's friend's house or watch them die.

Shad snorted. "I wouldn't call them friends."

Vaysa cracked a grin at Shad.

"Friend or not, they will die without my help," Zara said. Her voice was void of the earlier bubbly tone and had an edge to it. "Do you want that on your conscience?"

Vaysa sighed. No, she didn't. That was why she was still with them instead of a day's travel away. And Shad said Zara was one of the best healers. "Okay, how are we going to get two dying people back when it took you two a day?"

"Easy, we have the horses," Zara said, waving a hand toward the two.

Vaysa sneered at the beasts. She'd never ridden one, and hadn't ever had the urge, either.

AFTER HOURS OF TRAVEL, the sunlight waned. Plush green trees canopied them. The sweet smell of rain still lingered from a recent storm. They'd reached a tributary of the Peras River that flowed through the edge of the Silver Forest and the remnants of the Sea Swamp.

So far, Berla looked like Kennard. It had trees, dirt, water, and Zara. Nothing made it special compared to Kennard.

Vaysa had begrudgingly ridden behind Zara. She couldn't keep pace with the horses with her busted ribs. Shad carried Teo, as it was too unsafe for him to ride a horse. Solon rode one horse and held Gren between him and the horse's neck.

Zara pulled on the reins as they neared the stream. Vaysa sat down hard on the saddle and bit her lips together. She pressed a hand against her ribs and blinked to hide the pain. Maybe death by ants would have been better than traveling on a horse.

She looked at Shad. Shad always felt at ease in the forest. Although alert, she was more relaxed than at any point in Kennard. Vaysa rolled her tongue over her teeth. There was so much she didn't know about Shad. But that had always been the case. Just like Vaysa, Shad didn't reflect on her life in Berla. They had focused together on surviving and helping each other. Reminiscing about Shad's lost life only brought them sorrow.

Zara said, "This is a good spot. We'll have half a day's travel tomorrow."

Solon and Shad tended to Teo and Gren.

Vaysa cringed as she looked at the ground. Zara dismounted. Vaysa licked her lips. The vibrations from hitting the ground would be brutal. With nothing else to do, and refusing to ask for help, Vaysa braced for impact.

"Need help?" Solon asked her, startling her as he helped Gren to the ground.

She shot him a dark look. Shad stifled a laugh and heat crept onto Vaysa's cheeks.

"Hold his mane," Zara said.

Vaysa instinctively grabbed the mane before considering the direction. Zara tapped the horse's snout, and he lowered his rump to the ground. Vaysa tightened slightly against the downward momentum, and fire shot up her side, but she could touch her feet to the ground.

"I wouldn't want you to hurt your ribs more," Zara said with a smile and wink.

Vaysa seethed at the woman. She didn't need her help or Solon's. Curses curled on her tongue. She ran a hand over her mouth to stop herself from retorting.

Solon started to say something, but Zara shook her head. He sighed in defeat and started to help her build a fire.

Despite her anger, Vaysa helped Shad with Teo. Teo was awake but weak. His leg was swollen, and the ointments had seeped through the bandage.

Teo lifted his head to look Vaysa in the eyes.

A shaky breath escaped Vaysa before she forced the next one normal.

"Thank you," Teo whispered.

"All I did was force you to eat and drink against your wishes."

A small smile danced on his lips.

She looked away before she smiled back.

Gren was only slightly green, and his fever was almost broken.

Vaysa sat by the fire away from Solon and Zara, and Shad and Solon placed Gren and Teo around the fire.

Shad offered to take the first shift, and the other three threw their rolls down.

VAYSA'S EYES BOLTED OPEN. She stared in confusion at the flickering fire. A twig snapped and she looked toward Zara and caught her eye. Zara nodded once.

Vaysa rolled over as a shadow moved to the livestock. Zara gave her the slightest of nods and then Zara's harsh gaze fell to Shad. Shad snarled but stayed put.

Zara slid out of her bed and moved to the trees. She kicked the intruder's feet out beneath him and sent him sprawling to the cold ground. Before he could turn, Zara had him pinned and hog-tied, and she lifted him by the center knot. She hauled him back to the fire and held him toward it. The flames singed his clothes, hair, and exposed skin. He recoiled and shrieked as the embers burned tiny holes in his clothes.

"Zara," Solon said, sitting up in his bedroll.

She met his gaze and, rolling her eyes, moved the thief away from the fire.

"I didn't know Silvers could be so klutzy, or that they turned into thieves," she said as the Silver wiggled in his binds.

"I thought they were stealthy," Vaysa said. She tilted her head to scrutinize the man. He looked around Gren's age. His eyes were paler than Gren's and his hair a darker green.

"Supposed to be," Zara said. "But I'd guess drinking too much can change that."

"Ah... ah... a Cuma was chasing me," he wailed. "I just wanted a horse to escape."

"There isn't another Cuma for miles," snarled Shad.

The thief turned and gawked at Shad's hulking form across the flames. He screamed and tried to push away from Zara.

Teo rolled over and groggily asked, "Why is there yelling?"

"We have an issue with a Silver," Zara replied.

"What? What's Gren doing?" Teo asked, sitting up and rubbing his eyes.

"Gren?" shrieked the man. "Gren of the Red-Water house, Gren?"

Vaysa shrugged when Zara looked at her.

Gren rustled at hearing his name being yelled.

The four who were conscious glared at Teo. He gulped and looked away.

The man jerked his head toward Gren, trying to get a glimpse of him. "He's alive?"

"What is he talking about?" Vaysa asked the others.

"We thought he died in the attack," the thief said, squirming to get a full look at Gren.

"The coup." Zara sighed and pinched the bridge of her nose.

"Why's he with you?" the thief asked darkly.

The group stared uncertainly at each other. Zara shared a look with Shad and Shad conked the thief on the head. He slumped backwards.

"What is he talking about? What coup?" Vaysa asked.

Shad refused to meet her gaze and looked at Zara.

"That was years ago," Zara said and waved a dismissive hand backwards at the air.

"What happened?" Vaysa asked, ignoring Zara's focus on the shadows.

"There was an incident with the Silvers years ago after the coup. Many of them died," Zara said, turning to Vaysa.

"Gren said he left on his own," Vaysa said and looked at Gren. "He said he wanted to forget his dead family."

Teo asked, "Why was there a coup? Why were the Silvers killed?"

Zara said, "King Russom's family were not the rightful rulers. Each region used to govern itself. We still did for the most part despite Russom and his ways. The coup was Berlans taking back our country and our right to rule ourselves. It became the catalyst for the war. The Silvers had a monarchy. Other areas do too. Some have Chiefdoms, while others select their leaders, like Monoc. The Silvers were one of many species to be targeted by the Royal Guards and King Russom's soldiers before the Traitors stepped in."

Teo's lip curled up to the right, and he stared at the ground. He muttered, "The Traitors?"

Zara's amber eyes shone coldly toward him. He gulped when he looked up and saw her staring at him. "You know nothing about the Traitors. Whatever garbage the Royal Guard has taught you is likely all lies."

Teo stared back at her. His jaw twitched and he finally looked away and lay back down.

Vaysa watched the group. They referred to the war in the past, but looking at the hardened faces around her, the remnants of it pulsed as if it was only lurking in the shadows.

Chapter 19

VAYSA

Vaysa awoke to clanging swords. Her heartbeat quickened. Grabbing her sword, she slouched down to get a better view.

She laughed at seeing Shad clumsily holding a sword, trying to spar with Zara. Zara danced around, barely touching the ground. Shad was quicker, but she wasn't skilled with a sword. Finally, Shad growled and lunged forward, shoving Zara to the ground.

"Cheater!" Zara laughed.

Shad helped her back up, grinning, and they continued sparring. Solon sparred against a tree as if dancing. Vaysa sat up to watch better. They looked so normal together; it was odd. She let her gaze drift to the thief who was still conscious.

"Hey, sleepyhead, want to join?" Zara offered, turning to Vaysa with a toothy grin.

"What about her ribs?" Solon asked, frowning at Zara.

Shad shot Zara and Solon a disapproving look, but her gaze shifted to Vaysa's ribs.

"My ribs are fine. I'll get breakfast ready," Vaysa said and bit back the pain as she stood and headed into the woods. Her heart tightened, and she swallowed back her emotions. Shad was with her friends, her real friends. The ones she chose. Ones she hadn't found as children and taken in out of sympathy.

Vaysa paused at hearing Shad jogging behind her and leaned against a tree. She clutched her side and groaned. Shad wordlessly picked her up and carried her back to camp. Vaysa didn't bother protesting; Shad would win anyway.

Vaysa started to say, "I'm fine," but gasped instead.

"Don't try lying to me," Shad said.

Vaysa nodded and lay on her back as Shad rubbed a numbing ointment from Zara's collection over her ribs. Then Shad gave her a stick to bite on. Being careful not to break more, Shad wrapped Vaysa's ribs tightly. It hurt considerably less, but her motion was restricted.

Zara joined them and gave Vaysa a tight smile. Her hard eyes traced over Vaysa's injuries and scarred skin. With a blink, her expression softened, returning to the practiced, patient one.

Vaysa didn't return the smile. Her body stiffened at the perusal, and a flame licked her veins. Even here, people noticed. She didn't need Zara's pity or approval.

Shad offered Vaysa a hand up, breaking Vaysa's thoughts.

Zara handed Vaysa a bulging leather sack. "This might help with breakfast."

Vaysa stared at the sack and then Zara. Shad nudged Vaysa's arm. Vaysa scowled but took the sack. She peered inside and found dried meats, cheeses, and hard bread.

Shad cleared her throat. A reminder of her manners. They had helped in the town and kept attention off of her. Just another reminder she didn't belong with Shad's friends, like she didn't belong in town.

"Thanks," Vaysa mumbled without looking at Zara. Her stomach twisted and her nostrils flared.

Her face heated when the three exchanged glances. She scowled. She was supposed to exchange looks with Shad. Not these two strangers. It wasn't fair. She'd never heard of these two before, and now they seemed to know Shad better than she did. Her stomach twisted tighter. Instead of fire, a chill ran through her veins.

"Vaysa," Shad said.

"I gotta start breakfast," Vaysa said and willed her anger down. Her neck hairs rose as Shad watched her. Based on the silence, the others were watching her too. She avoided looking at them as she dug through the supplies attached to the horses' saddles. She didn't need to see their concern or curiosity. Or Shad's disapproval. She found a small pot and headed back to the campfire.

Shad brought Vaysa water from the stream to a boil, and Vaysa laid the bread and meat over the top to warm. Shad patted her shoulder and then wrapped an arm around her shoulders. Vaysa eased, the tightness in her heart loosening, and Shad bonked her head against Vaysa's before settling down by the fire.

Vaysa sat by Shad.

"Mm, food," Teo mumbled, waking up. Without opening his eyes, he followed the aroma to the fire. He greedily grabbed for the meat. He didn't stop even as the fire singed his fingers.

Vaysa chuckled. His amber eyes shot up, and when they met hers, he grinned. She couldn't stop the one that formed on her lips. She swallowed against it and averted her gaze.

Gren shifted and started mumbling. Everyone but Teo, who continued to eat, hurried over to Gren. His eyes were half-open but shot wide when he saw faces staring at him. He tried to sit up, but he swayed back down.

"Easy. You've been out for days," Zara said.

Gren groaned and his face fell as he stared at the group until his eyes fell on Vaysa. He nodded and gave a half-hearted smile. She returned it, thankful he was awake.

He ran a hand through his hair and looked away. He momentarily stiffened and cocked his head to the side. Vaysa followed his gaze to the dark forest but was unable to see anything unique. He returned his attention to the group.

Solon helped him sit up. Vaysa handed him what they had left of the silver tree fruit. He eyed it suspiciously but took a bite.

"What's going on?" Gren asked. "The last I remember we were in the Sea Swamp."

"You need rest," Zara said. "We're going to my place so I can properly tend to you."

Gren looked at Teo.

Teo nodded and looked away.

Vaysa frowned. Even with the diversion, she'd still somehow have to get Teo back to the Royal Guard. She swallowed back the bitterness in her mouth. Even if they helped each other, he was going back. The sooner, the better. It'd be one less person to feed or check on. Or have any weird reactions with.

A smile tugged on Gren's lips, but then his expression clouded over. He glared at the thief who was still hogged-tied and gagged, but unconscious due to an elixir. Gren pointed at him in question.

"He tried to steal our horses," Solon said.

"Free him," hissed Gren.

"He knows you," Vaysa said, studying his face. His expression belied nothing but anger. Uncertain if his rage was from the other Silver being bound, or from seeing him, she flicked her gaze to Shad.

Shad only glowered at the two Silvers.

Gren cursed and asked, "Does it matter?"

Zara shrugged. "Only if it matters to you. But he obviously needs help if he is stealing."

"What's his name?" Teo asked and shoved another bite of food into his mouth.

"You think I know every Silver?" Gren asked.

"Yes," Shad said and settled back with her food.

Vaysa stifled a chuckle.

"Shad," Zara warned and gave Vaysa a dark look.

Vaysa chuckled harder.

"What?" Shad asked.

Zara narrowed her eyes and shook her head.

"My parents were prominent people," Gren muttered. "I was known through them."

"What's his name?" Shad asked and pointed her fork at the thief.

Gren rolled his eyes, and gritted out, "Avil."

"See," Shad told Zara.

Vaysa laughed and didn't bother to hide it, earning a stern look from Zara.

Zara rolled her lips between her teeth to still her own smile.

Vaysa looked at Avil. If Gren had been healed, she'd offer to help to get Avil back to the Silver Forest with them. But Gren needed to heal, and it was Zara's home, not hers.

"What should we do with him?" she finally asked. "I agree with Zara. He needs help."

Gren furled and unfurled his fists as he stared into the trees. "We can't leave him here unprotected, and we can't risk running into the Royal Guard by going south to get him back."

"We can drop him off near the Traitors' fort. He should be safe there for the night," Zara said.

The group returned to their breakfast. Vaysa watched the others. Was the Traitor fort a good thing? Gren and Shad had been vague about them in Kennard and the few other times they mentioned them. Gren had only been willing to join them because she and Shad weren't Traitors since it'd break his oath to the Royal Guard. Shad had been adamant they weren't Traitors. Were the Traitors like the Royal Guard? How were they a safe option?

She started to ask but stopped when Solon glared at Zara and mouthed, "Traitors? Really?"

More of their secrets. But Solon seemed unhappy with them, too.

Zara's face darkened and Vaysa involuntarily leaned back to get distance from her. "Yes, Traitors," she mouthed back. Finally, Zara's expression cleared. Vaysa let her breath out but pushed herself a few inches away. She didn't care enough about the Traitors to get between Solon and Zara.

Shad placed a hand on Solon's shoulder, and he finally turned from Zara. Satisfied with his silence, Shad nodded, grabbed Avil, and bounded away with him toward the fort.

Vaysa put her unfinished breakfast down and started to clean the campsite.

"Leave it," Zara whispered harshly.

Vaysa turned to see if they were talking about the Traitors again but found Solon staring at her, and Zara staring between her and Solon. She growled when her face flushed. She slammed the last few items into the sacks to wait for Shad away from the others. Soon, they'd separate, and she wouldn't have to face them judging her just like the humans had.

ZARA'S HOME WAS A SMALL, quaint wooden cabin with no ornamentations, but her training grounds were immense and well-supplied. Vaysa's jaw dropped looking at the targets, obstacles, and weapons storage room. Nestled at the edge of the forest was a large black stone structure that dwarfed the cabin. It'd take weeks to explore everything.

Inside, the home was tidy but sparsely furnished. A large table filled the kitchen space. Bottles and canisters lined the wall-to-wall shelves. Beside the large fireplace were a few chairs and a cot. Some rooms lined the narrow hall.

"Well, you all stink," Zara said. "Shad, you can use the washbasin. It's out back. When she's done, Solon, you can wash up and then help Teo. I'll help Vaysa and Gren."

"I can take care of myself," Vaysa said, folding her arms. She grimaced at the pain from touching her side but stood her ground.

"I wouldn't say hygiene is your forte, and I doubt you can properly clean up with your busted ribs."

Vaysa fumed. She hated how bossy Zara was. She hated even more that she was right. "Whatever," she muttered.

Zara supplied each person with gear.

"I have to make a living somehow," she said to Vaysa's stare.

Zara burned Teo and Gren's Royal Guard uniforms in the fireplace but let them keep their boots since they were still in decent shape. She provided both of them with leather pants, a metal breastplate hidden beneath a tunic, and a fitted leather jacket. The complete leather look offered protection from weapons, weather, and animals. She also provided each of them with a new sword.

The garments Solon already wore were similar, except his jacket reached his ankles. The similarities between his attire and Teo and Gren's were unmistakable. Zara provided him with new pants and a tunic.

Since Shad could morph, Zara gave her a breastplate that could slide to meet size requirements. It appeared to be made specifically for a Cuma.

Shad hit the plate area over her wound and smiled when it didn't cause her to double over in pain.

Zara gave Shad a quiver of arrows and a bow made of strong wood. "You're a good fighter, but arrows will provide distance. We know what happens to Cumas in battle."

"What happens?" Teo asked with raised brows. He grimaced when he saw Shad's dark glare.

Vaysa had only witnessed her unbridled and uncontrolled fury a few times, and that was just with soldiers, not in actual battle.

"Leave it," Solon warned and gestured for Teo to move toward the door.

Teo rolled his eyes but obeyed.

Vaysa slipped the Koi teeth to Shad and winked. One more weapon for her friend.

Zara emptied the pockets and then burned Vaysa's jacket before she could protest.

"That was a perfectly good jacket," Vaysa fumed. She stared at the remains of one of her few possessions.

"Sure, but it stunk," Teo said and then clasped his hands over his mouth.

"About time," Shad said.

Solon hid his grin with a sharp cough.

Vaysa put her hands on her hips and tilted her head in challenge, embarrassment burning in her cheeks.

"Enough. Get into the tub," Zara said, directing Vaysa toward the wash area before jerking her head toward Solon and the door.

Solon smirked and held the door. Teo walked with him outside.

Zara helped Vaysa into the tub. The water turned brown from the dirt ground in her skin, and Zara had to replace the water twice. The warm water, meant to relax her muscles, only made her self-conscious, as her scars were on display. Each water refill showed more and more of her history.

Vaysa's mouth went dry when Zara noticed her gnarled arms. Zara ran a finger gently over them and blinked several times. Vaysa's chest tightened when the healer stole a dark glance at the shadows but kept quiet. Vaysa desperately wanted the protection of her jacket back.

"You were filthy," Zara said. She flashed her a smile, masking any other emotion, and draped a towel around her.

The previous concern on Zara's face was gone and Vaysa let out a breath. At least Zara was kind enough not to comment about her scars.

"Kept me safe," Vaysa mumbled.

Zara's eyes traced down the vibrant red scars, each looking like a fresh cut on her white skin.

"Perhaps it did."

Zara gave Vaysa new boots since her pilfered ones didn't fit right. She also gave her fitted pants, a tunic, breastplate, and jacket. She'd miss her favorite smith from Kennard, but Zara would put him to shame.

Vaysa's spirit lifted after the bath and a sense of normalcy warmed her when she and Shad practiced swords alone.

Gren was up, and as he practiced, he seemed to perk up. He'd soon be ready to go home. Vaysa's moral obligation was done.

Maybe Berla would be okay. Zara's place was exceptional. It was obvious why Shad liked her so much. It was a shame they'd have to leave it for Gillons and a dragon scale.

Chapter 20

CLOSS

General Closs' boots sank in the wetland. Looming in front of him was the start of the Silver Forest. The silver bark glistened in the sun, and the silver leaves swayed, creating a shimmering display. Silver wood was hard to burn, but he'd managed before.

His troops assembled along the shore.

He wasn't supposed to be here. This was General Xander's fight, and he'd specifically asked King Malik to exclude Closs.

Closs smirked. But he had Gren. Well, he'd had Gren when King Malik agreed to let General Closs come with a Berlan willing to guide him.

Now he didn't have Gren. Now he had a chance at something better.

If he could catch the girl, both Berla and Kennard would be his. He wouldn't need Gren or the prince. His men just couldn't know, or they'd try to steal what was his right. What he'd worked his life to claim.

Swinging his binoculars south, he stared at the landscape. The scenery was a distant memory. General Xander was already somewhere in there. Already headed to the prince. One less distraction. Word about him would reach Xander, but by then, it should be too late for his interference.

Closs knew the most logical place for the Traitors to hide the prince. It was the same place as his downfall in the war twenty years ago. He could get the prince quickly, with or without Gren. But as long as King Malik thought he had Gren, he had a free pass to be in Berla. And time to find what was his.

He growled as his mind flickered back to that Cuma. Closs knew of the rumors about a monster lurking in the Kennard woods. He hadn't cared. It kept travelers off the roads and troops from wandering off. The creature had gone after his troops a few times, singling out a weak one, but it toughened them up. Made them think harder. Made them afraid.

When he saw it in its full Cuma form the night it took Gren, he recognized it instantly. Had he known it was her, he'd have sent his men to hunt her down years ago. She was already supposed to be dead. He'd killed her fifteen years ago in Berla. The group she had been with was why he had failed. A stupid mistake he was still paying for.

He also hadn't known she had a companion. A companion that would make up for his failure.

Leaving the rest of the Royal Guard to burn the Silver Forest and start the systematic destruction on lower Berla, he led his troops north through the woods.

After traveling for two days, they came to a clearing. His men started to set camp. General Closs watched with little interest. He nodded at Ben to oversee the arrangements as he moved toward his tent. Ben was a good soldier. He followed orders, didn't accept weakness, and hated Berlans. Closs knew he had raised him well. He had saved him from a life in Berla.

As he sat down to eat, there was rustling in the bushes outside his tent. He pointed at a guard to check it out and started gnawing on a piece of meat. He spat the chunk out and threw the rest of the meat at the closest soldier.

"What's this crap?" he barked.

"What we caught," the soldier said weakly, trying to back up out of Closs's reach.

Closs snorted. "It's disgusting! Don't feed me this Berlan garbage. I want real food!"

The soldier stuttered. "But... but... that's all we have."

Closs narrowed his eyes and slowly approached the soldier. Grabbing the soldier by his neck, he pulled the man's face next to his own. "Find me something decent to eat, or you don't eat."

The soldier dully nodded. When Closs released him, he ran into the woods. Closs turned to give someone else orders when he noticed his men huddled together. Grunting, he stormed over to the group and yanked men out of the way. In the center of the group was a Silver.

Chapter 21

ZARA

As the others slept, Zara sat on her porch watching the few rays of the morning sun pierce the foliage. Time always had a way of repeating itself. War. Birth. Friends. Enemies. Death. Life. War.

With a sigh, she lifted her mug to her lips, the spicy brew biting at her tongue. She was supposed to be in the tunnels almost to the castle by now, but Solon had arrived on her doorstop like a ghost from the past here to warn her. To stop her. And it'd worked. She was already too late to get Kier and make sure he was never found. Other ideas popped into her mind, and she figured she'd settle on one once she arrived at the castle and saw Enat. Saw Prince Kier.

Her mind cycled to Yala. Whatever she did, protecting Yala was the most important. Even if it meant she joined Hans.

The shadows shifted. Zara shook her head and said, "Not now."

He always had an opinion. A warning to guide her to stay in the physical longer. His shadowy presence was almost constant. Alone, she didn't have to face others' looks about him. The piteous ones that turned her stomach. The shadows had resulted from one of her few failures.

It was possible to bring the dead back, but rarely did the results go as expected.

Another shift.

"I can't help them further," she mumbled into her mug. Her breath caused ripples across the steaming surface.

He shifted in disapproval, not believing her any more than she did.

A pang twisted in her heart. She had missed her friends. Now, Shad and Solon were back. Although she was happy to see them, it changed her plans. Changed her truths.

She'd told everyone they had died in the battle to get Solon's wife, Yala, and their child out of Berla. Zara knew they had left Berla, but Yala returned and didn't know where the rest were. Zara had hoped her friends' story wasn't done, but hope could be deadly.

Seeing Solon on her stoop, soaking wet and hopeful, had stirred the glimmer of hope she'd once felt. The hope before the coup, before the death of her husband Hans, before her son had left, before the Traitors had taken over the marshaling of Berla. Hope was dangerous but addictive. And no matter her history with Solon, she couldn't tell him no when he asked for help. His hopefulness could drown all pain.

He was just a complication, though, when it came to protecting Yala. Zara had helped her hide when she returned, and Berla was prosperous because of her return. Solon could ruin that. Yala would come out of hiding for him. He'd go after the Royal Guard and Traitors for her. Neither would help Berla. Berla needed Yala. Yala needed to stay hidden.

Zara considered taking Solon to Yala, but the risks were too high. The Royal Guard was infecting the land as they tried to find their prince, and they were destroying as much of the land as possible in their plight to find him.

It was a repeat of before. After the coup, everything was in chaos. They'd destroyed land, annihilated species, and after King Russom's human children had been killed, his half-human, half-non-human children had disappeared. Some were even rumored to have been taken by the Royal Guard. But that wasn't enough for them. Kennard wanted more from Berla. She wouldn't let it happen again.

She'd been gearing up to go after the prince before Solon's diversion. She'd heard the rumors on what the prince was after, where he had been last spotted, and she hoped he hadn't found it. The western Traitors had caught him first, but no other information had traveled to the eastern side. The silence was worrisome. Since there wasn't movement yet, she figured the prince hadn't shared anything. If they thought he had known nothing, the western Traitors would have sent him back to Kennard already.

It meant the prince likely knew where Yala was. Yala, the last Water Witch and Berla's protector. Zara had wanted to intervene. Dispose of him before he told his secret. But it was too late for a silent mission, and she couldn't just leave Shad and Solon.

If she could get to him before the western Traitors could get him to talk, she would still have a chance to protect Yala. Otherwise, the western Traitors could compromise her safety.

Her biggest concern was how to tell Shad and Solon that Yala was alive and in Berla. They'd sacrificed everything to get her out. They'd risk everything to do it again if they knew.

No matter how she looked at it, there was no winning situation.

Life was easier alone.

"Oh Hans, this is going to be messy," Zara whispered into the air.

Chapter 22

VAYSA

$\mathcal{V}$aysa followed the others to the table. She scratched her side and yawned as she straddled the chair. They each wore fresh tunics and trousers. Zara plopped down dishes of scrambled eggs, dried meat, and bread. Vaysa's stomach growled, and she shoved fresh bread into her mouth.

"Since when do you bake?" Solon asked and popped a piece of bread in his mouth.

Zara chuckled. "I don't."

"And you trust it?" Solon asked, holding a second piece of bread close to his mouth.

Zara popped a piece in her mouth and chewed dramatically.

Vaysa shrugged and took another piece. It wasn't as good as the baker's bread in Hark, but it was still edible.

Teo's knee bumped into the table while scooting closer to Zara, drawing their attention. Narrowing his eyes, he studied her face and asked, "Are you human?"

"Nope," she said with a laugh. He was brazen, but he'd learn.

"She's no island in the monster sea. She swims in the deepest trenches," Shad said and smiled as Teo's eyes bulged.

"What are you?" he asked, and then pulled back, color staining his cheeks.

"None of your business," Shad said and pointed at him.

He frowned at her but didn't push.

Vaysa stared at Zara, Shad's words running in her mind. She was half Gillon and half something... Her gaze slid to Shad. Shad only shook her head. Another fun secret.

Zara's eyes darted to the shadows. Shaking her head, she said, "Not now."

Teo turned to look at the shadows and then stared suspiciously at Zara.

"Who were you talking to?" Teo asked.

Zara ran her tongue over her teeth.

"It's her husband," Shad said, glaring at Teo. "Eat your food and shut up."

Teo stared at her and then the table. He mumbled, "She seemed normal, but of course she talks to ghosts."

Solon kicked Teo under the table, and when the human's eyes darted angrily to Solon, Solon shook his head at him. Teo sighed but stopped talking.

Keeping her head down, Vaysa cast a look at the shadows, but nothing moved in them.

"Come on." Solon pushed his chair back to draw everyone's attention. "Let's get some practice in."

Vaysa pushed her chair back and motioned for Teo and Gren to join them. They obliged and washed their plates.

Solon led them outside, headed toward the weapons building.

Vaysa turned to ask Shad if she was coming to find Shad and Zara talking. Her eyes darted back to the three outside. It was a private moment and she shouldn't listen, but she leaned against the wall and tilted her head toward the kitchen.

"Solon needs to ease up on Teo and Gren. They have no idea what happened," Zara said as she stood.

"When have you known Solon to ease up on anyone?" Shad said, leaning back in her chair. "What did you tell everyone?" Zara turned to put dishes away. Shad had provided her a chance to compose her face. Mask her emotions. Decide what she wanted to present.

"I said you all died."

Vaysa closed her eyes and steadied her breath. She shouldn't listen, but couldn't bring herself to move. This was about Solon and Shad knowing each other. About what happened before Vaysa met Shad. All their silent words, expressions. They spoke full sentences with a simple glance. They knew what Shad kept hidden. Knew more about her than Vaysa. They'd known who Shad was before she'd lost everything and ended up alone in Kennard.

And now they were going to talk about it.

All the questions Shad ignored.

"Did they believe you?" Shad asked.

Zara snorted.

"So, yes. Where's Lars?" Shad asked.

Another friend? Vaysa shook her head. How many were there?

"He's training with the Cumas. There're certain things I can't teach him," Zara said.

"I'm sure you miss your son," Shad said.

Vaysa's eyes flew open, but she suppressed a gasp. Shad hadn't mentioned any children.

Zara turned and gave Shad a brittle smile.

"Hans," Shad said and swallowed. Her eyes diverted to the tabletop and then back to Zara.

"Let's not," Zara said, joining Shad at the table.

Shad nodded and blinked repeatedly.

All names to ask Shad about later.

"Why'd you help Solon?" Shad asked, looking up to meet her eyes.

"What was I to do? I thought he was dead, and he shows up soaking wet and hopeful. He's his own worst enemy. His hope is addictive and dangerous. I feed off of it. And no matter my history with him, I couldn't tell him no when he asked for help. I see a different path looking at him."

"Look where that led," Shad deadpanned.

"The people who needed to escape did. The coup was successful."

Vaysa leaned in closer at the mention of the coup. It was the war. They all seemed involved, and yet no one would talk about it.

"We lost a lot." Shad slumped back in her chair.

"We gained more," Zara replied.

"Solon was on a Phantom Island."

"I didn't know," Zara said, meeting Shad's eyes. All pretenses washed from her face.

Shad nodded.

"Why'd you bring her here?" Zara asked.

Vaysa stilled. She had to be asking about her.

"We were wrong about Kennard," Shad murmured.

"How so?" Zara asked, leaning in.

"Powers can develop there."

They were talking about her. A lump bobbed in her throat and her chest tightened.

"No," Zara said, shaking her head. "They can't."

"Hers did."

Vaysa gasped. Why would Shad tell her that? She sucked in a ragged breath. Her vision swam, the fields turning into a blur. But... they were going to Zara's home. She'd know, anyway.

Zara's eyes darted back to Shad. "What?"

"Yea, the Royal Guard saw, too. We're going to Gillons," Shad said, rubbing her forehead.

Zara nodded and, pursing her lips, picking at a spot on the table. "They'll help her."

"Is Yala here?" Shad asked, and her eyes darted to the field. She frowned and scanned the horizon.

Vaysa cursed. Shad likely noticed she wasn't with the others. She pressed into the exterior wall and hoped Shad didn't hear her. These few glimpses were more than she'd ever heard before.

Zara sighed and rubbed her forehead.

"I see," Shad said, returning her gaze to Zara. "Is she safe?"

Zara gave a non-committal shrug.

"Are the fields fertile?" Shad asked, leaning toward Zara.

Zara's eyes narrowed and her jaw ticked. "Berla is more prosperous than ever."

"Are the rumors true? Is the prince here?"

"Yes," Zara said, nonplussed.

"If you're sharing that, it means he was caught, and not by you. Couldn't get to him first?" Shad asked.

"I need to silence him."

"He knows where Yala is?"

Zara took a long breath and licked her lips. "I can't be certain. The silence is worrisome, but there hasn't been movement with the Western Traitors."

"So, if he knows where she is, they haven't gotten it from him. But they haven't sent him home, so they think he does know."

Zara growled and nodded in agreement.

"So the prince knows where Yala is," Shad growled.

"Our last Water Witch."

So the prince wasn't kidnapped. He'd come here on his own. Found someone important and got caught.

Shad raised an eyebrow at Zara and glanced outside.

"Shad, you can't tell Solon."

"Zara," Shad breathed, leaning back with wide eyes.

"Not, yet, please," Zara said, clasping her hands over Shad's. "He'll only get himself killed, again."

VAYSA FOLLOWED the others in from practice. She barely looked at the soup and biscuits Zara made for the group for lunch.

She'd learned more about Berla in an overheard conversation than she had in fifteen years with Shad. There was a war, a coup, one remaining Water Witch, and a prince who knew the location of said witch, but the Western Traitors had him. Both Zara and Shad were keeping information from Solon.

"Do you want to come?" Zara said.

Vaysa looked up to everyone staring at her.

"What?" she asked, willing the heat from her face.

"I'm going to town. Do you want to come?"

"Why?"

Teo choked a laugh while the others smiled.

"Apparently you missed that part, too. We should go to town for horses. I need two for my cart."

"Why do we need horses?" Vaysa questioned.

"Do you want to walk a couple hundred miles with lots of gear?"

Vaysa growled. No one had mentioned that much distance. Her gaze fell to Solon and Shad. When they smiled in amusement, she grimaced and stabbed her food.

"Berla has towns?" Teo questioned, pulling the attention away from her. "How can you get horses in town?"

The group stared at him.

Gren finally said, "Why wouldn't there be towns?"

Teo stumbled, "Well, I... well I just... I don't know. The pamphlets... I guess I thought..."

"Monsters just roam freely?" Vaysa asked.

Teo met her hard glare with one of his own.

"You thought it was uncivilized," Zara said matter-of-factly. "Don't be deceived. If you're lucky, you'll miss most of the towns and the questions that ensue. Forts should be safe enough, though."

"I know, I'm human," Teo said and rolled his eyes.

"No, humans live here, too. You're a Royal Guard."

"Oh," he gulped and averted his eyes down.

Vaysa lingered in the doorway and waited until the others had gone back to practice. She had many questions, but doubted Zara would answer them.

Instead, she said, "We only agreed to come to Berla, but I need to get Gren back to the Silver Forest and Teo back to the Royal Guard. I'm not sure how."

Zara smiled in amusement. "Sure. After they heal up, I'll help get them where they need to be."

Vaysa scowled. "I promised to get Gren safely to Berla."

"And you did. The rest will happen as it's meant to."

Chapter 23

VAYSA

Vaysa trailed behind Zara and Solon on her horse. Shad insisted she go with them, so she did. Even if horses smelled and she didn't want to spend time with them.

It was another forest. The leaves were rounded instead of spade-shaped, and the large deciduous trees fanned them across the path, blocking the sun. The peridot leaves danced lightly in the breeze, rainwater from the night before rattling inside, and a few floated off in the wind in their final twirl of life, leaving dots of water on the dirt path.

Despite the cover and serene setting, something was off. Both Zara and Solon stared into the trees, frowns dominating their faces and their tense posture ready for attack.

A gentle breeze raced across Vaysa's arms. She turned around in her saddle to find an empty trail. She glanced back at Zara, who licked her dry lips and scanned the trees.

"What's going on?" Vaysa whispered.

Zara flicked her eyes to Vaysa and then Solon.

"Are we being followed?" Vaysa asked, straining to see through the flora.

"No, the opposite. It's silent," Zara said. "Silence is never good." Zara mumbled to the shadows, "Where are the scouts?"

"Scouts?" Solon groused. He stopped and sniffed the air.

"Oh, please no," Zara said, urging her horse into a gallop.

Before they reached the Traitor's fort, Vaysa smelled it. The scent of charred wood and burnt flesh drifted through the trees, assaulting her nose. The destroyed fort still smoldered when it came into view. Mostly gone in ash, the blackened walls glowed with embers. A once-two-story building was a heap of destruction. Most of the inhabitants had burned. A dozen or so charred bodies lay in the rubble. Several others had arrows protruding from their fleshy bodies. One body hung from a tree, dripping blackened flesh.

"What happened?" Vaysa asked, a lump in her throat making it hard to breathe.

"Royal Guard," Zara spat and hopped off her horse.

The Royal Guard. They were really here. And just as cruel as they had been in Kennard, if not more so. Now they were dealing with Berlans, non-humans. Any illusion of compassion and humanity they'd shown in Kennard had been drowned in the Spirit Strait.

"We should leave," Vaysa said, turning her horse.

"These were good people," Zara said, crouching as she observed the destruction, tears freely falling down her face.

Vaysa looked at Solon. Raw hatred darkened his expression.

He dismounted and walked to the person left hanging. A patch of green hair clung to their scorched scalp. The blackened flesh hid any other distinctive features.

"Was that the thief?" Vaysa asked, finally dismounting and joining them. Acid pooled in her stomach. They'd left him to be safe, but the Royal Guard had found him.

"Pretty sure," Solon whispered, emotion catching his words.

Tied around the victim's neck was a notice. It read:

WANTED – ALIVE!
The Silver by the name of Gren

Cuma – female, dark with yellow eyes

FIRE WITCH – FEMALE, BLACK HAIR WITH WHITE EYES
LAST SEEN WITH:
A GREEN-ARMORED WARRIOR HUMAN, AND HUMANOID
SEEK ROYAL GUARD
GOLD REWARD
HIDE THEM AND BE KILLED

SOLON SWALLOWED. "That was the thief. That sign's meant for us."

Zara rubbed her forehead. "Of course it is. They know the Traitors won't turn you in. It's meant to scare you."

"It doesn't reassure me."

"They came to Berla for the prince, and are still looking for us?" Vaysa asked. Shad had been right. Closs wanted her. "That doesn't make sense."

"What happened in Kennard?" Zara asked, staring at the poster.

Vaysa shrugged. "I messed up."

"Elaborate."

Vaysa remained quiet. She didn't owe them an explanation.

"They're putting posters up looking for you. We're on them as accomplices," Zara pointed out.

Vaysa ran a hand through her hair and blew out a breath. Zara was right. She'd pulled them into it. She owed them information to keep them safe. "I attacked a soldier when he challenged me. We decided to move. The Royal Guard caught up to us. We fled and... they burned the forest. We took Gren with us to protect him."

"So they want Gren?" Zara asked skeptically.

"He was going to lead them to the prince."

Solon and Zara exchanged a glance and Vaysa rolled her eyes. A spike of heat charged through her.

"What aren't you saying?" Zara asked.

Vaysa shook her head. "The only thing different was Gren. Soldiers don't pursue. I didn't even rob one of them that time."

"Shad let you target soldiers?" Solon asked, a dangerous hint in his voice.

"Let me?" Vaysa echoed. "They had the best supplies."

"How'd they know about you?" Zara asked.

"It went wrong," Vaysa said, folding her arms. Shad had already told her.

Zara turned to face Vaysa head on. Her amber eyes shimmered. Vaysa stepped back and fire coursed in her veins.

Both Solon and Zara flinched and stood up straighter, staring at her.

"What?" she seethed. Dark shadows edged around her vision, and whispers murmured around her.

"Did you start the fire?" Zara asked, scanning Vaysa.

"Yes," Vaysa snarled. Zara was asking questions she already knew the answers to. Angry fire rippled through her veins, her muscles constricted, and her fists clenched. The beginnings of an inferno churned in her core.

"Was there thunder that night, too?" Solon whispered, his face pinched in sorrow.

Thunder? Vaysa blinked. The world whirled around her, and both Zara and Solon came into normal focus.

They didn't look at each other, but their body language shifted in unison.

"What?" Vaysa asked.

"Was there thunder?" Zara asked, her face full of sympathy.

Vaysa's stomach coiled. It felt like a trap, but she had nothing to do with the weather. She snarled out, "Yea, so? What does it matter?"

Zara smiled brightly at her while Solon snorted in disbelief.

"Zara," Solon said, staring at Vaysa. "Why is the Royal Guard really here? Other than what the poster says?"

Vaysa blinked, glad for the conversation to move from her.

Zara rolled her eyes. "They think the Traitors kidnapped the prince."

"The Traitors, huh?" Solon asked. He didn't hide his anger.

"Yep," Zara said, turning back to mount her horse. "Your hatred is justified, but it doesn't matter. The Traitors are protecting Berla now."

"They started this war," Solon said through clenched teeth.

Zara whirled around and faced Solon. "What are you talking about? They're trying to fix our mistake. We can claim the other war ended when the Royal Guard left Berla, or when King Russom died, or even when the Royal Guard focused on the eastern mountains of Kennard, but we failed to bring unity and safety to Berla. Berla is still socially islanded. No one helps each other. The Traitors still have to be here. They continue to battle our failures."

"I never wanted the Traitors to continue."

"Too bad."

"Are the Traitors good or bad?" Vaysa asked, watching the other two.

Solon muttered, "Bad," but Zara raised a finger to him in warning.

"The Traitors aren't perfect, but they are defending Berla and are its only hope to survive," Zara explained.

"So, good enough," Vaysa said.

A loud crash broke the tension as a remaining section of the fort collapsed. Laughter drifted through the trees.

Vaysa shifted on her feet, reaching for her horse and mounting. All her habits in Kennard urged her to get away from the Royal Guard. Run. Hide. Regroup. Stay out of view.

Even in Berla she had to deal with them.

"They're coming back," Solon warned.

Vaysa blindly followed Zara as they bolted out of the ruined fort and headed back to Zara's base.

There was no choice now.

Faster than she realized they arrived back at Zara's compound. Gren and Teo practiced with swords while Shad shot arrows at a target.

The three practicing turned in confusion.

"Pack what you can grab!" Solon shouted and darted for the armory.

Despite not understanding why, the other three leapt to action and ran back toward Zara's house.

Vaysa followed Solon and Zara to the armory. After loading the cart with what would fit, they pushed aside a heavy worktable. Zara then opened a hidden compartment beneath it. The metal weapons that didn't fit in the cart, they jammed underneath. They shut it and pushed the thick table back.

"The table won't burn. Make sure it's all the way over the hatch," Zara instructed.

Vaysa checked the doors as Zara fastened the cart to the horses.

With a final glance at the cabin, Vaysa joined the others in the house in heavy silence. The others had gathered most of their items, and Zara haphazardly grabbed every vial and container of ingredients from her medicine cabinet.

The six regrouped at the cart. Zara wept as she went about setting her buildings to flames.

"The Royal Guard is here, and they know about all of us," Solon said, making a sweeping gesture. He glared at Shad, and said, "They want the three of you specifically. We need to go to Monoc and figure out a plan."

Just as Shad had said.

Zara shook her head. "I'll help get you across the river, but I will need to separate to deliver my goods."

Shad swallowed. She looked at Vaysa and mouthed, "We're still going to Gillons."

Vaysa stared at the fire she'd caused, not by her hand directly, but by her choices in Kennard. She bit back the tremors of power that pushed against her muscles. She had to get control. She couldn't let her powers out again. If Shad was right about its abilities, she needed the dragon scale. It was her only hope.

Chapter 24

VAYSA

The Royal Guard had burned another forest. Berla wasn't safe. It wasn't any better than Kennard. But Shad was more determined to keep moving, so she pushed them through the fading light of day.

Vaysa didn't bother protesting. Shad had been concerned about the soldiers' movement in Kennard. Vaysa had ignored her then, and now they were homeless in Berla.

Ahead lay the unknown, Gillons. A wasteland. Her chance at control. A hollow sensation sunk into her chest and a tight ball formed in her gut. She suppressed a whimper and chewed her lip.

She and Shad would look for a dragon scale. On the way, she needed to figure out how to get Teo back to the Royal Guard and Gren to the Silver Forest. They were in Berla and mostly healed. They didn't owe each other anything else, but she'd help Gren and Teo get where they needed. Even if Zara offered, it was her responsibility.

As Shad continued to push them through the night, Vaysa barely noticed as the Peras River energized her and helped her fully heal the more she drank. Her ribs healed, along with other pains she had grown accustomed to, and a few of her scars ebbed. New strength coursed through her.

They finally stopped to camp for the night under the cover of trees near the riverbank. Vaysa couldn't sleep with the surges of energy coursing through her and volunteered to take the first shift.

After several hours, laughter rang through the forest. A small band of the Royal Guard walked along the river.

She cursed inwardly. They'd made it this far into Berla already.

Silently she stood to check out the threat. The guards hadn't spotted her group yet, or they would've attacked already.

Perhaps she'd found a group for Teo to join. Then her promise would be met, and they could move on. Her stomach knotted, but she leapt into the trees and inhaled deeply. The air was fresh and clean, unlike the stale air that clung to the forest floor.

She skittered across the branches. The long, gnarled branches jutted out, giving her long lanes to run on. They didn't spring as much when she jumped, but she had a more solid footing on them than the Kennardian pines and deciduous.

The trees thinned at the river's edge where a wide traveling path, grooved with wheel marks, cut between the river and the trees. She slowed to take in the sight. A large object engulfed the sky above the tree line, but the dim moonlight hid the monstrous feature from her.

Vaysa listened to their conversation as she lingered in the trees. The soldiers discussed the new creatures and humanoids they were seeing. Their quips hinted at fearing the new land.

She smiled. Fears were easy to exploit.

Despite being easy targets, they weren't a threat to the sleeping group, and she was outnumbered. She rose to head back to camp. Soon, Shad would have them in a new home after Vaysa got a dragon scale, and she wouldn't have to worry about the Royal Guard anymore. She smiled at the thought.

She blew out a sigh to relax and prepared to dash for the next large branch.

"Did you see their faces?" a voice cackled.

A few nervous laughs joined in.

"I can't wait to see them all dead," the voice said again and laughed.

The others made throaty noises but didn't argue.

"Did you have to burn them inside it?"

"Of course. What good are they?"

Searing hot fire raced through Vaysa's veins. She gasped and a flame popped from her breath.

These were the monsters that had killed the people in the fort.

Soundlessly, Vaysa dove off the branch, flipping in the air. She landed behind the dumbfounded guards. They scurried to draw their weapons, but again she launched into the air. Sailing higher than ever before, she grabbed the shoulders of a guard while in the air, and as she came down, she used her strength to drop him. The guard lay gasping for breath, while the other four tried to encircle her.

"It's—it's—" one stammered and stepped back.

Vaysa gulped in air, her body heaving and her muscles constricting. Her arms bent and her hands curled to encircle invisible orbs. Her vision tunneled, only seeing the leader, his visage dancing against the shadows.

The soldiers gasped and backed up.

A shot of fire danced in front of her eyes and ripped out of her hand toward the leader.

He stumbled back, swatting at the flames consuming him.

She roundhouse-kicked the guard to her left and flung herself into a handstand to grab the head of the leader with her feet. Using her weight, she brought him down with her and a sickening crack filled the air.

The two remaining soldiers trembled and backed up together.

Vaysa was barely sweating, and her breathing normalized as the flickering flames receded around her. She licked her lips and gestured at the guards.

The guards gasped and stumbled over each other trying to get away.

Vaysa snorted in disgust as they disappeared back down the trail.

She crouched over the lifeless soldier the others had left behind.

He looked frail compared to when he had been reliving the terrors he bestowed on the fort.

Her body trembled as adrenaline fled her. She gasped for air and white pops of light danced in her eyes. She leaned her head over her knees and gulped in air.

The visage of the soldier danced in front of her face. She hadn't meant to kill him. Probably. Maybe. She had killed before, but only to defend herself and Shad.

She darted back to camp.

Zara was asleep and she growled when Vaysa shook her. Vaysa shook harder, and finally Zara barked, "What?" She rubbed a hand roughly over her face and through her hair. She blinked several times and asked, softer but still perturbed, "What?"

"I need your help," Vaysa whispered. She'd originally gone to ask Shad, but Zara was a healer. Her eyes darted to Shad, and she swallowed. Shad would understand.

Zara didn't question her and immediately got up. She followed Vaysa back to the soldier. She shuddered at the sight. Kneeling, she felt for a pulse.

"Oh, Vaysa. What happened?"

"There was a patrol unit. He was in the group that burned the fort. He was joking about the destruction. I couldn't control myself, and... I'm stronger than I've ever felt."

"Your powers came out?"

"Yeah," Vaysa said and stared at her hands. Gillons and a dragon scale offered hope, but they were so far away, and the Royal Guard was between her and it. Would she make it before bringing the Royal Guard down on them all?

Zara looked her up and down, her brows furrowed.

Heat crept up Vaysa's cheeks under Zara's scrutiny, but she didn't look away.

Sighing, Zara fumbled with her medicine pack. She mixed various vials together and then added river water to them. The liquid glimmered an eerie silver color, then turned dark. Zara forced the potion into the guard's mouth.

"He should be coughing and sputtering and then should shake violently," Zara said, looking at the vial and then back at the body. A muscle twitched in her jaw and sorrow marred her face.

Vaysa stared at the body. Nothing was happening. Zara's words seeped in. "Wait, you can bring people back from the dead?"

"I can, but that creates undead. He's unfortunately too far gone."

"What do we do? Do we dump him in the river?"

"No," Zara said too loudly. "It's best if we don't pollute the river."

"We can't just leave him," Vaysa said, scanning the path.

Zara smirked and clapped her hands. She expertly removed the soldier's uniform and possessions, leaving him in his undergarments.

"Grab his feet."

Vaysa did as Zara told her and helped drag him off the trail. "And?"

"Not much we can do. His captain will find him. Those were good people in that fort, and he murdered them for the fun of it."

"I'm no better. I killed him. But I still think he was a monster," Vaysa said. She wasn't sure she really felt guilt over the death. She licked her lips and wrapped her arms around her torso.

"It's not the same thing, and he was a monster. You'll meet many more, from both countries," Zara said. After collecting the uniform, she started walking back.

Vaysa followed her, and after a few minutes she said, "Please don't tell anyone."

"Sure."

For some reason, Vaysa believed her. Be it the secrets Shad had kept for so long, or knowing a secret of Zara's; that the last Water Witch was alive, and she didn't want Solon to know. And Zara had likely known Vaysa was listening.

Her powers were growing. Zara had seen it. She didn't need to worry the others. She needed a scale now.

Chapter 25

TEO

The group awoke before dawn to cross the river with some cover of darkness.

Teo stared across the river as they crossed an old animal path. The normal red dirt and plush green trees belied the magical nature of the land. The other side was just as densely packed with trees, but on the other side of the Peras River was also a long mountain range. The Royal Guard pamphlets had shown them riddled with horrors. They'd shown shadowy monsters, caverns that skimmed the abyss, pockets of darkness, and areas that just showed "do not enter." The group was headed to Monoc, one of the "do not enter" zones. There was nothing in the vast flora that belied the waiting terror. Just trees.

Since the forest had green trees, it meant they were in the Whismur Forest. Monoc bordered the green trees. North should be the Blue Plains and south the Silver Forest.

He didn't care where they went. He just needed to find the Royal Guard to join up with. He needed to get himself and Gren back with General Closs, fix his mistake, find the prince, and then go home.

His stomach turned. He needed to leave, but he couldn't risk the other's safety either. Not after all they did to protect him. But that didn't change his plans.

Now he had a deadline. If they went into Monoc, he'd never see the Royal Guard again.

He'd faced the Phantom Islands and the Cypress Ants, survived an ant bite, survived the Spirit Strait creatures, and still had Gren. It was time to finish it.

The pamphlets couldn't cover all the species, but if half of the Berlans he'd met so far weren't in the materials, most wouldn't be. Even the ones they covered had so much not listed in them, so much the Royal Guard had not informed him about.

Solon was likely a Monocian, a monster class, but didn't burn everything in sight. He'd breathed fire, but it had been to protect them.

Shad... she was even more off mark. She didn't fear water. She spoke intelligibly and showed compassion. She was supposed to be a beast, a monster that ate all things, regardless if they were alive or dead. But she'd saved them repeatedly.

He'd lost count of the times he'd stared at them, trying to see the pamphlet monsters lurking beneath. A fire-wielding, death-loving monster. A compassionless beast that sought destruction. The enemy. But they weren't there.

Instead, he saw the heroes of his youth. The beginning passage of the book he'd long ago memorized:

> *Dragons and Guardians protected all, by land and air,*
> *Grounds tremble beneath, but all be fair,*
> *Soaring above the land, a shield,*
> *So that all enemies may yield.*
>
> *Evil may come, but always by sea,*
> *For within the land, the protectors stand.*
> *Evil may come, but always by sea,*
> *For within the air, the protectors snare.*
> *Evil may come, but always will flee.*

. . .

HIS GRANDMA'S book didn't have any creatures, hero or destroyer, with white eyes. Zara looked human, and humans were protected by the creatures in the book.

Solon matched more closely to the lava warriors, land protectors. Creatures that were sculpted from lava and tended to the islands, keeping the land stable.

Shad was like the prowlers. A band of warriors that roamed in the trees, keeping guard from above. They were the most revered and honored of all for their objective justice.

Vaysa had glowed, had created fire, but her powers didn't seem consistent. More than that, she'd helped him. Stuck with him in Berla. Now she could continue into the depths of Berla. The areas yet to be explored. He'd never see her again. He frowned.

He rubbed his temples and tried to clear his mind. The trees swirled into a blur as he continued to trudge on. He had no idea what lay in wait. He wasn't even prepared for what he had already met.

BEFORE CROSSING THE RIVER, Zara wanted to unload some gear she had brought with the Traitors. Teo didn't know how to reconcile that Zara sold to them. They were his enemy. They stole his prince.

At least, the Royal Guard claimed they did.

But there wasn't a reason for the prince to be here to begin with. He wasn't the crowned prince. If they wanted a ransom, one of his older brothers would be worth more. He'd done something to make it happen.

Teo glanced at Gren. They needed to find a platoon to join up with. Then none of this mattered. They'd get the prince and go home and leave the Berlans alone.

His gaze bounced to Vaysa. It would be safer for all of them to separate.

The river narrowed several times, providing adequate places to cross, but they continued north, closer to Monoc, farther from the Royal Guard in the south.

Teo looked back down the trail, unsure how he and Gren were going to meet up with the guards heading away from them. Gren had declined every offer to go back. He could overpower Gren, but the others would intervene. He could disappear with Gren when it was his turn for the nightly watch, but it'd leave the others exposed. Even if they were Berlans, were supposed to be his enemies, it didn't sit right in his stomach. All they'd done was help him. He couldn't leave them with no lookout.

The day bled into night, and they rested. Rising again, long before the sun, they continued through the forest. After traveling an hour in the graying morning light, they came to another burned fort. Teo gasped at the carnage. Tacked on the blackened, crumbling wall was a wanted poster.

There'd been rumors of similar atrocities committed east of the mountains, but they'd been tales. Warnings to the citizens to obey.

The Royal Guard was responsible for these sins.

He looked down where his insignia would be if he wore his jacket and swallowed.

Sins he was connected to.

Vaysa snorted at her poster. "They're burning forts to find us?"

"I think so," Teo whispered. He cringed at Vaysa's dark look.

Closs had only asked for Gren back. He was whom they needed, but he had ranted about the woman and Cuma. Teo closed his eyes and cursed. Closs had seen her powers, like they all had. Closs was using him to bring in Vaysa and Shad, not just Gren. He'd destroy them.

A lump bobbed in his throat, and he took an unsteady breath. Bringing the two in weren't his orders. He didn't have to obey those. He could try to protect Vaysa.

"They're that upset I have fire powers?" Vaysa asked.

Teo's stomach turned, and he flinched when an odd emotion twisted his throat. He wanted to say something, to argue, to reassure Vaysa she was safe, but it'd only be lies. She'd kept him safe, healed him, and helped him. He couldn't even provide her with hope.

Shad growled, and said, "We'll get you the help you need."

Vaysa nodded dully in response. She looked at the poster and her jaw ticked. She balled her fist, crumpling the poster. She glanced back at Shad.

Shad closed her eyes and rubbed her forehead.

Solon said, "We're going to Monoc. We'll figure out a plan."

Monoc... One of the many places listed with a warning to not enter. Had Teo done his job, watched Gren, not let him out of his sight...

Now everyone was wanted. They'd brought Closs's attention to Vaysa.

"Dammit Gren," Teo growled.

Gren snapped his gaze from the trees to him... His lips pinched into a thin blue line.

Teo said, "I never should have let you walk by yourself. I should have followed."

Gren laughed. "You think that would have stopped all this?"

"They wouldn't be here," Teo said and gestured to the other Berlans. "They'd be safe. We could have gotten the prince and gotten out already. These forts wouldn't be burned."

"Doubtful. It is the Royal Guard."

"Why did you join them?" Teo asked.

"They wanted me as a guide through this land and didn't want others to find out. I had a secure way to get back to Berla. I took it."

"Then why'd you join us?" Shad snapped. "You'd be safer with the guards than us, and so would we." Her lip danced into a snarl, slightly revealing a fang. "Silvers always have a hidden agenda."

Gren snorted. "Well, I didn't really have a choice. You hog-tied me if I remember correctly."

"We freed you after we escaped the fire. You chose to come with us," Vaysa warned.

He growled and kicked a rock, then spread his arms and said, "But wouldn't you also rather go with other Berlans than the Royal Guard?"

Teo let out an annoyed breath and rolled his eyes.

"You're healing. Why don't you go home now?" Shad said. "The agreement was to get to Berla. You used us to get what you wanted. The Silver Forest is that way." Shad gestured south.

Gren snorted in disgust. "Look around. Berla is being invaded."

Teo stared at Gren. Gren got everything he wanted without the Royal Guard, and Teo had helped. He'd made an even bigger mess, but if he wanted to go home, he had to bring Gren in and that likely meant Closs would go after Shad and Vaysa. He swallowed. How could he protect them as they had him? Did he have to? The thought left as quickly as it came. Berlan or not, enemy or not, he couldn't let Closs reach them.

"Shad has a point," Solon said. "We don't need to stay together."

The six stared at each other.

"I can help Gren get to safety while you go to Monoc," Teo said, steeling his resolve. If he went slow enough, the Royal Guard wouldn't be able to catch up with the other four, even if he told them exactly where they were headed. They'd never be able to penetrate Monoc. "I promised to protect him."

"I don't need your help," Gren hissed.

"This is nonsense," Zara said, interrupting Teo's response, her voice vibrating. "They've made it farther than I thought. We're out in the open and in danger. I need to find a Traitors' fort and find out what's going on. From there, we can devise plans to get people where they need to go."

Chapter 26

VAYSA

Vaysa leaned against a tree when the group stopped about a half mile from the fort, out of its view. The trees had become sparse and the ground hillier with blue clovers starting to dot the land.

Odd hoots echoed in the distance, and Zara tilted toward them and licked her lips. Solon and Shad were fixated on Zara. The sounds weren't typical Royal Guard calls and didn't sound human. Based on Zara's reaction, Vaysa figured they were Traitor calls. They were likely being watched. If it was the Royal Guard, they'd have attacked.

Gren plopped down on the ground and leaned back in the sun. Teo oscillated between staring at Gren and back down the path. She followed his gaze down the well-traveled trail. It'd be easy to mistake it for Kennard with its functionality and green-treed forest.

Zara finally took her cart and moseyed up to the fort. She returned quickly with half the cart emptied. Her face was pale, and her eyes darted to the horizons as she approached the group.

"It's bad. The Royal Guard is burning forts going north on the river. The rumor is they plan to take over the Peras River and burn everything going west until they find the prince. It's a full invasion."

Zara paused and, taking a ragged breath, finished, "Sentinels have landed."

"No!" Solon and Shad screamed in unison.

A jolt rocketed through Vaysa. The Sentinels would make the current destruction look tame. They were Kennard's elite force. More accurately, mercenaries. She licked her lips and wrapped her arms around her torso. No place was safe.

A course of fire wove through her, and she closed her eyes, willing it to not shoot out. She was a liability to Shad here, too. She needed a dragon scale.

Shad gasped and Vaysa looked down. The dark red scars that laced her arms glowed gold as they pulsed with heat before the color dissipated back to red.

Her eyes darted to the others who were focused on Zara.

"We have to stop them!" Teo blurted out. He rubbed his forehead and took a shaky breath.

Vaysa looked at Shad, who pursed her lips.

Fire whispered through her veins again, flaring with her uncertainty.

"I thought you were a soldier," Solon finally questioned.

"I am," Teo said. He blinked and looked up at the group with glassy amber eyes.

"Then why do you care so much?" Solon asked.

"I... I..." Teo said, his gaze drifting to the ground.

"Teo, it's okay," Solon offered.

"No! It's not. They're burning homes and people for one person? No one's worth that." Teo clasped his hand over his mouth from his treason and stepped back from the group.

Solon glanced at Zara. She mirrored his worried expression.

Vaysa's stomach roiled, the bitter taste of bile clawing at her throat. She'd been the reason for multiple fires by the Royal Guard. They'd gone from burning forests to burning people. She swallowed, but the acid continued to rise. She'd interfered with their plans with Gren, exposed her powers, and others were paying. It was beyond just her group that were suffering because of her.

Shad wrapped an arm around Vaysa and pulled her tightly against her. In her hair, she mumbled, "You did not do this. The Royal Guard would have done this anyway, but chosen a different reason."

Vaysa swallowed and nodded, unable to find words. Shad's words sounded right, felt right, but still she knew her connection to what happened.

"Isn't that why you're here starting a war? For that one person?" Shad asked to Teo. Her body tightened, hatred emanating from her, but she didn't posture toward him.

"We're only here for the prince, not a war," Teo said. "Gren's supposed to help make it quick. If we give him back, maybe the Sentinels will stop?"

"Not a chance. This is a full war." Solon turned and stared at Gren. "Where were you headed?"

War... They were headed to Berla for war, and she'd got herself and Shad locked into it. Instead of fire, a chill ran through her veins, and she sucked in a rough breath.

"This was already in the works before we ran into the troop," Shad whispered to Vaysa.

"But we're here... with them, because—" Vaysa swallowed the rest of the words. Her chest tightened.

"Because I brought us here." Shad's fingers tightened around Vaysa's shoulder.

Gren shrugged and looked away.

"Where?" Solon repeated.

"The west," Gren muttered. His jaw ticked and his eyes narrowed.

Shad, Solon, and Zara looked at one another knowingly.

Vaysa snarled. More secrets. And even if she asked, they wouldn't answer. Besides, she didn't care if Solon or Zara had secrets. Voicing her questions in front of everyone would be like admitting she didn't know Shad.

Solon said, "Burning Berla is only a diversion. Gren was meant to help get the prince out to safety before the war."

Teo shook his head as if trying to remove the idea. "You're lying!

The Royal Guard doesn't want war. We don't have the resources. We're already hungry."

"So Kennard wants Berla's crops?" Vaysa asked. "Since the Traitors won't trade, and as you said, you're already hungry? So if they can't have them, they'll destroy them?"

Teo blinked. "No," he whimpered. "No, you're wrong. We don't want war. We're just here for the prince."

"Did you see the fort? You just said no one was worth that, and yet you defend who did it!" Vaysa spat, clenching her fists as heat licked at her resolve and pushed against her muscles.

"Vaysa," Teo started but stopped. The single word was like a punch to her stomach.

She'd been so foolish. He was a royal guard, not a Berlan trying to get passage across the Spirit Strait. She'd been ignoring it, avoiding it, but he was defending their cruelty. Now they also had to deal with the Sentinels.

"No, there's nothing you can say to me," Vaysa spat. Her stomach hardened.

Teo gasped for breath as tears streamed down his face. He spun around, his eyes not fixing on anything.

"Teo, think about it," Solon said. "Your Royal Guard burned that fort. There were people locked inside. I saw another fort just as bad. That's why we ran."

"No," Teo's shrill word pierced the air.

"The Royal Guard is spreading across this land to destroy it and everyone living here."

Teo backed up from the group. Pointing at Vaysa and Shad, he said, "You two! You did this. This is your fault. You should have just left Gren alone! The Royal Guard would be back in Kennard already."

Vaysa sucked in a hard breath, her vision tunneling. Fire tangled with ice in her veins. He blamed her, too, just like she did. But he didn't get the right if he was with the Royal Guard.

"Teo, I chose to go with them," Gren said calmly as he stepped closer to him. His red eyes flicked to Vaysa. His blue lips were pressed tightly, and he shook his head. "They offered to let me go multiple times, even in Kennard."

Vaysa met Teo's hard gaze. Instead of burning hatred, his amber eyes shone with fear. Teo's face scrunched in embarrassment. He opened his mouth but said nothing.

An odd pang shot through her heart. An odd ache of betrayal and pity. He needed help. He was frightened. But he was with the Royal Guard. Even if he had helped them in the Phantom Islands, the strait, and Berla. Even if...

"I came here by choice," Gren said, yanking Vaysa's attention away from her thoughts.

Teo's gaze shot to Gren. "Then you're responsible, too! Go rejoin the army so they'll stop! We can go together," Teo shrieked.

"You can rejoin, but I will stay here." Gren folded his arms over his chest and tilted his chin down.

"Fine!" Teo yelled, whirling around to find the path.

"South," Vaysa said and pointed. "Just keep walking that direction, and at some point, you'll find a group."

Her promise was fulfilled. She owed him nothing else.

"Vaysa," Teo sputtered.

"We're done," Vaysa growled.

"Just one question," Solon said. "How will you explain getting here and your lack of uniform? Or how you let us escape?"

Teo stopped and stared down at his clothes. His uniform was burned. He wore Zara's creations and looked like a Traitor.

Teo fell to his knees. He whimpered and rocked back and forth.

Vaysa stepped forward, but uncertainty stopped her.

What were they going to do now? Despite everything he said, they couldn't leave him in this state. He'd hurt himself in his panic.

Shad met Vaysa's eyes and sighed. She stepped behind Teo and clobbered him over the head with her fist. He tumbled forward, unconscious.

"He'll draw an audience with his rants," Shad said and stared defiantly at Zara. Her gaze jumped to Vaysa. "And we can't just leave him here. And he can't get to a Royal Guard group without help."

Zara sighed. "Put him in the cart."

"What do we do now?" Gren asked. He looked at Teo with disgust.

"Go to Monoc," Solon said and crossed his arms over his chest.

Vaysa sucked in a breath and rubbed her fingers together. Most of the heat was gone, but phantom pulses still tingled on her fingertips. A mixture of emotions swirled in her, forming a lump in her throat. She needed to go to Gillons. She needed a dragon scale. The group needed to hide from the Royal Guard looking for them. Teo... Teo needed help.

"I think Gren should go with Solon to Monoc," Shad said.

"What does that mean?" Solon asked and met Vaysa's eyes. Emotion skittered across his face and Vaysa's stomach twisted.

They'd made it to Berla as they'd agreed to, and even farther to make sure the others were safe. They'd met the agreement. Teo wanted to go back, all but begged. And yet hesitation twisted in her stomach. Vaysa licked her lips and looked at Shad.

"Where are you going?" Solon asked Shad.

She looked at Gren before meeting Solon's gaze. "We're going to Zara's home."

Gren's face scrunched as he stared between them, but he didn't interrupt.

Vaysa looked at Gren and said, "Gren, you don't have to go to Monoc. You can head to the Silver Forest. It is your home."

Gren shook his head. "There's a war. You invited me to go with you. It's safer. I'm going with the group, wherever that is."

Shad rolled her eyes and muttered under her breath, "Typical Silver."

Solon's jaw ticked and he focused back on Vaysa. "Zara's home is a safe place but too far to travel right now. We don't know where the Royal Guard is. You should go to Monoc."

Shad swallowed hard and said, "It doesn't matter. We need to go. The Royal Guard will be everywhere."

Vaysa wanted to punch something at seeing shame on Shad's face. The shame was Vaysa's. She was the one who had lost control in front of the Royal Guard and forced them into this situation.

Kennard wasn't safe. Berla wasn't safe. Every place was a threat.

Now the Royal Guard was intentionally burning people. As Shad said, this couldn't have escalated in just a few days. This had been building. She had to have missed something. Her stomach tightened thinking about the eastern progression to the lands on the other side of the mountains.

She needed a dragon scale now more than anything, and would once again risk Shad's life to get it.

Vaysa stared at the other members. She couldn't just abandon them without a plan.

She knew what they each wanted. Gren saw them as a safety net and wanted to follow them. Shad wanted to go to Gillons immediately. Solon wanted to hide in Monoc and form a plan; a plan that likely involved them staying in Monoc.

Her gaze fell on Zara.

Zara glanced between the ground and the fort. There was something going on between Zara and the Traitors even though she was silent. She'd originally said back at her home she didn't want to go to Monoc. She knew they were after a scale to control her powers, and the importance of it.

She was the objective voice in the group and knew more than any of them about the situation.

"Zara?" Vaysa asked.

Zara stared at Shad. Shad gave her a dark look and Zara rolled her eyes.

But Zara smiled brightly, though it didn't meet her eyes. "We'll separate at the Ash Fields. Vaysa and Shad can take the mountains north. Gren and Solon can decide to go in the mountain to Monoc, or wherever."

"What about Teo?" Vaysa asked, her eyes darting to the cart. Disappointment swirled in her stomach.

"I'll take care of him," Zara said.

Chapter 27

CLOSS

General Closs stared at the messengers. No bodies were at the warrior's house. Nor her weapons—a true loss. Instead, they'd found a soldier dead by a tree, apparently from intoxication. But he knew better. His army had been attacked unjustly.

He eyed the Berlan guide. His red skin was covered in dark blotches, and his eyes were swollen. Scraps of Traitor coat swung at his sides. Despite the beating, he was able to walk. The Tefs were thick-skinned, but not indestructible.

"They've been generous with you. I'd have broken you," General Closs sneered.

The Tef lowered his eyes and cringed. General Closs laughed. Pathetic.

"Get out of here!" he bellowed at the messengers.

The soldiers quickly shoved the Tef ahead of them. They needed him alive in order to get back to their own camp.

General Closs paced back and forth. He heard there were sightings of Gren. Gren was still alive, and Closs would destroy Berla to get him back. But Gren was with the girl. Gren had led him to an even bigger prize than the prince. Perhaps he'd make Gren's death quick as a reward.

The reports included a Monocian, though. Monoc was inhospitable, almost as bad as Phantom Islands. He'd managed to maim a Monocian and left it to die on one of the Phantom Islands, but it had still prevented him from getting the Water Witch.

He kicked the tree in front of him; he would not fail this time. He would destroy every civilization in Berla to ensure victory, and to finally destroy Kennard's largest enemy. And take what was his.

Looking at the crude map of Berla he'd found at a Traitors' fort, they were a few days' travel from Monoc's wasteland with several forts between them. If there were a Monocian in the group, then they would head there. He had to intercept them.

Chapter 28

VAYSA

They walked through the night and the next day, only taking a few hours to rest to put as much distance as possible between them and the Royal Guard. Crossing the river was easy. There was a gentle current, and the water seemed to slow for them. As they passed, Vaysa and Zara filled empty vials and canteens to replenish their supply.

The reprieve lasted until the sun crested the treetops and the heat increased. Vaysa pushed her sweaty hair from her face. Her clothes clung to her in a wet mess. The heat grew as they approached the Ash Fields, and she finally took her jacket off and tossed it in the cart despite Zara's protesting.

Sweat beads ran down her face into her eyes, mouth, and ears. They trudged on, scowling but silent despite the festering arguments.

When the forest ended abruptly, they stared in amazement at a giant volcano and mountain range in the distance. Unlike the blackened trails through a plush forest on the Phantom Islands volcano, this volcano was bare rock. The surrounding land was scorched, and an ashy haze hovered above the charred earth. The heat was incredible, and the air rippled with mirages. Burnt vegetation stubbled the ground.

The bleak land went into the horizon. The volcano, still a significant distance away, blocked most of the sky. It was at least a day's travel through ash with the horses.

Solon turned to the group with a large smile that was out of place in the dismal land.

He pointed to the bleakness and volcano beyond. "That's Monoc."

Gren stared back at the trees with longing and then turned toward the volcano and shook his head.

Vaysa watched Shad, her stomach twisting when she saw the trepidation in her friend's eyes.

"We'll all go to the base," Zara said.

"Why?" Vaysa asked.

"The mountains have many trails that will make it easy to go north. If you just go over the mountain here, you'll face the largest number of Royal Guards. North of that is the Drylands, which is a desert and doesn't have hiding places."

"Where is your home?" Gren asked, his red eyes fixing on Zara.

She smiled at him and said, "Whismur Forest."

"Enough," Shad said. "Let's move. We'll be in the open for a while."

Shad caught Vaysa watching and nodded toward the mountain. They were going to Gillons. The group was finally going to separate and start their own paths. Vaysa frowned and looked away but refrained from commenting.

The group trekked on. Zara put special masks on the horses to keep the ash out of their mouths and snouts. Vaysa laughed as she put goggles on their eyes.

"Don't laugh, you will be jealous."

Vaysa shrugged, but Zara was right. After several hours of ash settling in their mouth, nose, and eyes and creating a gray layer on their clothes and skin, a wind started.

It was gentle at first, but it sent Zara and Solon into motion. They stopped the horses and covered them head to tail with a blanket from the cart. Zara whispered something, and the horses lay down.

Zara and Solon then quickly shoved everyone into the cart. Vaysa groaned at the new special Berlan hell they'd get to encounter.

Teo lay in the cart, bound and tied to the wall. He was bruised from bumping against the wall and floor repeatedly. He watched as they entered. Shad quickly pulled the doors shut behind them and Zara pulled down a tarp from the roof.

"This can't be good," he mumbled.

He looked away when Vaysa glared at him. An unwelcome twisting in her stomach passed, a flush burning her neck. She didn't regret helping him, even despite his outburst, he'd been through a lot too and in a short time, but she didn't have the patience for his attitude.

Zara growled, and Vaysa turned from Teo to scoot next to Shad.

Shad wrapped around Vaysa and allowed Solon to huddle with them under a blanket. Gren snuggled next to Zara, and she pulled a blanket over their heads. Solon sliced Teo's tether to the wall and, yanked Teo by them.

Shad growled, but Solon shielded Teo's head.

A horrible, whiny howl filled the air. The cart shook, and the boards banged and squeaked. Vaysa braced against Shad and the floor.

The wind ripped off a board on the roof and a fine gray dust whipped into the cart, covering everything. After a few minutes, the commotion stopped. They sat in silence for a while longer, listening.

When they piled out, the landscape didn't look different except now the cart, too, was covered in gray ash.

"What was that?" Vaysa hissed, brushing ash from her clothes. Shad had to be insane if she thought Berla was safer than Kennard.

"A wind," Solon responded.

Shad pulled Teo from the cart. "You get to face this, too."

Chapter 29

TEO

Teo gasped at the sight. He had entered a barren hell.

The urge to look at Vaysa, meet her eyes, try to apologize burned in him but she refused to look at him. Acknowledge him. As soon as he could, he'd head south to find a group. Leave her in peace.

His hands were tied, and they had removed all his weapons. Shad trailed him. While sulking, he glimpsed a bright light. He kept his head down to not make a scene, but from the corner of his eye, he caught sight of a Royal Guard carriage coming from the south at great speed.

Six odd creatures pulled the carriage. Their long spindly legs covered massive ground as their large heads bobbed along. The pamphlets called them maris. A plume of ash billowed into the sky behind them.

Teo's stomach flipped. They would rescue him and Gren. They'd be back with the Royal Guard. The group could go on without them.

"What's wrong?" growled Shad.

Before Teo could answer, the group heard the cart. They didn't have time to respond before arrows sprung around them. The ground troops had weapons drawn, and archers clung to the carriage.

In the fray, Teo hid behind Zara's cart. He had no weapons and his hands were rebound. He scraped the bindings on the corner as he watched the others. His heart hammered in his chest and his ears.

Solon took on three of the guards on his own with a sword. Shad howled and leapt for the archers. Arrows protruded from her body in various places, but her armor protected her heart. Gren looked pale, but he took on a guard. Zara charged two guards. Four surrounded Vaysa.

Teo gulped. The Royal Guard wouldn't take prisoners to get Gren back. This wasn't like the ants. This was to the death. He had to warn the others to just leave Gren and run.

He scooted around the cart and realized his mistake. The Royal Guard was clearly outmatched. They would underestimate the five. Five who had non-human abilities.

He closed his eyes and shuddered. If the Guards backed away, he figured the group wouldn't pursue them. He wasn't sure how to warn the Royal Guards; they wouldn't listen to him in Traitors' gear.

The Royal Guard charged forward. There was no turning back.

Solon sliced through one guard, who howled then crumpled to the ground. The two comrades attacked with more vigor. They jabbed and lunged, but Solon was quicker on his feet. One ran his sword through Solon's shoulder. Solon yipped and whirled around. The sword dripped with his blood. Teo's stomach turned.

The two guards smiled and lunged. Solon dodged and then ran his sword through the stomach of the closest. The guard grabbed his oozing stomach and fell to the ground. The third one stumbled back, but Solon was quicker. He pounced on top of the soldier and slid his dagger into his heart.

He then ran to help Shad.

Shad had ripped three of the archers in half. Their broken bodies lay strewn around the cart in a bloody mess.

The seven remaining archers were trying to draw Shad to them.

Teo couldn't believe their stupidity. Shad was in her full Cuma form. She would easily destroy them.

"Closs wants them alive!" one yelled and poured a few drops from a vial on the arrow.

Teo recognized the elixir's bottle. The soldier thought it would sedate her. He snorted. There was no way that small amount would do anything but piss her off.

"Closs can come for us himself," Shad laughed and then roared at the maris. They reared back, sending an archer to the ground.

Shad easily dispatched the fallen archer. Her lips danced into a grin, and she gestured for the other to attack.

Teo stared at Shad. Closs was serious that he wanted Vaysa and Shad? He sent troops after them because they took Gren? It was stupid. Closs could find the prince without Gren. Especially with the Sentinels in Berla. But the Sentinels wouldn't be here if there wasn't a war. He swallowed, the reality chilling him. Solon had been right. They'd all been right. He closed his eyes to block the truth, but fire danced in his mind.

His eyes fluttered open.

Another archer fell to Shad, and one of the other archers tried to spur the harnessed creatures away, but Shad jumped in front of the cart, scaring the creatures and causing them to buck. The jarring motion sent the remaining archers to the ground.

Solon dove for the nearest one. He speared one and moved on to the next. The four remaining archers backed against each other. Shad smiled.

Teo shook his head. They were making it easy for Shad.

Gren grunted and Teo turned toward him. Gren sparred with his counterpart. The young soldier lunged and leapt, careful not to hurt Gren. Someone with sense.

"I'm here to rescue you," the Royal Guard said and deflected Gren's attack.

"Obviously, I don't want it," Gren said.

"Why?"

"My secret," Gren said and stabbed the soldier in the upper arm.

The soldier grasped his sword and swung at Gren, striking him in the upper shoulder.

Gren staggered from the blow as blood swelled from the wound. He whimpered and fell to his knees. The guard grinned and raised his sword high above Gren.

Teo sputtered. That soldier knew his duties and was defying them.

"Wait!" Teo yelled. "You are supposed to rescue him!"

"He traded sides, and now he dies!" the soldier spat.

"But we need him!" Teo pleaded.

"No we don't," the soldier said and brought his sword crashing down. It ricocheted off Zara's blade.

Zara's two foes lay lifeless. An amused smirk lit her face, like this was practice and she was taking notes.

"Playtime's done," Zara said, finally frowning and kicking the soldier in his knee. He stumbled back, and in his daze, Zara plunged her sword through him.

While Shad tore at two archers, Solon chased a third. The fourth, though, backed up to Zara's cart. He skirted Vaysa and her last target. The other three lay in the ash. His gaze fell on Teo. He smirked at Teo with bound wrists.

"How fitting," the soldier snarled.

"Run," Teo said. Maybe he could save one guard.

"You're Teo. You failed to protect Gren."

Teo stared at him. He was from his platoon. He barely recognized him now. Teo stammered, "He's still alive."

"You're a failure and will die a coward. We'll get those three back to Closs."

The archer sprang at Teo with sword raised.

Teo yelled.

"No," Vaysa yelled, turning toward him. She hurled her dagger into the archer's back. Her eyes flashed and a white fire haloed around her.

The archer toppled over Teo, and his eyes rolled back. Teo squirmed.

A scream pierced the air and thunder clapped above.

He looked up to see Vaysa's sparring partner's sword lodged in her back. He gagged as the foe twisted the sword. His demonic smile filled his face. Her blood ran down his hands.

Vaysa arched forward, her mouth open. The fire flickered and blinked out. She gasped, and her sword fell flatly into the dust with a puff of ash.

"No!" Zara roared, and a green aurora burst around her. The only sign he'd seen of her unknown powers.

Vaysa's attacker's head tumbled forward as Zara's sword sliced through his neck, and his body crumbled to the ground. His blood created darkened puddles in the ash.

Zara jumped for Vaysa, keeping her from hitting the ground.

A wind roared through the fields with a thunderous hiss. The odor of sulfur and age lingered after it.

Shad cringed and whimpered. She grasped the sword lodged in Vaysa and had to turn it again to pull it out. Her eyes glowed brightly as her body trembled.

Teo's stomach crept up his throat. Vaysa had tried to protect him. He had blamed her for the Royal Guards' actions, had even tried to leave them, and she had saved him.

Shad carried Vaysa to the cart and placed her on a blanket. Shad's body heaved as she sucked back sobs.

Solon tore across the field, fire swirling from his eyes and encasing his fists. He jumped into the wagon and pushed Shad aside. He put his hands on Vaysa's wound and started chanting. He grabbed his dagger and slit his arm on a vein. The blood pooled on Vaysa's wound, mixing with her blood. He put his hands back on the wounds and threw his head back. His eyes flashed with fire, and his voice vibrated. His face and arms grayed as he chanted louder.

Teo watched, knowing she was already gone. She had died saving him.

Electricity cracked and charged the air, the surge heating the cramped cart.

Teo turned when Gren's raspy breath reached him. Gren grunted as he hoisted Teo off the ground. Gren's face strained as his shoulder blossomed with new blood. When Teo was standing, Gren punched him in the gut.

Teo's breath escaped him as his stomach knotted in pain.

"You should've died, not her!" Gren screamed in a hoarse voice. He punched Teo in the stomach again. The same spot burst with pain. Teo doubled over and fell to his knees.

Teo folded, accepting all Gren gave. He deserved it and worse. His eyes burned as emotion and fear. Unable to hold back, he wept into the ash. He was responsible for Vaysa's death. He couldn't ever right that wrong. They could kill him. He wouldn't fight.

He sat wallowing when gasps emerged from the cart. He maneuvered to his knees, straining to right himself. Getting one leg in front of him, he stood up, wobbly.

In the cart, Vaysa was shallowly breathing. Relief swelled in his chest stealing his shaky breath. She was alive. Alive. His breath rushed from him taking in everything else. Blood was smeared everywhere. Solon breathed raggedly as Shad held him up. His head bobbed, and his eyes fluttered.

"They need rest," Zara said.

Zara hopped out of the cart. Shad lingered to stare at Vaysa and then joined them on the ground. Her eyes flickered to Teo and glowed with hatred. She threw her head back and roared.

Teo closed his eyes and took a deep breath in preparation. He opened them again to show Shad he was ready for his death, but Zara stood bracing her hands against Shad, invisible magic holding Shad back. Her power was somehow able to hold a Cuma back.

"He didn't make them attack," Zara yelled.

"I don't care. He's one of them. I'm going to kill him!" Shad bellowed, her frame heaving as saliva dripped from her fangs.

"Eat and then rethink it," Zara gritted out.

"With pleasure." Shad tried to step toward Teo, but Zara didn't loosen her hold.

"Shad!" Zara's voice echoed.

Shad flinched, and her gaze found Zara. She snarled.

"Don't make me do something," Zara said.

Shad glared back at Teo and then Zara. "Fine," she spat. "But you won't always be here to protect him."

Zara released her hold and pointed at the mass of bodies strewn around the ash.

Shad growled but walked toward them.

"It's my fault," Teo croaked.

"They would've attacked anyway," Zara said, turning to him.

"They didn't care about the orders to protect Gren. They were going to kill him."

"Yes, and you... a soldier."

Teo dropped his head and realized he didn't want to be one. He couldn't justify anything they'd done. He didn't want to, either. He couldn't unsee the crimes the Royal Guard had committed.

He could never return to the Royal Guard. He wasn't sure about home. He'd made a mess, and instead of fixing it, had decided to protect it. His family wouldn't understand.

Even more, he wasn't safe in the group that had protected him since the Phantom Islands. He'd been responsible for Vaysa's death. He'd led the Royal Guard to them.

He was alone.

Chapter 30

VAYSA

A hiss startled Vaysa awake. She blinked and a searing pain rocketed through her body. Fire singed her nerves, racing down her arms and legs. Curling through her fingers and toes. Her muscles tightened, clenching her frame. She convulsed and her body instinctively tried to fold into a fetal position. She gasped for air but found none, and her mouth trembled.

Another hiss pierced the air, and she tried to turn her head to see, but darkness surrounded her.

Her body lurched again, her lungs seeking air, and thankfully, painfully, they filled. Her body quivered.

The darkness beckoned to her, offering bliss. Offering coolness to quench the fire consuming her veins. She closed her eyes and tried to steady her breathing. She just needed to let go. Let it surround her. Let it end the pain.

"Stay with me," a voice whispered.

She wanted to ignore it. Defy it. Let the numbness take her, ease her pain.

But her heart pushed through the darkness, grasping at the words, demanding she focus. She clenched her eyes and tightened her fists, trying to concentrate on the voice; it was so familiar.

So comforting.

She wanted to hear it again. Answer it. She tried to open her mouth to call back, but nothing came out, not even the strained sound of air.

"Vaysa, stay," the voice pleaded as if hearing her wish.

Cold chilled her skin and ebbed her pain, and the lull of darkness pulled at her again. Offering permanent freedom. She wanted to succumb. Let it wash over her, take her pain, take her fears, take her.

A third hiss pierced the air, pulling her attention away from the darkness.

"Vaysa, I need you."

Her heart thumped in her chest, the echo pushing at the silent darkness. It was Shad's voice. Warmth coursed through her, stirring her limbs, unclenching her muscles.

Other voices swarmed, ones she recognized and some she forgot, but Shad's was the strongest.

"Vaysa, please." Shad's voice was louder and closer than before.

Vaysa gasped. The darkness vanished, and the smell of fear and sweat from the others filled her nostrils. The dim light of the cart reflected in the familiar golden eyes of Shad.

Chapter 31

ZARA

Zara touched Gren and motioned for him to follow. She took out ointment and went to work on his wounds.

"What happened in there?" Gren said as he nodded toward the cart. Despite the sun, a cold chill had fallen over the land.

"A strong magic."

"I didn't know Monocians knew healing magic."

He wasn't wrong, they didn't, it was something Solon learned from his wife, but it still wasn't Gren's business. "You'll learn a lot this trip."

"Why is Solon so tired?" His red eyes narrowed in on her.

"It's a special magic. He gave part of his life. He almost killed himself. She was way too far gone for one person to heal." It was magic not meant for him to harness. One he wasn't powerful enough to wield alone.

"She was dead. That wasn't just healing. Will he be okay?"

"Hopefully, but we need to get them to Monoc." Zara's expression remained jovial, despite the concern pooling inside her. It wasn't Solon alone that had saved Vaysa. Something else had intervened, and she doubted any of them were ready to face what that meant.

ZARA WATCHED as gray hazy light streaked through the cracks of the cart. Morning in the Ash Fields was not much different from the other parts of the day.

She pushed the other three that could move out of the carriage. The labored sleep from the night before did little to improve their moods, and she wanted space between Shad and the others.

The carnage of the night lay before them, but a thin layer of ash already covered the scene. She needed to get them moving. The Royal Guard would be here soon.

"What are we going to do?" Teo asked. He stretched and ran a hand through his disheveled hair.

"You have a choice," Zara said. "Join us and go to Monoc or start walking back to a guards' camp. All you have to do is head away from the volcano, cross the river, and head south. I even have a uniform you can use."

"No thanks."

Teo nodded and started to pack up the cart. Just as she figured.

She could feel Shad's glare bore into her, but she didn't acknowledge it. Shad shook her head and started to pilfer from the corpses.

"I thought soldiers were afraid to enter Monoc," Teo said to Zara as he helped Shad from a distance.

"Maris help, but the heart of Monoc is the volcano. This is like the wastelands."

Gren joined them. "That's why King Russom could never take over Monoc."

Teo whipped around to face Gren. "What? I thought the king controlled all of Berla."

Zara laughed. "They wanted everyone to believe that. Monoc can survive on its own. As long as they left it alone, Monoc wouldn't attack the army. King Russom tried to create diplomatic relations with Monoc."

Gren and Teo both stared at Zara, mouths agape. She watched as

Teo's face scrunched and he started to speak several times, but nothing came out.

"You'll be safe there," Zara said. She didn't hold the strong belief Shad and Solon did. Monoc was safe but was nowhere near impenetrable. History had proven that. However, Monoc was one of few places that would hold out the longest against the Royal Guard. Once she got them situated, hopefully, she could get the prince and then go to Yala before Monoc fell.

Chapter 32

VAYSA

Vaysa opened her eyes. Instead of pain, her body was numb. She tried to move her hands, but her fingers barely twitched. Fear soared up her throat, but she kept it from coming out in a yell.

Noises swarmed around her, and she looked in confusion around the room. The ceiling, about twenty feet above her, was carved from the rock. Sweet aromas lingered in the air but were not abrasive. A thick blanket was draped over her. She was in a soft bed.

She blinked slowly and tried to turn her head. It didn't cooperate much, but Shad's voice was distinguishable at the new angle. Her low rumble brought a smile to Vaysa's face, and her body eased back. If Shad was there, she was safe.

She opened her mouth to speak, but stopped when Shad said, "Zara."

Zara sauntered into the room, her form small but commanding. Her amber eyes shone brightly as she tied her black hair back. She wore a simple green leather outfit similar to the clothing she'd dressed them in.

She gnawed on a piece of meat and tossed Shad a piece. Shad took it with the hint of a smile.

"How are they?" Zara asked.

Vaysa scrunched her face. They? Her mind raced backwards, but the last thing she remembered was the windstorm.

She forced her head to obey, turning to the side, and noticed a second bed in the room. The large form was also draped in a blanket. Solon's hair and hard face were visible. Sleep did little to ease his features. Worry still clung to him.

"The Monocians are working their magic. They'll both have a scar but should recover. The power of home should expedite the recovery." Shad said and ran a hand over her cheek and let out a breath. Exhaustion slowed her motions and dimmed her eyes.

Monocians... Monoc. They were in Monoc. Vaysa blinked to focus through the cobwebs in her mind. They weren't supposed to be in Monoc.

Her gut rolled. She wanted to move, voice her concerns, but her body refused. Fatigue and pain kept her still.

"I've always been jealous that only Monocians can use Monoc magic. It seems so selfish."

"Others would abuse it," a voice shot back.

Vaysa stilled at the new voice. Concern flashed on both Shad and Zara's faces.

The two turned to the woman who had joined them. She was tall and slender with an angular face. She had the same bone-white skin as Solon, but her hair was snowy white and reached her knees. She wore a long coat similar to Solon's.

"Hello Te'ah." Zara said dryly.

Te'ah nodded. "Zara." Turning to Shad, she said, "Tell me why you came here."

Shad nodded and stepped in front of Vaysa. "We were headed west. Vaysa was... injured in the Ash Fields. Solon saved her. They both need your help."

Vaysa flinched. Solon had saved her?

"You said that at the entrance. Why are you in Berla? Weren't you in Kennard?" Te'ah asked.

"We were in Kennard," Shad replied. "Her powers should have been dormant there, but for the past few weeks they've been escalating."

"Past few weeks?" Zara asked.

"Yes," Shad said. "I think she's finally coming into her powers, Berla or not."

Te'ah snorted and sneered. "The impossible happens, and your first thought is to hide here in Monoc?"

Shad licked her lips. She said slowly, "We weren't planning to come here. We came because they were injured, and you can help."

"Past few weeks?" Zara reiterated, her eyes darting around the room.

Shad cut her eyes to Zara and frowned but returned her gaze back to Te'ah. "If we aren't welcome, I'll try the Fire Witches in Nacam."

"That's stupid," Te'ah chided.

"Which part? Not being welcomed or the Fire Witches?" Shad challenged and stepped closer.

Te'ah didn't step down but instead pulled her shoulders back.

Vaysa strained to sit up. They would leave if unwelcome. They weren't supposed to be here, anyway.

"I didn't say you weren't welcome. And the Fire Witches can't help, you know that."

Shad shrugged and smiled, revealing her fangs. "You could have fooled me on being welcome."

"You aren't dead," Te'ah said.

Vaysa held her breath for the "yet" part, but it didn't come.

"The Royal Guard is invading this land, and you bring one here," Te'ah said, cocking her head to the side. "Are you traveling with the Royal Guard nowadays?"

Shad's gold eyes flashed. "No."

"A Silver really joined the Royal Guard?" Te'ah asked, her voice deadly calm.

"He wanted a way home," Shad replied. Unlike the normal venom in her voice toward Gren, her voice was aloof and distant.

"And you agreed?"

"He was caught up in the fire. We didn't let him burn," Shad said.

"A Cuma and Silver playing nicely together? That doesn't seem likely," Te'ah said.

"It's amazing how Kennard can unite non-humans for a common cause," Shad said.

Te'ah snorted. "The human?"

Shad didn't respond.

"I see," Te'ah said, delight tingeing her words. "I will make sure he doesn't see tomorrow."

Raw heat curled in Vaysa's hands. Shad's image flickered and turned hazy as a shadow passed over it.

"No," Shad said, her movement stilling Vaysa.

"No?" Te'ah spat.

"No," Shad reiterated. "If he dies, it will be by my hands."

Vaysa blinked. What had Teo done? His rants alone weren't enough for her to kill him.

"Shad," Zara snapped.

"What?"

"He didn't cause them to attack," Zara said.

Vaysa looked over at Solon.

"Defending a Royal Guard soldier now?" Te'ah asked Zara.

"He's not a soldier anymore," Zara said and took a bite of her food.

Te'ah rolled her eyes and reached inside her jacket.

"So tell me, then," Te'ah said, pulling out a parchment and handing it to Shad. "Would this be your group the Royal Guard wants?"

It had to be a poster from the forts.

"Yes," Shad said, and her shoulders slumped.

"Why do they want her?" Te'ah asked.

"They saw her powers," Shad said.

"Which ones?"

Shad blinked at her. "She displayed fire powers."

"I see. Any others?" Te'ah asked.

"No," Shad said.

"Zara, you see any other powers?" Te'ah turned to face Zara.

Zara met Te'ah's eyes and scrunched her face. "No. What other powers would there be?"

Te'ah snorted. "Play fool. You're an expert at it. And Gren? They named him specifically. Why not give him up?"

"He isn't our prisoner. He wasn't special to them other than being a willing Berlan. They wanted him as a guide through Berla. They'll sadly find another," Zara said.

"A guide? Where? Mosa Plains, at Treble Lake?"

Zara stared at her. "Why must we play this game?"

Te'ah grinned darkly. "We all know that is where the prince is. It's a shame you couldn't have found him first and just ended it."

"I know."

"Are you going there?"

Shad and Zara exchanged a look. Shad closed her eyes and shook her head. "No, Vaysa and I are not."

"You plan to stay in Monoc?" Te'ah asked with a raised brow.

"No," Shad said.

"What? Where are you going then?" Disbelief darkened Te'ah's words.

"Not here," Shad said.

"And Solon?" Te'ah asked, her voice catching in her throat.

"What about me?" Solon asked groggy.

The startled three turned at Solon. He sat up slightly, and Vaysa could get a full look. He looked grayish beneath his sheets. He stared intently at them with his piercing black eyes. They each looked at one another.

"Going to Treble Lake?" Vaysa breathed after a long pause of silence, using all her energy. It was another weird secret, and she was tired of secrets. It was time to expose them all.

Solon rolled over to look at her. Shad was by her side.

Vaysa's eyes flickered shut and open from the strain to move.

"You're alive," Shad said.

"I am?"

Shad forced a smile at Vaysa's joke.

"We're in Monoc. You're in a hospital."

"What happened?" she choked. The effort to speak continued to tax her energy. Her eyes slid open and then shut again. Her breath came in raspy puffs.

"You protected Teo, but you... were injured," Shad muttered. Her jaw twitched.

"Him?" Vaysa asked and turned to see if Teo was in the room.

Her heart lurched at the possibilities of why he wasn't there. Had she failed to protect her group? Had Shad hurt him? Why did she care if he was part of the Royal Guard and wanted to rejoin? Her heart twisted at the last thought.

"He wants to talk when you're ready," Zara said, patting her hand. "We can discuss it when you're stronger."

Stronger. A phantom twist of heat licked in her veins. Her eyes scrunched at the sensation. They couldn't wait. Strong enough or not.

Chapter 33

TEO

Teo sat in his cell staring in the direction Zara and Shad had gone. The Monocians had allowed Zara and Shad to stay with Vaysa and Solon. He instead went with Gren to the prison.

At least Vaysa was still alive despite his betrayal. His screams had to have brought them. He slowed the group down and he couldn't help defending against the Royal Guard. Had considered going back with the Royal Guard.

Now, he justly sat in a prison. He'd let down the person who had helped him.

Despite it being a prison, the accommodations were quite appealing. The prison itself was a large cavern that had several small rooms attached.

The walls were worn smooth and intricate geometric carvings and paintings covered the rock, providing relief from the constant heat and humidity of the Ash Fields. Sweet aromas drifted about, and his stomach rumbled in anticipation.

A blue fire controlled by magic closed off each cell. Inside each room was a bed, blanket, and special water feature. The top part of the feature brought water in a prisoner could drink and bathe from. The bottom feature removed the water and any waste from the prisoner.

Te'ah appeared as Teo counted the number of circular designs on the ceiling for the eighth time. She sneered as she unlocked the cell. Although she dressed like all the other Monocians, she was the only one who engaged with him more than dropping off food. For what felt like days already, when others were with her, they gave her space and diverted to her for instruction. She'd yet to offer more than a frown.

He gulped at her expression. Her black eyes bore holes through him and she smiled. It was the smile that would be his undoing. Whatever was going to happen, it couldn't be good.

"Ready?" she asked and rubbed her fingers together, blue fire rippling across her knuckles.

Teo looked at Gren, who stared in confusion at Te'ah.

They were going to die. The Monocians were going to execute them, and the others were letting it happen.

Gren slowly got up, looking at Teo with wild eyes.

Teo shrugged in defeat but stood. Shad would finally have her way. She'd kill him. She was owed it. He was responsible for the Ash Fields, for Vaysa's injuries.

But why wasn't Shad here? He assumed she'd want to do it herself. Perhaps she was content with seeing it done? Or knowing it was done?

Teo quietly followed Te'ah through the maze of tunnels. His heart thumped in his ears as he tried to remember the twists they took. What did it matter though? He wouldn't need to remember a way out.

Te'ah stopped and gestured toward two openings. "Here," she barked.

Teo looked into the empty room and around the corridor. It was just the three of them, no weapons, no witnesses, no escape.

"Do we face the wall?" Teo asked.

"What?" Te'ah asked, a wicked smile teasing her lips.

"Aren't you going to…?" Teo's voice faded off.

"Going to what?" she prompted.

"Are you going to execute us?" Teo choked out.

Te'ah chuckled, the humorless laugh echoing in the cavern. "Not today," she said. "Today you've been released from the prison."

Teo turned back toward the path they'd come from. He had no clue how to get out. He swallowed back his fear and looked at Gren. Gren stared blankly at him, and anger tweaked Teo's stomach. The Monocians were releasing them from the prison, but they weren't free.

She was playing with them, enjoying their fear.

He balled his fists and entered one of the quarters. The room was spacious, including a bed area, a sectioned off restroom, a small seating area, and a corner that had running clean water and a small garden carved in the wall with various berries and plants. Small yellow fires glowed from pockets in the rocks around the room. It wasn't as bright as the white fire, but it provided a soothing, inviting light.

Te'ah nodded curtly at them and turned back before leaving. "Oh, I should clarify. Solon has spoken for you. You're allowed here because of him. If you show us disrespect or violate our laws, we will kill you without question."

Just as he expected.

"How long do you think we'll be here?" Teo asked Gren as he picked at his lunch tray. The spicy aroma watered his eyes, and he swirled the meal with his spoon.

Gren shrugged.

"Don't you want to get out of here?" Teo asked. He shoved a spoonful in his mouth and grimaced as he swallowed it whole.

"Why? We're safe here."

"But..." Teo's voice trailed off. "Don't you want to go home?"

Home. A place he had wanted to go back to...but how could he explain all that had happened?

"With the Royal Guard around? No," Gren snorted.

"So you plan on staying here?"

Gren shrugged again. "If Shad and Vaysa want to continue on, I'll likely go with them."

"Why?" Teo asked. "I thought you just said Monoc was safe."

Gren's red eyes flashed at Teo, and then he looked away.

"You plan on leaving?" Gren asked Teo after a long pause.

"I guess," Teo said. "I don't belong here, and they don't want me here."

He didn't belong anywhere. The thought settled hard in his heart. Berla wasn't home but even home now was skewed. He couldn't go back to a life that ignored what the Royal Guard did.

"You're going to join up with a Royal Guard troop?"

Teo shook his head and sighed. "I just don't know anymore."

"Because they tried to kill Vaysa?"

"They tried to kill you, too. They burned people."

"They're doing that on the other side of the mountains, too."

Something he had been ignorant of prior to joining. He knew of the war. His village sent people. However, he'd never known what the Royal Guard actually did. No wonder so few of them came back and those who did never spoke of it.

Teo stabbed his spoon into his food and growled.

"What are you going to do, then?" Gren asked.

Teo chewed his bite of food and met Gren's gaze. He didn't know. He wasn't welcome in Monoc, but the group didn't want him, either. He had caused too much pain. Now he didn't want to rejoin the Royal Guard. Maybe he could try to make up for what he'd done. Never could he undo what had happened, never could he unsee her being cut through. There was only one path that felt right.

He shrugged and said, "I guess I'm going to follow Vaysa and Shad if they let me."

Vaysa had invited him, even if it was just to Berla. She'd done everything to protect him, and he'd let her down. If she let him tag along, he'd do everything to make sure she wasn't hurt again. If she didn't let him, he'd follow from a distance and do his best to intercept anything that came her way.

A GRAY CHILD joined Teo and Gren later as they stood in the open foyer.

Teo's eyes shot to Gren and then back to the child. Gren shook his head at the unasked question.

Teo tried to recall the pamphlet. It hadn't listed Monocians ever being gray. They had a combination of either white or black hair, and white or black skin. All had black eyes with no exceptions. Perhaps the child was sick, since Solon had turned a faint gray in the Sea Swamp. But there was no way the Monocians would let him out if he was that sick. The question rolled on his tongue, but another sharp, disapproving look and quick head shake from Gren stopped him from asking it.

"Is something wrong?" the child asked.

"What's your name?" Gren said, pushing past Teo and shooting him a dark look.

"Joth," he replied.

"Are you here to take us to Vaysa and Shad?" Gren asked.

Joth's eyes narrowed and darted between the two. "No. That's not my decision. Te'ah or Solon would decide. I came to give you a tour of some of the caves you're welcome to explore."

"Oh, that's amazing," Teo said.

Gren shot Teo another warning look but stepped aside as Teo moved up.

Joth led them down the tunnels and honored Teo's request to only make right hand turns so they could follow them later.

Joth showed them a garden room, a meditation room, and a library.

"This fire in here is different," Teo said as he stared into the garden room.

"It's a stronger fire," Joth said, nodding. "The plants need more light."

"You have an entire room for plants?" Gren asked as he ran a hand over a blue fern with white bellflowers.

Joth shrugged. "Many families like to visit it," he said and turned around. "It is close to dinner time. I'll get you back to your corridors. I'm not sure which family will cook for you today."

Teo masked a grimace with a cough.

"That's great," he managed. Noticing Gren's attention on a purple bush, he asked, "Can I ask a personal question?"

Gren's head shot up and he waved his hand frantically "no."

"Yes, but I do not promise to answer," Joth said, looking between the two.

Teo smiled at the honesty.

Gren slapped a hand on his forehead and closed his eyes.

Teo asked, "Why do you have gray skin?"

Gren groaned.

Joth looked quizzically at Teo and said, "All of us children are gray. We don't get our colors until puberty."

"Are your colors based on your parents?"

Gren shook his head in disbelief. He mumbled, "Could you just shut up?"

"You know nothing of our people?"

"The pamphlet wasn't very informative or accurate," Teo said honestly.

"Our colors represent attributes. It's a long, complicated process," Joth said as he gestured back toward their rooms.

Beside each room was a tray with a cover. Each tray had a dish with meat. It smelled of spices and had an odd taste that hot flavors somewhat masked.

"Stop by later," Teo said as he sat down with his food.

Joth raised an eyebrow.

"We can play cards or something."

TEO LEANED in his chair as he looked at the cards in his hand. The cards were a gift from Zara to ward off boredom. It had helped the first couple days, but it was wearing thin on excitement.

His concern for Vaysa kept him edgy, and the lack of information was frustrating. Zara visited but rarely had news. He was tired of Gren, tired of Monoc, and tired of ambiguity. He was thankful for Joth and the friendship they were building, though.

Even if Joth was beating him at cards.

He smirked, watching Joth scrutinize his hand. Joth's black eyes looked up at Teo, and he tilted his head. Teo's grin faltered, and he squirmed in his seat. He shouldn't have taught Joth poker.

"I raise," Joth said and pushed in some bellberries.

It was a dirty trick. He loved the tangy but sweet fruit. It was a unique fruit that grew only in Monoc. "Jards, I fold."

Joth smirked and collected the pot.

"What d'ya have?"

"Garbage," Joth said and flipped his cards over.

"How do you bluff so well?"

"I'm just patient. This game really helps with my training."

"You're training to be patient?"

Joth nodded. "My parents want me to be an ambassador or council leader. To do so would require patience to listen to everyone fairly without showing bias."

Joth pushed his chair back and collected his winnings.

"You have to leave?" Teo asked with a frown.

"Yeah, I have my rotations. Oh, they gave me permission to tell you Vaysa is well enough for visitors. You can visit her this afternoon."

Teo's stomach flipped, and his hands shook. He wanted to talk to her, but what if she blamed him and wanted him dead?

"Thanks man. I should get ready," Teo mumbled.

Joth looked at him from the corner of his eye, his confusion evident. He nodded briefly and didn't ask his questions.

"Maybe afterwards, I can teach you some other card games or something," Teo offered.

Joth nodded and disappeared, leaving Teo with his thoughts.

Teo walked to Gren's room but turned away when Gren cursed at something inside.

Teo followed a tunnel he had explored earlier. It led to a large cavern full of different plants. Whenever his dad had made his mom mad, he brought home flowers from the fields since they didn't have money for gifts. Teo had some gold but figured it was useless here.

The tunnels were a labyrinth, but he navigated to the one Joth had shown them. The flower cavern had seats cut out of the wall for people to sit. There were pockets of glowing fire.

Clearing his throat loudly, he called to the hidden watchers. "I want to pick some of these flowers. I don't know if that is a crime or not. Please tell me before I offend you or break a law."

He waited, but no one came, and he was certain someone stifled a laugh. "Okay then, I am going to do it, three, two, one... zero."

He looked around again, and still no one had come to stop him. He reached to grab a purple flower that arched into six long petals.

He turned and bumped into a tall figure. The man had pitch-black skin and long white hair. He had a smile on his face, which seemed odd. Teo cursed to himself. He was in trouble now.

"That's a good selection for your sick friend. You might also want this one," the man said as he pointed to an orange bushy flower. It had a cinnamon aroma.

Teo stared at him, then the flowers, and back at the man.

"Are you going to arrest me for touching these?"

"I would get arrested, too, for aiding you if it was a crime. These are for people to enjoy."

"Teo," Teo said and extended his hand.

The man grinned and shook his hand. "I know," he said with a wink. "I'm Davak. I oversee the botanical gardens."

Teo smiled. He selected a third flower and followed Davak up to the infirmary. It was down an isolated hall. Probably in case someone was contagious. The patterns were different on these walls, relaxing and calm. Teo took a long breath and relaxed his shoulders.

Davak waited patiently.

"We designed them to help soothe the patients."

"Everything seems to have a purpose."

"As it should. We focus on necessity."

"But this is beautiful."

"Necessity can encompass beauty."

Teo stared at him. Davak half-smiled and continued down the tunnel. There were many empty rooms, and Teo figured that was a good thing.

Shad's form hovered in a doorway, and Teo's step faltered. She was in her human form.

Her eyes narrowed when she saw Teo, and her lip quivered into a snarl. Something caught her attention in the room, and she rolled her eyes but moved aside for him to enter. Goosebumps tingled his skin as he walked by her.

Zara saw Teo and clambered out of her seat. She pulled on Shad, who reluctantly followed her out. Solon and Vaysa lay in beds, Solon closest to the door. Solon's eyes followed Teo, hatred burning bright.

Teo's breath caught seeing Vaysa. Her eyes fixed on him and his heart hammered in his chest. Words escaped him as he held her gaze.

Vaysa was expressionless. A large pillow kept her sitting up.

"Teo?" Her scratchy voice pulled him from his thoughts.

The one word somehow calming his nerves while causing his pulse to kick up.

He laid the flowers on the table beside her. He awkwardly shuffled his feet and stared at the floor. His eyes flicked up to hers. They offered no reprieve but also no judgement. The Ash Fields flashed in his mind. Her gasp. The sword. The blood. His stomach roiled and he swallowed against it.

Solon cleared his throat, drawing Teo from the memory. Both Vaysa and Solon watched him.

They were waiting.

His voice came out in a squeaky stampede, "I'm so sorry. You didn't cause the Royal Guard to do this. I was wrong and angry and stupid. I'm sorry you almost died to save me. You should have just let them kill me. I'm really grateful that you saved me. I can't say that enough. I'm indebted to you."

His face flushed, and he heaved from not breathing. Sweat trickled down his back, and his hands shook at his sides. His mouth trembled, and he couldn't look at her.

"Teo." Once again, the one word pulled at his heart.

He forced himself to look up. Her mouth was set in a tight line, and she scrutinized him with narrowed eyes. Her expression finally softened, and he wasn't sure why.

"You saved Shad; I saved you. Our debts are paid."

The Phantom Islands seemed so long ago, but it had only been a few days. "But you saved me in the Sea Swamp, too."

A smile flicked across her lips before they returned to a thin line. "I forced you to eat against your will. You helped Solon there, too. We don't need to keep score."

"But... I said I would rejoin the Royal Guards with Gren."

"You still can rejoin them," she said.

He shook his head, a lump in his throat. "No, I don't think I can."

"Hm." She rolled the sound in her throat.

She wanted him gone. He was overstaying her mercy.

"I can leave, though," Teo said. "I don't want to..." His voice tapered off as his cheeks flamed in embarrassment.

"You're welcome to stay with us," Vaysa breathed.

He looked up at her. She was forgiving him? But why? He didn't deserve it.

"We've all made mistakes."

But he hadn't fixed any of his yet. He had to fix them to be forgiven. Isn't that what his dad had taught him?

Solon made a throaty growl, and Teo turned to him. Solon had done what Teo had failed to do. He'd saved Vaysa. Teo was why Solon was drained and Vaysa had been injured. He squashed a grimace at Solon's expression and turned back to Vaysa. Her eyes were different. There was a faint black circle outlining the iris and a thin vertical pupil. She looked eerily similar to the Monocians, but her eyes were like a reptile's. Solon barely shook his head at Teo, and Teo bit his tongue to stop from asking about her eyes.

"How are you feeling?"

"Better." She blinked slowly and refocused her gaze on him.

Teo eased up. She seemed like her old self despite being exhausted.

Teo looked at Solon. The words lodged in his throat, but he choked out, "How are you?"

Solon stared at him, his mouth twitching at the corners. His gaze fell on Zara's items in the corner, and he sighed heavily. "I'm fine. We'll be out in a few days to figure out what we'll do in Monoc and what's going to happen."

"You two are that much better?"

"It doesn't matter, we've already spent too much time idle," Vaysa said. "Even if we're safe here, the Royal Guard is near. We need to make sure we're ready."

Chapter 34

VAYSA

"Ow," Teo yelled as a blast of fire whizzed by his hand.

"Are you okay?" Vaysa asked, grimacing.

"Again," Teo said, waving off her concern.

"Are you burned?" Gren asked, walking over to him.

"It's fine," Teo said.

Vaysa blew out a breath and rolled her neck. Her powers had grown since the Ash Fields. Instead of tidal waves of force, a small current flowed within her. She hadn't yet figured out how to direct it.

"Are you working with Solon?" Gren asked.

Vaysa scoffed.

"How are you going to get better?" Teo asked and dodged a pop of fire by his face.

"Sorry," Vaysa gritted as the fire embers fell to the ground. Her powers came more freely and less forcefully, but she still didn't have control.

"I ask again, how are you going to get better?" Teo asked and ducked before the fire flew from her hand.

She growled. She had worked with Solon. He was too patient and too sympathetic. She'd worked with others who weren't as patient but didn't fare any better.

Monoc couldn't help with her powers, yet still they tried as she recovered. It was a futile endeavor that only flushed her face and twisted her stomach as she failed to control her powers.

"So, how long are we staying here?" Gren asked as he moved back to the wall and leaned against it, watching them.

"You can leave whenever you want," Vaysa said. She'd been out of the infirmary for two days. Shad said they needed to wait at least three for her to recover. Then they'd continue on to find a dragon scale.

"Oh come on," Teo said with a grin. "Who else would be willing to get blasted with fire accidents all day long as you heal?"

"Our tunnel has gotten more enjoyable since you four joined us," Gren said and chuckled at Teo's gesture.

"Do you think they found the prince?" Teo asked as he raised his fire shield up for the next sparring battle.

Vaysa's stomach twisted. He wanted to go back. She licked her lips, and her eyes darted to the side for a moment as she waited for the unpleasantness in her stomach to dissipate. He owed them nothing. She couldn't explain why she wanted him to stay with them. He didn't belong with them, anyway. She rolled her shoulders and said, "You can go back. We'll figure it out."

"That's not what I said," Teo said and pointed at her. Despite the shield, he ducked as a blast of fire shot forward.

"I don't know," Vaysa said and shrugged. "No one talks about him here."

"When are you going back to Kennard?" Gren asked Teo, his red eyes flashing.

Teo shrugged and looked to the ground. "I don't know."

"What about you?" Vaysa asked Gren. "When are you going back to the Silver Forest?"

Gren's jaw ticked and he stared at her. "I guess when the Royal Guard is gone."

"Are you staying in Monoc?" Teo asked Vaysa.

Vaysa shook her head. She needed a dragon scale. Monoc's failed attempts to help her were just a reminder of the hazard she was to their safety.

"How many Monocians have you worked with?" Teo asked and lunged at Vaysa.

Her eyes widened, but she righted her posture and thrust her fist up. A small arc of blue fire popped in an arch and fizzled out.

Although it didn't make contact, Teo stumbled backwards. Righting himself, he laughed.

"I've worked with three of them so far," Vaysa whispered.

"And?"

"I have a fourth one tomorrow."

"I see," Teo said.

Vaysa stopped the next comment. Both Gren and Teo already knew they were wasting time trying to help.

"Did the first one recover yet?" Gren asked from his spot on the wall.

Vaysa growled and looked away.

Teo made a gesture toward Gren and mouthed a curse at him.

"Hey," Shad said, walking into the training room. "It's time to eat."

Teo and Vaysa dropped their supplies on a shelf carved into the mountain and walked toward Shad.

"Teo, are you burned?" Shad asked, staring at his face and hands.

He hesitated at her concerned tone. "Uh..." Teo shrugged and skirted past Shad.

"Idiot," Gren chuckled.

Shad's eyes cut to Vaysa.

"It's fine," Teo said. "She's getting better."

Gren snorted a laugh, and both Teo and Vaysa shot him a dirty look while Shad hid a grin.

The four joined Zara and Solon in their tunnel. A table had been brought in so they could eat together.

Vaysa cleared her throat and asked, "So, any word on the prince?"

Shad, Solon, and Zara froze, not looking at anyone.

"What does that mean?" Teo asked around the bread in his mouth while pointing at their stiff features.

"It means they don't want to share," Vaysa said, her eyes boring into Shad.

"There's no word yet," Solon said, looking at the table.

Vaysa made a throaty growl and flicked her tongue against her teeth.

"We're fine here," Shad said. "We'll continue soon. I don't want to rush your recovery."

Shad's gold eyes flicked to Vaysa and then back down at her plate. If it wasn't for her uncontrolled powers, they could stay safely in Monoc until the Royal Guard left.

Vaysa's gaze darted to Zara. She'd been planning on going after the prince. Her eyes hadn't moved from a speck on the table and her muscles remained rigid.

Vaysa licked her lips to hide her smile and asked, "Zara, what are your plans?"

"What?" Zara asked, her eyes jumping to Vaysa.

"You weren't planning on staying in Monoc. What are your plans?"

"Oh," Zara said, and shook her head.

Vaysa, Teo, and Gren glanced at each other when she didn't continue.

"Elaborate," Vaysa said, mimicking Zara's command from the fort.

"I'm evaluating the situation."

"Vaysa," Shad warned.

"No, she's right," Zara said. "I do need to get moving. I have people I need to check on. I have supplies I need to deliver."

"So the Royal Guard is still here?" Vaysa asked.

Zara snorted in disbelief. "They aren't leaving anytime soon."

The others looked at Teo, waiting for his reaction.

He stared at Zara, face slackened and eyes glistening. "I... I..." he started.

Zara said, "Teo, why'd you join the Royal Guard?"

Teo flinched at the question and looked at the table. "My family. The drought hit us hard. We needed seed and food. The Royal Guard pays well."

"Did you know what it meant to join?" Zara asked.

Teo cocked his head. "What do you mean?"

"Did you know you were going to war?"

"Oh," Teo said and furrowed his brow. "The Royal Guard is always around. Others from my area have joined. It helped their family. The eastern side is something we've heard about, but not in detail. Soldiers are always patrolling. I guess I thought I'd join and march through Kennard."

"And do what?"

Teo shrugged. "Be a protector?"

"Protector?" Zara asked and pulled back.

"It's from his grandmother's book." Gren rolled his eyes.

"A book?" Zara asked, her gaze darting between the two.

Teo slumped down in his chair, color staining his cheeks. He rolled his eyes but repeated:

> Dragons and Guardians protected all, by land and air,
> Grounds tremble beneath, but all be fair,
> Soaring above the land, a shield,
> So that all enemies may yield.
>
> Evil may come, but always by sea,
> For within the land, the protectors stand.
> Evil may come, but always by sea,
> For within the air, the protectors snare.
> Evil may come, but always will flee.

"EVER CONSIDER that you're the sea?" Gren asked.

"I'm from the land," Teo said.

"Your grandma's book?" Zara choked.

"Yeah, it was pretty beat up. There were only a few pages remaining," Teo said.

Solon and Shad shared a look and then stared at Zara.

"Zara?" Vaysa finally said. "Are you okay?"

Zara nodded but didn't respond.

Chapter 35

VAYSA

*V*aysa growled and clenched her hands. The Monocian, her fifth trainer, and second of the morning, stared at her with indifference. His black eyes never wavered or belied his emotions.

"Again," he commanded.

Vaysa scrunched her lips together to stop the retort on her tongue. She breathed heavily out her nose and tightened her grip. She raised her hands in the air and tried to think about fire. Nothing happened. She tried to think about a flame flickering steadily, a fire warming her dinner, and the inferno that devoured her home. With the final thought, a shot of fire rocketed out of her hand and smashed into the wall. The orange embers faded in the air and landed as dark dots on the rock floor.

"Focus," he said again.

She raised her eyes to him and growled. She hated his one-word commands. She hated not being in control. She hated her surges of unrelenting chaos.

For some reason, the Monocians thought they could help her control her fire. This teacher was the closest to helping her, but only because he annoyed her. Her magic wasn't the same as theirs. No matter what she did, it flickered and sputtered and did as it pleased. No matter what they did.

For two of her teachers, she hadn't been able to produce any fire. One, she caused an inferno in the room and the Monocian had to put them in a magical blue orb bubble, and the fourth she'd burned with an unexpected burst. Vaysa didn't include Solon in the numbers. He hadn't quit her. She'd quit him.

Her center tightened, and she felt warmth building in her core, coursing through her veins and tunneling through her limbs. She released her fist in time and a pop of fire hovered above her hand.

She gasped, and a smile danced on her lips. Control! The light popped and extinguished, like the others had. She cursed. Failure. Again.

"How goes it?" Shad asked as she entered the training arena.

Vaysa grunted. She hated having witnesses to her failures, even if it was Shad.

"That well, huh?" Shad said, not hiding her smile.

"She doesn't focus," the Monocian said.

"Jarvyr," Vaysa started. He was the worst of them. He taunted and belittled her. Anger coursed through her, and her nose flared as she tried to keep it reined in.

"Yes?" he said and raised an eyebrow at her. While doing so, he flicked his hand in the air and pops of fire danced above it.

"You," Vaysa snarled, but she flinched when he flicked two fingers and his thumb together and the fire shot toward her. Her breath hitched.

She ducked and swiped her hand to the side. The fire swished and smashed into the wall.

She blinked in surprise at the control. A curl of excitement twisted through her.

"Good," he said.

"She does well angry," Shad said.

Vaysa whirled around and pointed a finger at Shad. Fire shot forward.

"Crap," Vaysa yelled.

Shad ducked and gave her a dark look but couldn't hide her amusement.

"As long as I keep you mad," Shad started, but was interrupted by footsteps rushing down the hall.

Zara skidded into the room with Solon close behind her. Her face was flushed with panic.

"Why are Monocians running?" Teo asked, pushing past Solon into the room. Gren appeared beside Solon, his arms crossed over his chest.

"What happened?" Shad asked and moved toward the door.

"Monoc is under attack. Closs is here," Zara said.

Jarvyr raced from the room.

"Closs?" Shad roared, her eyes flashing golden and her fangs dripped saliva.

"How?" Vaysa seethed. The Royal Guard had found them again. Everywhere she went, she brought their malice. Her vision blurred and dark shadows skittered across her vision. Heat rolled through her, melting her resolve and blasting out.

Solon threw his arms around Vaysa's, grabbing her hands and absorbing the flare. He redirected it toward the rock wall. It blasted on impact, sending embers into the air.

Vaysa sucked in air, her eyes un-focusing as her body shivered from sending the blast. She bit back the embarrassment of losing control, again. She was an endangerment to Monoc and those around her.

Solon slumped away, gasping for breath. His skin was ashen, and he blinked as he fell to one knee.

"What the jards," Teo mumbled. Vaysa turned toward them.

"This is what happened in Kennard?" Zara asked.

"Pretty much," Shad said the same time Teo and Gren said, "Yes."

Zara cut her eyes to them and then Vaysa.

Vaysa shook her head and blinked to clear the swimming images. She stared at her hands. They were unscathed by the fire. Her veins glowed before fading back beneath her opaque skin. Like her power issues, the Royal Guard had followed her. She needed to try for a dragon scale, anything, to help.

"Pack," Zara said, her eyes falling to Vaysa's hands.

"What?" Vaysa said. "I can hold it together. We need to fight back. We need to help Monoc before we leave. They helped us."

"We're leaving, now," Zara said and turned.

"No," Vaysa said.

"Vaysa," Shad warned.

"No, we brought them here. They're following us. We fight. I can't let the Royal Guard kill Monocians because they helped me," Vaysa said, fire welling in her again.

"You can't control your powers!" Shad yelled, and her eyes glowed gold. "You almost killed us."

"But—" Vaysa started.

"The Royal Guard won't get into Monoc," Solon said. Accepting Teo's extended hand, he stood. "They're blocked at the base in the Ash Fields. They can't make it anywhere close to Monoc."

"I can't just leave them," Vaysa said, a lump forming in her throat.

"Yes, you can," Shad said, moving toward her. "We need to hurry."

"Are you after a dragon scale?" Gren asked, his voice barely above a whisper.

Everyone in the room turned toward him.

"You are, aren't you? You're going to the northwest peninsula."

"There's a lot you just said, but I'll play along and pretend that dragons are real," Teo asked. "Why do you want a scale?"

"Their scales are rumored to have magical powers," Gren said, shifting his gaze solely to Vaysa. "They can help elemental wielders."

Vaysa licked her lips. Shad's concern was realized. Gren knew about the dragon scale myth. Now Teo did, too.

Teo whispered, "'Magic gathers, bit by bit. Through hazed fields it glows. With a mighty roar it yields.'"

"What?" Gren spat.

Teo shook his head.

"A dragon scale will help her control her powers?" Teo asked. "Then we should get one."

Shad made a throaty sound but didn't respond.

Shad was right. They had to leave. At least Vaysa did. Her powers were too unpredictable. Too uncontrollable.

"You don't have to come," Vaysa said. "Monoc is safe."

She'd only risk Monoc if she stayed. That didn't mean the others had to leave it.

Gren and Teo shared a look and crossed their arms.

Shad cocked her head and stared at them. She looked curiously back at Vaysa.

Impatience and conflict twisted Zara's expression. Her foot tapped the floor, and her fingers drummed at her side as she glared into the shadows.

"You still need rest, Vaysa," Solon said. "Monoc is safe from the Royal Guard."

Zara snorted earning a glare from Solon.

"But not from me," Vaysa said, swallowing hard and looking at Solon's gray flesh. He'd been hurt when he protected the others from her. She'd hurt another Monocian. She had to stop herself.

"We can help you," Solon said, flinching in the effort to stand up straight.

"No, you can't," Vaysa said.

JARVYR STOOD before Vaysa's corridors. His black arms folded around his torso as he leaned on the doorframe, his black hair pulled back.

"You don't have to leave," he said. His eyes followed her movements.

He hadn't seen her loss of control. Otherwise, he wouldn't be standing there.

"You can say more than one word at a time?" Vaysa asked, arching an eyebrow as she threw her few possessions into her satchel.

"Yes," he said and smiled.

Vaysa rolled her eyes. "I need to move on."

His brow furrowed. "No place is safer than Monoc."

She snorted. She faced him, arms at her side and jaw set. He was underestimating the Royal Guard. She'd done it once and now was trying to get a mythical dragon scale.

"Will you come back?" His voice was soft.

Vaysa shook her head. "No. There is no need."

"Oh." His face returned to a stoic expression.

"Ready?" Shad asked as she pushed past Jarvyr. She cut her eyes to him and looked back toward the hall.

He rolled his eyes but pushed off the frame and sauntered away.

Vaysa said, "Even Teo believes in dragons."

Shad snorted. "No he doesn't. He's pretending. Just like you."

"Shad," Vaysa started. Words and emotion lodged in her throat. Her lack of control was costing them to run again.

"It'll take us around a week to get to Gillons," Shad said, cutting Vaysa off. "Then I'll be proven right."

"What about Teo and Gren? Are they staying with Solon?"

"No, I think they should come with us. If they know where we're going anyway, it's safer if we can watch them."

"Teo, too?" Vaysa asked, recalling Shad's threats.

Shad sighed and looked away. She whispered, "How much did you hear?"

"Enough. I heard he'd die by your hands."

Shad met her gaze and nodded.

"Are you planning on killing him?"

Shad shrugged.

"Shad?"

Shad narrowed her eyes and said, "If I need to, I will."

Vaysa didn't bother to argue. She wouldn't win, and Shad would only do it if necessary. Even if the thought turned Vaysa's stomach.

Solon entered the room, drawing their attention. He scowled and said, "We don't have to leave."

"I do," Vaysa said and frowned at seeing a pack on his shoulder. "You don't have to, though."

Solon shared a look with Shad. Vaysa hoped he stayed. Then she wouldn't have to see their stupid looks.

Zara joined them, followed by Teo and Gren, each carrying their own sacks of goods.

Teo smiled when they neared but it fell when he saw Solon's expression.

"Vaysa," Teo started. He paused and his mouth worked but he spoke no words.

"Enough," Shad said. "It's time."

Solon growled but didn't argue.

Zara led the group to a large tunnel, her cart loaded down and the maris harnessed to it. They tethered the horses with a rope to the cart. "The Ice Caves aren't traveled. Stay on guard. Stay close to the group. If you see any creatures, speak up. I don't care if it's a small rodent. And don't look into the ice."

"What can a rodent or ice do?" Teo asked.

"It's better we don't find out," Zara said.

Gren blinked and looked at Vaysa, but otherwise his expression was impassive.

Vaysa stared back at the bulk of Monoc. Solon watched her but she refused to acknowledge it. She nodded at Zara's warning and walked toward an opening glowing in blue fire. Beyond lay a vast expanse of darkness.

Ten guards stood side-by-side in front of it. The guards on each end faced Monoc. The eight in the middle faced whatever may try to enter. Each guard held a bladeless sword and wore heavy armor in shining red.

Teo whispered, "Why don't they have blades?"

Solon whispered back, "They don't need blades. They use fire."

The formidable group scanned the mismatched group. A female guard wordlessly looked in the cart while a male guard stepped out of the line, and the rest filed together. The male guard walked up to Solon and pulled him into a hug. The guard was as tall as Solon but had black skin and shiny white hair.

Teo gasped.

Vaysa smiled at his reaction despite herself.

Shad leaned closely to her shocked group. "That's his brother, Sal. Teo, you met Sal's husband, Davak."

That brought on another set of gasps. Teo whipped around and stared, mouth agape, at Shad. She smirked back and returned her attention to the brothers.

"Be safe," Sal said.

"Take care of Davak and the kids," Solon said.

The two brothers parted, and Sal returned to the group.

Vaysa stared at him, but he focused forward. Why would he leave his family? He could stay. She looked back to Shad. Shad smiled sadly at her and walked through the exit.

Chapter 36

VAYSA

Vaysa hadn't seen ice yet, but her breath was thick in the air as the group trekked through the Ice Caves. The heat of Monoc was preferable to the damp, chilled air of the tunnels. Where she had lived in Kennard rarely froze, though other areas had. She'd purposely avoided those lands.

As they trudged on, she longed for the comforts of Monoc. Despite Monoc being made of rock walls, it felt cozy and buzzed with life. The hair on her neck prickled and her spine stiffened. She scanned the tunnel and checked behind her again, unsure what she expected to see following them.

She held in her protests when the group stopped after several hours to let the animals rest and eat. Her stomach growled, and she relented to the delay when she saw the Monocians had loaded them up with food. There were various meats, vegetables, breads, and fruits. She devoured her portion of the spicy food. It warmed her belly, and her anxiety lifted a bit.

She sprawled on her bedroll by the blue fire Solon created. Odd noises echoed in the cavern and the dampness added to their discomfort.

A hiss startled Vaysa awake. She rubbed her eyes and looking up lurched backwards against the cold, rocky path. The cave was lit by black fire, but the floor glowed on its own, showing only dancing shadows of objects on the path.

"What?" she whispered, her voice echoing off the cavern walls. Her hand fell to her dagger. Heat and something else welled in her core and pulsed through her limbs.

Whispers encircled her. She scrunched her shoulders as she crouched. Acid pooled in her stomach and burned her throat. The whispers moaned and whipped around her, but no matter where she turned, nothing materialized.

A hiss pierced the noise.

She blinked and startled awake. Rhythmic breathing and soft snores filled the cavern, and the orange firelight bathed the area in a warm glow.

Vaysa patted, finding herself on her bedroll and everything in place. Her eyes darted to Shad, and she sighed seeing her sitting by the fire, drinking from a canteen.

It had been a dream.

Shad's eyes flickered up to Vaysa and she frowned, then mouthed, "You okay?"

Vaysa paused a moment too long, and Shad started to stand up. Vaysa shook her head and waved at Shad to sit. She mouthed, "Fine."

Shad didn't look convinced, but she let it pass.

After a quick breakfast courtesy of the Monocians, the group packed up to leave. As Vaysa gathered her items, her body stiffened at the sensation of being watched again.

She scanned the dimly lit walls and tried to start a fire in her hands. The flash popped and echoed down the vast tunnel. The light sizzled out in her hand. The tunnel was more a prison than a help. There was nowhere to run if they were attacked.

She cursed and grabbed a torch from the cart and lit it, bathing the tunnel around her in light. The fire illuminated their area but made the surrounding areas that much darker.

The group silently flanked the cart and livestock with Solon in the front, Zara driving the cart, Vaysa, Teo, and Gren on the sides, and Shad in the back. Vaysa dropped into the pace. Solon looked back at Vaysa and then back toward Monoc. He set his jaw and shook his head. He looked back at Vaysa and rolled his eyes.

Vaysa started to make a comment that he could go back, but Shad placed a hand on her shoulder and nudged her forward. She turned and saw Shad was glaring at Solon and shaking her head.

Shad smiled back at her and gestured forward.

Vaysa looked back to Solon, but he was already walking with the cart. She smiled. Shad still had her back.

AFTER SEVERAL HOURS, the group rested in a larger hollow of the tunnel. They could build a bigger fire there, and they'd still have the horses, maris, and group mates close by but not atop each other.

"Any idea where we are in Berla?" Teo asked as he leaned against the tunnel wall.

"A tunnel," Vaysa said.

"The Ice Caves," Gren said at the same time.

"Ha, ha. I mean, are we going north? South? Up? Down?"

"We're headed northwest," Solon said.

"Where will we exit?" Teo asked.

"Why?" Gren barked. "Hoping to find Royal Guards?"

Teo growled and made a hand gesture.

"Gren," Solon warned.

Gren's eyes darted to Solon, but he pursed his lips and stopped talking.

Vaysa nodded at Solon and asked, "Where will we exit?"

Teo smiled at her. She rolled her eyes. A smile tugged on her own lips.

Solon met her eyes. "I don't know."

"What?" Vaysa asked. Her stomach tightened.

Both she and Teo shared a look.

Solon shrugged and looked toward Shad and Zara for backup.

"No one has mapped the Ice Caves," Zara said. "We prefer to avoid them."

And just like going to Gillons, they were in another Berlan hell for her. Vaysa rubbed her forehead.

"Why?" Teo asked, sitting up to listen.

Gren opened his mouth but shut it when Solon and Shad sent him a dark look.

Vaysa chuckled earning a scowl from Gren.

Zara shrugged. "It's a maze with a lot of nasty creatures inside. There's a lot of odd tales about them, and myth or not, we stay clear."

"Tales?" Teo pushed.

"I'd guess Kennard had tales to keep you from going into certain areas."

"Like your story about the scary sea." Gren grinned.

Teo made another gesture.

"Similar, yes," Zara said stiffly and looked away.

"Like you have room to talk," Vaysa said to Gren. "You were afraid of Shad when you first met her."

"She's a Cuma!" Gren yelled. "Teo was afraid too."

"Yea, but all Teo had to go on was a Royal Guard created pamphlet. You're from here. You knew better."

Gren's gaze drifted to Shad who met it with an evil smile. He snarled but remained quiet.

Teo grinned at her.

"Don't let it go to your head," Vaysa said but smirked back.

Zara blew a breath out. "Get some rest. We'll need our energy for whatever we find."

Vaysa slumped back in the new quiet. The heat from the fire filled the corridor and lifted the mustiness. She leaned against the cold wall and allowed her eyes to close. The warmth of the fire was inviting. Focusing on it helped her push thoughts about the Ice Caves and Gillons from her mind. Dwelling on the unchangeable would only dull her senses and distract her.

Her muscles relaxed, and she was almost asleep when a rough, furry thing brushed her hand. She bolted up, dagger drawn. She turned, but the area was clear.

She cursed and rubbed her hand against her leg to remove the sensation.

The group eyed her suspiciously.

Zara smiled. "You just dreamt it."

Shad whispered, "No, there's something here. I can smell it."

The group formed a circle around the fire. Shoulder to shoulder, weapons drawn, they faced the invisible invader.

Vaysa's breath puffed out around her. Heat snaked through her veins, and she rolled her fingers against her thumb.

The horses reared behind the cart, whining. They pranced, agitated despite the maris being at ease. Vaysa raised her brows in curiosity at the dichotomy, but her attention snapped to Shad as she ventured toward the horses, claws twitching.

Shad snarled and leapt effortlessly atop the cart, barely clearing the ceiling. The cart scarcely rocked despite her weight. She dove from the top and disappeared behind the cart.

Loud squeals, hisses, and growls echoed in the tunnels. A white bolt shot out from underneath the cart and headed straight for the group. It howled, and blood trailed it.

Vaysa fell back, staring at the furry blob unlike any creature in Kennard.

Shad bounded over the cart and landed with all four limbs on the ground. She zipped after the creature. She tumbled with it, and painful bellows filled the tunnel, but she finally wrapped her arms around the creature. It fought, squealing and snapping at her arms. She winced and growled at each bite.

Vaysa did a double take at the odd creature. It had a pointed snout, a bulky body, and black eyes.

Zara ventured closer but the group hung back. She leaned in, her large eyes staring at the creature. The creature stopped squirming as Zara softly spoke to it. It didn't look back, but its nose twitched. It went limp in Shad's arms and allowed Zara to pick it up.

Zara brought the dirty creature to the fire. There were gashes all over it, some fresh and some that had crusted over and scabbed. It had matted areas of brown and pink in its white fur. It nuzzled at Zara as she gently stroked its head.

"It's a baby vole," Zara said, cuddling it.

"A baby?" Teo shouted. "That thing's bigger than a cat!"

"Well, baby Giant Vole. I'd say it's an orphan. It's deathly thin. Most likely, most of these wounds came from whatever took its mama."

Shad stalked over. "I could put it out of its misery."

"No!" Zara, Vaysa, Teo, and Gren shouted.

Solon rolled his eyes at them, but a hint of a smile tugged his lips.

Shad slinked to a corner and washed her wounds, hiding her laugh with a grumble. Solon sat by Shad and watched the others with interest.

Zara tended to the vole. Gren dug through their provisions, gathering different tubers, fruit, and dried meats. He laid the food out by the vole.

The vole's attention diverted to the food. Zara calmed it down by talking to it.

Vaysa's eyes darted between the shadows and Zara. Zara's attention was split between the vole and shadows as she carried on a conversation with both. Vaysa's gaze tracked to Shad, but she and Solon were talking. She snorted and settled back to watch the vole dig at the food.

Its belly swelled as it ate the tubers and some meat. Finally finished, it rubbed against the trio, then curled up in Gren's lap and went to sleep.

Gren stared up with large, helpless eyes and held up his hands in question. Vaysa laughed at the odd show of emotion.

"What're we gonna do with it?" Teo whispered as he tentatively petted its head.

Gren looked at Vaysa, and he raised a brow.

Vaysa shrugged and whispered, "I'd hate to leave it unprotected. It's too young."

Gren and Teo exchanged a fake shocked look, and Vaysa rolled her eyes.

Zara smiled at Vaysa and said, "It can come with us. It wouldn't take up much room."

"Why are we whispering? It can't hear," Solon finally yelled from his spot. "And we should leave it here. This is its home."

"It can hear vibrations. It's just a baby, so shush up," Zara scolded in a whisper. Her face darkened and her eyes narrowed. "It'll die if we leave it! It's alone and can't fend for itself."

AFTER TRAVELING FOR MORE HOURS, the tunnels became damp and eerie sounds filled the void.

"Well?" Teo said to the group when the tunnel forked into three paths.

Vaysa stared uncertainly at the three options and blew out a sigh. They had simply followed the tunnel since leaving Monoc. Now three tunnels offered possibilities.

"No idea," Vaysa said. "We need to figure out which one is the best to take."

"Let's camp here as we decide," Gren said with a yawn.

"There are too many areas to protect," Teo protested.

"We could go into a tunnel half asleep see how we do," Gren said sarcastically.

"Gren's right," Zara said. "We'll stop here. We can scope out the different tunnels to find the most practical one. Let's eat for now."

The group started unpacking but stopped when they heard Gren yell from the cart. Vaysa hurried over, and found, to her horror, the vole had gnawed through their food bags. She sighed in annoyance. Maybe the vole wasn't a good idea, but she'd still make the same choice to bring it along.

The vole nuzzled Gren. Gren picked it up and handed it to Zara. It nuzzled her, content to be held. Zara smiled at it despite the new obstacle it had created.

Gren tossed out over half of the food sacks. The ones that remained would have to get them through the caves. Vaysa wasn't sure how much longer that would be. Gren sectioned the food into piles. Then he took a small helping and started preparing dinner.

Vaysa's stomach rumbled. The portion wouldn't be enough to fill the void. She bit her lip and groaned.

Still hungry after eating, Vaysa stared longing at the cart. Sighing, she turned her attention to Zara. Despite the small portions, Zara had shared part of hers with the vole even though it had consumed their food supply.

"It's the reason we have so little," Solon said, nodding toward the vole.

"It's a baby and doesn't know better. Solon, you've been alone too long," Zara replied.

Solon's mouth twitched, but he didn't argue.

Vaysa shivered and cursed at the cold. When the others grumbled in discomfort, Solon made an extra-large fire, but it didn't provide much more warmth, the heat swallowed by the biting cold. Resting against the wall, she closed her eyes to refocus and gather her thoughts.

Vaysa awoke abruptly. She scrambled back when she noticed she was alone again and that the cave was glowing black. She jumped into a crouch. Whirling around, she scanned the corridor, trying to figure out where her companions went. Tingles of fear raced up her spine and pinpricks of numbness danced in her veins.

She wasn't alone.

She whirled around, but the corridor was vacant.

"Jaeda," a voice hissed from the shadows. The air tightened around her. She squirmed against the sensation she was being hugged.

"You're not Jaeda," the voice cooed.

"So?" Vaysa growled.

"Where is Jaeda?" the voice snapped.

The words tingled down her spine.

"I don't know who Jaeda is."

There was a pause, and the air twisted around her.

Vaysa twirled, trying to see another person. Anything. She flexed her muscles, preparing for whatever the voice or Jaeda had in store. She willed for the fire within to obey, but it didn't come. She bit her lip and grasped for her dagger.

"I see time has passed," the voice rumbled. "You will be the one."

"What?"

"You will save me."

"How? Why?" Vaysa yelled into the darkening corridor.

"We are tied together. I see our bond has already saved you once."

An echo of a hiss filled Vaysa's mind, and she clasped her hands to her ears to block it.

"Who are you?" Vaysa yelled, her voice shrill and the bitter taste of panic creeping up her throat.

"I'll be waiting for you."

"Waiting for what? Show yourself!"

"Patience... Vaysa."

"How do you know me?" Vaysa screamed, waking herself up.

Startled, she realized she had been dreaming but her heart still hammered in her chest. Solon and Shad stared back with wide eyes. The others rubbed their eyes from being woken up. Vaysa turned away from the stares and lay back down.

Shad moved next to Vaysa.

Shad whispered, "What happened?"

"A nightmare."

"What was it about?"

Vaysa rolled toward Shad and shrugged. "It was odd. I woke up here, but everyone had vanished. The cave was black but brilliant. There was only a voice. It was inside my head but all around. It was scratchy but purring. It controlled the air. It said I would save it."

Shad gulped and nodded. She tried to smile at Vaysa, but it came out as a grimace.

"Have you heard it before?" Shad asked.

"No," Vaysa said, but added, "I saw the cavern before in my dream. Last time we slept."

Shad closed her eyes.

Vaysa took a ragged breath. "Do you think I'm crazy?"

"I think you need a dragon scale."

Vaysa pursed her lips and slightly nodded.

"This is related to my powers?"

"Probably," Shad mumbled and rubbed a hand over her face.

"What does it mean?"

"You need a dragon scale."

"That'll stop the dreams?"

Shad stilled and laughed humorlessly. "I don't know," she murmured.

"Oh, one more thing. It knew my name... but it called me a different name first."

Shad stiffened.

"It was Jae—"

"Sh," Shad said abruptly.

"What? What's wrong?" Vaysa asked. She looked around.

"Don't say that name."

"How do you know the name?"

"Leave the name in your dream. It will be safer."

Vaysa stared at Shad. Alarm exaggerated Shad's face and Vaysa knew things would never be the same. She was beginning to see why her mom had taken her from Berla.

Chapter 37

ZARA

After resting, they scanned the tunnels for the best solution. Shad took one tunnel, as did Zara and Solon. They each took a torch and weapon. Vaysa, Teo, and Gren lingered behind to pack up and watch the vole.

Zara went down the tunnel on the right. The light bounced off the ice-covered walls. She watched her reflection drift in and out of focus. Her head would become bulbous and then shrink into almost nothingness. She shivered as her footsteps echoed down the tunnel. At least it was deep and might not be a dead end.

The Ice Caves, an abandoned system of tunnels similar to those that veined across Berla, were cursed. Or at least, they were believed to be. Not even her ancestors, those who cursed them, ventured into them, the safe paths forgotten in time.

Her foot sent a rock skittering across the ground, and it ricocheted off a larger object. She stopped and found another rock. She inched further; her breath came out in cloud puffs that hovered in the air. Tingles race down her back. She wasn't alone.

"Crap…. Don't be a barbed spider, please don't be…" she muttered.

She blew out a sigh and sent another rock down into the darkness. A shatter sounded and she jumped.

A hiss escaped from the darkness.

"Jards," she said flatly. Shaking her head, she ripped off part of her skirt and wrapped it around another rock. She touched the material to her torch. It jumped to life with fire, and she hurled the rock toward the shadows.

As it flew, the ceiling lit up with dancing fire against icicle crystals. The rock bounced off a blob, and as it burned out, she caught the glint of a large fang. The spider was massive.

She turned and ran. Her heart pounded as she fled. She didn't know if it was following her or not. She came out of the tunnel at full speed and ran directly into Teo. The two plummeted to the ground and lay sprawled, gasping for air.

Chapter 38

VAYSA

Vaysa and Gren looked up from their work. Vaysa rushed to Zara and Teo's side, weapon drawn, and peered into the tunnel.

Fear and anger swarmed in her, igniting her core and sending pulses through her veins.

Trying to harness the power she felt, Vaysa concentrated on fire. Her eyes started to glow, and smoke twirled from their corners. Small flames sprung from her fingertips. She focused on them combining, becoming one. A small fireball the size of her hands formed. She pushed forward, and it flew into the darkness. It didn't go far, but the walls of ice shimmered, revealing a dark mass hovering down the trail.

Zara pulled herself up, and Teo slowly sat up, rubbing his head. Gren joined them and gasped.

"Looks like we have a fight coming," Teo said as he grabbed his sword.

"Move!" Shad roared as she bound out of her tunnel on all fours.

Vaysa whirled around to face her friend and whatever was pursuing her, leaving Zara, Gren, and Teo with their backs to her.

Behind Shad, the shadows shaped into dozens of toothy monsters. Shad crushed one of them beneath her as she sprang into the open area and scrambled around the cavern. The creature lashed with its claws and made an ear-piercing shriek. Shad kept leaping. Vaysa swore and the heat of a fireball warmed her palm as it formed.

The swarming beasts of dark fur, elongated limbs, and round heads with oversized teeth crawled against the rocks and made clicking noises with their jaws. Their nails scratched metallic beats as they scraped against the rocky wall, filling the cave with the sound. With them an odd odor, between a fart and burnt food, filled the cave.

Vaysa stepped in the path between the beasts and Shad, the fireball in her hand growing in size and heat.

"The smell alone will kill us," Teo gagged. He rushed to Vaysa's side, leaving Zara and Gren to the one tunnel.

Shad coughed and nodded, unable to speak. She hunched over coughing as a creature launched toward her back. She turned in time for it to land on her armor. Their gnashing teeth lashed at her face. Shad stumbled back and her heels caught on the rocky terrain.

Grabbing the beast with her claws, she ripped it from her body. Some of her fur ripped out as it tore its jaws away. Yelping in pain, she tossed the body toward the wall. It smacked with a thud and fell to the ground, limp.

Shad went to all fours and roared.

Not trusting her precision with fireballs, Vaysa shot the one still formed in her hand at a swarm rushing Shad. It splattered against them, sending a wave of embers over them. She regripped her sword.

"Protect the livestock," Shad told Teo. "I'll lead them away."

Teo opened his mouth to argue, but snapped it shut.

Vaysa met Teo's gaze. He nodded and rushed to the livestock. Vaysa watched as Gren ran to help Teo with the horses and maris.

"Help Zara," Shad said, lowering her head in preparation to take on the beasts. Vaysa knew this stance well.

"I'll help you."

"Keep that thing in the tunnel," Shad said with a head jerk toward Zara's tunnel.

Shad's eyes glowed gold. There was no point in arguing. Shad was past discussion. Vaysa growled and turned her attention to the beast in the tunnel.

Chapter 39

SOLON

Solon hated the cold. He hated the Ice Caves. Nasty, angry, hungry beasts roamed in them. They needed an exit.

Vaysa needed a dragon scale. He could admit it. She was so much like her mother, but with the Royal Guard covering Berla, going for a scale wasn't worth the risk. Monoc could handle her outbursts. There were more powerful wielders there than him. She could have had someone stationed with her at all times.

He snorted. There was no way she'd be okay with that.

But Closs had seen her powers, and he was coming for her, as he had her mother.

He growled and blue fire curled away from him, disappearing down the tunnel.

Screams interrupted his thoughts. He turned in circles but didn't hear the sound again. The stupid ice was playing tricks.

He continued, focusing on the path. He couldn't let the ice distract him.

Solon traveled half an hour and still had found nothing creepier than the ice, or a definite sign that this was the way out, so he shrugged and headed back. He shouldn't get too far from their campsite.

He caught sight of his reflection dancing dimly on the ice. His ageless black eyes and hair stood in contrast to his white flesh. He ran his hands over the rough leather of his duster. Red scars laced up his arms and torso, but the thick jacket kept them from view.

The darkness dwarfed his torch's light. His image popped from a bright light, and images materialized into view: Monoc from before his imprisonment over seventeen years ago, Berla while under the tyrannical king, and then the Traitors seizing power and killing the monarch.

It had been their chance, and they took it. Solon had killed Russom himself and ran with Yala, Solon's love, from the castle. It had been their one chance to get her out.

The coup hadn't mattered. Their marriage hadn't mattered. Even the Traitors had wanted Yala's powers. She was the Water Witch, the last of her kind. She had protected Berla with storms and patterned weather for crops. She'd been the lifeblood of the rivers. But her ultimate powers had come at a steep price.

Solon had called it a curse. Yala had called it her purpose. Now she was gone.

He ended up on the Phantom Islands alone and defeated. So many friends and allies had died trying to help them. A lump clogged his throat, and he tore his eyes from the ice.

There was a reason Monocians didn't travel the Ice Caves.

The image flashed next to the Ash Fields. The cart. Vaysa. There was no way his magic alone had saved Vaysa.

He'd heard Shad's words after Vaysa had fallen asleep. The cursed name. Vaysa had been called by the cursed name. But her eyes were still white. The curse didn't own her yet.

More screams echoed in the tunnel and he tore his eyes from the ice's images. He turned, trying to find the source. The sound kept growing louder. His pulse quickened, and rage warmed inside him realizing the screams were coming from the camp.

He cursed himself for ignoring them earlier and sped down the tunnel.

Intense heat greeted him as he neared the opening. The cart was ablaze, paralyzing the maris and horses in fear. They were smart enough to run, yet they stayed.

Vaysa was throwing fireballs down the left tunnel. A large, hulking black spider lashed at her. There were smoldering spots on it, and it hissed as a fireball landed on its head.

Shad had several odd-looking things attached to her. They were mostly teeth and claws and were trying to rip off chunks of flesh.

The same hellions surrounded the cart. Gren and Teo had torches and swung them wildly at the creatures trying to defend the frightened horses. Zara was trying to help Shad but had the same nasty things attacking her. A smile tugged on his lips when he saw the baby vole munching on one of the creatures trying to attack Zara.

Focusing, Solon's eyes rolled back, and smoke twirled from their corners. His chin touched his chest, and his eyes concentrated on the flaming cart. His arms stretched out and his hands danced in the fire's light. His fingers beckoned the fire. He started chanting, and the fire swirled toward him.

As he walked closer, the fire flickered and curved at him. Then it was floating in the air, leaving the cart blackened and smoking. The fireball was twice his size but bent to his whim.

Solon lowered his hands and made sweeping circles. His chanting grew louder and vibrated off the walls.

He roared.

The fire flew and engulfed the beasts attacking Gren, Teo, and the livestock. They burst in flames and the charred bodies fell to the floor.

Gren and Teo stood breathing heavily and soaking up the scene. They both looked at Solon in amazement. Solon turned his attention toward Shad. He had to stay focused.

Gren and Teo ran to help. He wanted to say, "Stay back," but it was too much energy. Teo and Gren tried ripping the fiends off, but the beasts then attached to them.

Solon clapped his hands, and sparks flew out. He inhaled deeply and blew into the sparks. Fire sprang to life in a small hailstorm of embers that covered the group. Teo and Gren were caught in the wave, but the embers only left small black dots on their heavy jackets.

The hellish creatures reared up, the embers consuming their bodies. They scrambled off in a blind rage and ran toward Solon, teeth bared and claws flying.

Solon waited until they were almost on him. Breathing heavily, he slowly backed up, drawing them further and further away from the group. He bellowed into the cave, and fire materialized from the air. The beasts were caught in the onslaught. They flailed and floundered and then withered into a black ashy mess.

Solon gasped for breath. He needed more fuel. More energy.

Shad and Zara whimpered in pain. Open gashes covered their bodies. Teo and Gren knelt by them. Solon heaved and clutched the wall. His body was spent. He pushed himself up and tried staggering to Vaysa's aid. Black dots popped in front of his eyes. He needed air.

Chapter 40

VAYSA

The black spider, with chunks of its hair on fire, lashed violently at Vaysa. She dodged and lost concentration on her fireball. It sizzled out as she stumbled. She cursed and dug in her heels to regroup.

Snorts and squeals of the other beasts were replaced with screeches and shrieks. The heat was welcoming, but she couldn't turn to see what was going on. They would attack her from the back if Zara and Shad failed. She'd die either way. She couldn't focus on that.

One of the beast's legs came close, and searing pain rocketed through Vaysa's body. Her leg gushed blood, and tiny barbs stuck out. White sparks burst in front of her eyes, and a wave of dizziness washed over her. She blinked, trying to clear her mind, but crumbled to her knees. Her voice caught in her throat and only a strangled cry came out.

A flash of silver cut in front of her, and then the creature reared back, slashing at the ceiling. Its cries deafened the shrieks and screams behind her. A sword stuck out of its head with dark goo bubbling and oozing down from its wound.

She tried to move, to stand or roll away, anything to get away from the beast, but her body refused to cooperate. Fear burned in her veins, constricting her muscles. Shadows crept over her eyes, dimming the cavern. Wind sounded around her, and the cavern flashed into the dark cave. Everyone was gone.

"No," she bellowed into the cavern. The word echoed around her, drowning out the silence.

She blinked and was back in the tunnel. The noises swarmed together into a cacophony of voices and screams.

Teo's gaze turned to her. His amber eyes were bright with concern. He knelt by her.

"Stay with me," Teo said. His words were garbled, but she heard next, "They're gray," as he pointed toward her eyes. Her brain couldn't register what that meant.

She didn't care. She pushed herself up, her feet on the ground, her hands braced on either side of the wall. She closed her eyes, digging for the heat in her core. Warmth rippled through her, and she stood, fire licking her hands.

She threw her head back and yelled. Fire raced over her and into the air with embers dropping to the ground. Her head fell forward, and she took gulping breaths. The barbs and poison in her leg had disintegrated in the inferno.

She looked up to find Teo staring at her. His amber eyes met hers and she smiled. Her stomach fluttered when he smiled back.

A welcoming heat took over. The pain melted. Nothing but a warm throb remained.

Chapter 41

VAYSA

"We have to take Solon's tunnel," Zara said. "We know Shad's opens into a chasm and mine has a spider's nest."

"Maybe we should rest longer," Teo said. His concerned eyes looked everywhere but at Vaysa.

"There's not enough food," Vaysa said and flexed her muscles. The power had receded, but she frowned at the phantom feeling of it racing through her.

The power had been controlled, precise, and intense, but she hadn't been the one in control of it. It had coursed through her, using her body as a marionette. Even if it had been to her benefit, she didn't like the idea that anything could be controlling her. Deciding for her.

Hopefully they could find a scale quickly. She didn't want to be anyone or anything's tool.

The others watched her, waiting to see if the powers showed again. They all needed rest, but staying meant starving. Staying meant her powers could rage again.

Everyone would be safer if they went back to Monoc and let her and Shad go to Gillons on their own. But Shad wanted to watch Teo and Gren. She wasn't sure what Gren and Teo could do with the knowledge of the scale.

Until she found a dragon scale, they'd all be in increasing danger.

"Can we hunt something?" Teo asked, breaking her thoughts.

"I don't know what we could eat. I also don't know how to find it here," Zara said.

"You could go back to Monoc," Solon said, staring at Vaysa.

Vaysa slid her gaze to him and then in the direction of Monoc. A growl sounded in her throat. She gritted out, "You don't have to be here."

"Neither do you," he countered, tilting his chin down.

"Doesn't she need a dragon scale?" Teo asked, rubbing a hand through his hair.

Solon growled.

Shad shot Teo a dark look and shook her head.

He lifted his palms up.

"You were attacked again," Solon yelled.

"We all were," Vaysa shouted. Her heart hammered in her chest. If she stayed, she'd do even worse to them. "It's too risky for me to go back."

"Monoc can help you."

"Does it have a dragon scale she could have?" Teo asked.

Vaysa smirked at Teo in approval.

Solon glared at Teo.

Shad bit her lip and sighed. She glanced between Vaysa and Solon and then in the direction of Monoc. She finally looked at Zara expectantly.

Vaysa crossed her arms. No matter what Zara said, she wasn't going back to Monoc. She couldn't risk the Monocians or her group. She'd go alone if need be.

"Enough," Zara said. "We either all go back to Monoc, or we all go forward. Anyone choosing to depart the group once we exit the caves is welcome to. But no one is going back alone. We need numbers."

"Are you going with us to the peninsula, Zara?" Gren asked.

"I'm not sure yet. It'll depend on what it looks like when we exit the caves," Zara said.

Vaysa tilted her head and gauged Zara. She was lying. She was certain of it.

"If," Solon muttered.

"I'm not going back to Monoc," Vaysa gritted out through clenched teeth.

"I'm with Vaysa," Shad said and stood beside her. "Besides, other than annoying her into power bursts, Monoc wasn't helping."

A look passed between Solon and Shad, one built on years of pain and hidden secrets.

Teo slid his gaze in the direction of Monoc and then Vaysa. Sadness and guilt drooped his eyes, but he said, "I'm with Vaysa."

Gren nodded.

Trepidation coiled in Vaysa's stomach. As much as their support was a comfort, it put them in danger. Again.

"Lovely," Zara said and raised an eyebrow at Solon.

Solon growled. He cursed under his breath but stood.

"They won't help," he mumbled.

"Who won't?" Gren asked, cocking his head.

Solon's gaze bore into him.

Teo yanked Gren backwards and pushed Gren behind him.

Vaysa turned her gaze to Shad and lifted a questioning eyebrow.

Shad shrugged. Despite her indifference, she probably knew who Solon was referring to but wouldn't share it around Gren and Teo. It wouldn't matter, anyway. Shad was set on them going. Even if Solon thought it was pointless.

Vaysa doubted this standoff was over, but it'd be something to face later.

Solon took the lead again, warning them to keep focused on what was ahead and not to stare at the ice. The group nodded but said nothing.

Vaysa kept her grip on her sword, trusting it more than her fireballs.

The time passed slowly as the tunnel snaked through the mountain. It was smaller than the previous one, cramped and cold.

Vaysa watched her breath linger in small clouds. The ice danced in the bright torchlight, and as she passed through, the ice reflected different shining colors.

An odd sensation tickled her spine. She felt a breath on her shoulder and heard her name.

She stiffened. It was the damn nightmare voice again. She whirled around and her stomach tightened upon seeing Zara's expression.

Chapter 42

Zara watched her reflection in the ice. Unlike the tunnel she had explored, her image here transformed and twisted. The image morphed into one of her younger self. She looked similar, but she had a large smile on her face instead of her forced one, and she was sparring with a handsome man. She caught her breath; it was her husband.

She still felt his presence with her now, nineteen years after he had passed. Then the castle popped into view, and then Solon and his beautiful wife were running through the woods.

Her heartbeat quickened, and tears stung her eyes. She watched in paralyzed horror as she and her husband followed them. They had started the war by killing King Russom and setting Yala free.

She wanted to shout "no, don't follow," but the words stuck painfully in her throat.

She yelped when a stabbing pain shot through her foot. The vole had bitten her, breaking her free from her nightmare early. The vole rubbed against her, and Zara smiled and picked it up.

She said, "Thank you, my friend. Hans likes you. He's my husband.

He says I should name you... I think Alice. It's what I wanted to name our child if he had been a girl."

Zara looked up to the group staring at her. She turned and walked on, refusing to say anything to them.

Life had been easier when she was alone. Once they exited the caves, she'd make sure they were safe and then head on. She'd lost time traveling with them, but how could she turn them away?

Now, what she needed to do had to be solo. She likely wouldn't return. A reality she'd accepted when Yala appeared on her doorstop all those years ago and she helped her hide. Hiding was never permanent. Only a delay. And now, time had passed.

Solon matched pace. His expression grim, he whispered, "Did you see the past?"

Zara nodded but wouldn't look at him. She had to swallow back the hatred that had surged up her throat. She couldn't blame Solon for her and Hans' choices.

"I saw it earlier, too. This place is odd," Solon said.

"We just need to watch everyone," Zara said and fell behind the group.

She paused when Vaysa fell behind to match pace with her.

Vaysa frowned and finally said, "Something's here with us."

Zara's brows shot up in surprise. "What do you mean?"

Before Vaysa could respond, Shad pounded on the ice, her glazed eyes fixated on it. She clawed at the air, and before Zara could stop her, Vaysa ran to her side.

Zara's spine stiffened when Vaysa's eyes flashed copper and then lavender as she placed a hand protectively on Shad's arm.

Zara swore and ran toward Vaysa. Vaysa didn't know the power of the curse or the ice. Zara ripped Vaysa's hand off Shad, and in the spot Vaysa's hand had been, a glowing handprint remained. Vaysa's eyes snapped copper again before the color faded to her white eyes. Zara braced for Vaysa's descent from the magic, and in doing so placed her hand on Shad.

A jolt shot through Zara. The memories she saw were not hers, but she felt like she was reliving them. Anger pulsed through her. It felt welcoming and controlled.

Zara turned in confusion and saw once-familiar land, but her gaze was pulled forward. Her pulse quickened when the castle loomed before her. Not the current decayed ruins it was now, but when it had washed stone with colored banners flapping, palace guards patrolled the grounds, and it held the general buzz of life.

She was in the siege on the monarch. Joy surged through her. Not her own. She'd felt terror during the operation. Shad had felt joy. Had Hans?

King Russom had tried to hunt the Cumas to extinction. Shad had helped Zara, Hans, Shad's brother and Zara's husband, and Solon with the coup.

Regret quickly replaced the joy. They had fled with Solon's wife, Yala. They hadn't known the other Traitors' plan included Yala and her powers. They wouldn't have helped had they known the Traitors wanted her.

Anger consumed her, and flashes of red popped across her vision so hot she gasped and clenched her fists to keep her rage in check. Betrayal burned in her belly and the need to escape constricted her muscles. It was not just Shad who had felt the betrayal. Zara would never forgive what happened. She may have moved on, but she would not forget.

The image skipped ahead in time, and she saw Solon crumble after an arrow ripped through him. Solon had used the last of his strength to beg Shad to leave with his family. Shad's remorse to leave Solon squeezed Zara's heart, but he was dead either way.

Next, the armies surrounded them. It took her a year, but Shad had gotten Solon's family to Berla's water edge. Yala would be fine in the strait. Water was her home; she was a Water Witch. She controlled water; powers given to her family centuries prior. Powers Berla still relied on. Powers monarchies waged wars to control.

Shad attacked the soldiers knowing they would capture her, but it meant saving Solon's family, her friends. That was what had mattered.

Relief flooded her knowing Yala was in the water. All would be okay. Shad was at peace. It didn't matter that she'd be captured. Her mission was accomplished.

Zara saw the Phantom Islands next, one of the few ancient Berlan relics she hadn't seen herself, and then Shad making it to Kennard alone. She found the partially burned village, and then the images skipped forward, and she found Vaysa alone in the woods. Yala was gone.

The next image was Vaysa losing control with the soldiers. Her fire powers rocketed from her, but it was the glowing light surrounding her that was the issue. Her eyes flashed copper, burning with metallic power. In her periphery, she could see Closs' expression. He knew.

Regret and fear clawed at her lungs, constricting her breathing and making her wheeze. She clutched her chest to ease the pressure. Vaysa's mother had been wrong; Vaysa's powers would develop in Kennard. A curse was a curse.

A cold wave washed over Zara, leaving her momentarily confused. The memories had run their course.

Shad looked at Zara. Her eyes were dim, and her shoulders slumped. So much had happened. Zara hugged her friend.

Zara looked into the ice over Shad's shoulder, but only their reflection showed.

Chapter 43

TEO

Teo watched the ice shimmer and change. The hues changed from orange to yellow to blue and then green, mesmerizing him. Images of his home, his family's farm, and then the years of drought flashed by. His family's farm dwindled. Everyone looked sad and thin. He had lost two siblings to the famine.

He saw himself a year ago. He was leaving for the army. Adrienne, his betrothed, refused to visit. Refused to see him off. She disagreed with his choice to leave. It had meant the end of their engagement. Instead of regret, relief flooded him.

His mother was crying, begging him not to go, her sweet voice pleading, "Teo, my boy, stay."

He had almost stayed, but his family needed his support and one less mouth to feed.

His dad wouldn't meet his eye. He just gazed off across the farm that Teo was leaving behind. Tight jawed, Teo had left with a small bag of items. He had a small canning jar of the farm's dirt, a hunting knife, and some scraps of food. He didn't have any money; neither did his family. He'd change that.

His twin sister, Mariah, had followed him to the border of the recruitment camp. None of his other siblings had come. She hadn't approved of his choice, but she supported him.

He wrote to his family regularly and sent all his pay home. The Royal Guard provided food, shelter, and clothing. His parents never wrote him. Mariah had sent him a cookie for each of their birthdays. It meant his money had provided enough they could afford some sugar.

His father was still furious at his decision to join the Royal Guard. Teo didn't know how to fix it. His family needed his stipend. Even if his father was too prideful to admit it.

The drought had passed, and the land was producing again. He felt an ache in his heart. He could go home now. He touched the image... home.

It vanished and was replaced with an image of the Phantom Islands and a head bobbing in the current. The next image was of him in Berla yelling at his group, and then Vaysa pierced by a sword and her eyes rolling back while protecting him. The same wave of sickness washed over him.

He heaved on the cold ground. The vision broke, but the image of Vaysa crumpling continued to flash before his eyes.

Then Vaysa was beside him. Shaking him.

"Teo... Teo... Answer me."

He looked up, startled to see Vaysa was alive and standing before him. He reached out and grasped her arm with his hand. She was alive. She hadn't died. Relief flooded him. He stopped himself from hugging her. His cheeks warmed. As much as he wanted to, he didn't want to imply something.

She was staring into his eyes. Her white eyes that once scared him now looked concerned. He'd do everything he could to keep her safe.

He mumbled, "I'm all right," and stood.

Vaysa gave Teo room but watched him as he righted himself.

His hands trembled as he brushed his clothes of dust and smoothed his hair and face.

She walked behind him, hovering, but they were both stopped when Gren's screams filled the tunnel.

He had drawn his sword and swung wildly at the ice. Small chips flicked off. His face turned red, and tears streamed down his face.

Chapter 44

VAYSA

Vaysa had reacted without thinking, her mind still reeling from the interaction with Zara.

The others hadn't noticed, but Zara had. Vaysa had heard the voice again.

She saw images of a foreign land. A castle. But they were ripped into blankness. Then a hiss.

She flinched when her mother's voice called to her from inside the ice, but then another voice drifted in her head, overpowering her mother's voice. It was the voice from the dream again. The air tightened around her in the same smothering fashion as in her dream and the voice called to her again, quieting all other sounds. Then harsh silence.

Gren screamed again.

She rushed to Gren and grabbed his arm. A jolt shot through her and then she heard the same deafening hiss. Blackness surrounded her, and then with a blinding flash, she found herself in a forest clearing.

It was the Silver Forest. The trees' bark was almost metallic. She squinted slightly, but the sight enamored her.

There were dozens if not hundreds of people who looked like Gren. They all had shocking blue skin and green hair. Their eyes varied from pink to deep red like Gren's.

Her gaze was forced up from the crowds. She wasn't in control of the image.

She took a breath and just paused. Faint whispers skimmed her ears. Like a lost thought.

It was Gren's voice. She gasped. She was in Gren's memories. She tried to close her eyes to make it stop, but the images remained. She had no choice. Eyes open or closed, the images flashed along.

Next was the image of an older man and woman. They looked eerily similar to Gren. The man had his same smirk, and the woman had his fiery red eyes and intense stare. They had to be Gren's parents. An odd emotion stirred in her stomach. It bordered on love, but there was more. Pride. Resentment. Longing.

Next, his family was having a feast. A celebration of sorts.

The people wore long black flowing garments made of a plush material. Intricate golden embroidered designs wove around the dress. Brilliantly polished gems were sprinkled throughout the elegant stitching and hung from their ears, necks, and wrists in cascades of colors. They threaded the same jewels in their hair. Each person wore a colored sash. Both of Gren's parents wore red sashes. The base material was covered in gems, red embroidery, and crimson flowers.

She looked to see if others wore the red colors, assuming it meant he was Gren of the Red-Water house, but felt a tightening and realized the voice was by her.

"You shouldn't be here," the voice said.

"How do I leave?" Vaysa asked.

"You can't once the images start."

"Then why are you here?"

"Do you pity him?" the voice asked.

"Why would I?"

"You are watching his most hated memory."

"Why? His family is celebrating," Vaysa said skeptically.

The voice laughed mockingly. "It is the anniversary of King Russom's monarchy being dismantled."

"Then he should be happy," Vaysa said, but dread pooled in her stomach. She blinked and realized it wasn't her own dread. She was feeling Gren's reaction to the memory.

"He should. The Traitor's promised a new government. Each region would be responsible for itself. His family was leading the charge to bring back the Silver monarchy."

"But Gren's family was..." Vaysa's eyes bulged.

Oh, no.

Her own dread crept up her throat. She tried to turn her head, to close her eyes, but she couldn't stop the image from playing before her.

Soldiers from both Russom's overthrown army and Kennard's Royal Guard and Sentinels rushed in, swarming the clearing. The Royal Guards wore the same green uniforms. She assumed the yellow uniforms belonged to Russom's army.

"They're working together?" Vaysa choked. Fire licked at her nerves and pulsed through her veins.

"Kennard benefited from King Russom's reign."

"But..."

"The Royal Guard and Sentinels came to support the fallen army."

"You mean to claim the land for King Malik?"

The voice laughed. "You know them well."

Nausea crept up her throat as she watched Gren's mother and father fall, necks slit, their lifeless bodies covered in a pool of blood.

The panicked people broke into chaos. They were fleeing, but they ran into guards and their swords. Hatred welled inside of her and burned her veins.

Gren jumped into the trees to hide. The carnage beneath was too much. His desire to escape flooded through her.

Beside his parents, his friends, council leaders, and civilians spread around in death. Their blood leached into the ground, darkening the soil and dulling the silver bark of the trees.

His fear and self-admonition curled in her stomach, and she

gasped for air. He felt like a coward. The bitter taste of hatred flooded her mouth.

Obligation and loyalty welled within her. His desire to avenge his family.

A whirl of images flashed by. Vaysa was disoriented seeing the foreign lands until she saw the Spirit Strait. It was odd to see it from an ocean vessel. Then, Kennard. Some faces she didn't recognize. All human. Then she saw Closs and her own rage bubbled to the surface. All she felt from Gren was a cold, dark emptiness.

There was a flash and then the campfire. The pique of curiosity when he met Vaysa. It was so odd to see it through his eyes. There was only fear when Shad flashed into focus. Primitive, uncontrolled fear that swarmed with anger.

Hope replaced the empty sensation. She brought hope to Gren? How was that possible?

Before she could think more about it, the image swirled and morphed again to the Phantom Islands. Shad carried Teo to the campsite. When Vaysa had been there, she'd felt anger and annoyance seeing a Royal Guard following them. Through Gren's eyes, she felt a mix of disbelief, anger, and something else

The next image was the horrid Sea Swamps and the welcoming signs of the Silver Forests. Gren wanted to go home, longed for it, but he couldn't. Not yet. A momentary pang of sympathy gripped her heart.

Quickly, she felt his emotions swell at seeing the thief. Anger. Sadness. Sense of responsibility. One of his species was reduced to crime.

She saw the thief's hatred mirrored in his eyes and felt Gren's shame.

Her arm suddenly ached and her hands throbbed. She looked around and realized she was feeling his pain. His physical pain.

A voice tugged at her, and she turned, expecting to see another horrific scene from his past.

Instead, Solon stood near him. "Gren, snap out of it!"

Vaysa jumped back and, looking around, realized she was back in the cave with Gren. She stared at him, open-mouthed.

"Vaysa," the voice hissed. "What you saw was not for you."

"What?" she whispered.

"You cannot speak of the images you saw. They were not for you."

Vaysa shook her head. She didn't know what to think of it, anyway. How could she explain she was in his head? His memories? She didn't believe it herself.

Chapter 45

VAYSA

The group continued, and after a couple of hours the ice started to dissipate, and small patches of wet rock covered the walls instead.

"Are we walking uphill?" Teo asked, kicking a rock to watch its trajectory.

"I think so," Gren said and leaned forward. He'd been silent since the ice and his gaze distant.

"How much longer do you think we have?" Teo asked, glancing at the cart.

"Days," Gren responded.

"Really?" Teo asked, pausing mid-step.

"No," Gren said. He waited until Teo looked at him and said, "Probably more like weeks."

Teo gave him a rude hand gesture.

"How far are we from Monoc?" Vaysa asked. Time had no meaning in the caves. It was an endless rocky path.

"We can go back," Solon offered.

Vaysa rolled her eyes, and Shad gave Solon a dark look.

"Couple days," Zara said and sent a withering look to Gren and Teo.

"Wait," Shad growled. The group fell silent and stopped. Shad sniffed the air and crept forward. She left for a few minutes and then came back frowning.

"We have visitors. Royal Guard are ahead," Shad said. "I also smell rain."

Vaysa growled. They couldn't have gotten around them in the tunnel, so they had to be close to an exit. They were going to have to face them again. Vaysa rubbed the healed injury on her abdomen. The phantom curl of pain twinged her stomach and made her grimace.

"How?" Gren asked.

"They probably went over the mountains and got trapped by the storm," Zara said.

"That means we are close to an exit," Teo said, relieved.

"That means we probably have another battle on our hands," Solon said.

"How many?" Zara asked.

"It's a small group. Looks like a scouting unit," Shad said.

"Is there a chance there's more hiding?" Vaysa asked with a glimmer of hope they'd not be injured in this attack.

Shad shrugged. "I didn't see or hear more."

"We're in a long corridor without hiding spots," Zara said. "We don't have a tactical advantage other than surprise."

Despite the acid in her stomach, Vaysa turned to Teo. "I know what you said in Monoc, but with time you may have reconsidered. You could join them."

Teo's jaw ticked. His eyes narrowed. "No."

Relief and something else twisted in her gut. She nodded and blinked. The cramped corridors were getting to her.

"Then let's get this done," Vaysa said. Waiting only meant worrying and provided a chance for the Royal Guard to find them.

Shad sketched in the dirt where the soldiers were. There was no way to sneak by them with the livestock and cart. The plan was simple: send a distraction and run.

The cart would be the distraction. The maris were better equipped to pull the cart while fleeing than the horses on the rocky terrain. Vaysa would ride a horse despite her protests. Gren and Teo rode on the other horse led by Shad. Solon and Zara would ride past the soldiers on the cart and draw them away from the entrance.

Vaysa steadied herself on the horse and patted its neck. She closed her eyes and let out a breath, steeling her resolve.

"Vaysa," Teo whispered.

She slid her gaze his way.

He held her eye contact a moment too long and color stained his cheeks before saying, "I know I've said a lot of things."

Vaysa snorted in agreement.

His gaze fell to his hands. "I don't know what will happen, or what the future holds long term, but I can't go back to the Royal Guard knowing what they've done."

She nodded not knowing what to say. He could change his mind again.

"That's nice, but focus you two," Shad mumbled.

When Solon and Zara gave the cue and started arguing loudly, Vaysa urged her horse forward. She gritted her teeth against the choppy gait but held the reins firmly.

Yells of surprise and the sound of running echoed down the tunnel.

The Royal Guards had taken the bait.

Rounding a curve, dim light of the outdoors spilled across the entryway. Vaysa blinked and shielded her eyes from the brightness. They'd found a way out.

"Wait," Shad gritted out when Vaysa and the others started to go through the soldiers' campsite.

Vaysa turned to Shad as the tunnels erupted with screams of terror.

The group drew their weapons and braced for attack. The soldiers came running back through, followed by the maris-pulled cart with toothy beasts attached to it, but the soldiers, in their confusion, didn't notice the four figures standing dumbfounded in their camp as they tore out of the cave and into the storm.

Vaysa, with the other three, galloped out of the cave. The soldiers stumbled down the path. Vaysa turned to the cave.

The toothy beasts swarmed the cart in a dark sea. Their sharp claws gouged the cart, and one jumped onto Solon's back.

Zara grabbed it by its neck and chucked it back into the darkness.

Two jumped toward Vaysa and she slashed her sword at them, slicing them in half. More came howling from the cave and leapt on the group.

Gren and Teo went back-to-back, and Shad jumped in front of them all. She roared into the cave. The beasts went silent and then filled the cave with shrill shrieks.

Vaysa focused on the heat stirring in her core and creeping down her arms and into her palms. A flash of fire popped, and a small fireball shot from her hand. The dismal display shot into the cave and sparks flew around harmlessly.

Teo gave her a sympathetic half-smile, which only infuriated her. She growled and drew on her power again. Before she could form another fireball, the sky lit up with a crackle of lightning, and thunder deafened all sound.

The toothy creatures clambered back into the tunnel, trampling each other to return to the dark haven as the sky split open in a downpour.

"That was awesome," Teo said and shielded his head.

"We didn't miss the storm," Vaysa said as she stared at the vacant path the soldiers had taken.

Gren pushed his hair from his face and cleared his throat to get Vaysa and Teo's attention. He nodded toward the dry cave. The two went back into the cave the guards had used for a campsite. Gren gave a last look down the trail and joined them.

"They'll be back with more soldiers and weapons," Solon said. He rubbed a hand over his face to wipe the rain away.

"It'll take them a while. We should leave in the dark so they don't see us," Zara said.

"Isn't that more dangerous?" Teo asked. He slumped against the wall.

"Trail-wise, yes. Avoiding Royal Guard-wise, no."

"They're more afraid of the monsters than the storm," Vaysa said. Understandable. She'd much rather face the elements than venture back into the tunnels.

"I guess we get some free provisions," Gren said as he pawed through the food.

In their haste the soldiers had left several sacks of food, some bedrolls, and pamphlets of creatures.

"Are these the pamphlets you were talking about?" Vaysa asked Teo, picking up several of them.

"Yeah," Teo said.

The pamphlets were hand-sketched and included various Berlan creatures, including the ones they had encountered.

"Those nasty teeth things are Jaw Crackers," Teo read and shuddered. "They hunt in packs. They rip flesh off of living or dead prey. They can chew through bone. What do you think is missing from it?"

"The smell," Shad and Teo said together.

Vaysa grabbed a different one. "The spider thing is a Barbed Spider. The legs have barbs that leave an itchy poison that can cause hallucinations."

Gren and Teo looked at it with her. Gren said, "It doesn't come close to stating how large it is."

"Oh, Alice is an Ice Cave Goliath Vole, or giant vole. She eats a variety of plants and insects and small prey. They reached the size of a large dog! How are we going to feed her?" Teo asked, looking at Zara.

Zara smiled and rolled her eyes. "We've got time for her to grow."

Shad laughed when she read the poster for Cumas out loud. "'Considered extremely dangerous, the animals were once hunted almost to extinction, but the crusade failed when the Traitors took over.' Also listed are various weapons that could bring us down. Included under 'additional facts' is that we can't be reasoned with, and that we only seek food."

"Hey Gren, here's one about you." Teo laughed as he read about the Silvers.

Vaysa leaned over and read it. "According to the poster, you are gluttonous humanoids that prefer celebrations and squandered resources. It doesn't say you can see in the dark," she said, looking up to Gren.

Gren's eyes narrowed and shot to Shad. "Not everyone knows that."

Solon laughed at the Monocian poster. "It just shows a dark figure burning trees and spearing faceless people. It says we can control fire and use it to destroy human creations. We're secretive and untrustworthy."

Zara said, "There's enough truth in the posters to make the rest seem reliable."

Vaysa picked up a poster in the pile. It was the same one that they'd seen tacked up at the fort listing all of them. In the margins, they'd written, "Spotted going into Monoc."

She looked at Shad, who was laughing at another poster with Zara. The Royal Guard was still looking for them. They'd known when they were at Zara's. They'd known they were in Monoc. They'd tried to invade Monoc. They'd been in the caves. They were everywhere.

Chapter 46

VAYSA

Vaysa stretched and ran a hand over her stomach. It no longer hurt, but the scar's ridge was still noticeable. So far, she'd been injured more severely in the past few weeks than in all the years she lived in Kennard. And yet, she continued to follow Zara's silhouette down the trail in the sliver of moonlight.

A pulse of fire coursed through her but ebbed when she constricted her fingers into a fist. It was the most control she'd had on her own, but it felt diminutive. Unnatural. She was suppressing the powers instead of learning them. But Monoc hadn't helped with it either. She'd just learned anger sparked a reaction. It wasn't less dangerous than not knowing, because all annoyance made her flinch to keep control.

They were moving at night to avoid the Royal Guard. The cold wind bit at Vaysa's face and she nestled into her jacket. She glanced into the dark horizon. The storm rumbled above the valley, blocking most of the moonlight. Large masses were visible in all directions.

She couldn't fathom how one person thought they could control all of it. And yet, armies were invading to find the prince. Hopefully they'd find him soon and leave or the Traitors would just force them out. They'd done it before.

They trekked through the night. The slow pace became unnerving, and Vaysa just wanted to find cover and relief from Gren and Teo's quarreling. Finally, she had enough when the first cracks of dawn sliced the horizon. As the morning came, dull gray light streaked through the storm, bringing color and distinction to the land features in the distance. The dismal light meant they'd be easier to spot.

"We need a campsite," Vaysa said to Solon as she scanned the trail.

Solon stopped and disappeared into a cave and then reappeared only to go further down into another.

Vaysa watched him go. He said nothing, nor did he look back at her. He had not spoken to her directly since they argued about Monoc.

She understood why he wanted her to go back to Monoc; she needed rest. They all did. But while her powers were growing, her control wasn't. She couldn't destroy Monoc just to stay away from the Royal Guard.

He finally emerged from one and motioned for them to join him. The cave was damp, and the floor was muddy from the pounding rains. Vaysa grimaced. Despite the cold, the tunnels had been dry and more stone than dirt. The smell of wet fur and excrement filled the small area. Vaysa held back a protest.

The others piled in with the same disdain on their faces.

Shad gagged and returned outside. She filled buckets from the cart with rainwater.

Vaysa made a base with rocks and started a small blue fire. The roof's moisture steamed, and the smells intensified. Vaysa ignored the groans of the others and made the fire bigger.

Gren cooked up some food they had confiscated. The aroma did nothing to block the mustiness.

The damp corridors made sleeping uncomfortable, so they crammed into the wagon to avoid the mud. Vaysa couldn't get comfortable and took guard at the cave's opening with Shad. The stormy air was refreshing from the foul, dank air of the cave.

Zara and Alice rested on the back rocks, where Zara angled herself and drifted off.

Vaysa surveyed around the opening. Solon had chosen a good tactical spot. The cave was small and had plenty of brush for cover. The curve of the mountain blocked the previous cave but had a good open view of the trail they took. She could spot any travelers from a far distance. She also had a good view of the valley.

"Where are we?" Vaysa asked, staring into the darkness.

"We're past the trees of the south. We're probably bordering the Drylands."

"Is that good?"

Shad snorted. "Anywhere not an Ice Cave is good."

"Is it safe?"

Shad's eyes flashed and she took a big breath. "I don't think any place is really safe right now. Not with the Royal Guard here."

A streak of blue lightning tore across the sky, veining through the clouds and flooding the barren land below in light. After a second burst, the valley was flooded in darkness again.

Vaysa groaned inwardly. There were no trees in sight. There would be no place to hide. Hopefully the cliffs would have better cover.

Vaysa shifted toward Shad, "We made it through the Ice Caves. Is the rest of the group separating now?"

Vaysa swallowed the lump in her throat and rested her elbow on her knee and her chin on her fist.

Shad's gaze slid to Vaysa and then back into the cave. She rubbed her forehead and closed her eyes. "I don't think so."

"Why?" Vaysa asked, sitting up. "Zara said..."

Shad slid an arm around Vaysa's shoulders and drew her to her side.

"Is this when you tell me all the secrets you've been keeping from me?"

Shad chuckled and pressed Vaysa closer. "No, it's not."

Vaysa growled, but Shad rocked slightly with her.

"Right now, not knowing is safer."

"How?"

"Because you'll run in sword drawn, fists blazing."

"So it's bad. Tell me."

"Vaysa," Shad sighed. "Right now, the absolute most important thing we can do is get you a dragon scale."

"What am I, then?"

Shad sat stiffly and quietly.

"Shad?" When Shad didn't respond, Vaysa added, "Closs thinks he knows what I am. You keep saying elemental wielder, but Monoc is full of them and Closs doesn't care. How can he know and you don't?"

Shad laughed humorlessly.

"You thought I'd miss that?"

Shad laughed again. "Zara's going with us to Gillons."

Vaysa pulled back and stared at Shad. "Really?"

"Yea."

"I thought she needed to sell her goods and check on things."

Shad shrugged. "She can get us there the fastest."

"I thought we were going through the Cliffs."

"We were when it was the two of us. She'll avoid the Cliffs. There're towns there she doesn't like. That means going way south or crossing the Drylands. Due to timing and safety, she'll risk the openness of the Drylands to get us there quicker."

Vaysa's gaze flicked to the Drylands, covered in unyielding darkness. There was nothing to protect them out there.

"Is it wise to bring them all with us?" Vaysa asked. Shad wanted to watch them because they knew about the dragon scale, but what would it really matter with a war going on? Who would believe it or really know where to go especially as it was considered an inhospitable wasteland.

"Not at all."

"They could go with Solon over the mountain back to Monoc. They'd be safer there than trekking into the unknown swarming with the Royal Guard."

"That is true."

"But you're letting them come with us?"

Shad cut her eyes to Vaysa. "Wouldn't you bring them anyway if they want to come?"

Vaysa chuckled.

"Solon can help you with your powers."

"What?" Vaysa spat. A spike of anger tore through her veins. Heat rose in her fingers, willing her to let it out. "You said he couldn't when we landed in Berla! And he was too nice in Monoc."

"You didn't have any control then. You have some now. He can help." Shad cast a look at her hands. A sigh lifted her frame, but she didn't comment.

"No he can't. We have different powers." She curled her fingers to control the welling power.

"Maybe, but he was trying too hard to be nice to you. He was able to help redirect your powers when you flared."

"Hey!"

"Vaysa, promise me you'll try to work with him."

Vaysa stared at Shad. Shad met her eyes, but her gaze was guarded and pained. Too many secrets and partial truths filled the space. Too many things to protect her and her powers. When the intensity of the heat finally receded, she eased back, her own breath unsteady from the strain to control the powers. Even she could see the reasons Shad kept the truth from her, despite how much it hurt.

"Tell me something first. A secret you've kept from me," Vaysa wagered.

"I know you heard my conversation with Zara about the Water Witch."

Vaysa sucked her teeth with her tongue and shrugged.

"You know we were a part of the coup. We rescued Yala the Water Witch, but we couldn't protect everyone."

"Yea, Solon was captured, and Zara's husband was killed."

Shad nodded. "Closs is the one who caught Solon."

"What?" Vaysa sputtered. "He came after the coup? But... is that how he knows my powers?"

Shad closed her eyes and nodded. Vaysa watched her. She wasn't saying something, but there were a lot of things she'd left out.

"Shad," Vaysa started.

Shad shook her head and said, "I don't care what it takes. I'll keep you safe."

THE STORM MADE it dark long before sunset, which provided additional traveling time. Shad had mapped out a descent plan while studying the terrain. She explained it to Solon, who nodded in agreement.

Vaysa watched the three older Berlans discuss the plan. They were good people, but her heart still tightened. She was reminded again of how little she knew of Shad's past, but it was obvious Shad didn't just hate Closs but feared him. And Vaysa had caught his attention. Separating from the others at the base with Shad would be logical, but they already knew where they were heading and having the extra support would be nice.

Vaysa hugged herself and leaned against the rocky surface. Her gaze drifted from the three to Teo and Gren. Gren's red eyes flicked to her. A tight smile tugged on his lips. She nodded and gave a weak smile back. Their familiarity was growing on her. It almost felt normal to be with them.

Teo ran a hand through his black hair. His expression was a mixture of sadness and hope. She caught him watching her and raised an eyebrow. He grinned at her, showing his white teeth. She couldn't stop herself from grinning back or the twist in her stomach.

Teo cleared his throat and, looking to Gren, asked, "Have you been here before?"

Gren watched Teo for a moment and then allowed his gaze to take in the rain-soaked path and the grayness that masked the land features beyond. Finally, he returned his gaze to Teo. "Not the Ice Caves. No one really wants to go through them."

"And..." Teo said, gesturing his arm widely to cover the horizon.

"Parts."

Teo rolled his eyes and narrowed his eyes on Gren. "Care to elaborate?"

Gren sighed. "I've been to parts of the Mosa River, but not all of that," he said, mocking Teo's gesture.

"You—" Teo started, but Solon stepped between the two of them.

"Let's move," Solon said, leaving no room for argument. He waited until Teo and Gren broke their glare and started down the path.

Shad shook her head, and Zara cracked a grin. Vaysa fell into step beside Shad. She patted her friend's shoulder. Bowing her head, she let her hair fall to block her smile. Some things never changed.

Chapter 47

CLOSS

Captain Closs watched as a group of soldiers clumsily descended the rocky terrain. They were drenched and had none of their supplies except for their swords. They weren't even in their entire uniforms.

He glared at them and noticed Ben approach the men. Anger twisted his features as he dealt with their incompetence. Closs knew he had raised him well. He had saved him from a life in Berla.

Ben clenched his fists and rigidly turned to Captain Closs. He pinched his lips tightly, and his mouth scrunched up to his nose. He stormed over to Closs. "A cart ambushed them in the caves. One was a Monocian. The other was a brunette woman."

It had to be them. No one willingly traveled in the tunnels. Only someone desperate would risk them. Even the Berlans were afraid of the hellish maze.

A dark smile passed quickly over his lips. They'd left the safety of Monoc.

Closs saw the shuffle of one of his messengers hiding in the corner. He slightly shook his head, sending him away. He already knew.

Soon the girl would be his.

Chapter 48

VAYSA

The Drylands weren't dry. Large pools of water covered the sandy land. The storm had soaked the sands, making it mushy and hard to travel on. Looking across the dunes, there was little cover once they left the mountain base.

The storm was finally easing after the three days it took to trek down the rest of the mountain to the hilly base, which meant the lands would likely be easier to traverse, but then it also meant it was easier for the Royal Guard, too.

Vaysa groaned as the rocky trail gave way to crumbling pebbles and sand and she slid on the loose ground. At least they'd finally be off the trail and have more space.

"Let's rest up and evaluate the conditions, I know everyone is tired and crabby," Zara said, breaking the silence. She pointed to a cave that had some shrubbery cover.

The others nodded.

Solon volunteered to check the connecting tunnels. If they had enough of an incline for water to run, they might stay dry.

Teo and Gren were silent as they leaned against the entrance. Vaysa noticed their shared glares. She rolled her eyes but appreciated the silence. Shad patted Vaysa's shoulder and then started to tug the cart into the cave's entrance but stopped when the standing water from the runoff pooled a few feet inside the cave.

"This isn't good," Teo said, staring at the pungent water.

"Not many options," Shad said and gave another pull. "We have to get out of sight."

"The water will be disease filled," Gren said.

"Worried about another fever?" Teo asked.

Gren gave Teo a withering look and a rude hand gesture.

"Enough you two," Shad said.

Both fell silent.

"Found a dry one," Solon said, emerging from the cave's recess. His gaze swept over the group, and he sighed loudly.

Zara smiled cheerfully. After looking sternly at each person individually, she said, "There's dry land inside, and the water will provide more protection. Get a move on."

It took all six tugging and coaxing to get the cart through the murky water and into the tunnel.

"I'll get clean water," Solon said and headed back out.

"I'll help," Vaysa said, desperate for another breath of fresh air.

She trailed behind Solon and helped bring in several buckets of rainwater. They boiled gallons of water to wash everything that had been through the stagnant water.

When they turned at the same time, Vaysa sucked in a breath. He'd been silent other than redirecting her. Try to get her to go back to Monoc. Now it sat, heavy and oppressive between them, devouring the air.

Even though she had questions bubbling up about Shad, the war, his willingness to leave his home, she let the silence remain between them. She was no privier to his past than he was to hers. He approved of nothing she'd done so far.

After bathing, Vaysa eased onto her bedroll. The warm, dry blankets from the cart were welcoming. She sighed, allowing herself to enjoy the simple moment.

SHE STARTED a fire in her hand and lit some brush on fire to start breakfast as she watched Zara leave the tunnel. She stretched and followed her through the caverns outside to offer her help to bring in fresh water.

She grimaced at the brightness of the sun and shielded her eyes. The storm had dissipated, and the water receded in the heavy heat of the Drylands.

Vaysa stopped when she realized Zara was talking to the shadows. She bowed her head and returned to the cave, not wanting to interrupt her private moment.

Zara came back in, a smile lighting her face up. Vaysa recognized the slight pinch of Zara's mouth to the right. It was a forced smile.

As they ate, Vaysa asked, "Are we still headed for Gillons?"

She bit back a curse when the three shared a look.

Teo caught her eye, and he rolled his eyes and gestured to the three older Berlans. Vaysa rolled her lips between her teeth to hide her smile.

"Wait!" Gren turned toward Zara, his eyes bright with fear. "Is that where we're headed? Gillons, not just the mountains in the peninsula?"

Zara nodded but focused on the shadows.

"You're from Gillons?" Gren's brow pinched as he stared at her.

"No."

Vaysa didn't correct the lie.

When Zara didn't continue, Gren flicked his confused gaze at Vaysa.

"Aren't the dragon scales from there?" Vaysa asked, steeling her expression.

With a frown, he let it drop. "I guess. How, though? Through the Cliffs?"

Zara snorted and glared at Gren. "We'll cross the Drylands."

"How are we going to find cover?" He gulped.

Zara growled.

Gren averted his eyes.

Vaysa chuckled to herself. At least he feared Zara enough to not push her.

"Gillons," Teo said. "That's one of the dangerous 'do-not-enter' zones in the pamphlets."

"Good," Zara said.

"Is it mentioned in your grandma's book?" Gren asked Teo, smiling.

Teo narrowed his eyes. "There weren't places listed, at least not in the pages that remained, but besides, her book is a book of tales."

"How many pages were in your book?" Vaysa asked.

"About a dozen or so remain but it had hundreds at one time according to my grandma."

"What else was in the book besides the poems?" Zara asked, leaning in.

"I don't know what all was there originally, but after the poem were short write-ups of different heroes and villains."

"Heroes and villains?" Zara prodded.

"There were poems for different ones."

"Were they illustrated?"

Teo looked up for a moment, and then said, "There were some, but it was mostly lands and some people. They were pretty worn down."

Zara nodded and smiled at him, but it didn't meet her eyes. Her eyes darted to the shadows before returning to Teo. "What are some of the heroes you remember?"

"Prowlers, night-watchers, cliff-climbers, and lava warriors," Teo said, his voice hitching. His gaze darted up the mountain. Guilt washed over his face, and he took a rugged breath. "If it wasn't for the Ash Fields, you'd already be in Gillons."

"We're all here because I lost control," Vaysa said.

"Your powers never should have materialized in Kennard," Zara said. "There is no blame. Your guilt will devour you and distort reality."

Vaysa snorted.

"If I hadn't freaked out before Monoc, I wouldn't have been bound and then you wouldn't have been—" Teo's voice broke.

"They would have attacked anyway," Vaysa said.

"But I could have helped."

"I'm sure you'll have more opportunities to help against the Royal Guard or whatever else Berla throws at us like the ants and spiders," Vaysa said. She offered Teo a wry smile. "No way we don't see something again."

He snorted in agreement. "We're like beacons to attacks."

"At least you're not on the wanted poster," Vaysa said.

"Only because they don't care if I'm alive. I'm just collateral damage in getting Gren back."

"They're not getting any of us alive," Vaysa said. "We'll go down fighting."

Gren made a throaty sound.

Vaysa looked up to find the older Berlans watching her. Sad agreement dimmed Shad, Solon, and Zara's faces. They'd fight to the end.

Determination stamped Teo's face as he stared at her.

"So how will we get across the Drylands?" Gren asked.

Solon made a raspy growl and crossed his arms over his chest.

Shad passed Solon a dark look and shook her head. Solon's jaw ticked and his nose flared, but he said nothing.

"I have some nomadic friends from the Drylands," Zara said. "We could probably stay with them for a night."

Vaysa swallowed. They'd be one step closer to a dragon scale, but more people would be at risk of her powers going awry.

Chapter 49

VAYSA

The group left as night fell. Calm air settled after the storm had passed. Stars and a full moon brightened the sky. Without the sun beating down on them, the desert air left goose-bumps on their skin.

Vaysa ignored the tension growing in her stomach. The group was silent, the uncertainty of what lay ahead wearing them down, too.

Shad laid an arm around her shoulders and squeezed. Vaysa leaned into her and let out a breath. She let Shad's warmth seep into her and calm her nerves.

"Get out of your head and be ready for what we will face," Shad murmured into Vaysa's hair.

Vaysa nodded and took a deep breath. She needed to focus.

They walked through the night until Alice started to squirm and squeak.

"Does she want to go back?" Solon asked, looking between Zara and the mountain range.

"We're too far," Zara said, worry pitching her words.

Alice continued fidgeting as they walked on. Her claws left lines on Zara's arms, and her nose twitched in agitation. Zara finally put her on the ground.

Alice ran in circles, trying to burrow in the sand. Her strong legs pounded, but each inch dug filled in with sand. Zara reached for Alice again but paused when the horses and maris started prancing. Zara swore and grasped her sword. Vaysa instinctively grabbed for her sword, too.

A gust of wind blew sand in her face, and she braced against the force. A black shadow blocked the moonlight, throwing them into darkness. A squawk filled the air and shook the ground.

"Get down!" Shad yelled and shoved Vaysa to the ground, covering her with her body.

Vaysa couldn't see anything around Shad, but Zara's panicked voice filled the air, sending fear rippling through her.

"Alice!" Zara yelled.

"Move," Shad roared. She scrambled to the top of the cart and soared off.

Vaysa sat up and looked around. A massive bird blocked the sky with Alice in its talon, and Shad was scrambling for both of them.

Vaysa cursed and stared helplessly. Shad slashed with her claws and caught the fleshy part by the bird's talon. The bird shrieked in pain and snatched Shad from the air.

Shad smiled triumphantly as it pulled her upward.

Fireballs sprang in Vaysa's palm without her trying. Her blood pounded in her ears. She needed to protect Shad. Her breath caught in her chest as she watched Shad struggle for air as the bird's grip tightened, and with each breath it squeezed her tighter.

Shad's eyes flashed and glowed gold.

Using her enormous size, Shad twisted until her legs could touch the bird. She dug her claws deep into the bird. It screeched again and dropped Shad.

Shad sprang into action. Shad grabbed and swung around the talon and launched herself onto the bird's leg. She dug in with her claws to keep from falling. The bird screeched and clawed at her.

Alice, who the bird dropped, was free falling. Shad released herself from the bird and dove for the vole. Snatching her gently with her claws, Shad rolled Alice against her chest.

The air current changed, and the bird swooped back toward Shad and Alice.

Shad balled herself up, with Alice cradled on her stomach. Talons snapped at her, and she grabbed at the extended talon and again flung herself toward the bird's body to hang on.

Shad climbed the bird, making long gashes up its leg. The pain caused the bird to soar higher.

Shad grabbed two long body feathers while holding Alice in her feet, and her weight pulled them out. She let herself fall with the feathers in hand. She held them in an arch over her head. Her arms barely covered the span of the huge feathers, and she used the feathers to glide toward the ground.

The bird squawked noisily in the sky but did not go after Shad again.

Shad landed roughly on top of the cart. She heaved and went limp. Alice lay next to her.

Vaysa stared in disbelief at Shad. Scolds swirled on her tongue, a reprimand for being reckless, but stayed. She'd have gone after Alice, too.

Zara climbed up and looked at both of them. She was smiling and tears of relief streamed down her face.

"Thank you, Shad!"

"She did her job warning us. Next time, I eat her."

Zara smiled at her friend, likely knowing she wouldn't eat Alice.

Shad righted herself and jumped off the cart.

"Let's get moving," Shad said. "Who knows who's out here."

Before the group could move on, the ground rumbled momentarily.

"What the?" Teo asked, staring at the ground. "Did it just move?"

"Jards," Zara said.

The others stared at her.

"What is it?" Vaysa asked. Dread pooled in her stomach.

"Someone's using the tunnels."

"What tunnels?" Vaysa asked.

"The underground tunnels are real?" Gren asked, staring at the ground.

"Move!" Zara yelled and urged the maris forward.

A loud roar deafened the night. A large creature fluttered in the air and landed in front of the cart. It made a strangled cawing noise showing its gaping beak that had rows of razor-sharp teeth.

"Get back," Shad ordered and thrust Vaysa behind her.

"No!" Vaysa roared and fire shot toward the creature. It hit squarely, causing the creature to stumble backwards.

Zara hopped from the cart and drew her sword.

Two cloaked figures hidden on the creature's back appeared in front of it. It screeched and flew into the air.

"You shouldn't have done that," one hissed. Their accent was scratchy.

Vaysa took ragged breaths but didn't back down. Another fireball materialized in her hand.

"Mercers," Gren breathed. His voice tinged with awe.

"What do you want?" Solon said. He flicked his hand and a blue shield of fire, like the Monocian cell fire, appeared around the group.

"Zara," the one hissed again.

"You can't have her," Shad said.

They tilted their heads in unison.

"Get back," Shad said, gesturing to the group without looking at them.

The Mercers let out a hollow whistle. The sand around Zara rumbled, and she started to sink.

"No!" Shad said and dove for Zara. She wrenched her from the sand and tossed her backwards.

The sand chasm pulled Shad to her knees and inched higher. Shad clawed at the ground but was pulled further below.

"NO!" Vaysa screamed. Her fear blinded her and tunneled her vision. She couldn't lose Shad. Shad was everything. Shad was her life.

Her mind ebbed, and the lull of darkness pulled at her. Whispers surrounded her, some in a language she didn't know but understood.

Power welled within her. Power that was hers. Power that wanted to be released. Power that promised to end the nightmare.

She let it out. She bellowed into the air. Her hands clutched invisible orbs, and she sank to her knees in the sand. A wave of fire spiraled out from her hands, disintegrating Solon's shields, flattening the Mercer's, and brightening the desert momentarily before flickering out over the sand.

"Vaysa, get the others to safety," Shad yelled but the creature with the Mercers screeched and then dove for Shad, and together they disappeared into the sand.

Chapter 50

VAYSA

"Shad!" Vaysa screamed and ran for the spot that had swallowed her.

"Vaysa, no," Zara said and ran after her. "It's too late."

Vaysa didn't listen. Tears blurred her vision, and the sand cut at her hands as she tried to dig.

Zara yanked at Vaysa's hand, but Vaysa pushed her back.

"I have to help her! It's my fault the thing got her." A pulse of heat coursed through her body, threatening to push forward.

Her powers, her stupid powers had done this. Losing homes was one thing, but now she'd lost Shad.

"Vaysa, stop!" Zara said. Her voice deepened and echoed. Her amber eyes glowed slightly, and she pulled Vaysa's arms up.

"What are you doing? Why aren't you helping?" A pop of fire shot from Vaysa's hand into the sand.

"They have her, you can't get to her the same way," Zara said. "You didn't do it. It would have gotten her through the sand, anyway."

"I don't care!" Vaysa roared and another wave of fire shot from her arms.

"Enough!" Zara yelled back. Her voice echoed, sending a chill down Vaysa's spine. "Shad is gone for now. We need to get everyone to safety."

Vaysa didn't care about the others' safety. She cared about Shad. Shad was as much a part of her life as breathing. Shad was the one who taught her how to hunt, how to scale trees, how to pickpocket from nobles sitting too close to the trees, and was the one she told stories to on the long winter nights.

She whirled around, her vision blurring as she stared at the endless sea of sand. There had to be an entrance somewhere in this Berlan hell hole.

"Vaysa," Zara said softly and touched her arms. "We need to get to Gillons, now."

Vaysa jerked but didn't pull her arm away. She finally looked into Zara's eyes and noticed Zara's unshed tears.

Her eyes darted over the rest of the group. Gren was staring at the downed Mercers while Solon restrained Teo from helping Vaysa.

These were people she cared about.

Vaysa said, her voice barely a whisper. "I need Shad."

"We'll find her," Zara whispered just to Vaysa.

"Vaysa, we'll figure it out," Teo said.

Vaysa blinked. The others needed her, too. Her heart was torn.

She needed to find Shad, but Shad hadn't left Solon or the others before. Vaysa hadn't, either.

"You killed two Mercers," Gren said in awe and looked approvingly at Vaysa.

"What's a Mercer?" Teo asked and yanked away from Solon.

"The Royal Guard didn't have a pamphlet?" Gren cocked an eyebrow.

Teo narrowed his eyes at Gren.

"They're not a monster class, but they'd be a villain in your grandma's book," Gren said.

Teo made a hand gesture.

"Well, what do you know about them then?" Vaysa demanded. "They took Shad."

Gren stepped back. He mumbled unintelligible words.

Zara said, "A sand being. They live in the south but can travel through the sand tunnels with the sandbirds. They're great hunters."

Teo shook his head. "Why do they want Shad?"

"She stopped them from getting Zara," Gren said. "Why do they want you?"

"We'll discuss it at the oasis. We can't be out here. Who knows what else will come looking for us.," Zara said.

"Like that?" Gren said as he pointed at large masses flying in the sky.

Giant birds were coming.

Zara swore. Pointing to the west, she yelled, "Move!"

Zara pulled Vaysa to her feet and jumped into the cart. Zara urged the maris into a wild gallop.

Solon tugged Vaysa into a sprint. The sand burned Vaysa's eyes and throat.

The birds' caws filled the air as they sped toward the horizon. She cared about none of it. She wanted to find Shad. She'd destroy any creature to find her.

Solon threw a blue fire orb above their heads. The sands and winds tore at them and the edge of the orb faltered. The strain to keep the hovering orb lit grayed his skin.

Vaysa glanced at the others. The fear that twisted her stomach was similar to the fear marring their faces, but now she didn't have Shad for comfort. Darkness blinded her for a second. Her fingers went cold, and hatred squeezed her heart. She blinked and pushed her anger into Solon's blue fire orb. It swelled and popped white before settling back to blue.

Brilliant gold lined the horizon, and the air ticked up in degrees. Dawn was coming, and so was the burning hot sun. She didn't notice the large cannon balls flying into the air until they came dangerously close. Large sprays of sand splashed over them.

A dark line loomed ahead of them as the sun peeked over the horizon, highlighting its uneven edge.

Zara slowed the cart, and the rest followed her. Zara yelled. "I know this camp. They'll help." Zara rushed to raise one of her blankets in the air. It was green and in the center was a triangle with circles for points. The rising sun shone off the gold emblem.

They advanced on the line. As they neared, the dark line gave way to distinct trees.

The perpetual aerial assault finally forced the birds to leave.

Vaysa and the group raced for the trees. The vibrant green vegetation stood in contrast to the barren sand dunes. Plush bushes with dark green leaves and lavender-colored berries grew at the bases of palm trees. The long pinnate leaves were bright green.

The oasis had a large watering hole and a small, nomadic village with maris moving about. Huts made from long, feathery leaves were tucked under the trees for protection.

Vaysa looked at the group. Sand coated them and stiffened their hair. Their eyes were red-rimmed and squinty, and their lips were cracked from the dryness.

A person emerged from a hut. He had a medium build, olive skin, and long tan hair. He wore long wispy robes with intricate copper bands running up his arms and around his neck, ending around his ears. He stood ramrod straight, and his dark brown eyes stared at the group curiously. The other villagers parted for him.

Vaysa looked at Zara for clues.

Zara whispered, "Chief Tikton."

Zara kept her eyes averted and lowered her head as he approached. Vaysa and the rest followed her lead, unsure of the village's customs.

The man made a raspy sound in his throat while making gestures toward the other villagers, then finally spoke to Zara, his voice gentle. "Zara, our friend, what trouble have you brought us?"

"We need rest."

"Why do you bring outsiders?"

Zara looked at her group and shrugged. "They're friends, and we are traveling together."

"Are you why there was Mercer activity?"

Zara shuffled nervously. "Yes."

"Do you know the western Traitors have questions for you?"

"I figured as much when the Mercers showed up."

Irritation fluttered in Vaysa's stomach, but she willed her anger down as a spike of heat coursed in her veins. The charade needed to end so they could find Shad.

Chief Tikton narrowed his eyes at Vaysa and turned back to Zara.

Zara looked at her knowingly and said, "We'll find her."

"Why do the western Traitors want you?" Solon asked, his voice soft but with an edge.

The others stared at her.

"They likely fear I'll go after the prince."

"No," Chief Tikton said. "They fear you'll kill him before he speaks."

"Zara?" Teo said. "Is that true?"

"Why would you kill him?" Solon asked. "Just give him back. He's useless."

"Later."

"No," Vaysa said, fire springing to her hands. "They took Shad because of this. Is this what you two were talking about at your compound?"

"What?" Solon asked.

Zara passed Vaysa a dark look and said, "Now is not the time. They won't hurt Shad. They'll use her as bait for me. I refused to meet with them and they're forcing my hand."

It was like Zara had punched her in the face. Shad had had a rich, complex life before their simple life in Kennard. Now she was bait? Vaysa's anger curled her toes, and she had to focus to keep it in check. Finally, she found her words. "So where is she then?"

"Likely, their strong point," Zara said and looked south.

"They're at the castle?" Gren asked.

"The Traitors have her at King Russom's old castle?" Teo asked. "With the prince?"

"Zara, what's going on?" Solon seethed.

"I'll get you guys to Gillons like Shad wanted and then fix this."

"No, I'm getting Shad," Vaysa said. "Now."

Zara stared at Vaysa and then Solon.

Solon arched an eyebrow.

Teo and Gren looked at each other and stepped toward Vaysa.

Zara sighed. "Fine, we'll leave at dusk."

Chapter 51

VAYSA

The chief agreed to harbor them for the day and night. In exchange, Zara gave him a sword for each of them, including the livestock as payment.

The village provided them with a place to wash up, generous helpings of food, and clean quarters to rest in. Young women in loose lavender robes with thickly braided tan hair came and put a salve on their lips and poured a cool liquid into their eyes.

Vaysa looked at the door of her hut and then the women. They had a few hours before night. Before she could leave to find Shad. Between the Royal Guard, the unknown Berlan threats and the heat, it wasn't wise to leave until later. With Zara leading them over familiar terrain, the cover of night would be safer.

Exhaustion from the morning slowed her movements, and Vaysa finally agreed the weary group should rest.

WHEN VAYSA AWOKE, she found the nomads had laid garments out for the group. The flimsy robes would help with the heat but would not provide protection from an attack.

She smiled, but it faltered when she imagined Shad seeing the garments. She tensed as fire sprang to her hands.

Shuffling at the entrance caught her attention, and in walked two women. They were shorter than everyone in the group and slender. Besides the light purple robes, they smelled of lavender. Their intricately-twisted tan hair framed their faces.

From Teo and Gren's sudden nervousness and breathing changes, Vaysa could guess that the women were very attractive. She rolled her eyes and pulled her jacket over her tunic and pants despite the heat.

Following behind the women was a young man also in robes. The top section of his long hair was pulled back and braided, running down his back. He smiled shyly at Vaysa and nodded at Gren and Teo.

Teo's expression darkened, but he stuck his hand out in greeting.

The man cleared his throat and stared uncertainly at Teo.

Gren stepped between them with a smirk. He bowed slightly and when the man bowed back, Gren winked at Teo.

Teo half-heartedly bowed.

The two women tugged at Vaysa's hand, and she quickly jerked back and turned defensively.

"I'm Rora and this is Trivala. We're here to help you; you'll get sick in those heavy clothes," Rora said.

"I'll be fine," Vaysa blurted and started for the door.

"We're here to take you to the group of us who're going to go cool off in the water," Trivala said. "You'll need to change."

Vaysa blinked. Her face flushed and she stepped toward the door. It didn't feel right. She needed to plan to find Shad.

"No thanks," she mumbled and rubbed her hands over her sleeves, her scars safely hidden beneath.

"Vaysa, you need some relaxation before tonight," Teo said.

"I need to plan," she said. She needed to focus, and swimming wouldn't help.

"Plan? We'll do what we always do. Head in the right direction and face what's there," Teo said.

Vaysa stared at him. Maybe that was part of her problem. She reacted instead of planned.

"You're here with two handsome men. More are down by the lake. And beautiful women," Rora said. "It'll be fun. You should change into the robes and join us. You'll be more comfortable."

Vaysa's eyes narrowed and twitched, but before she could retort, Teo stepped between them. "We can go down like we are. We'll cool off for a bit and then plan."

"But she'd be more comfortable with robes and a good scrubbing," Rora said and smiled widely at Teo. "As would you."

Teo blushed but looked back at Vaysa and jerked his head toward Rora. "We can go like this."

Vaysa arched an eyebrow and scanned Teo and then Gren. She couldn't waste time playing in the water when Shad needed her. Regardless of what Zara said, Shad was still being held captive. Being familiar, friendly hostiles didn't matter. They were hostiles, and Shad was being used as bait.

She forced a smile and said, "You two go and have fun."

"What's wrong with you?" Rora said.

Teo's smile faded.

Vaysa rolled her eyes and, shaking her head, left the hut.

Despite protests from the ladies, Teo followed Vaysa outside.

"Vaysa, wait," he called after her.

Vaysa paused but didn't turn around. She looked over her shoulder.

Teo ran a hand through his thick dark hair and opened his mouth but said nothing. He let out a hard breath.

"Teo, go back and have fun."

"I'll help plan."

Vaysa sighed. He didn't plan any better than she did. He'd gone by himself across the Spirit Strait. "It's okay, Teo. Go have fun and relax. We need to be ready for tonight."

"Vaysa, what happened to Shad isn't your fault. We're all here to help."

Vaysa flinched and spat, "Yes, it is. I lost control! I keep losing control!"

"No you're not. You've lost control a couple times, but you're in control most of the time. You helped Solon with the orb."

"Some of the time doesn't matter. It's when I lose control that I risk Shad. The Royal Guard started hunting us after I lost control in the forest. Shad wouldn't stay on Phantom Islands because she was afraid I'd burn it down. Monoc couldn't help me and now I lost control and people took Shad. I AM RESPONSIBLE!"

"No. The Royal Guard was coming, anyway. Zara said those Mercers would have gotten Shad anyway through the sand."

"I don't need her lies to feel better."

"You can't carry all of this on your shoulders. Shad made choices, too. She took you both out of Kennard. She left the Phantom Islands; you asked repeatedly to stay."

"My powers are the reason."

"Vaysa, you were alone in Kennard with Shad. How do you expect to learn them? She knew about the dragon scale. She could have left sooner."

"Are you blaming Shad?" Vaysa screamed, her face red with anger, fire popping from her fists into the sand.

"No," Teo said, shaking his head.

Her stomach curled, but she quickly squelched it. Vaysa turned from Teo.

"Then what are you saying?"

Teo stared at her, his mouth a thin pinched line. He shook his head. Finally, he said, "You need to stop blaming yourself."

If she did, then she'd only be lying to herself.

Chapter 52

VAYSA

Exhaling deeply, Vaysa stormed through the trees and surveyed the rest of the group. Her uneven breaths rippled through her body.

She found a solid tree, climbed into the welcoming canopy and slumped down. She leaned back and let out a breath. Her mind flashed with the recent events, and she opened her eyes to stop the mental show. Each loss of control and the resulting chaos played in her mind.

Vaysa rubbed her cheek and scanned the oasis. Her eyes grew heavy, and she let them close.

Snapping awake, she found the oasis gone. She was in a dark chamber. The air was damp and chilly. She swore and stiffened, waiting for the creepy voice. She cringed when it broke the silence.

"You do not listen well."

"Heartbreaking coming from you." The air constricted, and she choked on a cough.

"You bring me much concern."

"You don't bring me joy, either," Vaysa said, and a gush of air blew into her face. It tightened around her face, but she refused to back down. She was tired of being afraid of the voice.

"You're being reckless. You lost control."

Vaysa growled. She didn't need the voice to remind her of her mistakes, but she couldn't argue.

"We must work together."

We?

"We are not a 'we' or an 'our' or an 'us'. You are my mind playing tricks on me. Or a damned curse I somehow caught when I landed on Berla. You are a nuisance!"

Vaysa blinked when the air shifted again. A wave of anger coursed through her and then sadness pooled in her stomach. She gasped for breath as pain wretched her stomach.

"I cannot protect you if you are reckless."

"I have no idea what you're talking about. I never asked for your protection!" Vaysa's annoyance warmed her and coursed through her veins, melting the sadness and causing her to clench her fists.

"You wouldn't be alive without me!" the voice hissed back. "You'd have died on the Ash Fields."

VAYSA JOLTED AWAKE. The Ash Fields. She blinked and rubbed a hand over her eyes to clear the cobwebs and try to focus. The Ash Fields was where Solon saved her. Solon. The group said he saved her. Her mind screamed, and she tried to race her memories backwards, but she came up blank. Had he saved her?

From her position in the trees, she scoured the oasis until she found Solon sparring with some young warriors and giving them pointers.

Vaysa watched as he impressed the young warriors when he made a fire sword and did tricks, including sending fireballs through the sword as it still blazed.

He left Monoc with them, even though he had been home. Friendship was one thing, but he had family in Monoc. He owed the group nothing.

Shad trusted him. Why? Secrets were why Shad was abducted. Vaysa was tired of the secrets, of the mystery, of the repeated chaos caused by kept secrets. It was time to expose them.

She jumped down from the tree. As the warriors practiced, she crept up beside Solon. "I have some questions for you."

He looked at her from the corner of his eye. He sighed. "Let's talk in private."

They went to the tree line, which had a good view of the village, and of anyone approaching them. Solon leaned against a tree. He closed his eyes, pinched the bridge of his nose, and breathed deeply. Opening his eyes, he looked at Vaysa.

"What do you want to know?"

"How do you know Shad?" Guilt twisted her stomach at asking these questions without Shad present, but Shad said it was his truth to tell, and she needed to start at the beginning.

"She was a friend of mine in the past."

"Why does she keep your secrets?"

"She is a good friend."

"I can tell," Vaysa retorted. Jealousy stabbed her stomach and made her flinch.

He frowned at her but didn't comment.

"How long have you known her?" Vaysa asked.

Solon blinked and he said, "Decades. We met when I was an ambassador."

"She mentioned you were one."

"Did she?" Solon whispered and looked into the distance.

"Yea, she also mentioned you helped with the coup."

He nodded and picked at the dirt on his tunic.

"She said..." Vaysa's voice broke off. Shad had told her in private. Even if it was his history, she was privy to it in confidence.

"What'd she say?" Solon prompted, meeting Vaysa's eyes.

Vaysa stared back. Something about him was familiar. Like a lost memory. She shook her head. All their talk of history made her think she'd been there.

"Why'd you come with us?"

Solon furrowed his brow and searched her face. "Which location?"

"Here," Vaysa said, gesturing to the oasis and Drylands. "Why did you leave Monoc? Your family is there."

"Oh," Solon mumbled and rubbed his forehead.

"Oh?" Vaysa mimicked.

Solon sighed and looked toward the sky. "Monoc is where I was born. I will always have a place there, but it is not my home anymore."

"It's not? They welcomed you back with open arms. You don't owe us anything."

Solon laughed humorlessly.

"What?"

Solon pursed his lips and said, "My place will always be with you and Shad."

"What?" Vaysa said. "You care more about us than Monoc?"

"Yes."

Vaysa glared at him. He had a home. He had people, and he was giving it up. For them?

"If you two are so close, then why didn't she look for you on the Phantom Islands?"

"She thought I was dead."

"I know her. That wouldn't stop her."

"That is true," Solon agreed.

"Then why didn't she look for you?"

"She was getting others out of Berla."

Vaysa saw a flash of familiar dark water and faintly heard her mother's voice and a hiss. "Was I one of them?"

"Yes."

"What? Why?" Vaysa screamed.

Several people turned from the village to look.

"Russom's army, Royal Guards, Sentinels, and Traitors were searching for you. She had to get you to safety."

"Why?" she asked, more confused than angry. That didn't make sense, just like it didn't make sense that General Closs was still looking for her. "Why were they looking for me?"

"Because you are my daughter."

Vaysa jerked her head up and stared at him. He looked sheepish.

"You lie," she spat. She backed up slowly, shaking her head. The blood pounded in her ears. A hot wave coursed through her, and her fingers curled into fists. Fire ran from her fingers to her brain.

"You are— I—" Vaysa said, breathing raggedly. Turning, she darted away. Her heart hammered against her chest, and her mind went numb.

"Vaysa, wait," Solon called, his feet pounding after her.

Without turning, she lifted her hand to wave him away. An arc of fire rippled from her hand.

He cursed.

"Solon, don't," Zara called.

A tremor rippled beneath Vaysa's feet.

Heat pulsed in her veins, the flames licking at her fingers. She'd find Shad. Get a dragon scale. Then some answers.

Chapter 53

VAYSA

Vaysa swiftly covered ground despite the dunes. Her dark clothing and hair stood out in the golden sand.

She growled as Teo and Gren pulled up next to her on maris. She didn't need them to find Shad. They were safer with the others, anyway. They wouldn't be a casualty to her powers.

She snarled and fire shot out of her palms and dissipated in the hot sand.

Teo and Gren fell in step behind her.

After a while, she finally spat, "What do you want?"

Teo stammered, "You looked mad, and we were worried."

"I'm finding Shad," Vaysa said.

Teo and Gren looked in confusion at each other again.

"Aren't we going tonight?" Teo asked.

Vaysa growled in response.

"What happened?" Teo tried again.

Gren's eyes shot around and he shook his head violently. He mouthed, "Shut up!"

Vaysa stopped and turned around, and Teo pulled up short on the reins. Only concern reflected in his eyes. Concern she didn't want.

In a low growl she said, "I never want to see them again. I'm finding Shad, then a dragon scale, and then I'm finding a home without them."

Once she had a dragon scale, Shad would be content and Vaysa would possibly have some control. She owed Shad to try to get it.

Teo looked away and shifted on the maris.

Gren broke the silence. "That's fine, but we should look for shelter then. Night is fast approaching, and we don't know where we are. We need to plan."

Vaysa looked at the horizon, cursed, and nodded.

Gren said, "It might be quicker if you rode the maris."

She nodded dully and jumped on behind Gren.

THE DISTANT CRY of birds awoke Vaysa, Gren, and Teo. The night was still inky black with thousands of gleaming stars. Despite the bone-chilling bird screeches, they were safer under the brush of the rock formation they had found. The birds would notice their movement otherwise.

Vaysa's mind flickered to Shad. Was she safe? Her heart tightened, and she pressed her lips together. Guilt coursed through her and she had to swallow down revulsion.

She couldn't focus on the blame right now. It was all hers for getting Shad kidnapped, Gren and Teo lost in the desert, Zara away from her plans, and Solon from Monoc.

She wanted to delve into it. Sink into the abyss and let the emotions consume her, but she couldn't. She needed to focus on finding Shad and keeping Gren and Teo safe. Letting her emotions control her was how she got here.

Teo said, "I feel like a rabbit, huddling in terror from its predator." He pulled his knees tighter to his chin and let out a shaky breath.

Vaysa licked her lips and said, "We'll be fine."

"Uh huh."

"They notice movement," Vaysa said. She patted his knee before quickly pulling her hand back. An odd jolt coursed through her hand.

Teo just nodded and stared into the blackness.

Gren said, "Vaysa, what made you mad?"

"Solon."

"You realized he was your father?"

Vaysa and Teo both whipped their heads around to look at Gren. He stared back.

"It was pretty obvious."

Stunned, Teo said, "What're you talking about? I had no clue."

Gren snorted. "That's not surprising. Besides looking like you, he did that creepy magic thing."

Vaysa scrunched her face in confusion and slumped back. Everyone had known but her. Well, her and Teo.

She may have blood family, and she ran from him. Instead of feeling more complete, a hollowness consumed her.

The hardest part was that Shad knew. Shad knew he was her father and had said nothing. Vaysa closed her eyes. Shad had said it was for him to tell. Shad was loyal enough to Solon to keep even this secret from her.

But was it really for Shad to share? Vaysa rubbed her head. She didn't want to think about it anymore. She missed Shad and nothing made sense.

Gren sighed. "He really cared. When he saved you in the Ash Fields... he was angrier and more worried than a stranger should be. He also gave you his blood and almost killed himself saving you. Only family's that crazy."

"Or Shad," Teo said.

Vaysa couldn't help but smile. Shad was the best family.

Teo looked at Vaysa and then scanned the desert. His eyes settled south. "We'll help you find Shad."

Vaysa smiled at Teo.

"Didn't she hide the truth from you?" Gren asked.

Vaysa's eyes narrowed, and she glared at Gren. It didn't matter if he was right. "Don't talk about her."

An uneasy silence fell.

"Is it just the three of us now?" Gren asked.

Vaysa cut her eyes to him and then to Teo.

Teo shrugged and rested his head in his hands. "You're stuck with me."

She couldn't help the smile that flicked across her face.

She looked at Gren. He had been Kennard's guide to the castle. At least something was in her favor. Having him was easier than going blindly south.

A large crash followed by tremors startled them. Shrill whimpers pierced the night, and large gusts of sand floated their way. Vaysa motioned for them to stay. Whatever it was, she'd check it alone. She mounted a maris and trotted off in the direction of the sand gust.

As she headed in the direction of the sound, the ground shook. Pinpricks of fear raced up her spine when she topped the dune. A large bird lay in the sand. Open injuries oozed blood. It was the bird that had attacked them.

She galloped back to camp and yanked Teo onto the maris. Gren jumped on the other maris to follow.

Teo yelped when he saw the bird. He tugged on Vaysa and the reins to get them out of there.

"Vaysa, it will eat us," Teo whispered.

"It's in pain we caused."

"Sh—" Gren stopped himself when Vaysa cut him a dark look.

"Teo, get me the bottle to use and I'll go up to it. I just don't know what to use."

Teo grumbled but pulled out different bottles.

Vaysa crept up to it. The bird saw them and screeched in fear. It hobbled, but the sand tripped it.

Vaysa turned to Gren. "Get us some branches."

Gren left and returned shortly with the branches from their shelter. Vaysa made a fireball in her hand and inched closer to the bird. It focused on her, trying to avoid the fire. She drew its attention away from Teo and Gren.

Chapter 54

TEO

Teo whimpered as his hands, knees, and legs shook. The bird was too occupied with Vaysa and the fire to notice him. He waited until it squawked and then dumped the bottle's liquid into its beak.

The bird whirled around and thrust its beak at him. Teo jumped, but the beak grazed his arm and blood oozed from the sore.

The bird's head swirled and crashed to the ground with a puff of sand. Teo quickly went about putting ointment on the bird's sores.

"Why are we doing this?" Teo asked as he was finishing up. He'd known Vaysa's intent the second he saw the injured bird.

"It just wants to survive. It's not our enemy."

Teo shook his head at her. She baffled him most of the time. And yet, it was that same compassion that caused her to help on the Phantom Islands, with the ants, and everything else.

Gren watched, humored. To Vaysa he said, "You really don't like to see things suffer."

"Shut up, or we'll see about that."

Gren raised an eyebrow in amusement. He obviously wasn't concerned.

Teo stifled a groan when Gren's red eyes turned to him.

"You're a good soldier."

"What does that mean?" Teo asked dryly.

"You do as you're told."

Teo narrowed his eyes. Gren could jump off a cliff. He had followed evil blindly in the past, not questioning what they were doing. Although Vaysa was a thief, her intentions were to help. If Vaysa asked him to save a bird, he'd save a bird.

Chapter 55

VAYSA

Streaks of light cracked the darkness. Vaysa watched the bird all night to make sure it wasn't attacked as they waited for the maris to rest. She ignored the amusement that brightened Teo and Gren's faces. They smartly didn't make any more comments.

Her stomach ached with hunger, and she could hear the men's rumbling too, but they mounted the maris and started off again. There weren't any signs of food.

Gren said the castle was in the southwest. Vaysa had studied the stars to find the direction to head in.

The maris found another resting spot: another pile of rocks. Vaysa noticed bushier plants than before. They were finally getting out of the desert. Hopefully, cover would be easier to find.

The rocks formed a small cave and blocked the sultry sun. The three fit inside with the maris at the entrance. The coolness of the cave helped her and the others to drift off into sleep.

Cold washed over Vaysa and she wrapped her arms around her torso for warmth.

"Vaysa," the voice called.

She grimaced and closed her eyes. Maybe it would go away.

"Vaysa," the voice hissed louder.

"What?" she finally groaned.

"You keep going off path."

"What path?"

"I will lead you."

"No!" Vaysa yelled. "Tell me what the path is, what the goal is! Tell me and I'll choose."

"The choice isn't yours. This is your birthright."

"My what?"

Fire curled in her stomach and pulsed up her arms. She flexed her fingers and fire twirled around her hands. Her eyes opened

A crackly chuckle echoed in the cavern.

A tingle raced down her spine and Vaysa flexed her fingers. The fire stilled and then swayed with her hand motions.

She stared at her hands as she flipped them over, the fireball swooshing in obedience.

"You have much to learn."

"But…" Her voice drifted off. It was too late to learn. She needed a token of control.

"Vaysa, those with you cannot help you. I can."

Vaysa's eyes darted around the cave, looking for the source of the voice, but only shadows filled the area. She flexed her hand, and the fireball grew around her, controlled and ready.

"You were allowed to grow unencumbered in Kennard, but we need you now."

"Who are we?" she whispered.

"Your ancestors."

Gren shoved Vaysa awake. She punched him and sat up. He gripped his arm and cursed under his breath.

She breathed heavily, focusing on her surroundings. She was back in the cave she expected to be in. She licked her lips and shivered off the voice.

Shad had told her to leave the voice in the dreams, but the dreams weren't leaving her.

"Vaysa," Gren whispered, pulling her attention to him.

"What?" she asked, blinking to focus.

He gestured toward Teo, who was lying in a pool of sweat. His breaths were faint and ragged. White foam dripped from the corner of his mouth. His eyes were open, but only the whites were showing. His irises were rolled up under his eyelids. His visible flesh had swollen red blotches.

Vaysa fell back from the sight and landed against a maris. It was searing hot. Both maris were in the same comatose state as Teo.

"What happened?" Vaysa asked. She choked back fear. She absent-mindedly rubbed a hand over her arms and face to make sure she was still normal.

"It can't be food; we didn't eat anything."

A small giggle echoed in the cave. Vaysa sighed and closed her eyes. Another new fun Berlan creature. She opened her eyes and nodded at Gren. She then twirled her finger at the cave. He nodded, and they began searching.

The giggling increased into a full laugh that seemed to materialize from the air. Vaysa held her hand up to Gren, signaling for him to stop, and gestured at Teo, the maris, and the exit.

He nodded again, and they slowly backed up to the entrance, dragging Teo and then the maris out of the cave.

She let out a long breath to steady herself and allowed her frustration to boil up from her core. The heat radiated through her veins. She tossed her head back, mimicking the motions she saw Solon do.

A tingle charged through her, and her eyes flashed, and smoke swirled from their corners. Her hands danced in the air and flames licked the cave entrance.

She summoned a large ball of fire. It dwarfed the entrance and started to fill up the cave. The heat was welcoming in her hand. It was controlled. She pushed her anger into it and calmness took over, easing her muscles and her mind.

She pushed her anger about Shad's abduction, Solon's claims, and her lack of control into the fire. The fuel caused it to bulge and pop in her hand.

Vaysa turned and smiled at Gren as the heat magnified. Gren tilted his head slightly and gave her an odd look.

Her smile faltered when the fireball ebbed slightly and danced in the air. A hiss echoed and her stomach tightened. A quick flick of her wrist brought it back to the correct size.

She'd have to ask the voice next time what happened.

Coughing mixed with cursing caught her attention. She looked at Gren, who also looked confused.

Pink lightning bolts shot from a corner in the cave and sizzled through the flames. Vaysa lowered the magnitude of the ball but kept it glowing.

Gren went to the corner and knelt beside a pile of rocks and choked a laugh. He waved Vaysa over.

She kept the flame in her outstretched hand. It hovered in a red and orange orb. Its light bounced off the walls, casting long shadows.

Gren poked a small form. Before them was a small fairy. She was slightly bigger than Gren's hand. She had short, bright pink hair with chunks of magenta. Folded behind her were wings. Instead of delicate, shimmering, transparent pixie wings, hers were large, gray, leather-like and shaped like bat wings. She was trying hard to keep her orange eyes open. She coughed and pink light sprinkled around her.

The fairy snarled and cursed them. "What's wit' the fire?"

"What did you do to our friends?"

The fairy tried to laugh but sputtered and coughed. She squinted an eye at them and smirked, "Dead."

Vaysa scowled and put her face close to the fairy's face. "You'll be dead first."

The fairy snorted and a pink light zipped out and hit Vaysa in the nose. Vaysa reared back, swiping at the sting. The fairy tried to laugh.

Gren chuckled and picked up the fairy. "A Bamat. I thought they were a myth."

"A what?"

"Bamat. Basically, an evil fairy."

Vaysa raised an eyebrow at the creature. She'd seen scarier creatures. It may be evil, but she could squash it if necessary.

She might if it killed Teo.

The Bamat squirmed and tried to shoot pink light. Gren pinned her arms to her side and held her facing away from him.

She roared. "I no evil!"

"How about you save our friends to show us you're not evil and we'll free you," Gren offered.

"You don't got me caught."

"Vaysa will be happy to roast you."

The fairy broke into curses, and then she muttered, "Fine."

Vaysa breathed deeply. Her strength waned, but she focused on the dark cave, the voice, the hiss, and created a transparent orb of blue fire for the Bamat, and then she helped pull the three back inside the cave.

With a tremble of her fingers, the Bamat's orb disintegrated and Gren held the Bamat while Vaysa formed a fire dome over all of them. Gren gave Vaysa a concerned look, but he didn't point out that the spell was taxing her.

The Bamat cursed at them before pulling a few leaves from her skirt. The gray, withered leaves broke into dust as she touched them, floating over the three that were ill. She shot pink light at them and the leaf pieces burst into pink light and dissolved on the bodies.

"Done," she sang sarcastically.

"They don't look different," Vaysa said.

"Give 'em a few minutes."

Gren looked at Vaysa. His face pinched in unease.

Vaysa gave him a barely visible shake of the head. She didn't want his questions. Or concern on her strength. Her hands trembled and sweat beaded on her face. Her resolve shook and she focused on tightening her core. The strain weighed on her and a wave of dizziness washed over her. She gulped and blinked to regain focus.

"Vaysa, can you just corral her in fire again instead of all of us?"

The Bamat shrieked and tried to shoot lightning at Gren. He continued to hold her at bay, smirking.

Vaysa grunted, and the dome collapsed. She breathed heavily but turned toward the Bamat.

"You fine. Don't bother trappin' me."

Vaysa eyed her up and Gren nodded in agreement.

The Bamat was right. In a few minutes, Vaysa noticed the fevers had reduced and Teo and the maris were stirring.

"I'd give the night to rest," the fairy muttered.

Vaysa cursed. She was wasting too much time. She needed to find Shad.

"Shad would eat her," Gren said as if reading her mind.

Vaysa flinched at her friend's name and her nose flared.

"Is dat cha bird?" the Bamat quipped back.

"Bird? What bird?" Vaysa asked and whirled around.

Vaysa and Gren looked out of the cave and saw the injured bird nestled outside.

Chapter 56

VAYSA

Heat pulsed in her veins, not an urgent uncontrollable urge, but a promise of tappable power. She ran her thumbs over her fingers, reveling in the sensation of control. She flexed her hand, and a flame popped into it. She snapped her fist shut and the fire extinguished.

A smile flickered on her lips.

She had some control.

Her fire had obeyed… her.

For now.

But the voice had known of her powers. Known of her. Uncertain of how long the reprieve it provided would last, she wanted to push through the night, find Shad, and find a dragon scale, but she couldn't leave Teo.

The Bamat glowed pink in the darkness. When the Bamat wouldn't tell them her name, Vaysa named her Pinky. The Bamat hated the name, which made Vaysa call her it all the more for hurting her group.

As night settled, Vaysa set the entrance on fire. Her stomach ached with hunger, and her concentration waned, but she kept her tether to the fire. The invisible link charged the room and reminded her of Monoc.

She took guard through the night, too uncertain if the fire would give out if she slept, and watched as dawn light spilled across the sky.

Teo started to groan as the golden slivers of the sun danced across the sky, masking the stars and casting long shadows on the terrain.

He'd be hungry, too.

The bird squawked in discomfort. She cursed. It was still there and waiting.

"We need to deal with this," Vaysa said as Teo tossed fitfully. She grabbed her sword and flicked her hands toward the entrance, stopping the fire.

"You sure you want to do this?" Gren asked.

"If it wants to kill us, we can't escape. We'll starve."

"It could tire of waiting."

"We've got nothing to fight it with from a distance."

"You can shoot fire," Gren said.

"I can't guarantee I can control it," Vaysa said, standing up. The truth settled hard in her stomach. Even with more control of it still didn't mean it was reliable.

"Then I've been deceived, as it appears you've controlled it since leaving the oasis."

Vaysa rolled her eyes and asked, "Ready?"

Gren grabbed Pinky and nodded. She squirmed, but he held tight.

Vaysa created an orb of fire around her and crept toward the bird. As she approached, the bird swiveled its head toward her. Stepping aside, it unveiled a pile of food.

The bird preened as Vaysa watched it. It cocked its head at her and chirped. Uncertainty knotted in her stomach. She was sure the bird had brought them food.

She walked cautiously up to the pile. It looked like Royal Guard rations. The bird chirped and backed up a little from the food and her orb of fire. It bobbed its head slightly. Vaysa grabbed a few items, and the bird just watched her.

It was more than they had, and they needed it.

She took the food back to the cave and gave some to Gren and Teo.

Teo ate the food eagerly.

"It brought us food?" Gren questioned, holding up a food satchel.

"I guess," Vaysa said, not shocked by the event. Of all the things that had happened in Berla, this seemed fitting somehow.

Vaysa decided to test their luck.

Vaysa and Gren helped the maris and Teo out of the cave. Pinky trembled inside the cave and refused to go near the bird. The bird watched but did not attack as Vaysa walked back up to it without the orb of fire.

Walking up to the head, she extended her hand. She flinched when it moved to watch her. She relaxed when she still had her hand. She rubbed its neck and back. The bird jumped a little at the contact and turned to watch her. It settled down when Vaysa just stood there petting its feathers.

"It's worth a try to leave," she said, brushing her hands. "If it wants to follow us, I guess it can."

NIGHT SET AGAIN AND, using the stars, Vaysa directed the group to the southwest. Vaysa and Gren walked, helping to hold Teo up. They let the maris walk for a way to gain more strength before riding them. Pinky stayed in the cave, unwilling to go near the bird.

The bird waddled behind. It was not graceful on the sand and went slowly, but no matter the distance, the bird caught up.

As long as the bird didn't attack, she was fine with it following them. Its presence might ward off other predators, but either way, they needed to make ground. Shad was waiting.

After several hours in the heat, Vaysa tried the maris. They were frisky and already trotting along.

Midday warmed the air and brought the blinding sun. When they came to a small tributary, Vaysa called for a rest.

Gren and Teo looked relieved and willingly plopped down on the soft grassy ground. The maris eagerly drank and cooled off in the waters.

Teo looked at Gren and Vaysa, and finally asked, "Why aren't we afraid of the bird anymore?"

They both laughed.

"Because it brought us food," Vaysa said.

"So? Maybe it wants to fatten us before eating."

Vaysa rolled her eyes at him but couldn't hide her smile.

Vaysa watched as the huge bird fidgeted on the ground. She swallowed and looked back at Teo and Gren. Maybe the bird could make their travels easier. She'd learned to ride a horse. Maybe she could learn to ride a bird, too.

She walked over and again started petting it on the neck and working backwards. She took a deep breath and carefully wrapped a leg around the bird's body and eased herself into a sitting position.

The bird bristled and ripples raced down its back. She cautiously watched as the bird swiveled its head and watched her. She was about to slide off the bird's back when an arrow flew through the sky, skimming her arm. She jerked at the pain, and the bird flew up in fright of the soldiers charging at them.

Vaysa clung onto the bird's neck. Her breath stuck in her throat as air rushed around her.

Through the cover of the tall grasses, ten soldiers emerged in green uniforms. They surrounded Teo, Gren, and their maris. Teo and Gren both drew their weapons, but the soldiers outnumbered them.

They were too close to Shad. Had gone too far through Berla to end like this.

She had to think fast. She leaned, and the bird jerked forward.

The bird fluttered in fear, but Vaysa continued to urge it down. Vaysa clung to the bird with her knees and one arm. With the other she formed a fireball and lobbed it down. It smacked into a soldier's helmet. He yelped as his uniform caught fire.

They looked up at her, and terror marred their faces. She lobbed more fire orbs down and they hit the soldiers squarely. Gren and Teo used this advantage and lunged at the guards.

Vaysa yelled, "Cover!"

The guards looked at her in confusion, while Gren and Teo ducked and covered their faces.

She pulled on the bird's feathers and it reared back, pumping its wings. The force caused huge gusts of sand to fill the air. The soldiers were blinded and coughed as the sand filled their lungs. They scattered in different directions. When they had disappeared, Vaysa urged the bird to circle the area to confirm the guards were gone before the bird settled back to the ground.

She dismounted and smiled. "We have a new friend."

Teo looked at Vaysa, and then the bird. "It needs a name."

"Bird?" Gren offered.

"Grot," it cawed in a growly, odd voice.

Vaysa turned and stared at the bird. It understood them.

"You can talk?" Teo asked and stepped back.

Grot bobbed his head.

"Are you going to eat us?" Teo asked.

"No," Grot cawed.

"Good," Teo said with a nod.

Gren looked at Vaysa and rolled his eyes. She shrugged and smiled.

"What do we do from here?" asked Teo.

"It appears we're headed in the right direction," Vaysa said. "We're probably close to a Royal Guard camp. I didn't see any from above, but the group had to be from somewhere. We'll camp until nightfall. Grot and I can patrol from above."

"Won't the soldiers come back with more?"

Vaysa glanced at Grot. "I don't think so with Grot."

Gren and Teo nodded. The tributary had plush vegetation, including edible berries and roots. They feasted and rested in the shade of the bushes.

Grot nestled close to the group and squawked randomly. The

maris were restless next to the bird but munched happily on the plants.

Vaysa watched the other two drift off to sleep. With the quiet, her thoughts turned to Shad. They had not been apart from each other for this long. Her heart ached for her friend and sorrow sat heavy on her heart.

Chapter 57

ZARA

With Solon by her side, Zara sped through the desert. The Drylands' winds would destroy any trail the others left, so Zara went south in the direction Vaysa had first headed. Vaysa was headstrong enough to continue on to the castle without them.

Instead of going strategically to the castle and avoiding the Royal Guard routes she'd seen on the map, they were going full force into the lion's den.

As they crested a dune, relief flooded Zara seeing rock formations and brush in the distance. They were close to the grasslands and possibly Traitor forts. But more importantly, she could see the formations Chief Tikton had mentioned.

She'd needed the chief's help. She couldn't show her colors now for the western Traitors. They knew she'd come for Shad. It's why they took Shad. The western Traitors wanted to stop Zara. Now Vaysa was forcing her into the open with her reckless choices. It didn't matter if Solon hid something from her; it made rescuing Shad riskier.

She hoped Chief Tikton was true to his word. She'd supplied him with additional weapons for his support. She took the whistle the chief had given her and rubbed a thumb over the thin metal cylinder. She sent one long trill through the tube.

It didn't take long for the cry of a hawk to slice the silence of the desert. It circled twice and then veered sharply down, as if it spotted a mouse. She watched its descent and sent a silent "thank you" to Chief Tikton.

Zara followed the sighting to a large rock formation. The rocks had black soot around the cave entrance. Inside it smelled of fire, and soot covered the walls. There were piles of maris dung and some large bird feathers. From the looks of it, they were too late.

She mumbled to the air and nodded. It wasn't good. She licked her dry lips and tried to steady her breath.

Solon cursed and fell limp against the wall.

A shrewd laugh echoed off the walls. The two jumped and frantically looked around. The laugh grew louder until the echo was deafening.

Zara knew that laugh. She hated that evil, nasty laugh.

Solon clapped his hand and fire shot out into the corners.

A growl replaced the laughter. "What with the damn fire?"

They stopped and piqued their ears to listen.

"No more fire," the voice hissed.

Zara kicked a few rocks in its direction. The rocks ricocheted off the walls. Curses floated out of the pile and pink lightning zapped at Zara, but she quickly dodged it. It collided against the cave wall and showered pink embers. Zara cursed. It was a Bamat.

"Errrr, no more!" Pink light zipped in all directions. The two slowly backed up. Solon threw his head back. His eyes flashed and smoke twirled from the corners.

"Oh, no ya don't! The other did enough already!"

"What other?" Solon asked but threw up a blue fire shield as he scanned the cave.

"The nasty-eyed one."

Chief Tikton had held true to his word.

"Where is she now?" Zara asked.

"If she belongs with you, you should know."

Solon narrowed his eyes and mumbled under his breath. He threw his head back again.

"No, no, no. Don't do. With the bird."

"What bird?"

"A bird."

"Enough," Zara roared. The ground rumbled and her eyes glowed as she reached for the Bamat.

The Bamat was fast, but not fast enough. Zara pinned her down by her wings. The Bamat shot pink light at Zara's face. Zara didn't flinch but grabbed the Bamat.

"I'm done with your games!" Zara snarled.

"Zara," Solon said, alarmed.

"Wait, I know," the Bamat blurted.

Solon grabbed a pan from the cart. He gently took Pinky from Zara and placed her inside the pan. He chanted a few words, and a blue fire encircled the pan.

"You lead us to them, and you go free. If you don't, then..." Zara said, letting her threat taper off.

Despite her anger, Pinky settled in the pan, her body glowing with hatred.

Zara held Alice as she walked. The Bamat was from her native lands. They were evil and cunning, and they thrived in the gassy billows that covered Gillons. It was unsettling to see one so far south. Zara had met other types of fairies, but the Bamats were by far the meanest.

Pinky yelled profanities at Zara. She was likely waiting to be dismembered and used in a potion. Zara was Gillonite, a healer witch, even though only half. Gillonites were known for capturing Bamats and using them for lighting and magical elixirs. The angrier a Bamat became, the brighter they glowed and the more powerful they were. Pinky was fearful of her. Rightfully so. It didn't mean Zara felt bad for her.

Pinky's color was fading, as would her magic. In Gillons she would have deep magenta coloring. She had faded to a light purplish pink.

Pinky shouldn't be there, unless she'd been captured. It was probably by a warrior from the Red Ice lands northwest of Gillons. Traditionally, they carried a token Bamat into war. If they could capture one, they believed it would bring them luck.

She didn't know of any Red Ice Warriors this far south. She turned to scan the horizon, knowing she wouldn't find anything. The Warriors never left the peninsula. Their skills were in the bluff terrain and water. They even bred their horses to be fierce climbers and swimmers.

If the tome still had the pages, Teo's book would call them the cliff-climbers.

Zara looked back at Pinky. Pinky hissed at Zara when she saw her staring. Zara stuck her tongue out. Pinky shot pink lightning toward Zara, but it fizzled into the blue protective fire.

When she calmed down, she turned back to Zara. Zara didn't bother hiding her smile and said, "I take it you were a Warrior's good luck token?"

Pinky snorted and turned away.

"How did you escape?"

"I killed him."

"Doubtful. You're not fat with his blood."

Pinky buzzed around, shooting lightning and profanities at Zara. Zara half smiled and shook her head. At least some things didn't change.

Solon's shouting interrupted the one-sided confrontation. Zara turned to see what the issue was and swore. He pointed to the western sky. Dark, ominous clouds covered the sky. Another storm. This wasn't normal.

Chapter 58

TEO

Teo stared below as the group soared about the path Vaysa and Grot had scouted out. Small glowing fires were visible in the distance, and the rocks probably masked more.

He took the sights in, the land eerily similar to the plains of Kennard, but these fields were notorious for plentiful harvests, unlike the often drought-stricken plains of Kennard. The plains his family had lived on for generations.

The forest to the south was visible as a large, jagged line across the horizon. They were close to the castle and Shad. Guilt for helping his once-believed enemy had evaporated on the Ash Fields along with his allegiance to the Royal Guard. He wasn't sure where that left him, but his heart was at peace knowing he was doing the right thing.

The group crammed inside of a cave. Grot was resistant at first but folded up in a corner. He softly cooed in the cool shade as he drifted off to sleep.

Gren stretched and grumbled about his aching body and hungry stomach.

At least he was safe.

Teo ran a hand through his dark hair and bit the inside of his cheek. He sighed and kicked a rock. He was covered in sand, hungry, traveling with a carnivorous bird, and lost three powerful group mates. Yet, he was still alive.

He watched as Vaysa lay next to Grot and finally dozed off and let his breath out. He'd do anything to keep her safe. He wasn't sure if they were friends, but he was her ally, and she was stuck with him.

With Vaysa asleep, he and Gren were on guard duty. His body was stiff and he needed to relax. Grabbing his sword, he started sparring against an invisible foe.

His mind wandered back to his family and his stomach tightened. He missed them so much. He wanted to make them proud, but he wasn't sure he could anymore. He'd left against his parents' wishes. He was helping a Berlan. Sure, he was honoring his promise to protect Gren and would continue to. He wouldn't go back on his word.

But he'd also promised his allegiance to Kennard, and here he was helping Berlans. It was the right thing to do, but he wasn't sure his family would see it the same way. They hadn't seen the Ash Fields or the burned villages.

He was helping Zara, who was looking for the prince. She hadn't denied trying to kill him, but she hadn't shown malice toward him, either. She probably wanted to protect Berla, but finding the prince likely wouldn't do that anymore.

Nothing he had seen so far matched with what they had told him in the base camp in Kennard. The quick mission with other Royal Guard as cover was a lie. This was a full out war. Either he had missed the message, or it had never been told.

Teo clasped his forehead. The what ifs would undermine the mission. He needed a distraction. He needed to release some of his energy. He turned to offer to practice with Gren.

He swiveled around and realized Gren was gone. Cursing, he darted out of the cave. Gren was such a pain in the jards.

The sun blinded Teo, and he recoiled against the rock. Scanning the horizon, he couldn't see Gren. He scrambled to the top of the rock formation for a better view. They were in the Grass Lands, just east of the Mosa Plains and Treble Lake. The foliage was thicker and greener here but wouldn't provide a lot of cover.

Movement to the north caught his attention. A glint of metal in the mute scenery. Gren's blue skin stood out among the rocks. More movement skuttled to the west. The bushes moved without wind.

He squinted to see. They were far away, but four soldiers were patrolling the grounds. Bolting toward Gren, he hoped the soldiers wouldn't notice his movement. He stayed low to the ground. The sandy dirt was more solid and didn't make as large of a plume.

Gren groaned as Teo approached. Glaring, he grabbed his sack full of food and started toward Teo.

"Gren," Teo hissed.

"Food, you idiot," Gren shot back while holding up the sack to show some berries, wild onions, and tubers. "Let's just get back."

Teo pinched his mouth tightly together to stop himself from yelling. His nostrils flared, and he balled his fists. He leapt on Gren and knocked him to the ground.

Gren balled his fist and aimed for Teo's face. Teo blocked it and put a silent finger to his lips. His eyes bore into Gren. In a snarl he whispered, "Shut up, soldiers aren't far."

Gren's anger turned to concern. He twisted around to where Teo was pointing.

"We're too far from the cave." Turning back to Teo, Gren's face was tinted red. "They probably saw you. Did you want to face them alone?"

Gren growled but didn't argue.

Gren and Teo crouched in their spots. Teo stayed huddled, curling his toes to stay still. The anticipation wore him down. He hated not knowing, not being able to move.

Vibrations rolled through his feet. He grasped his sword. Something was coming. He took several deep breaths and silently prayed.

Gren cut his eyes to Teo and opened his mouth to speak. Then he shook his head and cursed under his breath.

As Teo rose, Gren slipped on his jacket. Gren seethed, "Be patient. We could live longer."

Teo brushed him off and went into a defensive stance. Teo's determined expression changed to confusion, his eyes grew large, and his mouth gaped open.

Gren slowly rose to his knees and stared in the same direction as Teo. Coming at them was a billow of dust. Running ahead of the plume was a Kennardian war carriage. Horsemen and smaller war carts flanked it.

Gren stared back at him. What were they going to do?

Arrows darkened the skies and landed around them. Teo cried out as they pierced his flesh. He fell. He rolled to cover his head next to Gren. Blood covered Gren and several arrows protruded from his back.

Jards, he'd failed to protect Gren.

Teo had several arrows sticking out of his own arm and the pain made his eyes water and he gasped for air. He would die. Yet he was more angered by his failure than afraid of his death.

The arrows stopped, but the sky remained dark. Teo braced for the next attack, and nausea crept up his throat. The ground rumbled again as foot soldiers scurried over, surrounding him and Gren.

Through the blinding pain, Teo saw dark figures jeering at him. He would die with Gren. He tried to block Gren with his body, even though it was useless.

If Vaysa stayed back, she could finish the rescue without them.

Thunder cracked in the sky, pulling everyone's attention up.

A thunderhead blocked the sun and darkened the earth.

The soldiers looked back at the war carriage.

A soldier with light hair pushed his way through the throngs of men. He looked so familiar. He smiled darkly at them, and Teo searched his memory for the face.

"Bind them," the familiar soldier barked. The others quickly obeyed.

Rain pelted their heads and a crack of lightning ripped across the sky.

The familiar soldier growled and ordered, "Get them back to the carriage." His honey-colored eyes shimmered in the cold rain.

They had a stay of interrogations. The soldiers wanted to get out of the storm's path. Teo forced himself not to look back at the cave Vaysa was sleeping in.

They were tossed in the cart, and Teo slowly blinked at seeing General Closs, like a mirage, sneering at the soldiers.

"Ben! Why did you bring prisoners?" General Closs bellowed.

The familiarity of it was almost welcoming. If he closed his eyes, perhaps he'd be back in Kennard.

Teo reopened his eyes and frowned. Ben. Ben had been the one originally in charge of Gren. He was Closs's favorite.

Ben barked orders at the men, and the troops piled back into the cart. Ben glanced in Closs's direction and smiled.

Closs followed his gaze and saw the blue face of Gren. A wicked smile spread across his lips. "Is that Gren?"

"Yes, sir," Ben said.

Closs's face darkened looking at Teo. "Is that Teo?"

"Yes, sir," Ben said, his smile faltering.

"Where's the girl?"

"Girl?" Ben questioned and looked back at Teo and Gren.

Closs's blue eyes flashed in annoyance, and a scowl twisted his lips. He faced Teo and spat, "All of you will lose provisions over this. As long as he is alive, you will pay! Find out where the girl is first!"

Closs slammed the divider shut, leaving the soldiers alone with Teo and Gren.

The group grumbled and several drew their daggers while staring at Teo.

"Sheathe them." Ben's quiet voice filled the cart. "We've been looking too long to kill them before getting information."

Teo rolled over through his pain to look at the soldiers.

"Besides, he was looking for a reason to cut our provisions, anyway. The Berlan fields have been destroyed by the rains."

"Yeah, so let's kill 'em so we can eat what little we have. We ain't getting replacements."

Ben smiled sympathetically at the angry men. "Don't you recognize our own men?" he asked the few original remaining soldiers while pointing at Gren and Teo. So many of the faces were new. "They're from our platoon. This is the Silver we've been looking for."

The men stared at the ragged two.

Teo looked at Gren and then down at his own gear. They wore Traitor's gear instead of their uniforms. They looked like Traitors. Teo blinked. Maybe he was one. He had sided with Vaysa, a Berlan, he was traveling with Berlans, and he was being held by the Royal Guard.

A soldier stood up and kicked Teo and Gren, forcing Teo from his thoughts and sending both him and Gren into coughing fits. "You idiots, this is your fault! Teo, you're human. You're supposed to be on our side. Jards!"

The disgruntled soldier went back to kicking the two. Several soldiers pulled him off. He turned to his comrades. "Don't you get it? If they hadn't left our side, we'd have the prince back, we wouldn't be in a war, and our friends wouldn't be dead!"

The gravity of his words hung in the air. Hardened faces turned to the two. Teo licked his lips and met their gaze. If the roles were reversed, he'd blame him and Gren, too. Maybe his death would bring some of them peace.

Chapter 59

VAYSA

A voice called to Vaysa. She shook her head, trying to go back to sleep. The voice grew louder, more urgent.

Groaning, she rubbed her face. Focusing, she saw mist surrounding her. She tensed and looked around.

A sharp comment flicked across her tongue, but her curiosity spiked, and she asked, "Did you help me with my powers?"

The air swished and ebbed around her. The smell of the sea tinged the air.

"Yes," the voice finally replied.

"Why?"

"Our future is changing. You were growing dangerous."

Vaysa snorted a chuckle. "How did you help me?"

A soft hum echoed off the walls. The sound was humanoid. Vaysa tilted her head to listen, the melodic sound familiar and comforting.

"I am tied to your ancestors."

"What does that mean?" Vaysa asked, scrunching her face.

A shrill call cut the air.

Vaysa startled awake. Grot screeched.

The smell of rain bathed the cave and dark clouds blocked the sun through the entrance. Another storm was coming.

She looked around and found the maris pawing nervously at the ground.

Grot swiveled his head and screeched again. His gravelly voice filled the shelter, "Soldiers."

Vaysa whirled around. Gren and Teo were gone. Her stomach tightened.

She was alone.

She mounted Grot, and they soared into the air. From the air, the dark blob of the war machine marred the ground, resembling a scar. Grot flew directly toward the fleeing army.

Chapter 60

ZARA

Solon and Zara sprinted into the darkening horizon. They topped a dune and saw in the distance a small gathering of tents. Unlike the green Kennardian tents, these were dark purple. The people milling about were purple with orange hair.

The purple people ignored them as they bustled about, reinforcing their tents and building shelters for their horses. The horses were also unique in appearance. The horses were various shades of black, brown, and tan. However, each had spikes growing out of their haunches and running down their snouts. The purple people also had three spiked bands on each upper arm. They were the Red Ice Warriors.

Zara walked toward them. By then, the people were watching them approach. They didn't gather weapons, but cautiously watched Zara.

Zara called to the small camp, "Is Darez present?"

There was a small shuffle, and a large man emerged from the group. His eyes were orange like his hair. He stood between the group and his people.

"What business do you have?" he barked.

"Darez, it's me, Zara."

The people relaxed and went back to work. Darez approached smiling. "I suppose you'd like shelter from the storm?"

Zara smiled. It was good to see Berlans organizing and supporting other species. She gestured toward her dilapidated cart. "I have items for trade."

Darez's smile faded. "We don't need them. We're depleted. We shouldn't have left the bluffs. We're going to head back, but you're welcome here tonight."

"But you're warriors!" Zara said. "You don't cower."

Darez shook his head. "We need to go home and protect our land. Berla will have to defend itself region by region. You should go home and help your kind. The Royal Guard'll be there soon."

Darez led the group into the camp and offered them a purple tent. Zara stared at the once-passionate soldier. This was not the battle-ready warrior she trained with years ago. He was a man who sought out battle, dared death. He loved to display his power, not cower in fear.

Fear would keep Berla apart.

"How will this protect us from the rains? Shouldn't we find a cave?" Solon asked, running a hand on the purple tent's leathery material.

Zara shot Solon a dark look, but let her protests go unvoiced for the time.

"In Red Ice, we have constant rain and sleet storms. These are made of a special material to protect against the rains," Darez explained.

From the pan came thunderous claps and the entire pan glowed pink. Zara peered in to find Pinky almost a magenta color from head to toe. Her orange eyes shot orange lightning while pink lightning zipped from her hands and feet.

Solon leaned over Zara and blew into the fire, which engulfed Pinky. Her frenzy ceased, and she glared back at both of them. She was still glowing and roared, "Ask 'em what material!"

Solon looked at Darez. "What's the material?"

Darez expressionlessly stared back. "Bamat wings."

Again, pink and orange lightning filled the pan.

Solon turned back to Darez. "I thought they were good luck charms?"

"When their luck wears off, they continue to help us as protection."

"That's disgusting," Solon said.

Zara nodded but wouldn't meet Solon's eyes.

Zara put their horses and maris in the shelter with the Red Ice horses. She then trailed back to the tents as the thunder pounded in the sky and lightning streaked through the dark clouds. The rain started softly but quickly picked up. The tents rippled under the fierce winds and downpour, but remained sturdy.

Solon and Zara set up their tent so it joined with Darez's. The three sat around a fire Solon created in the center. The warmth was welcoming.

Zara turned to Darez and finally asked, "Why are you quitting?"

He turned away and rubbed his arms. "We aren't quitting. We're going home to fight."

"The Royal Guard is already there?" she asked incredulously.

"Not yet, but soon. They're covering this land like a virus. They ambushed us."

Zara stared at him in disbelief. "How could they ambush you? You are the strongest warriors on Berla."

"Whoever is helping them is strong and knowledgeable. We believe they have guides from most of the lands."

"You mean prisoners," Zara murmured.

Darez sighed.

"Have they found the prince yet?" Solon asked.

"He's at the castle. But any Berlan would know that, Traitor or not. There are more guards moving toward the castle grounds, but none have infiltrated yet. The guards are everywhere, spreading us thin. There are rumors the Sentinels have arrived at the castle."

Solon shook his head. Swallowing, he asked, "What damage have they done?"

Darez sighed and looked off into the distance. "They're burning a path. They started in the Silver Forest and burned a path going north on the Peras River, including the jungle and Sea Swamp, and then they started over the mountains. That's been the saving grace." He looked directly at Solon. "Your people have been the biggest aid. The volcanoes have been constantly erupting, blocking a southern path and forcing the soldiers to go way north over the mountains. That's been slowing them down. That and the storms."

Zara said, "For how long they have been here, I'd expect more damage."

Darez nodded dully. "The last storm slowed the Royal Guard down. It raged for over a week. No one could travel much of the western side."

"What about this storm now? This is odd. One storm of this magnitude is rare, but two storms…" Solon noted.

Darez shrugged and looked away.

"What do you know?" Solon asked. His gaze tightened and then moved momentarily to Zara. His expression darkened.

"Not much… The weather here was always predictable. It has been for centuries… except during the war," Darez said.

Solon stared at Zara but did not interrupt.

"The first storm flooded the growing plains in the southwest. They never flood. Well, again, since the war. The storms in Red Ice are worse than usual…" His voice drifted off and he stared at the ground.

Solon prodded, "What does that mean?"

"The storms from the war resulted in the death of the Mosa Plains. It was lifeless. The humans had to be moved. Everyone abandoned the old castle area. A few years later, it flowed again with life, and the plains were bountiful. We had regular harvests. Now things are getting bad again."

"You mean the Mosa River is back to the way it was twenty years ago? I didn't realize it…" Solon's voice faded off. Finally, looking at Zara, he said, "You didn't mention that."

Zara turned her face away.

"Yes, about fifteen years ago, things improved," Darez said.

"Fifteen years," Solon parroted.

"Yes. We had four years of starvation, chaos, erratic storms, and terror. Many blamed the Traitors and thought they had killed the Water Witch. Some had even thought they should bring the monarchy back."

"And then things just got better?" Solon asked.

"One day the Mosa flowed with clean water again. The storms stopped. The Traitors forced out the remaining Royal Guard and Russom's soldiers in a few weeks. The Traitors have kept the lands peaceful since."

"How is that possible?" Solon whispered.

Zara shook her head and closed her eyes, trying to avoid Solon's stare. From the way Solon's eyes bore into her, he already knew why.

"The Water Witch returned. No one knows where she is, but the only way life could return to the river is if the Water Witch returned. It's a true blessing for Berla."

Zara flinched. "Solon, I wanted to tell you."

Solon said nothing as he glared at Zara. Fire sprang to his clenched fists and smoke curled around his eyes.

Zara didn't bother to defend her choices. She'd hid that his wife was alive and had returned. Nothing she could say would help.

Darez narrowed his eyes and finally broke the silence. "Zara, I thought you preferred solitude. Are you why the Mercers are active?"

Zara sighed. Who didn't know?

"Aren't you also looking for the prince?"

Solon looked at her expectantly. He rolled his eyes when she lied and said, "No."

His hard stare bore into her. Something glinted behind his eyes. Understanding. Knowing. He had likely pieced together the bits she'd shared. His wife was in danger. Everyone was looking for her... including the prince.

"What do you know about the prince?" Solon asked when Zara became silent. Despite his light tone, Zara could feel the accusations beneath.

Darez said, "He came looking for the Water Witch. Some of us think he actually knows where she's hiding. My contacts say he hasn't admitted anything yet, though."

"And the prince knows where Yala is?" Solon said between clenched teeth.

"We aren't sure, but if he does, Kennard will destroy us. Even if the Kennardian masses didn't know about the Water Witch, they knew about the fertile fields and their eastern movement hasn't gained them many crops.

"The Royal Guard is infesting Berla. The biggest obstacle is that the Traitors need more troops, but only a few are joining after their area's been destroyed. It's not enough to hold back the Royal Guard and Sentinels. It's why some of us came down, but..." Darez tapered off. "We need to go home and defend our lands."

Solon's eyes bore into Zara. His voice was cold when he said, "Yala is alive and hiding. A prince of Kennard possibly knows where. Both armies will go after Yala again. You know that."

"Solon..." Zara started but shook her head. She'd hidden the truth from him. Her reasons didn't matter.

"I doubt Prince Kier is the only one who knows her location," Solon said.

Zara sighed, and Solon looked away in disgust.

"Do you know where she is hiding?" Solon asked.

"I'd guess either the Nepta Ocean since the Mosa River is back, or more likely the Wind Ocean since it's the source of the Mosa and Peras rivers."

"The location doesn't matter," Solon mumbled. "She always could control both."

Darez stared quizzically at Solon. "What're you talking about?"

Zara looked at Solon and realized he would not answer. She pushed her guilt down and lied, "Nothing. It was only rumors."

Some secrets had to be kept. Yala'd always had power. She hid it to reduce King Russom's power. He could have destroyed all opposition, including the Monocians, emptied the Sea Swamp and navigated across the Spirit Strait. He could have conquered Kennard and the lands to the east. But Yala had wanted no one to have that much power, including herself.

Darez nodded. "I never understood why she just didn't kill King Russom."

"Nothing's that easy," Zara said. She couldn't explain the curse that followed Yala or how it bound her to follow whoever claimed her loyalty.

If only Zara had been the original person to find the prince, none of this would have happened. The Traitors would have continued on in ignorant bliss. His body would have washed up quietly in Kennard, and her secrets would have remained buried.

Chapter 61

TEO

Teo and Gren groaned as bodies fell on top of them. Teo tried to sit up but couldn't get his bearings.

"What was that?" Ben asked.

Voices called into the chaos, followed by screams. Something rocked the carriage.

Teo heard more confusion from outside. Then there was a reverberating caw. He squashed the small curl of joy that flittered in his stomach. He didn't want to get his hopes up that it was Grot, and then it turned out to be a group of birds that feasted on humans.

The next explosion sent the carriage toppling over, and the men flew to the side. The weight on the arrows broke the shafts, and the extra pressure sent sparks bursting in front of Teo's eyes.

The world darkened around him.

He awoke to Gren shoving him off.

Gren scrambled to get to the top of the pile. He had found a dagger in someone's sheath. He slashed his binds and then worked on Teo's. Teo couldn't understand why Gren was trying to help him. Unless Gren knew he needed Teo to get out of this alive.

The next explosion scattered them again. Teo blinked several times to gain focus and swallowed down his nausea. This time, Teo noticed the upturned side of the carriage was darkening and fire was licking its way through.

Gren smiled. Teo stared in horror at him. They would be burned alive.

"Vaysa's here," Gren said. He left Teo amidst the men and scurried to a corner, protecting his head.

Vaysa? She'd followed them?

Teo watched Gren. As the screeches outside turned into frenzied bellows, he braced himself. Embers rained on top of the men as Vaysa ripped the inflamed side off the cart and tossed it at the fleeing soldiers.

The men inside shuddered from the sight above.

Flames consumed Vaysa, and a glowing blue orb surrounded Grot. The Royal Guard war carts lay in shambles around them, the pieces either completely charred or still ablaze. Vaysa lobbed more fireballs at the toppled carts. The wood jumped to life with fire.

She was in complete control, and Teo just stared in awe.

In the blazing heat, her gaze fell on Gren and Teo. She breathed a sigh of relief and steered Grot down. Delicately with his talons, he picked up Teo and Gren. Then he reared back into the air.

Teo let out a breath, realizing he was safe. He was safe with Vaysa.

The four sped back to their cave.

Teo turned to look. The orb of blue fire shielded them from the soldiers' aerial attacks and the biting rains. His stomach flipped when he saw Closs crawl from a shattered cart and watch them soar away.

Chapter 62

Grot swooped and ducked back inside their shelter. Even if soldiers saw the flying bird, there was little they could do in the storm.

Vaysa dismounted and set to work. She threw her head back, and her hands danced as she chanted. Her eyes narrowed and the flicker of smoke twirled in the corners of her eyes. Blue fire danced from her fingers and engulfed the shelter.

She then turned her focus to Gren and Teo. They were both conscious, but Teo was in shock. He was shivering and had a glassy look in his eyes.

Since he looked worse, she focused first on him. An unwelcome emotion curled in her stomach again and she growled at it. She didn't have time for foolishness. Focusing, she carefully twisted the arrow shafts out of his arm.

He screamed in pain and jerked from her touch. He was too weak to push her off but tried to fumble in his medicine pouch.

Vaysa grimaced as she tugged each arrow out. Finishing, she extended her hand for the vial to use on the wounds.

The medicine bag fell from his hands as his eyes rolled back. Some vials that spilled out were ones she had given him, and others were new. None were labeled well.

She grabbed his head and turned it to the vials.

"Which one?" she screamed, trying to make him focus.

He slumped back.

Panic crept up her throat. She would not be responsible for his death or anyone's death from her group. She couldn't control much in her world, but she would not let her group die.

"Teo, you have to help me here," Vaysa pleaded.

He mumbled unintelligible words and feebly felt for a bottle and pointed to a few on the floor.

Knowing he would be of no help, she scanned the different salves and liquids. She noticed one bottle with an antique, tarnished silver top with intricate decals. The liquid shimmered red in the dim cave. The air thickened around her, and she heard murky, indistinguishable voices.

She whirled around when Teo coughed. Teo's breathing was raspy, and Gren groaned as he fought to stay conscious. Fear clouded her vision, and she stared back at the bottle.

She followed the urge and uncorked it. The sweet smell made her smile for a second and calmness coursed through her. She applied the elixir to his wounds and then stared at the vial and then Teo. She wasn't sure why she had followed the sensation, but it was too late to undo it.

She turned to Gren, who was still semi-cognitive. He took shallow breaths but could barely focus on Vaysa.

He moaned. "Don't put that stuff on me. Just cauterize it."

"It'll hurt."

"Don't care."

Vaysa shrugged. Flicking her thumb and pointer finger, her finger burned in red flames. She touched the tip of her finger to Gren's lacerations.

The flesh sizzled, and he closed his eyes and clamped his mouth shut, rocking against the pain. Beads of sweat dripped from his pinched face. He remained clenched and rocked after Vaysa finished.

Vaysa watched as Gren finally drifted off to sleep. Teo was already asleep. Grot chirped and preened in the corner and eventually settled into sleep. The storm raged on outside, but the fires kept the inside warm and dry.

JERKING AWAKE, Vaysa realized she had fallen asleep. The fire was low, and she quickly stoked it. She groggily got up and rifled through the few rations they had. That was when she noticed Teo.

Vaysa stared in amazement at Teo and then laughed. Several of his wounds were healing nicely. However, sprouting from his back were long white wings. They arched dramatically from his back and draped down to his feet. He didn't appear human anymore.

She stared at the vial she'd used on him. She wasn't sure what type of cure, or possibly curse, this was, but she hoped, for Teo's sake, it ran its course quickly. There was no way he could go back to Kennard like that.

Her stomach tightened, and she felt the unwelcome stir of emotion. His going back to Kennard shouldn't bother her. They'd never intended to stay as a group, anyway. They were supposed to split up when they first landed in Berla. She had no long-term plans. She would find Shad and make a home. His home was in Kennard. Hers was now in Berla.

She closed her eyes and pushed the thoughts down. She didn't want the distraction.

Checking his forehead, she sighed, finding that his fever had diminished. He should be okay. She'd have to ask Zara about the vial if she saw her again. Her stomach rolled again, and she looked around for something else to focus on.

Gren sat in the corner with his hand over his mouth. Snorts of laughter escaped his lips.

She snarled in his direction and then walked over.

"Don't bother with me. I see what your help can do," he said, still rippling with laughter.

Her white eyes narrowed, but she ignored the comment. "Make dinner for the two of you."

"What about you?" Gren asked.

"I ate already."

"You were sleeping."

She glared at him and walked away.

Gren got up to start food.

"We're running low on supplies," Gren said.

"I know. Grot and I'll get some."

"It's pouring!"

"We'll be fine. Just watch over Teo."

Gren rolled his eyes but didn't argue.

Vaysa put a blue orb of fire around herself and Grot as they left the shelter. She sighed, looking back at the humble place. Things were so different now. She missed Shad. She could handle the Royal Guard, Berla's odd creatures, and make a home anywhere, if she had Shad.

If anything happened to her, both sides would pay.

The rain continued to provide cover as they soared into the air. Looking below, Vaysa saw larger pockets of the Royal Guard.

Grot pulled up hard when the castle came into view. The behemoth dark stone structure stood defiantly in the torrential rains. King Malik's personal guards, the Sentinels, surrounded the castle's moat. The Sentinels wore black armor, green face visors, lances, and shields.

The Sentinels were part of the Royal Guard, but only fought for royalty. The prince was inside.

Scurrying on the castle's outer wall were Traitors dressed in heavy battle gear. The towers had cannons and archers standing ready. Despite the display, there did not appear to be many Traitors.

Vaysa guessed the rains had stopped a major battle. The moat was overflowing, and the Sentinels were slowly being pushed back. It wouldn't hold them for long. They would regroup and find a way around the moat. Why didn't the Traitors give over the prince? It would end the war.

Looking over her shoulder, she could see the distant splotches of troops. It wouldn't matter. Too much had happened. Returning the prince wasn't enough.

She turned back to the castle and stared at the Traitors.

Why would the Traitors take Shad to the castle? It seemed illogical if it was being invaded. Zara said they were using Shad as bait. Why would they lure her to the castle if they knew she was after the prince?

A hiss echoed in her ears, and she looked around. She was awake and not in the cave. Heat coursed through her, contained and strong. Her heart lurched and an invisible string pulled toward the castle. Were the Traitors trying to lure them to the castle?

It didn't matter the reason. Shad was there, so she was going. She'd face both armies if she had to.

Chapter 63

TEO

Teo crouched down with Gren behind a boulder in the cave. The blue firewall rippled at the entrance, both protecting and imprisoning them.

Three silhouettes wavered beyond the flames.

They were trapped. As long as Vaysa's magic held, they'd be safe, but then what? He and Gren had swords, but who knew how many people there were?

"Stay down," Gren hissed as the flames wavered and flickered out.

Teo's stomach dropped, his body both wanting to run and stay put as Vaysa's magic gave way to the three. They'd come so far. Survived so much.

Teo tugged Gren lower as three figures and a horse entered the cave.

A blue flame shield popped up around the newcomers, the same as around the entrance, and Zara's voice rang out, "Gren, Teo, it's us— Solon and Zara."

Teo floated out, his long white wings trailing behind him, his ragged dark hair and facial stubble in contrast to their pristine image.

Gren walked next to him trying to hide his smirk. His wings had been a Berlan surprise. At first, he thought he was dreaming but it faded into a Berlan reality. Whatever vial Vaysa used had caused it, but Zara would have the antidote.

"What happened?" Solon asked, aghast.

"Vaysa mended our wounds," Gren responded, lowering his sword. He smiled at the reinforcements. His blue skin was dirty, and his green hair mussed.

Zara chuckled, but managed to spit out, "If that was from my collection..." before erupting into laughter again.

Teo stared back and, gulping, asked, "What about it?"

"The side effects can be... permanent."

Teo smiled at her joke. "How long will they really last?"

Zara licked her lips. Something flickered behind her eyes before she smiled. "As long as you want them. When you're ready to be done with them, I can help."

Just as he had figured.

"He says they remind him of a picture in his grandma's book," Gren said.

"'Soaring above the land, a shield,'" Zara said with a pointed expression.

"Huh," Teo said. "I thought the dragons soared."

"Maybe your book is wrong," Gren said.

"Or the dragons cause the land to tremble," Zara said.

Teo shrugged. "It's just a storybook."

"Or not," Zara mumbled.

Gren's gaze drifted from Teo and his wings to Darez standing behind the group. His smile dropped and his eyes flashed with anger. Unsheathing his sword, he dove for the purple man.

Darez blocked the blow with an arm spike. The clicking sound echoed off the cave's walls. Solon lunged for Gren. The motion set Gren off-balance, and he slammed into Teo. Teo landed with a thud on the ground. He saw stars and feared he'd injured his wings. Despite the oddity, they were his for the moment. Something he'd never wanted and yet felt natural, made him feel whole.

392

Roaring laughter, reminding him of the Bamat, echoed from the cart.

Zara ran to Gren and Teo's side, with a smile still tugging at her lips. "The wings will take some getting used to. Let me introduce you to our friend, Darez from Red Ice."

Teo stood up in a daze and, shaking the dancing lights from his eyes, focused on the new addition to the group. He had formidable spikes protruding from his thickly muscled arms and he was purple. He was similar in height to Solon, but whereas Solon was wiry, Darez was sinewy. Teo had never seen a poster about a non-human from Red Ice, but his demeanor screamed warrior.

Darez cleared his throat and directed his attention toward Gren. "How is it a Silver is involved in war... at least, not just passively?"

The insult was clear to Teo. Gren narrowed his eyes toward the Red Ice Warrior, his voice tight, and said, "We don't run from battle. We just don't seek them out when unnecessary."

Teo glanced between the two and rolled his eyes. "Are you serious? Your people are enemies, too?" Sighing heavily, he slouched against the wall. Berla wasn't any better than Kennard. "This is getting old!"

The group stared wide-eyed at him.

"What?" Teo hollered at the group. "Everyone hates humans. 'Oh, they're evil doers who all want bloodshed and destruction.' Except Zara, who says that's the Royal Guard.

"Monocians hate everyone. Except they were fine with Shad and Zara. Silvers hate Cumas and apparently just about every other species is beneath them, too. Cumas will eat any species, except their own..." Teo paused. "Well, I can't verify that one." The desert people hate outsiders and shoot cannons. The animals here eat every other species. There are evil fairies that shoot lightning, and it looks like you brought her with you." He shuddered and deadpanned, "Great."

Teo continued, "The Red Ice people obviously hate Silvers and who knows who else? There are countless other species I haven't met, but I'm sure they hate each other. No wonder the Traitors don't want to unite anyone."

The group was silent as their gaze drifted from Teo.

Teo stood. His wings fluttered behind him. He stared directly at Zara. "How do you do it? You trade with everyone. You're friendly toward everyone, and you learn their customs. How do you not go insane catering to egos?"

Zara laughed loudly, breaking some tension. "Once you realize that a war took place, you understand why people are so skeptical of others. It's not hate, but fear of living through another war. Our group alone shows how much Berla has grown. A Cuma and Silver traveling together. Who'd have thought it?"

Darez cleared his throat. "He's right. If Berlans worked together, the Royal Guard would be easier to defeat. Yes, we all battle them, but we haven't joined together in any effort except the few who have joined the Traitors. Once the Royal Guard leave an area, that region quits fighting, and possibly a few join the Traitors."

"What about you? How'd you come to join our group?" Teo said. "Most likely you're like the rest."

Darez met Teo's eyes. "Despite your anger and quick judgment, you're right. My group's going back home to defend our land instead of Berla as a whole. We're just as much to blame."

"Deciding who's to blame now won't help end the war," Vaysa said, catching them all off guard.

Grot entered, unsettling the new members.

Solon, Zara, and Darez drew weapons and tried to block Gren and Teo from Grot.

Vaysa sighed loudly and threw an orb around her and Grot. "All right, everyone. Grot's with us. Grot, leave them alone. Everyone leave Grot alone."

"You named a crow?" Darez asked, still holding his weapon, his eyes darting between Vaysa and Grot.

"He came with it," Vaysa seethed.

Teo gulped as he watched Vaysa. Fire sprang to her hands and her eyes flashed. Her raw anger darkened her face.

"Drop your weapons, whoever you are," Vaysa said to Darez, releasing the blue fire orb. "I'm sure you came with a name, too."

"This is Darez," Zara said.

"You're controlling the fire?" Solon said, staring at her hands.

"We need to talk," Vaysa said, glaring at Zara and ignoring Solon.

Teo's heart leapt to his throat. Vaysa was back. The group was reunited, but based on her dark expression and the anguish on Solon's, they were anything but okay.

Chapter 64

VAYSA

Zara stared back at Vaysa.

"You're after the prince, but didn't want to tell us?" Vaysa asked, but she already knew the answer.

Zara blinked slowly at her, her face stoic. Vaysa took it as a yes.

"The Mercers caught up to you because of us," Vaysa stated. The Mercers were why they had learned about Zara's real plans. Otherwise, she'd have kept them secret after getting them to Gillons.

Zara continued to stare at her.

"We delayed you, didn't we?" Again, she already knew the answer.

Zara's face softened, and she stole a glance at Solon and sighed.

"The Traitors already had him when Solon came looking for you. You still wanted to silence him."

"Yes," Zara breathed.

"It's why you wanted us to get horses and go without you. So, we stopped you from going directly there. We stopped you from protecting the Water Witch," Vaysa said as an unwelcome curl of guilt twisted in her stomach.

"She knows about Yala?" Solon asked, his eyes darting to Zara.

Zara growled softly in her throat and looked away.

"I know Yala is the last Water Witch, whatever that is, and that the prince likely knows her location."

"What's a Water Witch?" Teo whispered.

"Sh," Gren hissed, waving him off.

Teo made a hand gesture but remained quiet.

"But you still helped us?" That was the part that confused Vaysa.

"Of course!" Zara yelled, her voice deep and echoing. Her eyes flashed bright amber.

"Why? It risked everything. You said Berla was prosperous because of her."

"How did you find this out?" Solon asked, his face hardened and eyes unblinking.

"She overheard a conversation," Zara said, not meeting his eyes. Turning to Vaysa, she asked, "Why are you traipsing through an unknown land to find Shad?"

"She's family!" Vaysa yelled.

"Exactly," Zara said.

Vaysa looked at Solon. His dark eyes were bright as he stared at her. He'd risked his life for her in the Sea Swamp, Ash Fields, and who knew where else.

She looked at Gren and Teo. Her choices hadn't been logical to keep them safe, either.

"What's a Water Witch?" Teo asked again and dodged Gren's swat.

Darez said, "She controls the waters, including ground and sky. Once there were several Water Witches, even one in Kennard, but Yala is the last one."

Solon shook his head. "We shouldn't talk about Yala."

Teo scrunched his face in confusion. "I never heard of one. Why's there only one left?"

"Humans killed the others hundreds of years ago. Before King Russom's family took control. One particular reason humans aren't liked."

Teo did not miss Darez's meaning and mimicked his face.

Gren added, "If she dies, so do all the waters."

"What does that mean for us?" Vaysa asked.

"She's the key to the success of Berla," Darez said. "Without her we will perish. She's beyond powerful. She now controls the North Ocean and the water that flows from it."

"I thought you didn't know where she was," Solon snapped.

Darez glanced at Solon but didn't respond.

Gren turned to Darez. "I thought she was unreachable."

"Shouldn't she stay hidden?" Teo asked.

"She wants to stay hidden, but greedy people don't want her to," Solon said.

"Don't the Traitors have her?" Teo asked. "They're in control. They should protect her."

Zara shook her head. "No. She escaped before the Traitors could catch her. When she came back and returned life to the waters, she did so undetected. The Traitors never pursued her since the lands were fertile and people were fed. Also, they didn't want it to be obvious where she was or make her run again. However, if the prince finds her, there'll be havoc, and Kennard will control both lands. The Traitors want to stop that."

"Why doesn't she just refuse, then?" Vaysa asked.

Solon replied, "The Water Witch has had her role for centuries. She has unlimited powers but must yield to the ruling person when asked to. It's a stipulation of her position as it has been for those who preceded her."

"Some call it a curse," Zara said, staring defiantly at Solon.

"A curse?" Vaysa mumbled.

"Then how's she controlling the weather now?" Teo asked. "Doesn't she have to obey someone?"

Solon sighed. "Teo, she has free will. When not controlled by someone, she does what she thinks is best for the lands."

Gren shifted and looked at Solon. "How do you know so much about her?"

He shrugged and, looking away, said, "I've been alive a long time."

"Hmm," Gren said and gave Solon a skeptical look. Then he glanced at Vaysa.

"How'd she get away, then?" Teo asked.

"When we laid siege on the castle, King Russom, who'd claimed her, was killed," Zara said. "The Traitors couldn't claim her before she fled."

"Sounds complicated. What's the plan?" Teo asked, looking toward Vaysa.

Vaysa looked at the others. It was obvious they should help this woman. She felt it in her soul. Zara was risking everything to protect her, but was it her fight too?

"We find Shad." Vaysa stared at the others. "And then we can help Zara find the Water Witch."

"What about your powers?" Teo asked. "Don't you need a dragon scale?"

Vaysa licked her lips. She didn't know how long the voice would help her, and she couldn't tell the others about it. She didn't want the help to evaporate by mentioning it.

Zara forced a smile at Vaysa. "It was a solo journey anyway."

Vaysa nodded and said, "Shad, and then the dragon scale."

Chapter 65

VAYSA

The storm still pounded on when the group awoke from their rest. They had somber faces as they started prepping. Vaysa rubbed her arms, a chill settling over her flesh. She'd… they'd get Shad back, no matter the cost. She swallowed back the reservations against seeing the castle. The Royal Guard. The Traitors. None of them mattered until she had Shad.

Despite the twist of her heart, she forced her feet and body forward.

Teo's alarmed voice filled the cave. "Where's Darez?"

Solon mumbled, "He asked to leave."

"I guess he really is a coward," Gren retorted.

Zara shot him a dark look and sighed.

Coward didn't seem to fit. Protective. Defeated. But not cowardly. Vaysa had seen what the Royal Guard had done, and it was likely only part of the destruction they'd reigned over the land. The others could say Berla needed to unite against the Royal Guard, become one army instead of separated pockets, but in the past, she and Shad had always fled instead of facing them. And that was why they were here.

The twist turned to a full body numbness. A sigh dropped her frame. She needed out of her head. She needed to stay focused. Shad needed her to stay focused. With that thought, she finished packing up.

While the rest packed, Solon moved to Vaysa.

"We should talk," he murmured. His dark eyes searched her face.

A slither of betrayal tightened around her spine. They probably needed to talk, despite how acidic it sat in her throat, but now wasn't the time for those truths. She needed her mind focused.

"After we have Shad."

He swallowed but nodded.

Solon and Zara secured the maris in the cave. Then they, Vaysa and Gren climbed on Grot, and Teo floated safely beside them. They'd decided on splitting into two groups when they arrived. Zara and Solon would be the decoys.

Despite the extra weight, Grot still took off with ease. The rain provided cover from the enemy's eyes. Solon and Vaysa held a blue orb around the group, and Grot glided into the black clouds.

Below them swirled the dark formations of the Royal Guard coming to aid the Sentinels. Into the horizon, the torrential rains pounded on the stalled army.

To the northwest, Treble Lake rippled in the wind. It was close to overflowing. The Mosa River separated them from the castle. It snaked beneath, swollen with rainwater. The usually clear waters were raging with debris and darkened by the storm. The castle itself was ablaze with activity. The Sentinels' camp showed activity despite the downpour.

The castle was on a hill and the surrounding land had been flattened for protection.

The Sentinels stood blockaded a few hundred feet outside the entrance.

Grot dropped Solon and Zara behind the Sentinels line. He then soared back up into the sky and started circling the castle. To Vaysa's surprise, he let out high-pitched caws that sliced through the storm. Vaysa's eyes flashed, and her heart panged with anger.

Grot had betrayed her?

Taking deep breaths, she climbed up to Grot's head for him to hear her. That's when she noticed the dark objects moving in. Swarms of large crows were fighting the rain to join Grot at the castle, and below, all activity had frozen. The Traitors stood watching, as did the Sentinels.

Grot had called his kind to aid them.

Chapter 66

ZARA

Zara stared into the sky with awe. The caws of the approaching swarm were deafening and blocked out the thunder. Zara hoped the birds would be on their side.

Taking advantage of the distraction, Solon pulled out the pan that was imprisoning Pinky. The pan no longer glowed pink, but she was inside, cowering in a corner from the cawing birds.

He handed it to Zara and nodded. His lips pressed into a thin line.

Zara peered inside, smiling. "Hello there!"

Pinky met her stare with cursing, growling, and pink lightning zapped in her direction.

"Tsk, tsk. That's not very nice. Perhaps I should give you to Darez to replace his dead good luck charm," Zara said in a saccharine voice.

"Ya wouldn't!" Pinky's face scrunched up in anger, and her eyes squinted at Zara. They started glowing bright orange and small electrical charges snapped at the corners. Pink lightning crackled from her hands and toes, and her hair sparked at the ends.

Zara laughed at her. "If you don't want to be a good luck charm, you could protect him as part of his tent." The fake sweetness dripped on every word.

Pinky's growls grew to roars, and lightning shot from her body. Her color deepened, and the pan glowed orange. The heat rolled in waves off the pan and the vibrations of her rage made it hard to hold on to.

Zara looked at Solon and asked, "Ready?"

He nodded.

Zara leaned back and threw the pan toward the assembled Sentinels. Solon swiped his hands in the air and the blue protection orb dissipated. The pan landed with a clank on the rocky terrain.

The Sentinels barely noticed the new object as they watched the crows draw closer. Solon and Zara looked at each other in anticipation. With the sound of thunder, the pan blew apart, and the shrapnel flew into the nearest Sentinels, pulling their attention away.

Pink and orange lightning exploded from the spot. Rods larger than six men tall flew into the crowd. The core center, Pinky, was glowing like a small sun.

Whipping around to the first person she saw, she attacked. Her target flew to the ground, charred, and broke into ash. She turned, looking for her next victim.

The Sentinels drew their weapons. The closest one to her tried clubbing her with his sword. Pink lightning zapped the sword and charged the Sentinel. He clasped at his heart. An orange bolt zapped him, and he, too, disintegrated into ash.

The Sentinels nearest her tried to give her a large berth, and one tried shooting arrows at her. She whirled in his direction. He screamed when pink lightning zapped him. She laughed as they reared around and darted in all directions. Her laugh grew into a screech. The ground beneath her vibrated and waves of intense heat and electricity rolled from her. The charge built until a vociferous pop filled the air and the moat sizzled pink.

The air cooled and smoke coiled off the lapping moat. Around where Pinky had been lay dozens of ashy bodies and abandoned weapons. The moat crackled with residual energy.

The Sentinels were in disarray as the crows dive-bombed them. The birds snatched bodies from the ground, crunching and gulping them. They dropped bits of flesh on the remaining soldiers. The panicked soldiers tried to regroup away from the castle, but the birds continued to pick at them.

Grot used the diversion from the other birds' attack as a cover to sidle next to a turret. Vaysa, Gren, and Teo scurried off and ducked into the tower.

Chapter 67

VAYSA

Adrenaline coursed through Vaysa as they entered through the window into a dark room. She curled her fingers and toes to maintain control. Finally, she'd get Shad back. Then everything else could unfold.

They'd entered on the opposite side of the castle as Solon and Zara and the Sentinels. The Royal Guard dotted the landscape in all directions, hunkered down by the storm and birds.

Prickles ran down her back and she slightly shivered to get a grip as she stepped into the room. She extended her hand, and a flame popped into life, illuminating the room. Dust and cobwebs covered the red-stone walls. The once grand suite was empty. It was void of furniture, likely burned for fuel. The odor of gunpowder lingered.

Peeking out of the room, she saw the room was in a long corridor void of ornamentation, but torches burned every few paces. Creeping farther down, they found patrolling Traitors on the walkways firing cannons and arrows at the attacking birds.

If Shad was in prison, she should be in a dungeon, which would be beneath ground. They needed to go down.

"Soon," she whispered.

The three kept to the stairs and fled to an interior section of the castle. A few Traitors running with additional weapons filled the corridors. Besides that, they were empty.

The three looked at each other.

Maybe they'd make it undetected.

Teo whispered, "Shouldn't there be more Traitors if this is a battle?"

"I think they weren't planning on one," Gren responded.

"Or the Traitors are that depleted from fighting all the other battles," Vaysa offered.

If the rest of Berla would fight, then the Traitors wouldn't be depleted fighting at the outposts. Vaysa realized that was the Royal Guards' plan. They were exploiting the estranged Berla.

The Traitors communicated between the species while the species governed themselves. It stopped Berla from fighting amongst itself and brought peace. However, none of the species worked together, and the Traitors didn't have to deal with skirmishes between Berlans because the Berlans didn't associate with one another. Their so-called peace would lead to their destruction.

Teo smacked her arm and brought her out of her thoughts. She went to hit him back when he motioned for her to be quiet. They could hear voices arguing in a room. Teo and Gren crept closer to hear better.

Her gaze flicked to the stairwell. They needed to move. Find Shad.

"This is crazy! We will never win against the Sentinels and the damn birds!"

"If we find the witch, then it doesn't matter."

"We were fine with her missing."

"Yeah, but Kennard won't stop. With the prince dead, they'll kill us. With the prince, they'll find the witch and kill us."

Vaysa snarled and darkness curled within her. She kept the flames in her hand controlled, but she couldn't control the anger coursing through her.

The three peeked into the room with the arguing Berlans. They were loading cannon balls into a cannon. The two weren't aiming, just firing and hoping to hit an enemy.

Vaysa blinked at seeing the species in the room. One had red skin without hair, and the other had olive skin and tan hair like the desert people.

"Shad," Vaysa mouthed to Gren and Teo.

They left the two Traitors undisturbed as they ventured further down the hall.

"She has to be in the dungeon," Vaysa said. "We need to head down."

"No, too obvious," Gren responded.

Vaysa and Teo looked at him.

Gren continued, "Anyone breaking in would think that. Zara said they knew she'd come for Shad, and they wouldn't hurt Shad. We need to find where the most guards are. Most likely a secluded area, not easily accessible."

"Due to so few Traitors, I'd think they'd have the same guards with her and the prince. Where would the prince be?" Vaysa asked.

"The place they think is the strongest," Teo said.

"The keep?" Gren asked.

Teo nodded. "Everyplace else would be too hard to secure. Its purpose is to keep royalty safe."

Vaysa nodded. It sounded like as good a theory as any.

Gren sighed and relented.

"Fabulous, how do we get there?" Vaysa said.

"Look for the kitchen," Gren said. "They are usually together. Kitchen should be at the bottom of it."

"How would you know?" Vaysa asked incredulously.

"I just do," Gren said and walked off.

Teo raised a questioning eyebrow to Vaysa. She shrugged.

Teo and Vaysa followed him down the halls. Various rooms had different Traitors in them arming the artillery. Some had desert nomads, the red men, a few Silvers, and many others.

"Why are there so many different people?" Teo asked.

"What do you mean?" Gren retorted.

"I figured it was a few species that joined the Traitors."

"Traitors were people who didn't think a monarchy for all was right nor was isolation of the species. Any Berlan can join."

"We fit in well, then," Teo whispered.

Vaysa nodded. Even if Solon had valid reasons to hate them, Berla needed the Traitors.

Chapter 68

ZARA

G rot pulled back to join the outside battle.

Zara turned with her weapon drawn. Solon raised his hand to stop her.

The remaining soldiers regrouped from Grot and Pinky's attacks while the birds battled against the Traitors' cannons.

There were roughly two hundred Sentinels left that Solon could count.

Their plan was simple: attack from a distance.

Solon took deep, focusing breaths.

Zara loaded arrows with different vials of potions. She focused mostly on fire and poison elixirs.

The two separated.

Solon flanked the north side and Zara, the south. The Traitors had the west side if they regrouped after the bird attacks. Grot pumped his wings and loudly cawed into the group of soldiers. They screamed and grabbed their weapons.

The Sentinels were trained soldiers. The surprise attack had weakened them, but they were quick to regroup. The leader, who was tall and thickly muscled, grabbed a conch shell from his waist. He blew quick short notes that came out dull and raspy.

The rest of the Sentinels snapped to attention and became silent.

Solon swore. They had fought the Sentinels before. Silence was never good.

A few more notes shot from the shell, this time long and high-pitched. The mass of mercenaries formed into lines. Despite the continuous onslaught of fire and weaponry that sent individual soldiers screaming to the ground, the remaining soldiers stood silently in rows of ten.

Solon nodded to Zara, and they focused their attack on the front line.

The soldiers behind them seemed oblivious to the carnage in front of them. They lifted black leather-covered shields. They were as long as the soldiers' bodies and just as wide. In the center was a spear for ramming. Surrounding the point was a green dragon, the symbol of Kennardian power. Solon snorted at the irony. They had killed almost all their dragons.

The Sentinels interlocked their shields, forming a wall of leathered metal around the front. The front line of unshielded soldiers had been a decoy to protect the rest of the troops.

The soldiers behind the front line held their shields over their heads. The ones on the sides positioned their shields interlocking toward the back. The back line turned and held their shields facing the rear. They formed a walking shield.

Solon grimaced. He knew this formation. The Sentinels would wait them out. The shields were unique and seemed to repel everything. It was a waste of his energy to continue lobbing fireballs at them. The dragon skin-coated shields would repel any heat attack.

ZARA WATCHED the fireballs bounce harmlessly to the ground, and the potions drip off the shields. She always wanted dragon skin items. However, she wouldn't kill a dragon to get the skins.

She was one of the few that knew Berla had dragons left. They mostly inhabited the northwestern cliffs and the islands in the North Ocean. Little could harm their skins. There were a few things that could, but she wasn't willing to kill Bamats to kill dragons, either.

An eerie whistle filled the air. The soldiers stomped their feet in place, and a vibrating hum filled their silence. Then they started a slow march toward them.

Another sharp whistle pierced the air. The formation broke into two. One line veered toward Solon, and the other section reformed into a smaller version of the impenetrable shield and veered toward her.

A deep, long whistle interrupted the humming. The Sentinels yelled in the air and again became silent as the middle sections lowered and interlocked their shields. The back row drew their bows and arrows. To Zara's horror, they did not have flaming arrows, which Solon would have been able to manipulate. Instead, the Sentinels' arrows glowed white, and steam curled from the tips.

The arrows filled the sky and landed around them. The ground cracked and contorted as the tips froze the area where they landed.

LETTING OUT A LONG BREATH, Solon threw his head back and started chanting. Smoke curled from his eyes and blue lightning sizzled in the corners. He would not let his friend down again. His voice drowned out the cawing of the crows, the steady downpour, and the pounding beat of his heart.

His hands swiveled and danced, and arcs of purple, blue, white, and yellow fire flew from his hands. They whipped at the Sentinels, licking the shields but leaving them unscathed. However, the arcing flames hit their target. Flames engulfed the Sentinels holding bows unprotected in the back. Their screams filled in the air, and they quickly tried to pass the frozen arrows to the next in line.

Solon prepared his next attack, but Zara's screaming distracted him. One of the frozen arrows had caught her arm. Her arm was beet red, and she held it, panting. Perspiration beaded on her brow. She slumped to the ground, clutching her frozen arm and rocking from the pain.

ZARA STAGGERED TO HER FEET. Her arm hung at her side. The weight pulled her down slightly. The pain sent searing reminders throughout her body, but she fumbled in her bag.

She turned and saw Solon was not faring better. Some Sentinels lay charred on the battlefield and others were smoldering, but the rest were almost on top of him. He was graying from the exertion.

Their remaining time was short. She smiled despite herself and whispered to the shadows, "I'll be with you soon, Hans."

She didn't notice the earth's tremors because of the battle, nor did she notice the first onset of arrows. When battle horns sounded behind her, she turned and faced the reinforcements.

Coming quickly were purple warriors on spiked horses. Leading the charge was Darez.

Arrows, maces, and spears shredded the Sentinels. Darez had not abandoned them. He had gone for reinforcements.

The horses and warriors went without hesitation into the lines of defense, the bulky horses trampling them. The Sentinels thrust shields at them, but the dragon skin was defenseless toward the Bamat-reinforced weapons of the Red Ice Warriors.

Solon left his post and ran toward Zara. The Sentinels were too engaged with the Red Ice Warriors to notice that he had escaped.

He gently held Zara's arm. He rubbed the gash and quickly warmed up her arm. It still throbbed in pain, but it no longer weighed her down or hurt as badly. Solon put the ointment Zara handed him on the wound.

Zara nodded at the shadows. Now wasn't their time.

"I know what will help." Zara put her thumb and forefinger to her lips and blew.

The shrill whistle caught Grot's attention again. He flew back to them, and with a quick dive, grabbed hold of them. Solon expanded his blue fire shield to Grot as they lobbed arrows at him.

Grot flew them to the original line the Sentinels had been holding.

Pink sparks sputtered on the ground. Zara recognized the charged blob as Pinky. Looking at the limp body, Zara couldn't leave Pinky here to die. Not after she had helped, even if it had been inadvertent.

Sighing, she bent down. Using an arrow tip, she picked up Pinky by her tattered clothes. Zara only had her leather quiver case, but she figured Pinky was too weak for another big attack. Settling her inside, she slung the quiver over her shoulder and faced the castle.

Chapter 69

VAYSA

$\mathcal{V}$aysa, Gren, and Teo crept through the castle. If anyone noticed, they didn't seem to care.

Vaysa figured their attire helped them. Zara supplied the Traitors, and she had given them the same gear. Hope clawed her heart, each step bringing her closer, but too much history with the Royal Guard prevented her from grabbing hold of it. Even if they were with Traitors, she wasn't really one of them.

"You know they're attacking Grot's friends?" Gren whispered as they passed another cannon room.

Vaysa sucked back a wave of guilt. She couldn't focus on what she couldn't control. And Shad needed her full attention.

"What's your point?" Teo asked.

"Aren't they our friends?"

"Grot's our friend. His species are probably our ally," Vaysa said.

"Are Silvers your ally?" Gren asked her directly.

Vaysa stared at him. Her eyes narrowed, and she sucked her cheeks in. He was wasting time. "What are you getting at? I don't care. We need to find Shad." Her voice held an edge.

"I might be able to speed us along."

Without telling them his plan, he walked into a cannon room. Vaysa and Teo watched him go.

Vaysa glanced at the long, dark corridors. Many rooms laced the path, not one a better option than the others. No smells lingered to give notice of a kitchen. Shad was somewhere in this labyrinth. They didn't need to waste time chatting.

When Vaysa went to continue one, Teo touched her arm. Her eyes lingered a moment too long before lifting to meet his.

"One minute," he said. "Let's see if he can help."

She snarled but flicked her eyes back to the room.

Gunpowder streaked the room's walls and tanged the air, and boxes of cannons lay strewn about. Even with light, the room would have been dark. Torches were lit on the wall away from the cannons and the blazes danced in the shadows. Despite the low light, Vaysa could tell the person manning the cannon was a Silver, and his comrade looked human except instead of hair, he had bumpy plating.

The Silver was shorter than Gren. His green hair was long and tangled, and his blue skin was smeared with black soot. When he turned to face Gren, his eyes were almost pink in the dim light. Shock etched his face at seeing Gren.

Vaysa and Teo watched as Gren and the other Silver stood in silence, watching each other. Vaysa held her breath, waiting for the reunion. Based on the sneer on the other Silver's face, it wouldn't be like Shad's reunion with Solon or Zara.

The other Traitor looked back and forth at them and finally broke the silence. "Lev, what's the matter?"

Lev nodded toward Gren. "He abandoned us."

Gren cleared his throat. "Clak, I know I left our people, but it was for good reason. I wanted to seek revenge on those who tried to destroy us."

"Silvers don't seek revenge."

Vaysa frowned. That was news. Clak wouldn't be of help. This was a waste of time.

Teo lifted a finger to still her.

Gren looked at Lev and the cannons and raised his eyebrows. "Then why are you fighting?"

Lev snorted. "This isn't revenge. Someone needs to protect this land. Most Silvers have joined."

"What?" Gren bellowed. His outburst surprised Vaysa and Teo. "Who's defending the land?"

"Why do you care? Besides, they burned most of it."

Vaysa flinched. After everything they'd done, Gren didn't have a home anymore. That meant they burned Shad's home, too. She swallowed the bile in her throat.

Gren ran a hand over his forehead. His eyes darted around. "But... how?"

"There were very few Silvers left when you left us, and there are even fewer now. The Traitors offered us safety if we joined. There was nothing left."

Gren's face flashed different hues of purple and red.

"Why'd you join the Traitors?" Clak asked Gren as he continued to set off cannons.

"I didn't. I've been traveling with your tailor."

"Zara's here?" they both said, whipping around to look in the hall.

Vaysa's spine stiffened. Her fingers curled. Fire danced in her veins, ready for whatever may happen.

Gren shook his head. "She's out there where you're launching cannon balls."

The two stared at each other. Through the window, all that was visible was smoke, fog, rain, and large flying birds.

"We must warn the others!" The two ran into the hall. Their eyes took in Vaysa, but they kept pace. She wasn't a threat to them.

Vaysa watched as they ran past toward the towers. Then she looked at Gren.

Gren ran after Clak and Lev.

"No!" Vaysa roared. "Shad!"

She turned in the opposite direction as Gren followed them to a turret of the castle.

Clak and Lev rang the cords of a large bell filling the tower. Vaysa grasped her ears. The sound chipped away at her thoughts. Her resolve. Her control.

She heaved for breath. Smoke twirled in her vision.

The cannons ceased. The following silence was enough to hear pockets of birds cawing and swords clashing.

Voices sounded in her head, but not from those around her.

Teo sided up to Vaysa. His touch shot a jolt through her. She blinked and took in the scene around her.

Clak and Lev used torches to wave different signs toward the other towers. The drawbridge lowered.

Gren turned to Lev and Clak. "Why did you let them in?"

"Zara has many things to answer for. As do you," Lev said, drawing his sword.

Fire raced through her. A pulse of heat and anger conjured a fireball in her hand. Willing herself not to lob it at them, to hurt more Traitors trying to protect Berla, she forced her feet to move away from them. To Shad. Her mind scrambled for thought, for direction. Find a kitchen.

"Let's go," Vaysa yelled to Teo and Gren, her voice raspy.

But when they turned to run, she saw the Traitors were emptying out of the cannon rooms and headed their way. So much for finding Shad quickly and stealthily.

"Damn it!" Teo yelled. He pumped his wings and rose in the air. "Why are we always a target?"

Chapter 70

ZARA

Solon and Zara looked around. It had been decades since Solon had been in the castle. Instead of the ostentatious display of wealth, the castle was dingy and in decay.

Zara turned toward the clamor of Traitors coming down the stairwell. By the rushed sound, she figured she and Solon weren't welcome. Zara stood in front of Solon. The Traitors wanted her. Zara raised her hands up to show Solon she didn't want to fight, nor did she want him to.

Twenty Traitors quickly surrounded them. They all had various weapons drawn, and they were all her work.

She didn't draw her weapon or protest. She looked at the angry faces around her and said, "I will answer any questions you have."

Three forms emerged from the group. An imposing figure walked toward Solon. The humanoid was as tall as Shad, with silver and black striped skin, long silvery hair, and fangs. Zara recognized the man immediately. He was half-Cuma and Enat's righthand man.

Instead of long claws like Shad, his arms tapered into long bony fingers with razor-sharp nails. A red man also walked up to Solon. He was a Tef from the Teffar Mud Pits. They were known for their strength.

Solon allowed him to put restraints on him. His hands lay bound together in front of him where the captures could see them. The two stood on either side of him.

Zara's escort was a tall woman. Her eyes had flames inside, and the ends of her scarlet hair sparked into embers. She didn't put restraints on Zara, but looped her arm with Zara's injured one.

Zara braced herself and forced a stoic expression despite her annoyance.

The woman's voice sounded like a purr as she drew out each syllable. "Zara, you have traded with many people."

"Your point, Enat?"

The woman chuckled, but her eyes narrowed at Zara. "You worked with, or should I say led, the eastern posts that are now burned."

"Do you have a point?"

The woman turned, and the fires in her eyes danced in dark oranges and yellows. Despite her stoic expression, her hair snapped with flames. "Whom did you sell our locations to? Is that direct enough for you?"

"I sold your location to no one, and yes."

"Then how did they find our forts?"

"They're scouring the country for Traitors and forts. My guess is they tortured others."

"You're traveling with the Silver that our sources say was to lead them to the prince. You're already rumored to want to kill the prince."

"That was by coincidence, and you should know not to trust rumors."

"Enlighten us, then."

"A friend came to me for help to save his traveling partners. I thought he was dead and couldn't refuse to help him. I was too happy to see him alive, although he was very sick. I helped heal his friends. There was no plan for me to travel with them. The Royal Guard then went after my home. I had no choice but to run."

"You're too you. Everything you said was true while also being a lie. You know things have gone too far. You simply can't return or kill him."

"You would never allow him to leave since he knows where the Water Witch is."

Enat growled. "If we find her, then we can protect her and our lands. Hiding is no longer an option. He can leave once we have her and relocate her."

"She won't let you find her."

Enat laughed. "How would you know? We are the best solution for this land."

"She will not willingly join an army."

"She's wise. She'll do what's best for the people. It's her job."

"She's doing her job now. Besides, you don't have the right bargaining tool."

Enat stopped and, eyeing up Zara, asked, "And what would that be?"

Zara smiled.

Chapter 71

VAYSA

Vaysa stared at the assailants as darkness encroached on her mind. She agreed with Teo, and she'd had enough. She'd faced the Royal Guards, caused her and Shad to run, protected Gren and Teo, been speared, lost Shad, found out Solon was her father and other secrets, there were so many more secrets she didn't know yet, and these people stood between her and Shad.

She allowed the darkness in her mind to wash over her, to sharpen her anger. Her anger at losing Shad, the Royal Guard, and the obstacles since arriving in Berla. Her body tingled and pulsated. She clenched her fists tight and threw back her head.

The power flooded her, drowning all reasoning.

Instead of smoke circles, purple charged lightning zipped across her eyes. Fire sprang to her hands, and when she couldn't hold it in anymore, she arched her body forward and then quickly flung it back.

From her hands and eyes shot blue lightning that arced around the trio. She didn't want to hurt the Traitors, but she would not let them hurt her or her group.

Whispers tugged at her and darkness seeped in her mind. The

power that welled inside her was intoxicating. It promised so much. Fueled her. Dulled her pain and thoughts.

She swiveled to face Lev. Concentrating, she twisted her hand around as if she was grabbing a suspended object. A blue orb lifted Lev off the ground with Lev suspended in the empty middle of it.

He shrieked and clawed toward Clak, who reared back.

"Vaysa," Teo breathed.

Vaysa pulled Lev into the orb with them. Vaysa's voice echoed like it was coming from a tunnel. "You will take us to Shad."

Lev shook his head and twisted, trying to get away.

"That's not an option." Vaysa flicked her fingers, and a bolt of electricity shot out and struck Clak. He crumpled to the floor, twitching.

Vaysa looked to Lev. "You do not have a choice."

Vaysa walked into the hall. The other Traitors stepped back with gaping mouths and wide eyes. Vaysa turned toward Lev. "Tell us now."

Lev shook his head. His eyes pinched shut and streams of sweat rolled down his face.

Vaysa glared at him and flung her hand toward a wall. A fireball zipped out and slammed into the wall. The floor, walls, and ceiling shook from the impact, and it left a crater at the blast sight.

Lev gulped and looked at Gren.

Gren sighed and smoothed his hair. He sauntered over to Vaysa. Touching her arm, he said, "You can't do this. He's one of my people."

Vaysa snorted at Gren and brushed him off. "Shad's more important."

Gren's face flashed red, and his eyes darkened. He reached for his weapon but stopped.

Vaysa turned toward Gren. White and purple charges zipped across her eyes. Was he betraying her?

Teo glided next to Vaysa. He put his hand on her shoulder. "Gren's not your enemy, even though his ego and anger are slowing us down." Teo ignored the vulgar gesture from Gren, and continued, "I agree, this person should get it. However, we'll then have new enemies."

"We have them now," she said and tilted her head toward the Traitors. The whispers in the darkness deepened. Her mind clouded with the noise.

"Nah, I think they're being protective. We are the ones who snuck in."

Vaysa glanced at Teo. Her mind screamed against the whispers and the blackness. He sounded right, but her anger didn't care.

"Vaysa, focus," Teo said, fear creeping into his voice.

Her power surged up. She wanted to release it. Let it free. Crush the enemy.

"Vaysa!" Teo screamed. He gripped her shoulders.

She blinked and stared at him. The power curled and receded. She flexed her fingers, control returning, and focused on Teo and the others.

She looked at Lev and the worried faces of the Traitors. She sighed. Teo was right.

She released Lev and rubbed her hands.

Gren glared at her but helped Lev up. Turning to Lev, Gren whispered in his ear.

Lev nodded, and a sly smile spread across his face. "I'll show you."

Chapter 72

CLOSS

Smoke and dirt hung in the air. The thick smell of blood and death clung to the castle and grounds. Endless cawing rattled Closs's ears.

The group had infiltrated the castle. The Sentinels were picked apart by the crows. Like locusts, the Royal Guard swarmed the castle, but with help from the crows, the Traitors held them off.

"Sir," Ben whispered next to him. "I sent for another dozen."

Closs narrowed his gaze as he scanned the troops. A dozen had survived the attack. He'd need a new batch of troops. Maybe two.

A rumble in the distance drew his gaze. A reminder of the power that would be his. With a smirk, he turned from the scene. The other Royal Guard could deal with the prince. A distraction. As long as the girl survived, Closs had the bounty that would bring him two countries. And with her, he could take the east, too.

She'd survive. Just like she always seemed to do.

And he'd be waiting.

Chapter 73

ZARA

Zara looked at Enat and then at Solon. "I doubt you'd believe me if I told you."

Enat growled. "Don't toy with me!"

"Solon, of course," Zara said, gesturing grandly at Solon.

Enat swiveled to stare at Solon. She scrutinized his face and nodded. "Well, I'll be, that is Solon under the guise of Traitor gear. Aren't you supposed to be dead?"

"By you or the humans?"

"Oh, Solon."

"You betrayed me."

"Solon, we were looking out for Berla, not one man."

"You wanted her to be your prisoner."

"Solon, we saw the big picture. You saw blinding love."

"What big picture was that?"

"Berla can never govern itself. It needs a mediator. You didn't want to see it."

Solon scowled and cocked his head back. Smoke curled from his eyes and he balled his fists.

Enat ignored his threat and asked, "Why did you pretend to be dead?"

"He didn't. I thought he was," Zara said, stepping between Enat and Solon. "I hid Yala's return."

Solon's anger flashed toward Zara. "About time you admit it."

"I was looking out for Berla."

Enat watched the argument with an amused smile. "Zara, it seems you can make enemies as easily as friends."

Solon's anger turned to Enat. "She saved my wife's life. I caused the death of her husband. I think she's still the better one."

Enat's face contorted in confusion. "That's right, he was responsible for Hans' death. Why are you helping him?"

"My husband's death was his own fault. As hard as that is to say, it was his anger that led him to death. And his belief in justice. For some reason, he thought a person should be free, not a tool of an army."

A sudden burst of yelling interrupted their banter. They turned to see a group of Traitors racing toward them. "Enat! Enat! Enat! Lev is leading them to the prince."

"Damn it!" Enat roared. Her hair burst into flames, and embers showered the floor. Common for a Nacam Fire Witch.

She gestured to her group to follow the messenger back to Lev. Before trailing after them, she turned to Zara. With a sneer, she said, "Zara, you've always helped us and vice versa. Make sure the people you're with are worth the sacrifice. The Royal Guard and Sentinels will hunt you to the death, again. Pick a side."

They left Solon and Zara with their two original guards and three extras.

Solon looked at Zara. "She's still unpleasant. Is she your friend or not?"

Zara laughed. "Fire Witches are hard to read, but they're not our enemy."

Solon nodded. "I've never trusted her. But I know what's going on now with the Traitors and Berla. Even if you've hidden it."

If only Solon could trust her. She would keep Yala safe. Even from the Traitors.

She looked at Solon and realized how mistaken she had been. She'd been trying to keep Solon from Yala until everything was resolved. She'd been afraid he'd undermine her work, but Solon was the one person who would stop at nothing to protect Yala. He'd given his life once to do it already. Maybe Solon was the best solution.

The prince was a lost cause. The western Traitors had him and would face annihilation to keep his secrets safe. She'd treated Solon and the Traitors like competition. She needed a new plan.

Vaysa was right; they needed to find Yala.

Suddenly, Solon lashed around and kicked the half-Cuma guarding him and sent a fireball into his face. The half-Cuma doubled over, clutching his face. His mouth gasped for air.

"Since you're not my enemy, I won't kill you," Solon warned.

With a flick of his wrist, a blue orb enclosed the two. Solon looked at his constraints; they smoked and disintegrated. The three extra guards slowly backed up from them.

"Sorry, we can't trust you to not come after us," Zara said as she bound their hands and legs with their own restraints. "However, you aren't our enemy. We're actually on the same side."

"You know they're only leading us into a trap," Solon said to Zara, gesturing in the direction Enat and the others ran.

"I know, but I'd guess they're in Yala's old quarters. That's worse than any prison."

They raced through the halls. As they neared the familiar room, Zara heard the other pursuit coming toward them. They ran toward the center tower.

Solon grabbed Zara and forced her to stop.

She turned in confusion. "What?"

"I know a special passage."

"Of course you do," she said with a smile.

Solon pushed on a block by the base of the stairwell. A small passage opened, and the two slipped inside. Solon re-centered the block, and the passage closed.

Beyond the wall, the flurry of Vaysa, Gren, and Teo being pursued rushed past.

Solon closed his eyes, and conflict warred on his face.

Zara placed a hand on his shoulder. Opening his eyes, he stepped forward.

"She needs us to do this."

Inside the wall was a secret staircase that led up to the tower.

"Why is this here?" Zara asked.

Solon said, "In case of attack. They wanted to get Yala to safety. We weren't supposed to know this was here."

As they ascended the steps, the sounds of traps sprung as the others climbed the steps on the other side of the wall provided a muffled soundtrack. Gren screamed in annoyance, Teo cursed, and Vaysa growled.

"They made it through one trap," Zara said, trying to sound encouraging.

As they moved forward, they continued to be serenaded by the others springing more traps from the other side.

At the top of the staircase was another cement wall. Solon took a deep breath and drew his arms back, holding his hands wrist to wrist and palms opened out he pushed. A large white fireball rocketed out and slammed into the wall.

The blast pushed the hidden entrance back and revealed Yala's old room. Solon threw up a blue shield and walked in front of Zara. They peeked into the room and saw that it was empty except for two figures: a lone man sitting in a chair in the corner looking curiously at them and Shad. Shad slumped against a wall, holding her head.

"Solon?" Shad asked, opening her eyes.

"Are you all right?" He stepped toward her.

She shrugged and nodded toward the center of the room. "Seems the Traitors learned magic and are afraid I'll hurt him."

"So some Monocians have joined," Solon said, seeing the blue fire divider.

"More than Monoc will admit," Zara said.

"Well, I wasn't expecting my rescuers to come in through the wall. Nor to be in Traitor gear." The lone man smirked and tilted his head in amusement. "Or to be Berlans."

Solon and Zara turned to look at Prince Kier. Besides his smirk, he had pale skin, hazel eyes, and mahogany hair. Despite being in captivity, he was well groomed. He wore brown leather pants and a black shirt.

Shad growled at him and revealed her fangs.

He pulled back. "You're not going to let her near me, are you?" His voice tinged with fear.

"You don't get to choose your rescuers," Solon said. With a quick swish of his hand, the fire barrier dissolved.

Shad stood and rolled her neck. Her eyes flashed gold, and she nodded toward Prince Kier. "See what he has?"

"What am I supposed to see?" Zara asked, scanning him over.

"She's infatuated with my necklace," Prince Kier said and smirked when Shad gave him a dark look.

Zara raised an eyebrow toward Shad.

"Tell them where you got it."

"I found it."

"Found it?" Solon asked and stepped closer. "Is that...?"

Prince Kier leaned back, uncertainty shining in his eyes.

"It looks like a rock," Zara said but leaned closer and her eyes widened. Her stomach dropped and a chill skimmed her bones. "Is that a scale?"

"Yep," Shad said. "He found it a few weeks ago."

Found it? And the dragons hadn't stopped him? It was worse than she thought. She needed to get to Yala.

"Isn't that when Vaysa's powers..." Solon didn't finish.

"Yep," Shad confirmed. "They're calling her back."

"But she was safer in Kennard. Safer not having powers."

"Was she?" Shad asked.

A large crash sounded outside of the door, followed by sounds of fighting. The prince flinched as the door shook with bodies thrown against it.

Solon walked over to the door and pulled on the handle.

"Good luck. I'm not here willingly. Besides, you want to let your enemies in?" Prince Kier said.

"They're with us," Zara said overly sweetly as she walked to the prince. He didn't know it yet, but he was going with them, too.

Shad joined Zara.

The prince tried to scoot away nonchalantly. Shad chuckled and stood between him and the door.

"You'll thank me later," she growled. Facing the door, she threw her head back and bellowed, "Vaysa!"

Chapter 74

VAYSA

Shad's voice sounded through the wall. Vaysa's heart clenched and her vision blurred. She blinked to focus. Around her were half a dozen Traitors unconscious on the floor and another half-dozen still standing.

"Enough," she seethed, and an orb of purple fire popped around her. The remaining Traitors fell. She cocooned Gren and Teo inside blue orbs.

Vaysa took a breath and looked at the door. She pulled from her core, allowing the darkness to edge away her hesitation, and when she felt it took too much, she pushed the energy forward. It rocketed forward in a blue ball of fire.

The door bulged inward and blue sparks scattered on the floor. She pulled from her core again and sent another fireball at the door. The blast sent the door flying back into a blue shield controlled by Solon. The door ricocheted off it and bounced on the floor. Solon's blue shield dissolved and faded under the pressure of Vaysa's fireball.

Vaysa's heart went to her throat seeing Shad unscathed. She ignored all the others as she raced to Shad. Vaysa threw her arms around her, and all was right. Everything was possible. She could face anything.

Shad returned the embrace and rocked them.

"Well, you're something," a new voice broke the moment. Although he spoke the common language of Berla, he had a light Kennardian accent on the words. "I could use you on my side."

Vaysa pulled back from Shad and noticed a figure sitting behind them. She sucked in a breath. It was the prince. He matched the face on the posters.

They'd found him, too. The source of all her recent issues. She had been expecting to feel something else. Some fear or excitement, but instead, she was empty. This victory meant nothing. She could kill him, and no one could stop her. This would not stop what was happening in the castle. It wouldn't help the Water Witch. It'd probably make it worse.

Having him only meant having enemies.

Her gaze flickered to Zara and back to the prince. He was the key to finding the Water Witch, to making the Royal Guard leave.

"Shad, it's good to see you're okay," Teo said.

Shad half-smiled and rolled her eyes. "I like the wings."

Teo smiled.

"Zara, how is that possible?" Shad asked, her smile growing.

"Just is," Zara said and gave Shad a silencing look.

"I see you kept each other alive," Shad said toward Vaysa, Teo, and Gren. She nodded at Teo. "Good."

"Are you okay?" Vaysa asked Shad, her eyes assessing her for injuries.

"I'm not hurt," Shad laughed, and pulled Vaysa in for another hug. She sucked back a sob. "I'm glad to see you."

"Same," Vaysa muffled into her fur coat. Whatever happened, she had Shad now.

Teo flushed and turned to Solon and Zara. "How'd you get in here?"

Solon cleared his throat. "We've been here before."

"Ah…" Teo floated around and turned to them. "Is this where the Water Witch was kept?"

"Yes," Zara murmured.

Tingles raced down Vaysa's back and she turned to see what the threat was. She saw nothing but the brick walls covered in weathered tapestries.

"What's so special about it? Well, besides the booby traps?" Teo asked.

"Try getting out," Solon said.

Teo shrugged and tried to walk out the door. He bounced back off an invisible force field. "I see."

Familiar faint whispers tugged at Vaysa's ears, but she shook her head to clear it. Nothing was there. She wanted out of this place. She could leave. She had Shad.

"Vaysa, what are you saying?" Teo asked and reached for her.

"What?" Vaysa asked and stepped back. "I didn't say anything."

The others looked at each other.

"Vaysa, your dream you had," Shad said, her eyes bright with emotion.

Vaysa's gaze snapped to Shad's.

"I didn't understand," Shad said, her voice thick.

"What didn't you understand?" Vaysa asked.

"They're calling you, aren't they?"

Vaysa blinked at Shad and swallowed. Her body was simultaneously numb and on fire.

"Who's calling her?" Teo asked.

"Is that why she's gotten control of her powers?" Solon asked.

"You got control?" Shad asked, her eyes bulged in surprise and fear.

Vaysa licked her lips and wrapped her arms around her torso. "Something like that," she mumbled.

"Something like that?" Gren echoed. "She lifted a person up with a fire orb but didn't hurt them like they were in a bubble. She's gone to almost mastery."

"When exactly?" Shad asked Gren.

"When she left the oasis to come here," he said, brow furrowed.

Shad nodded and gulped. "When you obeyed their wishes."

"What are you talking about?" Vaysa asked, stepping backwards.

Shad nodded to Prince Kier.

He ducked back, his hand instinctively going to his necklace.

"I misunderstood," Shad said again, head bowed, her body deflated. "I thought you needed a dragon scale, but I was wrong."

"What do you mean?" Vaysa asked.

"It's not a dragon scale, but that dragon scale," Shad said, pointing to Prince Kier. "He took it. They called you back to get it."

"They?" Gren whispered.

"Who and why?" Vaysa asked.

Shad looked at Solon.

He closed his eyes and grimaced.

They still needed to talk. To define their boundaries and if they wanted a relationship clear of secrets, but as with everything, there wasn't time. But there was one secret that would change everything.

"Solon, what is my mother?" Vaysa choked out.

The others in the room turned to him.

Solon whispered, "You're from a race that is almost extinct. They called themselves the Dracas. They were close to the dragons and still live with them. Though most others don't know the dragons still exist. Even the old nests can seem mythical."

He looked at Zara.

"The what?" Gren repeated. His red eyes cut to Solon and then Vaysa.

"Dracas." Zara nodded. "They use shed dragon scales in their armor."

"Never heard of it," Teo said.

"Me neither." Gren frowned.

"Almost extinct," Shad repeated. Her eyes flicked to Vaysa. "Other species have been lost to time and myth, too."

"And the dragons are still... alive?" Gren asked.

"A few," Zara hedged.

"I thought dragon scales work for all elemental wielders," Vaysa said and looked to Shad.

Shad shrugged. "They do."

"I don't understand," Vaysa said, looking between Shad and Solon.

Solon said, "Your people protected the dragons and vice versa. They often bonded. The link between you is magnified. You are more connected to the scales and their powers. When the prince stole the dragon scale, the dragons summoned you back."

"Why was I taken from them in the first place?"

"Soldiers were hunting you and you needed to go to a place where dragons were myth."

"And now?" Vaysa asked.

Shad stepped toward Prince Kier. "I'll give you a chance to hand it over, or I'll take it."

Kier looked at the others and took off his necklace.

Shad snatched it from him and held it out for Vaysa.

Vaysa's mind ebbed, and whispers ripped around her. The others moved behind a shimmering mirage, silhouettes yet distinctive.

She grasped the dragon scale and dug it into her palm.

"Finally, Vaysa, finally," the voice echoed in her brain. She wasn't in the cave like before, but in an isolated room. The darkened walls with inky shadows were gone, and instead, walls with intricate tapestries and relics surrounded her. A large pool stretched before her; the shimmering image fed from a stream of water. The reflective surface rippled and an image of the Water Witch's room came into focus with the others around her. A familiar presence was beside her, but it wasn't the same as the voice.

She blinked and she was back with the others.

The thunder of boots pounding up the steps broke the silence.

"We need to leave," Solon said.

Gren's red eyes scanned Vaysa, his face pinched in concern, and asked Solon, "What about the way you came in?"

"They're swarming the bottom of it. We'd be stuck in the wall."

"What about the window then?" Teo asked.

The others turned and stared at him.

"What?" he asked.

"Teo, we're twenty floors up," Solon said.

"So?"

"We don't have wings like you," the prince said.

Hearing the prince's voice again forced Vaysa to focus. They didn't have wings, but Grot did. She had to get his attention.

"We need to go," Vaysa said and moved toward Prince Kier.

"Where are we going?" Teo asked.

Vaysa looked at Prince Kier and then Zara.

"Does the Water Witch need our help?"

Zara and Solon shared a look. Solon's face darkened and Zara raised an eyebrow at him.

It meant yes.

"Vaysa," Solon groaned and slapped his hand on his forehead. "It's suicide."

Zara laughed.

"Hasn't stopped me yet."

"It's not your…" Solon didn't finish his sentence. He hung his head and sighed.

"Vaysa," Zara said, her voice tinged with fear.

Vaysa paused and turned to Zara.

"Are you sure you want to help with the Water Witch?"

Vaysa nodded.

"What?" Shad roared.

"Do you want to help her?" Vaysa asked Shad.

"Of course," Shad said without hesitation. Looking at Vaysa, guilt and sorrow contorted her face. "Vaysa… I'm sorry… You need to know…"

"They'll never stop looking for you," Zara cut her off.

Shad growled. "Maybe we shouldn't help."

Shad obviously didn't believe it.

Vaysa blinked and let the words sink in. She looked out the window at the Royal Guard below and back toward the stairwell that would fill with Traitors soon.

This was all for the prince who knew the location of the Water Witch.

She had her dragon scale.

"If you move the Water Witch, they'll hunt you, too," Shad said. Defeat sagged her expression.

They already were.

Vaysa looked at Zara and saw sympathy mar her face. She bit back the revulsion creeping up her throat. She would never be safe. If she had done nothing but hide in Monoc, she'd still be hiding. Still running on fear. Finding the Water Witch meant whoever wanted her powers would pursue her. But she'd be in charge of her choices.

Either way, she wasn't safe. She'd wanted to hide. Wanted it to be over. But that didn't feel like a choice. Her heart decided for her.

"I know," she whispered.

Shad closed her eyes and cursed. She looked back at Vaysa, her eyes glossy with emotion. "Then let's go. We'll grab Alice and the maris."

"It's your lucky day," Vaysa said to Prince Kier, and threw a fireball through the window. Silver sparks replaced the glass shards.

The faint caw of a bird echoed in the distance and Vaysa threw another fireball out. It exploded into a shower of sparks. Suddenly, Grot appeared by the window.

Vaysa shoved Prince Kier toward the window and said, "Congratulations, Your Highness. You're free from the Traitors."

ACKNOWLEDGMENTS

This is the first book I ever finished writing. I drafted it in the summer of 2009 after turning in my Master's project. It was my first break from a decade of academia, but the first few (dozen) drafts sounded like a research paper more than a novel. Fifteen years after finishing the first draft, it is published. I can honestly say I both hate and love this book after this long of reworking it.

Each draft chronologizes my progression as a writer. The imperfect characters showed me how to stop writers' block by listening to them instead of the narrative in my head. Although each one has changed from the first draft, some including their name, their spirit never has.

Eight years after finishing it, I had my first reader. Hearing and applying feedback is always a learning process. Now, I seek readers earlier in the process.

So many people have read earlier drafts. Some loved it while others hated it. All of which was a lesson on how I won't make everyone happy.

To the many people who have helped shape it into the book it is today, THANK YOU. Many editors and authors have read it along the way. There are few who made significant impacts to it, whether they know it or not.

I won an auction in 2019 for feedback on the first ten pages and synopsis from Kat E. Based on the synopsis, Kat offered structural changes that completely changed the focus of the book. Their insights changed everything from the catalyst onward.

Tory Hunter, development editor at Tory Hunter Books, who read it multiple times, stopped me from shelving it, and provided encouragement the whole way. She has a critical eye and great insights.

Emilie H, a beta reader who helped me fall back in love with the story. By now, you already know what happens in Book 2 and I am sorry ;).

This book isn't for everyone. The feedback I've received along the way has proven that. For those that hated it, I hope you find the story that brings you joy. To those who enjoyed it, I hope to see you back with the second book in the series.

ABOUT THE AUTHOR

Amelia J. Rivers is a bitter cinnamon roll who lives in the Midwest with her husband, a legion of demonic cats, and a pampered dog. Data diver by day, writer by night. She also spends as much time with her nieces as she can. She is an emerging author of paranormal and epic fantasies. This is Amelia's second book.

- Author website
- Join Newsletter
- All links

ALSO BY AMELIA J. RIVERS

<u>Stand Alones</u>

When Shadows Bleed

Washed Up

Twisted Beauty

<u>Series</u>

Legends of Berla

Book 1: Harnessing Fire

www.ingramcontent.com/pod-product-compliance
Lightning Source LLC
Chambersburg PA
CBHW030755260626
47169CB00001B/66